The House On The Marsh

A Romance

by

Florence Warden

Double9
BOOKS

The House On The Marsh
A Romance
by Florence Warden

ISBN: 978-93-62760-45-6

Published by

DOUBLE 9 BOOKS

2/13-B, Ansari Road
Daryaganj, New Delhi – 110002
info@double9books.com
www.double9books.com
Tel. 011-40042856

ABOUT THE AUTHOR

Florence Warden was an English actress and writer who published numerous novels under her stage name. Her real name was Florence Alice Price, and her marital name was Mrs G.E. James. Warden began her life as Florence Alice Price, the daughter of a stockbroker. She was born in Hanworth, Middlesex, and educated in both Brighton and France. In 1877, her debut novel, The Wolf at the Door, was published anonymously in Boston, Massachusetts. Warden worked as an actress between 1880 and 1885, and she also published stories and novels under her stage persona. In 1885, her mystery novel The House on the Marsh (1884) was adapted into a play in which she played the lead. Warden married an actor named George Edward James in 1887 in St Pancras. She continued to create novels, but she abandoned her acting profession. One of her sisters also became a writer, going by the name Gertrude Warden. Warden and her husband had two sons, Godfrey Warden James, born in St Pancras in 1888, and Rupert Warden, born in Ramsgate in 1893; and two daughters, Leslie Gertrude, born in London in 1890, and Olivia Mary, born in Ramsgate, Kent, in 1891. Warden's son, Godfrey Warden James (1888-1963), was educated at Oxford, qualified as a barrister, served as a schoolmaster and tutor, and as an Administrative Officer in Sierre Leone. He was also a novelist under the name Adam Broome.

CONTENTS

CHAPTER I

"Wanted, a Governess; must be young." I cut out the advertisement thus headed eagerly from the *Times*. I was eighteen, and my youth had been the great obstacle to my getting an engagement; now here was some delightful advertiser who considered it an advantage. I wrote to the address given, enclosing my photograph and the list of my qualifications. Within a week I was travelling down to Geldham, Norfolk, engaged to teach "one little girl, aged six," at a salary of thirty-five pounds a year. The correspondence had been carried on by my future pupil's father, who said he would meet me at the station at Beaconsburgh, the market-town nearest to Geldham.

It was about five o'clock on an afternoon in early August that I sat, trembling with excitement and fright, at the window of the railway-carriage, as the train steamed slowly into Beaconsburgh station. I looked out on to the platform. There were very few people on it, and there was no one who appeared at all like the gentleman I had pictured to myself as my future employer. There were two or three red-faced men who gave one the impression of being farmers, and at one end there were two young men engaged in securing a large mastiff, which was bounding about in great excitement at sight of the train. I got out and spoke to the station-master.

"There is Mr. Rayner himself, ma'am," said he, pointing towards the two young men with the dog.

One of them was now looking about, as if in search of somebody; and I walked timidly towards him. He seemed puzzled as his eyes fell upon me; then suddenly he raised his hat.

"Miss Christie?" he said interrogatively, growing very red.

"Yes," said I, bowing and blushing too.

"Will you come and show me which is your luggage?"

I was surprised and rather confused to find Mr. Rayner so much younger and less self-possessed than I had expected. I followed him and pointed out my boxes.

"The dog-cart is waiting outside," said he; "let me carry your bag."

I followed him through the station. Three or four big dogs began jumping up upon him and upon me as we came out.

"Down, Rover! Down, Luke! Get down, Tray!" said he, raising his voice.

I had noticed what a very pleasant rich voice he had when he first spoke to me, and now I remembered how particular he had been in his letters about my music; so I concluded that Mr. Rayner sang. He helped me into the dog-cart, carefully wrapped me up with a rug, and then, instead of getting in himself, patted the neck of the brown mare, who turned her head and put her nose into her master's hand. I was trying to get over my bewilderment. Of course I might have expected that the father of my six-year-old pupil would not be the middle-aged gray-haired man I had pictured to myself; but for him to be a man who did not look more than three or four and twenty was a surprise; and to find him so shy and deferential did not seem quite right, considering our respective positions. He was big and broad, and rather massive, had dark hair and mustache, gray eyes, and a kind simplicity of expression, which perhaps, I thought, with his habit of blushing, made him look younger than he was. He left the mare and stood by me again.

"I am afraid you will find the country dull. You will miss the gayety of London."

"I haven't led a very gay life," said I; "I don't think poor people are very gay anywhere."

"But you have not been shut up in a schoolroom before. I can't think how you will stand it. I always hated schoolrooms; and it's a fact that I was never in a school without being told that I was a disgrace to it."

Mr. Rayner did not seem much distressed as he made this confession.

"I dare say you were great at cricket, or rowing, or—or—fighting," I hazarded, feeling that some rejoinder was expected.

"No, I wasn't. I remember giving a boy a black eye once for calling me a dunce. He was quite right, you know. And I remember being surprised that I hurt him so much; for I generally got the worst of it in a fight. They used to say it took a good deal to rouse me; and I didn't do much harm when I was roused," he added, laughing.

"I hope your daughter does not share her father's dislike of school routine," I broke out anxiously.

He started and looked up at me, coloring vividly, and then said, with some amusement in his tones—

"Did you take me for Mr. Rayner?" The next moment he seemed sorry for my evident confusion, and added, looking away, "My name is Reade.

Mrs. Rayner sent her brougham for you; but a wagon ran into it and took one of the wheels off; so I put my cart at your disposal. I hope you don't mind driving in a thing like this?"

"Oh, no!" I said.

"That was Mr. Rayner on the platform with me," he went on. "His dog rushed out just as the train came up, and he asked me to see to your luggage while he held him. I don't know why he is so long."

As he spoke, Mr. Rayner himself came out of the station, letting his mastiff loose at the door. I saw in a moment that he was a few years older than my companion, and that, while they both wore round hats and Norfolk jackets, he bore the impress of town breeding as clearly as Mr. Reade did that of the country. He was slight, well made, with delicate features and a dark golden beard and mustache. He came up, raising his hat, and shook hands with me.

"You have been marvelling at the barbarism of Norfolk-manners, Miss Christie, and asking 'When is the next train back to London?' But I have been warned by my wife not to make my reappearance at home without a certain parcel from the 'Stores' which has been due at this station about ten days, but has, for some unaccountable reason, failed to turn up hitherto. By the way, I hope my sprightly young friend has been entertaining you well?"

"Miss Christie took me for you, Mr. Rayner," said Mr. Reade, shyly reddening again.

"And has now to suffer the awful disappointment of finding that Mr. Rayner is an old fogy after all. Miss Christie, forgive my gray hairs. You will find me a great deal more trustworthy than any of these gay deceiving Norfolk lads. Now, Laurence, my boy, if you want us to get home before the mist rises, we had better start."

Mr. Rayner sprang up behind; Mr. Reade got up in front by my side, and took the reins; and off we started, with the five dogs bounding, barking, and growling along the road as we went. We had to drive right through Beaconsburgh; up a long hill to the market-place, which was lively and busy, as it was market-day; down another long hill, lined with the dreary old houses of the *élite* of a provincial town; past a tan-yard, over a small bridge crowded with cattle returning from market, and then along two miles of straight willow-bordered road over a marsh. The scenery was not particularly pretty; but I had never lived in the country, and everything was new and interesting to me. Mr. Rayner was occupied at the back with letters and papers, and Mr. Reade at my side listened to my comments with flattering interest and appreciation.

"How beautifully green everything is!" I remarked presently.

"Yes, rather too green," Mr. Reade rejoined ruefully. "We have had a wet summer, and now we are going to have a wet autumn, I believe, and this place will be nothing but a swamp."

"Don't set Miss Christie against the place, Laurence," said Mr. Rayner rather sharply.

We passed through a low-lying village—some of the houses of which were flooded in winter, Mr. Reade told me—up a hill, down a hill, and up another sloping road, at the side of which stretched the marsh again.

"There is the Alders, Miss Christie," said he, pointing with his whip to a pretty red house, half covered with ivy and surrounded by trees, which stood below the road, on the borders of the marsh.

"Here, Laurence, I'll get down and take the short cut," said Mr Rayner.

There was a foot-path which led from this point of the road straight to the house through a couple of fields and a plantation. After Mr. Rayner had alighted, Mr. Reade and I drove on by the road.

"What a lovely place!" I cried enthusiastically.

My companion remained silent.

"And, oh, what a beautiful pond! I do believe it has water-lilies!" I exclaimed, turning round half breathless at such a glorious discovery.

"I wouldn't have that stagnant water near my house for my children to play about for something!" said he, in an energetic growl which surprised me.

I said no more until we drove slowly down the sloping carriage-drive through the trees which led to the house; then again my admiration broke out.

"Oh, how delightfully cool it looks, with the ivy all over it to keep out the hot sun!"

"Yes, and to keep in the cold moisture, Miss Christie. That ivy hasn't been cut for the last five years; and it ought to be torn down altogether to make the place fit to live in. It is no better than a pest-house!" he went on, getting more and more excited. "I wouldn't let a laborer live in it!"

"A laborer won't have a chance until my lease is up, Laurence," said Mr. Rayner dryly, coming out of a path among the trees. And the two men exchanged looks which showed that at the bottom of their hearts they were not friends.

But then it was not likely that Mr. Rayner would care to hear his beautiful home called a pest-house!

We drove slowly down to the hall door, which was open, and a gaunt untidy-looking servant came out and carried in my boxes. Mr. Reade helped me down and stood by me, apparently examining the harness, while I looked in an ecstasy of admiration at the dark red house thickly covered with ivy, and at the gray stone portico, the pillars of which were stained with picturesque patches of green, while the capitals were overgrown with soft bronze and brown moss. Then he seized a moment, when Mr. Rayner was speaking to the servant, to stoop and say to me quickly, in a low voice—

"Don't let them put you near Mrs. Rayner's room."

I could not answer, could not ask why, for the next moment he was calling out good-by to Mr. Rayner, and, raising his hat to me, was walking by the side of the dog-cart up the steep drive that led through the garden to the road. I was sorry he was gone. I wanted to ask what he meant by his strange warning, and to thank him for his kindness. A distressing sense of loneliness came over me. Mr. Rayner, who had grown grave and silent and deeply occupied with his letters during the last part of the drive, had gone into the house forgetting to invite me in; the servant had disappeared with my last box. Instead of following her, I stood watching the dog-cart and its owner out of sight, until a harsh woman's voice startled me.

"Won't you come in? I'm to show you to your room."

It was the gaunt servant who addressed me. I turned, blushing, and followed her into a low long hall, dark, cool, and old-fashioned, such as the outside of the house had prepared me for; up an oak-lined staircase; through a few of those short and inconvenient passages which abound in old houses that have been added to from time to time, to a corner-room, shabby, dark, and bare-looking, where my boxes were already installed. I sat down on one of these, the only friendly things I had about me, and began to cry. Somebody might at least have come to the door to meet me! I thought of Mr. Reade's words, and began to wonder with a new sense of dread what Mrs. Rayner was like. Was she an invalid? Was she—mad? If not, why had she left the correspondence about her child's governess entirely to her husband? My tears dried slowly as I went on puzzling myself uselessly about this mystery which must be so very soon solved; and I was scarcely ready when the servant returned to tell me that tea was waiting for me. But my curiosity was only to be sharpened. Tea was prepared for me alone, the servant saying that Mr. Rayner was busy, and had had his taken into the study. Not a word about Mrs. Rayner—no sign of a pupil! So great were my anxiety and curiosity that I forgot how hungry I was, and in a few minutes I had finished my tea, and was standing by the window looking out into the garden.

It was not yet seven o'clock and a bright summer evening. A light breeze had sprung up and was swaying the tops of the trees that grew thickly round the house. On the side of the dining-room a mossy lawn stretched from the roots of the trees right up to the French windows. I opened one of these and went out. I had never been in such a beautiful garden before. The grass was soft and springy and well kept; there were no stiff beds of geraniums and verbenas, but under the trees and against the house, and wherever there was a spare corner, grew clumps of Scotch and monthly roses, Canterbury bells, prince's feather, and such simple flowers. The house was built on the very border of the marsh, at the bottom of a hill which sloped down, covered with trees, towards the dining-room side of the house. I made my way round to the front and the moss-grown portico—from here one caught glimpses of the marsh through the thick trees. I followed a grass-path cut through them, facing the front of the house, until I came to the pond which had excited my admiration from the dog-cart. Here the vegetation grew unchecked. The water was half covered with smooth green duckweed and water-lilies, and the reeds and rushes, which grew tall and thick round the margin, had encroached much upon the little sheet of water. The path I had followed was continued through the trees, within a few feet of the pond, to the outer edge of the little wood which enclosed the house and garden; there a few rough steps over the fence connected it with the foot-path along the borders of the marsh, which joined the road at the descent of the hill. This was the short cut by which Mr. Rayner had reached the house before us that afternoon.

I had turned back towards the garden, and was close to the pond, when I heard a low crooning sound which seemed to come out of the ground at my feet. Looking about, I saw sitting among the reeds, at the very edge of the water—so close to it that her little shoes kept slipping in the moist yielding earth—a tiny elfish-looking child, about two years old, in a dirty white frock and pinafore, with a small pale wrinkled face and thin straight red hair, who rocked herself to and fro and went on with her monotonous chant without seeming at all disturbed by the appearance of a stranger. She only stared at me, without altering her position, when I told her that she must not sit so near the water, or she would fall in and be drowned; but, when I stooped to lift her up, she proved her humanity by screaming loudly and reproaching me in baby language too indistinct for me to understand. I supposed her to be the child of the gardener or of some neighboring cottager, and, not quite knowing what to do with her, I carried her, still screaming, to the house, where I met the servant whom I had already seen.

"I found this child sitting with her feet nearly in the pond!" I said tragically.

"Oh, yes, miss, there's no keeping her away from the pond! She's there pretty nearly all day by herself. Come now, Mona, it's time for you to go to bed. Dirty little girl, look at your pinafore!"

She took the child from me, thankful to have been spared the trouble of hunting and catching the little wild thing, and carried her off, leaving me wondering whether my pupil would be as eerie a creature as her sister. As there was nothing to invite me to stay indoors, I went out again, this time to explore the side of the house which faced the marsh. Here the grass grew untrimmed and rank up to the very walls; and, as I made my way through it, my feet sank from time to time into little unseen pools and swamps, which wetted them up to the ankles after a few steps. However, I went on as carefully as I could, past a tangle of shrubs, yew-trees, and straggling briers, until, pushing aside the low-hanging branches of a barberry-tree, I found myself within a few feet of a window so heavily shaded by gnarled and knotted ivy that for a few moments I did not notice a woman's face staring at me intently through the glass. As soon as I caught sight of the sunken face and large lustreless gray eyes, I knew, by her likeness to the child at the pond, that this was Mrs. Rayner. I retreated in as leisurely a manner as I could, trying to look as if I had not seen her; for there was something in the eager, hopeless stare of her eyes as mine met them which made me feel like a spy.

I crept back into the house and up to my room, unpacked my boxes, and sat down to write to my mother an account of my journey and arrival. I did not tell her quite all that I had seen, or all the strange impressions this first evening had made upon me. I felt very anxious to communicate them to somebody; but my mother was a gentle nervous woman, whom I had already, young as I was, learned to lead rather than be led by; I knew that the least suggestion of mystery would cause her an agony of doubt and anxiety about her child which I could not allay by letter; so I contented myself with a description of the picturesque beauty of the place and of Mr. Rayner's kindness. I had to finish this by candle-light, and, when I had ended, I rose and went to the window to give one more look at the scene under a new aspect. My window, I afterwards found, was over the one at which I had seen Mrs. Rayner's face; it was high enough from the ground for me to have, through the gaps between the trees, a good view of the marsh and the hills beyond.

A low cry of admiration burst from me as I looked out. Over all the wide expanse of marsh, which seemed to stretch for miles on either hand, lay a white mist, rising only a few feet from the ground, but so thick as to look like a silver lake in the moonlight; a range of hills two or three miles off seemed to mark the opposite shore. The mist was dense under my window, too, on the very grass that I had waded through a couple of hours before. As I looked out and tried to imagine little fairy boats in the elders which rose here and there out of the mist-hidden marsh, a shiver passed over me; and I drew in my head with a sudden change of thought.

"How cold it is! Mr. and Mrs. Rayner must be devoted admirers of the picturesque to live in a house that must be so very damp!"

CHAPTER II

I was down in the dining-room the next morning, with the unfailing punctuality of a new-comer, at the sound of the breakfast-bell, before any one else was there. Mr. Rayner came in in a few minutes, handsome, cheerful, but rather preoccupied; and I was listening to his bright small-talk with the polite stranger's smile, when I discovered, without having heard any sound, that Mrs. Rayner was in the room. She had glided in like a ghost, and, without more interest in the life around her than a ghost might show, she was standing at the table, waiting. I was thankful to see that there was no trace in her eyes now of the steadfast eager gaze which had disconcerted me on the night before, nothing but the limpest indifference to me in the way in which she held out her hand when her husband introduced me.

"She must have been pretty ten years ago," I thought, as I looked at her thin face, with the fair faded complexion and dull gray eyes. There was a gentleness about her which would have been grace still, if she had taken any pains to set off by a little womanly coquetry her slim girl-like figure, small thin hands, and the masses of long brown hair which were carelessly and unbecomingly dragged away from her forehead and twisted up on her head.

Then the door opened, and the servants came in to prayers, with the elfish baby and a pretty delicate-looking child, blue-eyed and fair-haired, who was presented to me before breakfast as Haidee, my pupil.

Nobody talked during the meal but Mr. Rayner, and the only other noticeable thing was the improper behavior of the baby, who kept throwing bits of bread at her father when he was not looking, and aimed a blow with a spoon at him when he passed her chair to cut himself some cold meat. He saw it and laughed at her.

"It is a most extraordinary thing, Miss Christie," said he; "but that child hates me."

I thought he spoke in fun; but, before I had been long at the Alders, I found that it was true that this most unpleasant baby's strongest feeling was dislike of her father, though there seemed to be no reason for it, since he never did anything harsher than laugh at her. She would not even take sweets from his hand.

"You do not yet know what primitive people you have come among, Miss Christie," said Mr. Rayner during breakfast. "We dine here at half-past one. If we were to suggest late dinner, we should have to prepare our own food, like excommunicated persons. It is hard as it is to keep our modest staff of three servants. They say the place is damp, which, being interpreted, means that it is too far for their 'young men' in the town to come and see them. Were you not surprised at the wording of my advertisement?"

"Yes, Mr. Rayner."

"My wife was afraid that it would frighten off many desirable young ladies by its ogreish abruptness. The fact is, the lady who has just left us, quite a typical instructress of forty, with prominent teeth and glasses, nearly frightened our lives out. She wouldn't talk, and my wife wants a cheerful companion; and she said she was dying of rheumatism, and threatened to prosecute me for decoying her to such a damp place. So we registered a solemn vow that we would have nothing to do with hoar antiquity again."

"How could she say anything against such a lovely place?" said I.

"Well, now, Miss Christie, I grant she had a show of reason on her side. I have sometimes thought the place damp myself; but my wife has got attached to it; haven't you, Lola?"

"Yes," said she, without a sign of feeling or interest.

"And so we remain," he went on. "A lady's wishes must be considered; and there are special reasons why they should be in this case. You must know, Miss Christie, that I am a penniless wretch, dependent on my wife; am I not, Lola?" He turned playfully to her.

"Not quite that," said she gently, but with no more warmth than before.

"Practically I am," he persisted. "She was an heiress, I a ruined spendthrift, when she married me. Yet she trusted me; and the only condition she would allow her friends to make was that I should settle in the country—out of the reach of temptation, you see, Miss Christie."

He spoke with some feeling, and looked affectionately at his wife at the end of this unexpectedly frank confession; but she remained as impassive as ever.

I could not help feeling rather sorry for Mr. Rayner. He was always kind and attentive to his wife; but, whether he was in a bright mood, and tried to make her smile, or silent, and needing to be roused out of his gravity, she was always the same, limp, nerveless, apathetic, speaking when necessary in a low soft voice, slowly, with many pauses. She had a habit of letting the last words of a sentence die away upon her lips, and then, after a few moments, as if by an effort, she would say them aloud. I soon grew quite afraid of her, started if I met her unexpectedly, and felt more restrained in her presence than if she had been one of those brilliant satirical women who take the color out of the rest of their sex. Anxious to shake off this strange diffidence, which was beginning to cast a shadow over my life, I offered to read to her when my short hours of study with my pupil were over.

She accepted my offer, and I went into the drawing-room that very afternoon and read her some chapters of *Adam Bede,* while she sat in a rocking-chair, with a piece of embroidery making slow progress in the thin white fingers. I stopped at the end of each chapter, waiting for the comment which never came, and rather hoping for some little compliment upon my reading, an accomplishment I took pride in. But she only said "Thank you" very gently, and, when I asked her if I should go on, "Yes, if it will not tire you."

Presently I found out that she was not listening, except for a few minutes at a time, but that she was sitting with her hands in her lap listlessly playing with her embroidery, while her eyes were fixed on the garden outside, with a deep sadness in them which contrasted strangely with her usual apathetic indifference to all things. Still I read on, pretending not to notice her mood, until such a heavy despairing sigh broke from her pale lips that my heart beat fast for pity, and I involuntarily stopped short in my reading, and raised my eyes, with tears in them, to hers. She started, and, turning towards me, seemed to hold my eyes for a moment fixed on hers by the fascination of a gaze which seemed anxious to penetrate to the deepest recesses of my thoughts. A little color came to her cheeks; I could see her breast heaving through the muslin gown she wore; she half stretched out one hand towards me, and in another moment I believe she would have called me to her side, when a voice from behind her chair startled us both.

Mr. Rayner had entered the room so softly that we had not heard him.

"You look tired, my dearest Lola," said he gently; "you had better go and lie down for a little while."

At the sound of her husband's voice Mrs. Rayner had shrunk back into her usual statuesque self, like a sensitive plant touched by rough fingers—so quickly too that for a moment I almost thought, as I glanced at the placid expressionless face, that I must have imagined the look of despair and the gesture of invitation. I timidly offered to read her to sleep, but she declined at once, almost abruptly for her, and, with some conventional thanks for my trouble, took the arm her husband held out, thanked him as he carefully wrapped round her a little shawl that she generally wore, and left the room with him.

After that, her reserve towards me was greater than ever; she seemed reluctant to accept the smallest service of common courtesy at my hands, and refused my offers to read to her again, under the plea that it was wasting my time, as she was hardly well enough to listen with full attention. I was hurt as well as puzzled by this; and, being too young and timid to make any further advances, the distance between me and the silent sad lady grew greater than ever.

An attempt that Mr. Rayner made two days after the above scene to draw us together only sent us farther apart. He came into the schoolroom just as Haidee and I were finishing the day's lessons, and, after a few playful questions about her studies, dismissed her into the garden.

"The child is very like her mother in face; don't you think so?" said he. "But I am afraid she will never have her mother's strength of intellect. I see you cannot help looking surprised, Miss Christie. My wife does not give herself the airs of a clever woman. But you would not have doubted it if you had known her five years ago."

He was in one of those moods of almost embarrassing frankness, during which the only thing possible was to sit and listen quietly, with such sparing comment as would content him.

"I dare say," he continued, "it will seem almost incredible to you, who have never heard her say more than is absolutely necessary, but she was one of the most brilliant talkers I have ever met, and four years ago she wrote a book which took London by storm. If I were to tell you the *nom de plume* under which she wrote, you would be afraid of her, for it became at once a sort of proverb for daring of thought and expression. People who did not know her made a bogy of her, and many people who did looked with a sort of superstitious awe upon this slight fair woman who dared to write out what she thought and believed. But they had no idea what a sensitive nature lay under the almost masculine intellect. We had a boy then"—his voice seemed to tremble a little—"two years older than Haidee. The two children had been left in the country—in the best of care, mind—while my wife and I spent the season in town; it was a duty she owed to society then, as one of its brightest ornaments. We heard that the boy was not well; but we had no idea that his illness was serious. I assure you, Miss Christie"—and he spoke with touching earnestness—"that, if my wife had known there was the slightest danger, she would have flown to her child's side without a thought of the pleasures and excitements she was leaving. Well—I can scarcely speak of it even now—the child died, after only two days' illness, away from us. It was on her return from a ball that my wife heard of it. She sank down into a chair, dumb and shivering, without a word or a tear.

When at last we succeeded in rousing her from this state, she took off her beautiful jewels—you have heard she was an heiress—and flung them from her with a shudder of disgust. She has never looked at them since."

He paused for a few minutes, and I sat waiting for him to continue, too much interested to say much.

"I hoped that the depression into which she sank would wear off; but, instead, it only grew deeper. I have told you before that by an arrangement on our marriage our settled home was in the country; after her boy's death, my wife would never even visit town again. When Mona was born, just before we came to this place, a change came, but not the change I had expected. I had hoped she would reawaken to interest in life, and perhaps, if the child had been a boy to replace the one she had lost, it would have been so. Instead of that, her apathy deepened, until now, as you see, she shuts herself from all the world and raises a barrier between herself and the life around her which to strangers is often insurmountable. I have been looking for an opportunity to tell you this, Miss Christie, as I was afraid you might have been puzzled, and perhaps offended, by her strange manner the other day when you were reading to her. When I came in, I thought you looked rather frightened, and I supposed that something you had read had recalled the grief which is always slumbering at her heart, and perhaps led to one of those outbreaks which sometimes cause me the gravest, the very gravest anxiety."

I understood what he meant; but I would not allow myself to appear alarmed by the suggestion. Mr. Rayner went on—

"I fancied I caught sight of a wild look in her eyes, which is sometimes called up in them by a reference to the past, or even by a sudden vivid flash of memory. At such times only I, with the power of my long-tried affection, can calm her instantly. Do not imagine that she would ever be violent, but she might be incoherent enough to frighten you. Tell me, had she said anything that day before I came in which alarmed or puzzled you?"

"No, Mr. Rayner; she scarcely spoke while I read to her."

"Was there anything in what you were reading likely to call up memories of the dreadful time to which I have alluded?"

"I think not. No—none."

"I need not warn you, my dear Miss Christie, to avoid all reference to that subject, or anything that might suggest it, in talking to her, but of course without any appearance of constraint. And I am sure such a sensible girl as you are will not take needless fright at this unhappy disclosure, which I thought it safer to make to you, trusting in your discretion. I still hope that in time she may recover her old health and spirits, consent to see people, and even move away from this place for a little change, which I am sure would do her good. I have begged her to do so over and over again, always unsuccessfully. I cannot bear to be harsh to her; but there is an iron strength of resistance in that woman of strong intellect and weak frame which, I confess, even I have not yet been able to overcome. If you will allow me to advise you, do not mention that subject either to her. One of my reasons for wishing for a young governess was that I might provide her in an unobtrusive manner with cheerful society and let her get accustomed to seeing a bright young face about her; but I am afraid her obstinate reserve has so far defeated my object. However, I don't despair. Now that you know something of her history, you are more likely to sympathize with her and to make some allowance for her seeming coldness. Believe me, underneath all she has a warm heart still. And I am sure you will spare a little sympathy for me, condemned to see the wife I adore living a shut-up life, as it were, seeming to ignore the undying affection of which she must still be conscious."

There was something so winning in his voice and manner as he said these last words that I felt for the moment even more sorry for him than for her, and I took the hand he held out as he rose to go, and looked up with all the frank sympathy I felt. He seemed touched by it, for, as if by a sudden impulse, he stooped and let his lips lightly touch my hand; then, pressing it once more in his, with a look of almost grateful kindliness, he left the room.

I was a little surprised by this demonstration, which I thought rather out of place to a dependant. But he was an impulsive man, the very opposite in all things to his cold statuesque wife, and the union between them seemed sometimes like a bond between the dead and the living.

When I thought over all that he had told me, after he had left the room, it was impossible, even setting apart my natural inclination as a woman to put the blame on the woman, not to come to the conclusion that the fault in this most uncomfortable household was chiefly on the side of Mrs. Rayner. I had never seen a more attentive, long-suffering husband, nor a more coldly irritating wife. From all I had seen, I judged that Mr. Rayner was a sociable man, particularly alive to sympathy, fond of conversation and the society of his fellow-men. To such a man the sort of exile his wife's obstinate reserve and dislike to society condemned him to must have been specially hard to bear with patience. It was true he scoffed at the society the neighborhood afforded, and made me laugh by his description of a country dinner-party, where one could almost predict with certainty what each lady would wear, and where more than half the gentlemen were clergymen, and how the talk would drift after dinner into clerical "shop," and one of the ladies would play a colorless drawing-room piece on the piano, and one of the gentlemen—a curate nearly always—would sing an unintelligible song, in a husky voice, and, when told—by a lady—how well it suited his style, would reply modestly that Santley's songs always did.

But I fancied that, dull as it might be, Mr. Rayner would have been glad of more of even such society as the neighborhood afforded; and, from the bitterness with which he laughed at the paltry pride of small country gentlemen, I soon began to imagine that he must have been snubbed by some among them.

The first Sunday after my arrival was so wet that we could not go to church, so that I had been there a fortnight before I saw a general gathering of the inhabitants. But on the very day previous to this event I had an encounter with two of the ladies of the neighborhood which left a most unpleasant impression upon my mind. Haidee and I were taking our morning walk, when a big Newfoundland dog rushed through a gap in the hedge and frightened my poor little pupil so much that she began to scream. Then a young girl of about fourteen or fifteen, to whom the dog belonged, came up to the hedge, and said that she was sorry he had frightened the child, but that he would not hurt her. And she and I, having soothed Haidee, exchanged a little talk about the fields and her dog, and where the first blackberries were to be found, before we parted, my pupil and I going on by the road while the girl remained in the field. We were only a few steps away when I heard the voice of another girl addressing her rather sharply.

"Who was that you were talking to, Alice?"

The answer was given in a lower voice.

"Well," the other went on, "you should not have spoken to her. Don't you know she comes from the house on the marsh?"

CHAPTER III

The shock given me by those few overheard words—"You should not have spoken to her. Don't you know she comes from the house on the marsh?"—was so great that I lay awake half the night, at first trying to reconcile Mr. Rayner's pathetic story with the horror of everything connected with the Alders expressed by the girl to her companion, and then asking myself whether it would be wise to stay in a house to which it was plain that a mystery of some sort was clinging. At last, when my nerves were calmed somewhat and I began to feel sleepy, I made up my mind to set down those unlucky words as the prejudiced utterance of some narrow-minded country-girl, to whom the least touch of unconventionality seemed a dreadful thing. However, I could not dismiss the incident at once from my mind, and the remembrance of it sharpened my attention to the manner of the salutations that Mr. Rayner exchanged with his neighbors the next day.

Although Geldham church was only a short distance from the Alders, Mrs. Rayner was not strong enough to walk; so she and her husband drove there in the brougham, while Haidee and I went on foot. We started before them, and Mr. Rayner was carefully helping his wife out of the carriage as we got to the gate. There was nothing noticeable in the way in which they bowed to one person, shook hands with another, exchanged a few words with a third; then we all went into the little church, which had been erected but a few years, and of which one aisle was still unbuilt.

There was a square family-pew just in front of ours, which was empty when we took our seats; but, when I rose from my knees, I found fixed upon me, with a straightforward and not very friendly stare, the round gray eyes of a girl two or three years older than myself, whom I recognized as the owner of the voice which had said of me, "Don't you know she comes from the house on the marsh?" By her side, therefore also facing me, was the younger sister, with whom I had talked; she avoided meeting my eyes, and looked rather uncomfortable. As for me, I felt that I hated them both, and was glad when the gentleman who was evidently their father changed his position so that he almost hid them from my sight. Next to him sat a stout lady, who wore a black silk mantle covered with lace and beads and a white bonnet trimmed with yellow bows and unlikely clusters of roses.

My heart sank curiously when I caught sight of the third person in the row, at the farther end of the pew. It was Mr. Laurence Reade, my friend of the dog-cart; and I felt as if a trusted ally had suddenly proved to be an officer in the enemy's camp. Having found myself in an uncongenial household, I had unconsciously looked forward to seeing again, at some time or other, the only person I had met since I came to Norfolk to whom no associations of mystery or melancholy were attached. And now to meet him with those horrid girls! He was their brother evidently, for the elder harpooned him sharply with her sunshade several times for dozing during the service; but, when the sermon began and he had settled himself sideways in the corner with the plain intention of sleeping through the entire discourse, and the devout girl made a desperate lunge at him to rouse him once for all, he quietly took the weapon from her and kicked it under the seat. I rejoiced at this, and so missed the text, which was given out during the struggle. And then I missed a great deal of the sermon, for I was growing unhappy in my new home, and, as the preaching of one clergyman, especially if you are not listening particularly, sounds much like the preaching of another, it was easy to shut my eyes and fancy myself sitting with my mother in church at home in London. Presently, happening to glance round me, I caught sight of Mr. Laurence Reade in the corner of the next pew, with his arms folded, his legs crossed, and his head thrown back; and, if it had not been so very unlikely, I should have thought that he was not really asleep, but that through his half-shut eyelids he was looking at me.

When the sermon was over, and we filed out of church, I noticed that old Mr. Reade exchanged a few words with Mr. Rayner rather stiffly, while the two girls deliberately turned their heads away from us. But Mr. Laurence Reade hung back behind the rest of his family, and stooped to speak to Haidee, who was holding my hand. He asked her to give him a kiss, and she refused—and I was very glad. Of course it was my duty to rebuke her for rudeness, and to tell her to accept the attention with gratitude; but, instead, I looked carefully the other way and pretended not to be aware of the little comedy.

"Oh, Haidee, you shouldn't turn away from your friends!" said he, in his musical voice, with rather more of grave reproach than the occasion required—to a child.

Mr. Rayner was on the churchyard path a little way in front of us, talking to the schoolmaster, the clergyman, and two or three of the gentlemen of the parish. He was trying to persuade them to start a penny bank, and was pointing out to them the encouragement it would give to habits of thrift, and offering to take most of the trouble of starting it into his own hands.

The spirit of inactivity ruled at Geldham; there was no energetic curate to scandalize people by insisting that to doze through one sermon a week was but a negligent way of caring for their souls; the last vestry-meeting had dwindled into a spelling-bee, at which the doctor had been ruled out for putting only one "t" in "committee," and gone home vehemently affirming that his was the right way, and that of the schoolmaster, his colleagues, and the dictionary, the wrong.

It was curious to note now how they all listened coldly at first, with an aversion to the proposal, strengthened by their dislike to the man who proposed it, and how, overcome by an irresistible charm in his manner of arguing as much as by the arguments themselves, they one by one from listless became interested, and not only agreed to the scheme being started, but to taking each some small share in setting it on foot. Then, parting cordially from the man they had greeted so coldly, they all dispersed; and Mr. Rayner, handsome, bright, pleased with his little triumph, turned to his wife and led her to the carriage, while Haidee and I returned as we came— on foot.

He was very severe indeed upon rustic wits and rustic governors during dinner, calling them sheep and donkeys and other things. Then he grew merry and made jokes about them, and I laughed; and, finding in me an appreciative listener, his spirits rose still higher, and I thought before dinner was over that I had never heard any one talk more amusingly. I think Mrs. Rayner made only one remark, and that was when I was furtively wiping some tears of laughter from my eyes; she asked me—

"Do you care to go to church this afternoon, Miss Christie?"

I suppose I looked rather snubbed, for Mr. Rayner broke in—

"Poor girl, how frightened you look at the thought! Know then, Miss Christie, that it is not one of the conditions of residence under this moist but hospitable roof that you should trudge backwards and forwards to church all Sunday, with intervals of pious meditation. We never go ourselves more than once. Our last governess did, because she liked it, not because she was 'druv to it,' I assure you; and I don't suppose, I don't even hope, that the excellent Miss Parker's mantle has fallen on your quarter-of-a-century younger shoulders."

But I had quickly made up my mind that I had better go. Indeed I liked going to church; and, even if I had not acquired the taste already, the dulness of the Sunday before—which I had spent in the drawing-room with Mrs. Rayner and Haidee, hearing my pupil repeat one of the Thirty-nine Articles, which I was sure she did not understand, and which I myself did not understand well enough to explain to her, and stifling my yawns for the rest of the time behind Goulburn's *Personal Religion*—would have made me love it. So I said I should like to go, and they said that there was no afternoon service at Geldham; but Mr. Rayner told me the way to the church at Gullingborough, the next parish, which was not far off.

It was a sultry summer afternoon, with a heavy clouded sky; but it was pleasant to be out of doors, and it was pleasant to be alone; for I found the society of little Haidee, whose shyness and reserve with me had not worn off yet, rather depressing sometimes—I had even cried a little at night over the difficulty I had in making the child fond of me. So that to be quite alone and out of the sombre atmosphere of the Alders was a relief. I passed the gates of a park, among the trees of which I saw a big square white house surrounded by a flower-garden; and a little farther on I saw an American chair on the grass under the park trees, and a young man in a light suit, with his cravat hanging loose and his hat off, lying at full length in it. He had a cigar in his mouth and a gaudy-covered book in his hand, and on a rustic table beside him was a half-empty glass containing some liquid; and I could see that there was ice in it. Of course I only glanced that way, but I recognized the gentleman as Mr. Laurence Reade; and I could not help smiling to myself as I went on. He saw me, I think, for he started up and coughed; but I was looking the other way, and I thought it best not to hear him. As I turned the angle of the park, I glanced again at the white house, and I saw, with a little surprise, Mr. Reade running towards it.

I got to church in very good time, and, being given a seat in the chancel, I could watch the country-people as they filed in; and, just as the last wheezy sound from the organ was dying away before service began, Mr. Laurence Reade, having exchanged his light suit for church-going attire, strode up the middle aisle and banged the door of his pew upon himself. And, remembering how nice the iced drink looked and how cosey the arm-chair appeared, I thought it did him great credit to come to church the second time.

The sky had grown very dark by the time service was over, and the occasional rolling of distant thunder threatened a storm. A few heavy drops fell as I stepped out of the church door, and my heart sank at the thought of the ruin a good shower would work upon my best gown, a light gray merino. It was nearly half an hour's walk to the Alders; my way lay along lanes and across fields where there was little or no shelter, and my umbrella was a small one. However, there was nothing to be done but to start, hoping that the storm might not break with any violence before I got home. I had left all chance of shelter well behind me, when the rain came pouring down like sheets of water, with a sharp hissing sound which made my heart sink within me. I stopped, gathered up my skirt round me, gave a glance round to see that no one was in sight, being aware that my appearance would be neither graceful nor decorous, and then ran for my life. Before I had gone many yards, I heard some one running after me, and then Mr. Reade's voice calling, "Miss Christie!" I ran on without heeding him, ashamed of my plight; but he would not take the rebuff, and in a few more steps he had caught me up, and, taking away my small umbrella, was holding his large one over me. He opened a gate to the right that led into a field with a rough cart-track alongside the hedge.

"But this is the wrong way. I have to turn to the left, I know," said I.

"There is a shed for carts here where we shall get shelter," said he.

And in a few minutes we reached it, and I found myself sitting under a low roof on the red shaft of a cart, watching the downpour outside, while Mr. Reade shook the rain from our umbrellas. A few days before I might have found something to enjoy in this curious encounter with my friend of the dog-cart; but the rudeness and suspicion of his sisters had made me shy with him. So I merely sat there and looked straight in front of me, while he, infected by my reserve, leant against the side of the shed and looked at me. I could see—as one sees so many things, without looking—the rain-drops falling one by one from the low roof on to his hat; but I would not tell him of it.

Things went on like this for some minutes, until a bright flash of lightning dazzled me and made me cry "Oh!"

"You are frightened. Let me stand in front of you," said my companion, starting forward.

"Oh, no, thank you—I am not nervous!" I replied contemptuously, when a loud peal of thunder startled me so much that I nearly fell off my seat.

He said nothing, did not even smile at my crestfallen look; but he took up his stand in front of me, giving me a fine view of his profile against the dark sky. Every minute of this awkward silence was making it more difficult to me to think of something to say.

"I wish it would leave off," I remarked stupidly, at length.

"Are you in such a hurry to get back to the Alders? It is no drier there than it is here."

"But at least one can change one's boots."

"Have you got your feet wet? Why, you have on little toy town-boots, not fit to walk down a country-lane in! You will be laid up with rheumatic fever, or something of the kind," said he anxiously, looking vaguely about him for dry boots.

"Oh, no, no—they are much thicker than they look!" said I. "It isn't that. But Mr. Rayner will be anxious."

"Mr. Rayner; and Mrs. Rayner, won't she be anxious too?"

"Oh, Mrs. Rayner is never anything! At least—I mean," said I, annoyed at having spoken without thinking, "she is so reserved that—"

"That you like Mr. Rayner best?"

"Oh, yes!"

He drew himself up rather coldly.

"So do most ladies, I believe."

"One can't help liking a person who talks and laughs, and is bright and kind, better than one who never speaks, and glides about like a ghost, and looks coldly at you if you speak to her," I burst out, apologetically at first, but warming into vehemence towards the close of my speech.

"Perhaps she means to be kind," said he gently.

"Then she ought to make her meaning plainer. She can't think it is kind to fix her eyes upon me as if I were something not human, if I laugh; to give me her hand so coldly and unresponsively that it seems like a dead hand in mine, and at other times to take no more notice of me than if I were not there. Besides, she knows that it is the first time I have ever left home, and she must see sometimes that I am not happy."

Mr. Reade suddenly stooped towards me, and then straightened himself again just as suddenly, without any remark; but he cleared his throat. I remembered that I had no right to make this confession to a comparative stranger, and I added quickly—

"I ought not to talk as if I were ill-treated. I am not at all. If she would only not be quite so cold!"

"Perhaps her own troubles are very heavy and hard to bear."

"Oh, no, they are not!" I replied confidently. "At least, she has a kind husband and a pretty home, and everything she can wish for. And I think it is very selfish of her to give herself up to brooding over the memory of her dead child, instead of trying to please her living husband."

"Her dead child?"

"Yes. She had a boy who died some years ago, and she has never got over it. That is why she is so reserved."

"Oh! How long ago did this boy die?" asked he, in a curiously incredulous tone.

"About five years ago, I think Mr. Rayner said."

"Oh, then it was Mr. Rayner who told you?"

"Yes."

"And Mrs. Rayner has never got over it?"

"No. It seems difficult to believe, doesn't it, that a brilliant woman who wrote books and was much admired should fade like that into a kind of shadow? I wonder she doesn't write more books to divert her thoughts from brooding over the past."

"Oh, she wrote books! Did she tell you so herself?"

"No—Mr. Rayner."

"Oh! Did Mr. Rayner tell you any more?"

The irony in his tone was now so unmistakable that I hesitated and looked up at him inquiringly.

"I am sure he must have told you that he is a very ill-used man and a very long-suffering husband, and asked you to pity him. Didn't he, Miss Christie? Ah, I see he did!" he cried.

I could feel the blood rushing to my cheeks; but I was indignant at having to submit to this catechism.

"Mr. Rayner never asks impertinent questions," I said severely.

The young man drew back, muttered "I beg your pardon," and, turning to watch the rain, began to hum something without any tune to cover his discomfiture. I was sorry directly; but my dignity forbade my calling him back to retract the snub. Yet I was dying to know the reason of his violent prejudice against Mr. Rayner. To my relief, in a few minutes he came back to me of his own accord.

"Miss Christie," he began nervously, "I am afraid I have offended you. Won't you forgive me for being carried a little too far by my interest in a lady who herself confessed that she is away from her friends for the first time and not—very happy?"

I could not resist such an appeal as that; I looked up smiling, with tears in my eyes.

"Oh, I am not at all offended! But I should like to know what reason you have for thinking so ill, as you seem to do, of Mr. Rayner."

"Perhaps I am wrong. I really have no proof that he is anything but what he wishes every one to think him—a light-hearted accomplished man, of idle life and pleasant temper. It is not his fault that, with all his cleverness, his ease of manner is not quite the ease of a gentleman."

I was scarcely experienced enough to have found that out for myself. I considered for a moment, and then said rather timidly—

"Won't you tell me anything more? You can if you will, I think, and, alone in the world as I am, I want all the knowledge I can get of the people I live among, to guide me in my conduct."

He seemed to debate with himself for a moment; then he sat down beside me on the other shaft of the cart, and said very earnestly—

"Seriously, then, Miss Christie, I would advise you to leave the Alders as soon as you possibly can, even before you have got another engagement. You are in the midst of more dangers than you can possibly know of, more probably than I know of myself, more certainly than I can warn you against."

His voice was very low as he finished, and, while we both sat silent, he with his eyes intently fixed on my face, mine staring out fearfully at the sky, a dark figure suddenly appeared before us, blocking out the light. It was Mr. Rayner. Mr. Reade and I started guiltily. The new-comer had approached so quietly that we had not heard him; had he heard us?

CHAPTER IV

In spite of the rain and the mud, Mr. Rayner was in the brightest of humors; and his first words dispelled my fear that he might have overheard the warning Mr. Reade had just given me not to stay at the Alders. He caught sight of me first as he came under the roof of the dark shed.

"At last, Miss Christie! It was a happy thought of mine to look for you here. But how in the world did you discover this place of refuge?" Then, turning, he saw my companion. "Hallo, Laurence! Ah, this explains the mystery! You have been playing knight-errant, I see, and I am too late in the field; but I shall carry off the lady, after all. My wife noticed that you started without your ulster, Miss Christie, and, as soon as service was over, she sent me off with it to meet you."

He helped me on with it, and then I stood between them, silent and rather shy at receiving so much unaccustomed attention, until the rain began to fall less heavily, and we seized the opportunity to escape. When we got in sight of the park, Mr. Reade wanted to take a short cut through it to the house; but Mr. Rayner pointed out that there was no object to be gained by catching a bad cold wading through the long wet grass, so we all went together as far as the park gates, where Mr. Reade left us.

"Nice young fellow, that," said Mr. Rayner, as soon as the other was out of earshot. "Just the kind of open frank lad I should have liked to have for a son in a few years' time. Handsome too, and good-natured. There's not a girl in all the country-side who hasn't a smile and a blush for Laurence."

I did not think this so great a recommendation as it seemed to Mr. Rayner, but I said nothing; and he went on—

"He is worth all the rest of his family put together. Father—self-important, narrow-minded old simpleton; mother—ill-dressed vegetable, kept alive by a sense of her own dignity as the penniless daughter of an earl; sisters—plain stuck-up nonentities; younger brother—dunce at Eton. But they haven't been able to spoil Laurence. He may have a few of their prejudices, but he has none of their narrow-minded pig-headedness. You don't understand the rustic mind yet, Miss Christie. I assure you there are plenty of people in this parish who have condemned me to eternal punishment because I am fond of racing and, worse than all, play the violin."

"Do you play the violin? Oh, I am so fond of it!"

"Are you? Poor child, you had better not acknowledge the taste as long as you remain in this benighted spot; they class it with the black art. I believe I am popularly supposed to have bewitched the Alders with my playing. Some of the rustics think that the reeds round the pond play all by themselves about midnight, if they are accidentally touched."

"Oh, Mr. Rayner, aren't you rather hard upon the rustics?" I said, laughing.

"Not a bit, as you will find out soon enough. However, if you are not afraid of being bewitched too, you shall hear my violin some evening, and give me your opinion of it."

We were within the garden gates by this time, and, as we walked down the path, I saw a woman's figure among the trees on our right. The storm had left the evening sky so dark and she was so well hidden that, if I had not been very sharp-sighted, I should not have noticed her. As it was, I could not recognize her, and could only guess that it was Mrs. Rayner. The idea of those great weird eyes being upon me, watching me, just as they had been on the evening of my arrival, made me uncomfortable. I was glad Mr. Rayner did not look that way, but went on quietly chatting till we reached the house. He left me in the hall, and went straight into his study, while I, before going upstairs to take off my bonnet, went into our little schoolroom to put my church-service away. The French window had not been closed, and I walked up to it to see whether the rain had come in. The sky was still heavy with rain-clouds, so that it was quite dark indoors, and, while I could plainly see the woman I had noticed among the trees forcing her way through the wet branches, stepping over the flower-beds on to the lawn, and making her way to the front of the house, she could not see me. When she came near enough for me to distinguish her figure, I saw that it was not Mrs. Rayner, but Sarah the housemaid. I stood, without acknowledging it to myself, rather in awe of this woman; she was so tall and so thin, and had such big eager eyes and such a curiously constrained manner. She was only a few steps from the window where I stood completely hidden by the curtain, when Mr. Rayner passed quickly and caught her arm from behind. She did not turn or cry out, but only stopped short with a sort of gasp.

"What were you doing in the shrubbery just now, Sarah?" he asked quietly. "If you want to take fresh air in the garden, you must keep to the lawn and the paths. By forcing your way through the trees and walking over the beds you do damage to the flowers—and to yourself. If you cannot remember these simple rules, you will have to look out for another situation."

She turned round sharply.

"Another situation! Me!"

"Yes, you. Though I should be sorry to part with such an old servant, yet one may keep a servant too long."

"Old! I wasn't always old!" she broke out passionately.

"Therefore you were not always in receipt of such good wages as you get now. Now go in and get tea ready. And take care the toast is not burnt again."

I could see that she glared at him with her great black eyes like a tigress at bay, but she did not dare to answer again, but slunk away cowed into the house. I was not surprised, for the tone of cold command with which he spoke those last insignificant words inspired me with a sudden sense of fear of him, with a feeling that I was face to face with an irresistible will, such as I should have thought it impossible for light-hearted Mr. Rayner to inspire.

The whole scene had puzzled me a little. What did Sarah the housemaid want to stand like a spy in the shrubbery for? How had Mr. Rayner seen and recognized her without seeming even to look in that direction? Was there any deeper meaning under the words that had passed between them? There was suppressed passion in the woman's manner which could hardly have been stirred by her master's orders to keep to the garden paths and not to burn the toast; and there was a hard decision in Mr. Rayner's which I had never noticed before, even when he was seriously displeased. I waited behind the curtain by the window until long after he had gone back towards the study, feeling guiltily that his sharp eyes must find me out, innocently as I had played the spy. If he were to speak to me in the tone that he had used to Sarah, I felt that I should run away or burst into tears, or do something else equally foolish and unbecoming in an instructress of youth. But no one molested me. When I crept away from the window and went softly upstairs to my room, there was no one about, and no sound to be heard in the house save a faint clatter of tea-things in the servants' hall. At tea-time Mr. Rayner was as bright as usual, and laughingly declared that they should never trust me to go to church by myself again.

That night I pondered Mr. Reade's warning to me to leave the Alders; but I soon decided that the suggestion was quite unpractical. For, putting aside the fact that I had no stronger grounds than other people's prejudice and suspicion for thinking it imprudent to stay, and that I could see no sign of the dangers Mr. Reade had hinted at so vaguely, what reason could I offer either to my employers or to my mother for wishing to go? This sort of diffidence at inventing excuses is a strong barrier to action in young people. And, if I had overcome this diffidence sufficiently to offer a plausible motive for leaving the Alders, where was I to go?

My father was dead; my mother, who had been left with very little to live upon, had been glad, at the time when it was agreed that I should begin to earn my own living, to accept an offer to superintend the household of a brother of hers who had not long lost his wife. My uncle would, I know, give me a home while I looked out for another situation; but I understood now how few people seemed to want the services of "a young lady, aged eighteen, who preferred children under twelve."

And what a bad recommendation it would be to have left my first situation within a month! And what could I say I did it for? If I said, Because the house was damp, people would think I was too particular. And, if I said I was afraid my pupil's mother was mad, they would want some better reason than the fact that she talked very little and moved very softly for believing me. And, if I said I had been told the place was dangerous, and so thought I had better go, they would think I was mad myself. And, besides these objections to my leaving, was there not, to a young mind, an unacknowledged attraction in the faint air of mystery that hung about the place, which would have made the ordinary British middle-class household seem rather uninteresting after it? So I decided to pay no attention to vague warnings, but to stay where I was certainly, on the whole, well off.

The next morning, as I put on a dainty china-blue cotton frock that I had never worn before, I could not help noticing how much better I was looking than when I lived in London. Instead of being pale, I had now a pink color in my cheeks, and my eyes seemed to look larger and brighter than they used to do. After a minute's pleased contemplation of my altered appearance, I turned from the glass in shame. What would my mother say if she could see how vain her daughter was growing? Without another look even to see whether I had put in my brooch straight, I went downstairs. Mr. Rayner was already in the dining-room, but no one else was there yet. He put down his newspaper and smiled at me.

"Come into the garden for a few minutes until the rest of the family assembles," said he; and I followed him through the French window on to the lawn.

The morning sun left this side of the house in shade. The birds were twittering in the ivy and stirring the heavy leaves as they flew out frightened at the noise of the opening window; the dew was sparkling on the grass, and the scent of the flowers was deliciously sweet.

"Looks pretty, doesn't it?" said Mr. Rayner.

"Pretty! It looks and smells like Paradise! I mean—" I stopped and blushed, afraid that he would think the speech profane.

But he only laughed very pleasantly. I was smelling a rose while I tried to recover the staid demeanor I cultivated as most suitable to my profession. When I raised my eyes, he was looking at me and still laughing.

"You are fond of roses?"

"Yes, very, Mr. Rayner."

I might own so much without any derogation from my dignity.

"But don't you think it was very silly of Beauty to choose only a rose, when her father asked what he should bring her? I have always thought that ostentation of humility spoilt an otherwise amiable character."

I laughed.

"Poor girl, think how hard her punishment was! I don't think, if I had married the prince, I could ever have forgotten that he had been a beast, and I should have always been in fear of his changing back again."

"The true story is, you know, that he always remained a beast, but he gave her so many diamonds and beautiful things that she overlooked his ugliness. Like that the story happens every day."

I only shook my head gently; I could not contradict Mr. Rayner, but I would not believe him.

"Now, if you were Beauty, what would you ask papa to bring you?"

I laughed shyly.

"A prince?" I blushed and shook my head.

"No, not yet," I said, smiling rather mischievously.

"A ring, a bracelet, a brooch?"

"Oh, no!"

"A Murray's Grammar, a pair of globes, a black-board?"

"No, Mr. Rayner. I should say a rose like Beauty—a beautiful Marshal Niel rose. I couldn't think of anything lovelier than that."

"That is a large pale yellow rose, isn't it? I can't get it to grow here. What a pity we are not in a fairy tale, Miss Christie, and then the soil wouldn't matter! We would have Marshal Niel roses growing up to the chimney-pots."

We had sauntered back to the dining-room window, and there, staring out upon us in a strange fixed way, was Mrs. Rayner. She continued to look at us, and especially at me, as if fascinated, until we were close to the window, when she turned with a start; and when we entered the room the intent expression had faded from her lustreless eyes, and she was her usual lifeless self again.

At dinner-time Mr. Rayner did not appear; I was too shy to ask Mrs. Rayner the reason, and I could only guess, when tea-time came and again there was no place laid for him, that he had gone away somewhere. I was sure of it when he had not reappeared the next morning, and then I became conscious of a slow but sure change, a kind of gradual lightening, in Mrs. Rayner's manner. She did not become talkative or animated like any other woman; but it was as if a statue of stone had become a statue of flesh, feeling the life in its own veins and grown conscious of the life around it. This change brought one strange symptom: she had grown nervous. Instead of wearing always an unruffled stolidity, she started at any unexpected sound, and a faint tinge of color would mount to her white face at the opening of a distant door or at a step in the passage. This change must certainly, I thought, be due to her husband's departure; but it was hard to tell whether his absence made her glad or sorry, or whether any such vivid feeling as gladness or grief caused the alteration in her manner.

On the second day of Mr. Rayner's absence Sarah came to the schoolroom, saying that a gentleman wished to speak to me. In the drawing-room I found Mr. Laurence Reade.

"I have come on business with Mr. Rayner; but, as they told me he was out, I ventured to trouble you with a commission for him, Miss Christie."

"I don't know anything about business, especially Mr. Rayner's," I began doubtfully. "Perhaps Mrs. Rayner—"

"Oh, I couldn't trouble her with such a small matter! I know she is an invalid. It is only that two of the village boys want to open an account with the penny bank. So I offered to bring the money."

He felt in his pockets and produced one penny.

"I must have lost the other," he said gravely. "Can you give me change for a threepenny-piece?"

I left him and returned with two halfpennies. He had forgotten the names of the boys, and it was some time before he remembered them. Then I made a formal note of their names and of the amounts, and Mr. Reade examined it, and made me write it out again in a more business-like manner. Then he put the date, and wrote one of the names again, because I had misspelt it, and then smoothed the paper with the blotting-paper and folded it, making, I thought, an unnecessarily long performance of the whole matter.

"It seems a great deal of fuss to make about twopence, doesn't it?" I asked innocently.

And Mr. Reade, who was bending over the writing-table, suddenly began to laugh, then checked himself and said—

"One cannot be too particular, even about trifles, where other people's money is concerned."

And I said, "Oh, no! I see," with an uncomfortable feeling that he was making fun of my ignorance of business-matters. He talked a little about Sunday, and hoped I had not caught cold; and then he went away. And I found, by the amount of hemming Haidee had got through when I went back to the schoolroom, that he had stayed quite a long time.

Nothing happened after that until Saturday, which was the day on which I generally wrote to my mother. After tea, I took my desk upstairs to my own room; it was pleasanter there than in the schoolroom; I liked the view of the marsh between the trees, and the sighing of the wind among the poplars. I had not written many lines before another sound overpowered the rustle of the leaves—the faint tones of a violin. At first I could distinguish only a few notes of the melody, then there was a pause and a sound as of an opening window; after that, Schubert's beautiful "Aufenthalt" rang out clearly and held me as if enchanted. It must be Mr. Rayner come back. I had not thought, when he said he played the violin, that he could play like that. I must hear better. When the last long sighing note of the "Aufenthalt" had died away, I shut up my half-finished letter hastily in my desk and slipped downstairs with it. The music had begun again. This time it was the "Ständchen." I stole softly through the hall, meaning to finish my letter in the schoolroom, where, with the door ajar, I could hear the violin quite well. But, as I passed the drawing-room door, Mr. Rayner, without pausing in his playing, cried "Come in!" I was startled by this, for I had made no noise; but I put my desk down on the hall table and went in. Mrs. Rayner and Haidee were there, the former with a handsome shawl, brought by her husband, on a chair beside her, and my pupil holding a big wax doll, which she was not looking at—the child never cared for her dolls. Mr. Rayner, looking handsomer than ever, sunburnt, with his chestnut hair in disorder, smiled at me and said, without stopping the music—

"I have not forgotten you. There is a *souvenir* of your dear London for you," and nodded towards a rough wooden box, nailed down.

I opened it without much difficulty; it was from Covent Garden, and in it, lying among ferns and moss and cotton-wool, were a dozen heavy beautiful Marshal Niel roses. I sat playing with them in an ecstasy of pleasure, intoxicated with music and flowers, until Mr. Rayner put away his violin and I rose to say good-night.

"Lucky Beauty!" he said, laughing, as he opened the door for me. "There is no beast for you to sacrifice yourself to in return for the roses."

I laughed back and left the room, and, putting my desk under my flowers, went towards the staircase. Sarah was standing near the foot of it, wearing a very forbidding expression.

"So you're bewitched too!" she said, with a short laugh, and turned sharply towards the servants' hall.

And I wondered what she meant, and why Mr. and Mrs. Rayner kept in their service such a very rude and disagreeable person.

CHAPTER V

The next day was Sunday, to which I had already begun to look forward eagerly, as one does in the country, as a break in the monotonous round of days. Old Mr. Reade was not at church, and his son sat in his place with his back to me. Instead of putting his elbows on his knees through the prayers as he had done on the Sunday before, he would turn right round and kneel in front of his seat, facing me—which was a little disconcerting, for, as he knelt with his chin on his hands and his head back, he seemed to be saying all the responses to me, and I could not raise my eyes for a minute from my book without having my attention distracted in spite of myself.

After service, as we stood about in the churchyard, I heard Mr. Rayner telling the doctor and two of the farmers about the races he had been to the week before, and of his having won fifteen pounds on a horse the name of which I forget; and he took out of his pocket a torn race-card, seeming surprised to find it there, and said it must have been that which had caused his thoughts to wander during the sermon. He asked Mrs. Reade whether her husband was ill, and did not seem at all affected by the cool manner in which she answered his inquiries.

"I had the pleasure of lunching with a relative of yours, Mrs. Reade, on the course at Newmarket last week—Lord Bramley. He is a cousin of yours, is he not?"

"Hardly a cousin; but he is connected with my family, Mr. Rayner," she answered more graciously.

"He thinks more of the connection than you seem to do, for he asked me particularly how you were, and whether you thought of going up to town this autumn. I told him I could not give him any information as to your intended movements, but that you had never looked better than when I saw you last."

And Mrs. Reade was still talking to Mr. Rayner, with more affability in her haughtiness, when Haidee and I started on our walk home.

At dinner Mr. Rayner gave us part of their conversation, with an excellent parody of the lady's manner and a funny exaggeration of the humility of his own. He was always particularly bright on Sunday at dinner, the contact with duller wits in the morning seeming to give edge to his own.

On that afternoon I was scarcely outside the gate on my way to church when he joined me.

"No, no, Miss Christie; we are not going to trust you to go to church by yourself again."

I blushed, feeling a little annoyed, though I scarcely knew why. But surely I could take care of myself, and did not want surveillance, especially Mr. Rayner's.

"Don't be angry; I spoke only in fun. I want to see Boggett about some fencing, and I know I shall catch him at church. But, if you object to my company—"

"Oh, no, Mr. Rayner, of course not!" said I, overwhelmed with terror at the thought of such impertinence being attributed to me.

The shock of this made conversation difficult to me, and I listened while Mr. Rayner talked, with even less of "Yes" and "No" and simple comment than usual. When we passed the park, I saw Mr. Laurence Reade, dressed for church, tossing a small prayer-book—men never burden themselves with the big church-service we women carry—and finishing a cigar, with his back against a tree. I think he must have seen us for some time before I caught sight of him, for I was looking at an oak-leaf in my hand while Mr. Rayner explained its structure to me. I had never seen Mr. Reade look cross before, and I thought it a pity he should spoil his nice kind face by such a frown; and I wondered whether he was ill-tempered, and, if not, what had annoyed him.

When one sees people playing with prayer-books and dressed for church, one cannot help expecting to see them there; and I had an unreasonable and absurd feeling almost like disappointment as the little organ droned out a dismal voluntary and the service began, and still Mr. Laurence Reade did not appear; and I caught myself looking up whenever the door creaked and a late worshipper came in, and glancing towards the pew he had occupied on the Sunday before, which I suddenly remembered was very unbecoming in me. But he did not come.

The heat and this absurd little trifle, and my penitence for it, so distracted my attention that I scarcely heard a word of the sermon. But then it was the curate who preached on that afternoon, and his discourses were never of the exciting kind. I just heard him say that it was his intention to give a course of six sermons, of which this was to be the first; and after that I listened only now and then; and presently I noticed that Mr. Rayner, who always looked more devout than anybody else in church, was really asleep all the time. It was a heavily-built little Norman church, very old and dark, and he was sitting in a corner in such an attentive attitude that I thought at first I must be mistaken; but I looked at him twice, and then I was quite sure.

When service was over, he stayed behind to talk to Boggett, while I went on alone. He overtook me in a few minutes; but, when he said the sermon was good of its kind, I had to turn away my head that he might not see me smiling. But I was not quick enough for Mr. Rayner.

"I didn't say of what kind, Miss Christie. I may have meant it was good as a lullaby. One must be on one's guard with you demure people. I have never yet been to afternoon service without going to sleep, and I have never before been discovered. Now the spell is broken, and I shall feel that the eyes of the whole congregation are upon me. Are you shocked Miss Christie?"

"Oh, no, Mr. Rayner!"

"You wouldn't take such a liberty as to be shocked at anything I might do; would you, Miss Christie?"

His tone of grave mischief woke an answering spirit in me.

"Certainly not, Mr. Rayner."

"Where did you pick up a sense of humor, most rare gift of your sex, and why do you hide it away so carefully, Miss Christie?"

"Indeed I don't know; and I don't mean to hide anything," I answered rather foolishly.

"And how did you like the sermon?"

"I—I wasn't listening much, Mr. Rayner."

"Not listening! A religious little girl like you not listening! I'm surprised—I really am."

His manner grew suddenly so grave, and he really seemed so much surprised, that I felt called upon to make a sort of profession.

"I'm not really religious," I said hurriedly. "I haven't meant ever to pretend to be. But I do respect religion and religious people very much, and I hope some day I shall be able to enter into their feelings better than I can now. I do pray for it," I ended, almost in a whisper.

Mr. Rayner took my hand very kindly.

"It will come, child, it will come," he said gravely and quite paternally. "Go on quietly doing your duty as you do, and the blessing will come in due time."

He said it so simply, without any attempt at preaching, that I felt I looked up to him more naturally than even to a clergyman, being quite sure now that he acquitted me of any intention to be hypocritical. And when, after tea, he asked me to accompany his violin on the piano while he played Mozart's Twelfth Mass, the fervor which he put into the beautiful music inspired me with a corresponding exaltation of feeling, such as no sacred music had ever woke in me before. At the end of the evening Mrs. Rayner wished me good-night and glided softly from the room before I had finished putting the music in order, as Mr. Rayner had asked me to do. When I rose from bending over the canterbury, still flushed with the excitement caused by the music, Mr. Rayner held out his hand with a grave smile.

"You are the best accompanist I have ever met; you catch the spirit of this sacred music perfectly. To-morrow night I shall prove whether you are so accomplished a reader of secular music. Good night, my dear child."

And he bent down to kiss me. But I shrank back slightly, and so evaded him, trying at the same time to make my movement seem unconscious; and, with a smiling "Good-night," I left the room.

As soon as I had done so, my heart sank within me. What had I done? Probably offended Mr. Rayner beyond recall by what must seem to him an absurdly strained piece of prudery. It looked as if I thought myself a person of such attractions that he wanted to kiss me to please himself, instead of an insignificant little girl whom he was going to kiss good-naturedly, as he might have done if he had been her father. But then he was not my father, and not nearly old enough to be so, however paternal and kind his manner might be; if he had been forty or fifty, I should have submitted without a moment's hesitation. But, if Sarah or Mrs. Rayner, neither of whom seemed to like me very much, had suddenly come in and found Mr. Rayner kissing me, she might have mistaken, in a way which would have been very unpleasant for me, the feeling which prompted him to do so. So I comforted myself as well as I could with the thought that, after all, I had done only what was right and prudent; and, if he was offended, well, there was no help for it.

The next morning, to my great relief, his manner was just the same as usual; of course what had caused so much thought and anxiety to the girl of eighteen had seemed but a trifle to the man of three-and-thirty. I wondered whether I should be summoned to the drawing-room to accompany him on the violin, as he had spoken on the previous night of wishing me to do. But at tea he was much preoccupied, and told Sarah that a gentleman would be coming to see him presently, who was to be shown into the study.

As he turned to say this, I noticed a sudden flash of horror pass over Mrs. Rayner's pale features and disappear in a moment, before her husband could see her face again; and I thought I saw on Sarah's dark face a look of intelligence when the order was given her, as if she too knew something about the expected visitor. I hope I am not very inquisitive; but, in a quiet country-house to which, rightly or wrongly, some suspicion of mystery is attached, one cannot help noticing even trifles connected with unaccustomed events, and wondering whether there is some meaning in them.

I tried not to think any more about it, as it certainly did not concern me; but I did not succeed very well in banishing it from my mind until I sat down in the empty schoolroom to my evening task, set by myself, of translating a page of Markham's English History into German. I was very anxious to improve myself, so that by and by I might be an accomplished woman and able to take an engagement as finishing governess, which at that time seemed to me quite a lofty ambition. When the translation was finished, I had still to read a chapter of Guizot's French History; but that was pleasant, easy work, and might be enjoyed in the garden. I had seen the stranger as I was crossing the hall after tea. He was a small slight man, with a fair mustache, who might be old or young; and, although he wore only a gray travelling-suit, he gave one the impression of being very well dressed indeed. I had forgotten all about him long before I made my way, with a heavy volume of history in my arms, to the pond, near the prettiest, reediest corner of which I had made myself a nice little nest. There was here a willow-tree which had been forced by an aggressive oak to grow in a slanting position, and one of its lowest branches hung parallel to the ground. This made my seat, and a piece of cord fastened from branch to branch a foot and a half above made a rest for my back; so, with a couple of old bricks to raise my feet out of the damp grass, I could injudiciously sit there and enjoy the summer evening till quite late. I read my Guizot, conscientiously hunting out in the dictionary all the words I did not know, until the light began to fade, and I was thinking it was time to go in, when I heard voices that seemed to be coming towards me from the house.

I have mentioned a path which led, by a short cut through the plantation, from the house to the high-road to Beaconsburgh. The speakers, a man and a woman, as I could already make out, seemed to be coming along the path. Whoever they might be, I would wait until they had gone by before I went in. I could not see them, nor could they see me, I knew. When they came a little nearer, I recognized Sarah's voice; the other was that of a man of a class much higher than her own. Could it be the stranger? He was talking familiarly and seriously with her; I could tell that before I heard any words. Sarah was speaking in a tone of bitter complaint, and the first words I heard were hers.

"I won't stand it much longer—and so I tell you."

"Tell him, my dear Sally—if you dare. And now oblige me by speaking a little lower, for there is nothing like trees for carrying tales."

She began again in a lower voice, but in the same tone, and, from the occasional words I heard—for I could not help listening—I gathered that she was angry because some unknown "he" paid too much attention to some unknown "her." But I could guess who they were. Sarah, it was well known in the house, had an admirer, a man some years younger than herself, who lived a long way off—in London, I think I had heard it said—and who paid her visits at irregular intervals. Mr. Rayner took great interest in this love-affair, and derived much amusement from it; he had somehow discovered that the admirer, whose name was Tom Parkes, was inclined to pay more attention than was meet to the kitchen-maid, Jane; and it was Mr. Rayner's opinion that there would be very little left of Jane if she encouraged the fickle swain's attentions.

So Sarah was giving vent to her jealousy in an earnest and intimate conversation with her master's guest. It seemed a very strange proceeding. I knew that men in the position of gentlemen do treat women of a lower class with more consideration than is necessary when they are young and pretty; but Sarah's face, which looked as if it was worn and lined before its time with hard work and strong passions, was more repellent than attractive, and I was glad I could not see it as I heard her fierce words more plainly, and knew how her great black eyes must be flashing and her mouth twitching, as they did whenever she was annoyed.

"Look what I've done for him; think how I've worked for him!" she said. "He would never be where he is now if it wasn't for me. Does he think his new fancy will plan for him and plot for him, and risk—"

"Hush, hush—don't speak so loud! Where's your old discretion, Sally?"

"Let him look for discretion in Miss Baby, with her round face and her child's eyes. Does he think he can make use of her? Nonsense! It wants a woman that's strong in her head and strong in her limbs to do the work he wants done, and not a soft little chit like that!"

"Depend upon it, however useful she might be, he would never compare her services with yours, Sally. He is only amusing himself with this little simpleton," the man said soothingly.

But she interrupted him in a tone of half-suppressed savagery that made me shudder, out of her sight though I was.

"Amusing himself, do you say? Only amusing himself! Looking at her, talking to her, not because he wants to make use of her, but because he likes her, loves her"—she hissed—"as he has never loved any of his poor tools, though they were handsomer a thousand times than this wretched girl! If I thought that, if I really believed that, he'd find me more than his match for once. I'd spoil her beauty for her, and for him, if I hanged for it!"

Oh, what an awful woman! And all because poor little Jane was younger and prettier than herself, and had had the misfortune—for it was indeed a misfortune—to attract the attention of her unprincipled lover!

The man spoke again, this time very gravely. I had to listen with all my attention to hear him, for they had now passed the place where I sat.

"Sally, don't do anything foolish," said he. "Jim isn't a fool, and he knows how to repay services like yours, though he may be a trifle harsh sometimes. Why, he might have thrown you over with the rest when—"

I could hear no more; they had gone too far. I waited till their voices had died away, and then dashed from my perch, through the plantation and the hall, up to my room, as fast as I could, locked the door, and sat down appalled.

What a terrible tragedy in the servants' hall we were likely to have if things went on like this! If Mrs. Rayner had been only a woman, not a statue, I would have confessed all to her; but, as she was, it would do no good. It was not the sort of thing I could tell Mr. Rayner, and there was no way of letting him know without telling him. There was nothing for it but to hope that little Jane would be wise and leave off provoking Sarah, and that Providence would bring Sarah herself to a better mind.

But what a dreadful woman to have in the house! And why had the stranger spoken of Tom Parkes as "Jim"?

CHAPTER VI

The next morning I woke up with that strange feeling of oppression which is caused by something unpleasant heard the night before. I soon remembered what it was, and tried to shake off the recollection of the talk in the plantation and of Sarah's vindictive tones. I looked at her searchingly as she came in demurely to prayers with the cook and poor little Jane, and I could not help thinking that Tom Parkes, or "Jim" as the stranger had called him—but then a man of such a desperate character as they had described him to be would have a dozen *aliases*—might be excused in preferring the simple little kitchen-maid Jane to that forbidding-looking shrew. But perhaps, when he first made love to her, she was young and comparatively fair; and, if so, he ought not to desert her just because she had grown thin and hard-looking in doing the wicked things he made her do. What were those wicked things? I wondered. I had seen Tom Parkes, a strongly-made thick-set young man, two or three times, and he had seemed to me to have a stolid but rather good-humored expression; I should have thought him to be more stupid than wicked, and certainly not the sort of man to rule with a rod of iron the formidable Sarah.

That very day I had an opportunity of comparing my impression of Tom, when I thought him a harmless and inoffensive person, with my impression of him now that I knew him to be a rogue of the most determined kind. When Haidee and I returned from our walk, we came into the garden by a side-gate at the back of the house, and had to pass by the servants' entrance. Tom Parkes was sitting outside the door in as easy an attitude as the broken chair he sat on would permit, eating bread and cheese; while opposite to him stood Jane and Sarah, both apparently in high good humor. One held a jug, the other a glass, and they seemed united in the desire to please him by ministering to his wants, and by a rough kind of humor to which he was not slow in replying. They were talking about kisses, and I think they were going to illustrate the subject, when Tom suddenly became aware of our presence, and, taking his arm from round Jane's waist, pulled his cap off apologetically and remained standing until we had gone by.

What a strange contradiction this scene seemed to give to what I had overheard on the night before! Sarah was scarcely the sort of woman to exercise great self-control when among her equals; yet here she was, all laughter and rough gayety, submitting in the best of tempers to receive a share only, and evidently the smaller share, of Tom's attention with her rival Jane! I was rather ashamed of my strong interest in this low-class love-affair; but Sarah was such an exceptional woman, and her admirer, from what I had heard, such an exceptional man, that I could not help puzzling myself as to whether she had been only acting good humor, or whether the love-affairs of the uneducated were conducted on different principles from those of other people.

That evening, after tea, when, my translation finished, the time came for Guizot, I remembered, with a pang of conscience, that I had left that nicely-bound book out in the damp all night, forgotten in my hasty flight. I hurried through the plantation, eager to see whether it was much injured; but, when I got within a few yards of my nest, I saw Mr. Rayner there before me, standing with the unlucky volume in his hand.

If I had been conscience-stricken before, when my guilt was known only to myself, what did I feel now that it was discovered? I had not the courage to face him, but turned, and was sneaking back towards the house, when he called me—

"Miss Christie!"

I might have known I should not escape his sharp eyes and ears. I went back slowly, murmuring, "Yes, Mr. Rayner," and blushing with mortification. It was only a trifle, after all, but it was a most vexatious one. To Mr. Rayner, to whom I could not explain that I was too much occupied in listening to a strictly private *tête-à-tête* to think of his book, it must seem a most reprehensible piece of carelessness on the part of a responsible member of his household; it would serve me right if he requested me not to touch any of his books in future. He was turning over the leaves with his eyes bent on the book as I came up; but I have since thought that he took a mischievous pleasure in my discomfiture.

"I am very sorry, Mr. Rayner," I began, in a low voice which almost threatened tears; "I brought that book out here to read yesterday evening, and I—I forgot to take it with me when I went in. I know it was most inexcusable carelessness—indeed I will never bring one of the library-books out again."

"And why not, Miss Christie?" said he, suddenly dispelling my anxiety by looking up with his usual kindly smile. "I am sure Guizot is dry enough to stand a little moisture, and, if you were to throw him into the pond, you would be his only mourner, for nobody takes him off his shelf but you. But what makes you spoil your young eyes by plodding through such heavy stuff as this? It is very laudable of you, I know; but, if you were to bring out a volume of poetry or a novel, that would run no risk of being forgotten."

"I am so ignorant," said I humbly, "and I want some day to be able to teach girls much older than Haidee, so that I have to read to improve myself. And I don't read only dry things. This morning I found time to read nearly the whole of yesterday's paper."

"Well, that was dry enough; there was nothing in it, was there?"

"Yes, there was an account of another murder in Ireland, and a long article on the present position of the Eastern difficulty, and the latest details about that big burglary."

"What burglary?"

"Haven't you read about it? A large house in Derbyshire, belonging to Lord Dalston, was broken into last Wednesday, and a quantity of valuable things stolen. They say they've got a clue, but they haven't been able to find any of the thieves yet."

"And they won't either. They never do, except by a fluke."

"They say that the robbery must have been most carefully planned, and that it was most skilfully carried out."

"They always say that. That is to excuse the utter incompetency of the police in face of a little daring and dexterity."

"And they say that it looks like the work of the same hand that committed several large jewel robberies some years ago."

"Whose hand was that?"

"Ah, they don't know! The man was never discovered."

"That is another newspaper commonplace. To say that the way one ladder was placed against a window, the window opened and entered, and the diamonds taken away, looks very like the way another ladder was placed against another window, and another set of diamonds taken away, sounds very cute indeed; and to imply that there is only one thief in England with skill enough to baffle them raises that uncaught thief into a half divinity whom it is quite excusable in mere human policemen to fail to catch."

"Well, I hope they will catch this one, whether he is a half divinity or not."

"Why, what harm has the poor thief done you? You have nothing to fear from diamond-robbers, because you have no diamonds."

"I believe you have more sympathy with the thieves than with the policemen," said I, laughing.

"I have, infinitely more. I have just the same admiration for the successful diamond-robber that you have for Robin Hood and Jack Sheppard, and just the same contempt for the policeman that you have for the Sheriff of Nottingham and Jack's gaol."

"Oh, but that is different!" I broke in hotly—for I always put down "Robin Hood" in confession-books as "my favorite hero," and I was not without a weakness for Jack.

"Oh, yes, it is very different, I know!" said Mr. Rayner maliciously. "Robin Hood wore Lincoln green and carried a picturesque bow and arrow, while Sheppard's costume, in colored prints, is enough of itself to win any woman's heart. And then the pretty story about Maid Marian! Jack Sheppard had a sweetheart too, hadn't he? Some dainty little lady whose mild reproaches for his crimes proved gentle incentives to more, and who was never really sorry for her lover's sins until he was hanged for them."

"Well, Mr. Rayner, their very appearance, which you laugh at, shows them to be superior to the modern burglar."

"Have you ever seen a modern burglar?"

"No; but I know what they look like. They have fustian caps and long protruding upper lips, and their eyes are quite close together, and their lady-loves are like Nancy Sykes."

"I see. Then you don't sympathize with a criminal unless he is good looking, nicely dressed, and in love with a lady of beauty and refinement?"

"Oh, Mr. Rayner," I cried, exasperated at having my words misconstrued in this mischievous manner, "you know I don't sympathize with criminals at all! But Robin Hood and Jack Sheppard lived in different ages, when people were not so enlightened as they are now; and, besides," said I, brightening in triumph as a new idea flashed across me, "I don't know what the real Robin and Jack did; but the Robin Hood and Jack Sheppard of the novels and poems that I can't help liking and admiring robbed only rich people who could afford to lose some of their ill-gotten wealth."

"But all wealth is not ill-gotten," interposed Mr. Rayner mildly.

"It was then," I went on hastily—"at least, generally. And Robin Hood didn't rob the good rich people, only the bad ones; and most of his spoil he distributed among the poor, you know," I finished triumphantly.

"It won't do, Miss Christie; I must destroy your edifice of argument at a blow," said he, shaking his head mournfully. "I happen to know something about this Lord Dalston whose house was broken into; and he is a very bad rich person indeed, much more so than the poor old abbots whom your favorite Robin Hood treated so roughly. He ill-treated his mother, stole and squandered his sisters' fortunes, neglected his wife, and tried to shut her up in a lunatic asylum, knocked out in a passion the left eye of one of his own grooms, had embezzled money before he was twenty-one, and now owes heavy debts to half the big tradesmen in London. So that he is something like a thief. Now, if you were to find out that the man who had the chief hand—for, of course, there were dozens at work over it—in planning the robbery of this wicked rich man's property was young, good-looking, well dressed, a large subscriber to charities, and in love with a pretty lady-like girl, you ought, if you were logical, to admire him as much as you do Robin Hood, and more than you do Jack Sheppard."

"Oh, Mr. Rayner," said I, joining in his laughter, "how absurd! But it is too bad of you to make fun of my logic. I can't put it properly; but what I mean is this. In those days the laws were unjust, so that even good men were forced into defiance of them; but now that the laws are really, upon the whole, fair, it is only wicked people who disobey them."

"Then you don't like wicked people, Miss Christie?"

"Oh, Mr. Rayner, of course not!" said I, aghast at such a question, which he asked quite seriously.

"Ah, you must know some before you decide too hastily that you don't like them!" said he.

"Know some wicked people, Mr. Rayner?" I gasped.

He nodded gravely; and then I saw that he was amusing himself with my horror-struck expression.

"You won't like all of them, any more than you dislike all the good people you know. But you will find that those you do like beat the good people hollow."

"Indeed I am sure I shouldn't like them at all. I wouldn't speak to a wicked person if I could help it."

"But you can't. You won't be able to tell them from the good ones, except, as I said before, that they are nicer; and by the time you find out they are wicked you will like them too much to go back."

It was too bad of Mr. Rayner to tease me like this; but, though I saw he was enjoying my indignation, I could not help getting indignant.

"You are quite mistaken in me indeed," I said, trying to keep down my annoyance. "I can prove it to you by something that happened to me not very long ago. I knew a person against whom I had heard nothing who always seemed to me to look good-natured and simple. And then I found out that he was really a most wicked man; and when I saw him after that his very face seemed changed to me, to look evil and cunning; and the sight of him made me shrink."

I was thinking of Tom Parkes and the change I had seemed to see in him that morning. Mr. Rayner looked at me keenly while I said this; but I was not afraid of his finding out whom I meant in such a cautious statement.

"And what would you do if, in the course of your career as a governess, you found yourself in a family of whose morals you could not approve? Would you give them lectures on the error of their ways and try to convert them all round, Miss Christie?"

"Oh, no, I couldn't do that!" said I humbly. "If I found myself among very dreadful people, I should just run away back to my uncle's house, where my mother lives, on the first opportunity, without saying anything to any one till I was gone, and without even writing to say I was coming, lest my letter should be intercepted. I should be so horribly afraid of them."

"Well, child, I hope you will never have to do anything so desperate as that; but the profession of teaching has its dangers for a beautiful woman," he said gravely.

The last words gave a shock to me. I had never heard them applied to me before, and for a moment I was without an answer. He had been sitting on my seat, and I had been standing with my back against a young oak-tree, a few feet from him and nearer to the pond. He got up and came towards me, when a shrill little cry as from out of the ground caused him to start. It was the only sound that ever drew forth such a display of ordinary human weakness from self-possessed Mr. Rayner. It came from the lips of his baby-daughter Mona, who, ragged, dirty, and withered-looking as usual, had walked or crawled through the mud and rushes till she had silently taken her place in the long grass a little way from us, and who now, seeing her father approach, had given vent to her extraordinary dislike of him in her usual undutiful manner.

For one moment I saw in the dusk a look pass over Mr. Rayner's face which made me catch my breath; it reminded me instantly of his tone on that Sunday night when he had caught Sarah in the garden; and, quickly as it passed and gave place to a light laugh, it had frightened me and made me long to escape. Mona was an excuse.

"Oh, you naughty little girl to be out so late at night—and without a hat! Sarah must have forgotten you. Come—I must take you in now. Be a good girl, and come with me."

Mona had somehow come to regard me with less animosity than she did most of the household. So she let me take her in my arms without much opposition, and gave only one more yell when her father, while wishing me good-night, shook hands with me and accidentally touched her dirty little shoe. I took her into the house and gave her to Sarah in the hall; then I went into the schoolroom to replace the dissipated volume of Guizot that had been out all night among its more sober brethren, and then, moved by some spring of vanity, took my candle to the mantelpiece and looked at myself in the glass above it.

I suppose no girl can hear herself called a beautiful woman for the first time, no matter by whom, without a slight thrill of gratification. To be called pretty falls, I suppose, at some time or other, to the lot of most girls; but the other term implies a higher measure of attractiveness, and I certainly was not insensible to the pleasure of hearing it applied to me. I had lived such a very quiet life with my mother, and had had so few acquaintances, that I had never known flattery of any kind. The thought that flashed through my mind as I looked at my dark gray eyes, brighter than usual, and at my cheeks, flushed with gratified vanity, was—"Does Mr. Laurence Reade think me—beautiful?"

I was too much absorbed in my vain contemplation of myself, and in the foolish thoughts to which it gave rise, to notice that I was not alone in the room. Suddenly I was startled, as I well deserved to be, by a harsh ironical voice breaking in upon the silence of the room.

"Yes, it's a pretty face enough now, and you do right to set store by it, for it won't last pretty long—not long; in a few years it will be all lines and wrinkles, and not worth looking at; and you'll turn away in disgust from the glass, thinking of how you used to look, and how the men used to look at you—the fools!"

I had turned, and was looking at Sarah's hard, cruel face as she stood, with Mona still in her arms, her eyes flashing scornfully on me as she hissed out the spiteful words. I felt ashamed of my vanity, though, after all, it seemed harmless enough; and I felt sorry for her, for she spoke so bitterly that I was sure she must be thinking of the changes a few years of anxiety and hard work had wrought in herself; so I said gently—

"I suppose we women all think more than we ought about our looks sometimes, Sarah; but, after all, they are a very important matter to every woman, and make a great deal of difference to her life. You know you must be glad not to be ugly, Sarah."

I own this was a little bit of innocent flattery, for I did think her very ugly—and I thought I had never seen her look so hideous as she did as she stood there glaring at me—but I was anxious to soothe her at all hazards, and I was thankful to see that the bait took.

"Handsome is that handsome does," she said less viciously; and, with a toss of her head, she left the room.

CHAPTER VII

Very soon after Sarah's somewhat harsh and uncalled-for reproof of my vanity I began to suffer a punishment for it. The country air, which had brought unwonted roses to my cheeks while the weather was fine and dry, affected me very differently when, in the first days of September, the rain fell daily in a steady, continuous downpour that soon swelled the river and turned part of the marsh from a swamp into a stagnant unwholesome lake. The air round the house seemed never free from mist; the pond overflowed and covered the bricks that had formed the footstool of my nest; the lower part of the garden that touched the marsh was a bog; the moss grew greener and thicker on the pillars of the portico, the untrimmed ivy that clung round the house and made it so beautiful dripped all day long, and bright green stains grew broader and broader down the side of that wing of the house where Mr. and Mrs. Rayner's room was.

I often wondered why they slept there. I knew by the doors and windows that the ground-floor of that wing contained two rooms, a large and a small one. My own was in the same wing, but on the story above; and over mine was a turret that looked out high above the trees, but which was not used, so far as I knew. Haidee slept on the ground-floor in a cot in the dressing-room next to her parents' bedroom, I knew, while the nursery and servants' rooms and several spare-rooms were on the upper story besides my own. Why did not Mr. and Mrs. Rayner make one of these their own, and lift themselves out of the reeking damp which must be poisonous to delicate Mrs. Rayner? Even I, who slept in the upper story, soon began to lose my color and my appetite, and to feel at first languid, and then really ill. I showed the change more quickly than any one, being less used to the place; but little fragile Haidee soon followed suit, and grew more wan and listless than ever, until the lustre of her large blue eyes and the unhealthy flush that began to burn in her thin little cheeks frightened me and drew me to the child as her strange reserve had prevented my being drawn before. She answered to the change in my manner as sensitive children do, and one day, putting her little dry hand in mine, she said—

"You are getting thin and white too, like mamma and me. We'll all go away and be angels together, Miss Christie, now you have begun to love me."

I burst into tears; I had begun to love the fairy-like little creature long before, if she had only known it. Now I took her up in my arms and rested her flaxen head on my breast, and she said her lessons there that day. And after that, without any more explanation or comment, the sympathy between the child and me was perfect.

But as, on the one hand, the little one's friendship was a great solace to me, so, on the other, it brought me fresh trouble. For in Mrs. Rayner's indifferent eyes I could see now a dull flame of jealousy whenever Haidee put her languid little head upon my knee, or came up and said, "Tell me a story, Miss Christie—about fairies and the good Prince Caramel." I began, from merely pitying, almost to dislike Mrs. Rayner. Why, if she was so fond of Haidee, did she not come into the schoolroom to see her, or take her out during her play-hours, instead of leaving her the whole day with me, without coming to see her until bedtime, when the child was put to bed in the room next to hers, while she herself went into the drawing-room? It was unreasonable to expect to keep the child's undivided love like that; and yet at meals, when we all met together, she seemed to look at Haidee with strained wistful eyes, as if she loved the child, yet dared not show it. But what was there to prevent her, except the shroud of reserve she seemed to have wrapped round herself?

The weather had been so bad that for two Sundays we had not been able to go to church at all, for which I was very sorry, more sorry than I can tell; one misses church dreadfully in the country. So we knew nothing of what was going on in the parish for two whole weeks. We did not have to wait until the church-porch gathering on the following Sunday, though; for on the second day after the weather had at last grown fine again, when we were all in the drawing-room reading the morning papers over our coffee, as we always did after our early dinner, we heard the sound of a horse's hoofs coming down the drive. Mr. Rayner threw open the window and stepped out on to the broad space of gravel before the front of the house.

"Hallo, Laurence, you are as welcome as the dove was to the ark! Come in, come in; the ladies will make even more of you than usual. We have had no visitors lately, but an occasional mermaid came up the river from the sea and overflowed into our garden."

"Can't come in, thanks, Mr. Rayner—I'm too much splashed; the roads are awful still. I've only come with a note from Mrs. Manners to Mrs. Rayner."

"Nonsense! Come in, mud and all."

So he tied up his horse and came in.

Mrs. Manners was the clergyman's wife, and generally sent her notes by one of her half-dozen boys; and I confess I thought, when I heard what a flimsy sort of errand had brought Mr. Reade, that perhaps—that perhaps some other silly motive had helped to bring him too. But my only half-acknowledged fancy was disappointed. Not only did Mr. Reade devote all his conversation to Mr. and Mrs. Rayner, with an occasional word to Haidee, but, when I made a remark, he did not even look at me. I confess I was piqued; I certainly did not want Mr. Reade either to look at me or speak to me, but surely common courtesy, especially to a dependant, demanded that he should not ignore my presence altogether. So I thought I would take a small and impotent revenge by ignoring his, and, when Haidee got up and slipped out of the window to look at Mr. Reade's horse, I followed her. She was not a bit afraid of him, but ran into the house for some sugar, and then, flattening out her small hand with a piece on it, fed him, and talked to him in a language which he seemed to understand, though I could not.

"Would you like to give him a piece, Miss Christie?" she asked.

But I would not have bestowed such an attention on a horse of Mr. Reade's for worlds; and, leaving the child and her four-footed friend to continue their conversation, I walked away to gather some flowers for the tea-table, as it was the day for renewing them.

I had my hands half full by the time I heard the voices of the gentlemen at the window and the grinding of soft gravel under the horse's hoofs as Mr. Reade mounted him. I was near the bottom of the drive, pulling off some small branches of copper beech to put among the flowers, when I heard Mr. Reade ride by behind me. I did not even look round until he called out, "Good-afternoon, Miss Christie;" and then I just turned my head over my shoulder and said stiffly, "Good afternoon," and went on with my task. He had half pulled up his horse. I dare say he thought I wanted to talk to him. I was not going to let him make such an absurd mistake as that. So he rode on to the gate, and then he stopped, and presently I heard him utter impatient ejaculations, and I looked and saw that he was fumbling with his whip at the fastening of the gate.

"How stupid he is not to get off and open it with his fingers!" I thought contemptuously. "It is quite an easy fastening too. I believe I could do it on horseback directly."

However, he still continued to make ineffectual efforts to raise the heavy latch, but each time the restive horse swerved or the whip slipped, until I stood watching the struggle intently, and grew quite excited and half inclined to call out to him "Now!" when the horse stood still for a minute. It seemed to me that he deliberately missed all the best opportunities, and I was frowning with impatience, when he suddenly looked up and his eyes met mine. There was nothing for it then but in common civility to go and open the gate for him myself; so I walked up the drive very reluctantly and opened it wide without a smile.

"Thank you, thank you—so much obliged to you! I wouldn't have given you so much trouble for worlds. If only this brute would stand still!"

"Pray don't mention it. It is no trouble at all," I said icily, occupied in keeping my armful of flowers together.

And he raised his hat and rode off at a walking pace, while I shut the gate and turned to go down the drive again. I had such a curiously hurt and disappointed feeling—I could not tell why; but I supposed that, being a dependant, I was naturally very sensitive, and it was surely a slight on Mr. Reade's part not even to speak to me when we were all in the drawing-room.

"I dare say he wouldn't have let me open the gate for him if I hadn't been only a governess," I thought, as a lump came into my throat. "I wish I hadn't—oh, I wish I hadn't! I wish I had let him get off his horse, or jump over it, or anything rather than make me play groom for him."

And the flowers I was looking at began to grow misty, when again I heard hoofs behind me and the latch of the gate go, and, glancing round, I saw Mr. Reade on horseback inside the gate. He had opened it without any difficulty this time. He seemed to look a little embarrassed, "ashamed of his own clumsiness the first time," I thought severely; and, jumping off his horse, he led him towards me, saying—

"I must apologize for returning so soon, but I find I have lost a stone from my ring, and I think it must have dropped out while I was fumbling at the gate just now. It is much easier to open from the outside."

"Do you think so? We don't find any difference," I said simply.

He gave me a quick inquisitive glance and a half smile, as if to see what I meant, and then, finding that I returned his look quite gravely, he turned back to the gate and began searching about in the gravel. Politeness obliged me to help him. He fastened his horse's rein round the gate-post and showed me the ring, and I saw the hole where there was a stone missing. Suddenly it flashed through my mind that, while we stood under the shed on that Sunday in the rain, I had noticed the very same hole in the very same ring, and I was just going to tell him that it was of no use for him to look, for he had lost the stone much longer than he fancied, when another thought, which brought the color swiftly to my face and made my lips quiver and my heart beat faster, flashed into my mind and stopped me. And the thought was that Mr. Reade must know how long ago he had lost that stone, at least as well as I did. And from that moment a spirit of daring mischief came into me—I don't know how—and I would not condescend to pretend to look about any longer; but I patted the horse's neck and glanced every now and then at his master, and thought how foolish he looked hunting about so carefully for what he knew he should not find. Then he looked up, red with stooping, and caught me smiling, and he had to bite his lip in order not to smile himself as he walked up to me.

"I can't find it. It isn't of any consequence; I sha'n't look any longer," he said.

"Oh, but it would be such a pity to lose such a large stone, Mr. Reade!" I said boldly. "I'll tell the gardener to hunt for it, and Sam the boy, and—"

"No, no—indeed it doesn't matter."

"And Jane the kitchen-maid. She has sharp eyes; she might spend an hour or two hunting," I murmured confidentially, while he protested.

And I think he began to suspect my good faith; and we both got into such a giggling excited state that it was very difficult to go on talking, and I was glad when some of my flowers fell down and Mr. Reade had to pick them up, and we had time to regain a little of our lost composure.

"You are fond of flowers, Miss Christie?"

"Oh, yes! But the best of them are over now; the rain has spoilt them all."

"The rain spoils a good many things here," he said, with sudden gravity. "You don't look nearly so well as you did a fortnight ago, Miss Christie, and I expect it is the damp of this place. You might as well live in a cave, you know, as in that house in a rainy season," he added, dropping his voice. "Don't you find yourself that your health is affected by it?"

I hesitated.

"It is damp, I know; but it isn't half so bad for me, who am strong, as it is for Mrs. Rayner or for little Haidee."

"But they can't help themselves, poor things, while it lies in your own power whether you will put up with it or not."

"You mean that I ought to go away?"

"No, no, I don't mean that," said he hastily.

"But that is what you advised me to do," said I, looking up, surprised.

"Did I? Ah, yes! But, now that you have grown attached to—to—the place, and—and Mrs. Rayner—"

"No, indeed I haven't," I interrupted. "I don't like her at all."

"Well, to Haidee, or the baby. You must have grown attached to something or to somebody, or you wouldn't talk as if you didn't want to leave the place," he said, with such abrupt earnestness as to be almost rude.

"I like the house, in spite of the damp, and I love the garden even when it is a swamp, and I like Haidee, and Jane the kitchen-maid, and Mr. Rayner," I said quietly.

With nervous fingers Mr. Reade began playing with his horse's bridle.

"You like Mr. Rayner, you say? Then I suppose our sympathies must be as far apart as the poles. For he seems to me the most intolerable snob that ever existed, and so selfish and heartless as to be almost outside the pale of humanity."

This tirade amazed me; but it also made me angry. I could not let him abuse a person whom I liked, and who had been consistently kind to me, without protest.

"You surely cannot judge him so well as I, a member of his household," said I coolly. "Whether he is a snob or not I cannot tell, because I don't quite know what it means. But I do know that he is kind to his wife and his children and servants and dependants, and—"

"Kind to his wife, do you say? I should not call it kindness to shut up my wife in the darkest, dampest corner of a dark, damp house, until she is as spiritless and silent as a spectre, and then invent absurd lies to account for the very natural change in her looks and spirits."

"What do you mean? What lies?"

"The stories he told you about her when you first came. He would never have tried them on any one but an unsuspecting girl, and of course he never thought you would repeat them to me."

"I wish I hadn't!" said I indignantly. "You have known Mr. and Mrs. Rayner only during the three years they have lived here. What proof have you that the things he told me were not true?"

"No proof, Miss Christie, but a man's common-sense," said he excitedly—"no more proof than of another fact of which I am equally certain, that he is as surely killing his wife as if he were making her drink poison."

"How dare you say such a thing?" I cried. "You have no right to utter it even if you think it. You are giving way to the most cruel prejudice against a man whose only fault is that he cannot contentedly lead the dull life his neighbors do. I suppose you think, like the villagers, that to play the violin is an impious action, and that it is a shocking thing for him to go to races."

"If he did nothing worse than that, I should think no worse of him than you do, Miss Christie. But I think you will allow that a man who has lived within half a mile of another man for nearly three years must know more of his character than a young innocent girl who has seen him at his best only for a month."

"But you cannot judge a man fairly until you have seen him continually in his own home. I have seen Mr. Rayner among his family; I have played for him, walked with him, had long talks with him; and I must surely know him better than you, who have only an ordinary outside acquaintance with him."

Mr. Reade drew himself up very stiffly, and the color rushed to his forehead. He was getting really angry.

"No doubt, Miss Christie, you know him a great deal better than I do. I have never played for him, and I have not found either talks or walks with him particularly delightful. But then I dare say he did not try so hard to be agreeable to me as he did to you."

He said this in a sneering tone, which brought the hot blood to my face. I tried to answer, but my voice would not come. I turned away sharply, and left him, with an agony of anger and pain at my heart which would have made him remorseful indeed if he could have guessed what his words had inflicted. As it was, he followed me a few steps down the drive, with apologies to which I was too angry and too much hurt to listen.

"Don't speak to me now," I said—"I can't bear it;" and, turning off rapidly into a side-path, I left him, and fled away through the alleys into the house.

Luckily I managed to keep back tears, so that I could return to the drawing-room with the flowers I had gathered before they began to wonder why I had been so long. Mrs. Rayner told me that the note from Mrs. Manners which Mr. Reade had brought was to ask that the articles which we were preparing for the "sale"—a sort of bazaar on a small scale which was one of the attractions of the annual school-treat—should be sent in to her within a week, as they had to be ticketed and arranged before the sale-day arrived, and whether Miss Christie would be so kind as to give her services at the stall; and, if so, whether she would call upon Mrs. Manners within the next few days to settle what should be her share of the work. I was delighted at the thought of this little excitement, and, although Mr. Rayner warned me that I should have nothing nicer to do than to see the pretty trifles I had worked fingered by dirty old women who would not buy them, and to have hot tea poured over me by clumsy children if I helped at the feast, I would not be frightened by the prospect.

That evening I debated with myself whether it was not too damp and swampy still for me to go and peep at my nest and see if the water had subsided and left the top of the bricks dry. I chose afterwards to think that it was some supernatural instinct which led me to decide that I would put on my goloshes and go.

When I got there, I found on the bough which formed my seat a basket of Gloire de Dijon roses, and the stalk of the uppermost one was stuck through a little note. I never doubted those roses were for me; I only wondered who had put them there. I looked searchingly around me in all directions before I took up the rose which carried the note and carefully slipped it off. It contained these words—

> "For Miss Christie, with the sincere apologies of some one who would not willingly have offended her for the whole world."

I did not know the writing, but I knew whom it was from. I think, if I had been quite sure that no one could have seen me, I should have raised the note to my lips, I was so happy. But, though I could see no one, the fact of the basket arriving so surely at my secret haunt seemed to argue the existence of a supernatural agency in dealing with which one could not be too discreet; so I only put the note into my pocket and returned to the house with my flowers. I put them in water as soon as I had sneaked upstairs to my room with them.

The supernatural agency could not follow me there, so I slept that night with the note under my pillow.

CHAPTER VIII

"You are getting pale again, my dear child," said Mr. Rayner to me the very next morning—he met me, at the foot of the stairs, dressed for my walk with Haidee. "We must find some means of bringing those most becoming roses back to your cheeks again. You work too hard at those self-imposed evening tasks, I am afraid."

"Oh, no, indeed I don't, Mr. Rayner! I am getting very lazy; I haven't done anything for two or three nights."

The fact was that I had felt too languid even to sit down and write, and had wasted the last two evenings listlessly turning over the pages of a book I did not read.

"Ah, then you want change of air! Now how to give it you without letting you go away—for we can't spare you even for a week! You will think me a magician if I procure you change of air without leaving this house, won't you, Miss Christie? Yet I think I can manage it. You must give me a few days to look about for my wand, and then, hey, presto, the thing will be done!"

I laughed at these promises, looking upon them as the lightest of jests; but the very next day I met a workman upon the staircase, and Mr. Rayner asked me mysteriously at dinner whether I had seen his familiar spirit about, adding that the spirit wore a paper cap and a dirty artisan's suit, and smelt of beer. That spirit pervaded the house for two days. I met him in the garden holding very unspiritual converse with Jane; I met him in my room taking the measure of my bedstead; I met him in the passage carrying what looked like thin sheets of tin and rolls of wall-paper, and I heard sounds of heavy boots in the turret above my room. Then I saw no more of him; but still there were unaccustomed sounds over my head, sounds of footsteps and knocking, and I met sometimes Jane and sometimes Sarah coming out of a door which I had never known unlocked before, but which I now discovered led to a narrow staircase that I guessed was the way to the turret.

On the fourth day, when I went to my room to dress for tea, I found it all dismantled, the bed and most of the furniture gone, and little Jane pulling down my books from their shelf and enjoying my discomfiture with delighted giggles, not at all disconcerted at being caught taking an unheard-of liberty.

"What does this mean, Jane? I can't sleep on the floor; and what are you doing with my books?" I cried in one breath.

"I don't know nothing about it, miss; it's Mr. Rayner's orders," said she, with another irrepressible snigger at my bewildered face.

I was turning to the door to wander forth, I did not know exactly whither, to try to find an explanation of this most extraordinary state of things, when Sarah came in, her dark frowning face offering a strong contrast to that of the laughing Jane.

"Sarah, can you tell me what this means?" said I.

"Mr. Rayner has ordered the room in the turret to be prepared for you," said she shortly. "Perhaps you will be kind enough to manage down here till after tea, as it's his orders that you shouldn't be shown up till the room is quite ready."

I answered that I could manage very well, and they left the room. I said nothing at tea about my adventure, reflecting that perhaps some surprise for me was intended, which would be sprung upon me at a fitting time. And so it proved. While I was quietly writing in the schoolroom, after tea, Mr. and Mrs. Rayner and Haidee, who had not yet gone to bed, came in and conducted me in a formal procession upstairs, up the narrow winding turret-staircase that I had so often wanted to explore, and, opening the door of the one room the turret contained, Mr. Rayner, in a short but elaborate speech, begged to install me without further ceremony as the "imprisoned princess of the enchanted tower."

I gave a cry of delight. It was an octagonal room, the four sides which overlooked the marsh containing each a window, while in one of the other sides was a small fireplace with a bright fire burning. The carpet was new, the wall-paper was new; there were two easy-chairs, one on each side of the fire, a writing-table and a Japanese screen, besides the furniture of my old room. It looked so bright and so pretty that my eyes danced with pleasure at the sight, and I could not speak while Mr. Rayner explained that now I should be high and dry out of the damp, and he expected me to become red-faced and healthy-looking immediately—that he had had tinfoil put behind the paper in one of the cupboards which was considered damp, that the picturesque ivy had been torn down—all but a little bit to hide the unsightly chimney—and that I was to have a fire whenever I liked now, and one every day when it began to grow colder.

"I don't know what to say. I don't know how to thank you," said I, almost pained by the extent of the kindness showered upon me.

I tried to include Mrs. Rayner in my thanks; but she hung back almost ungraciously, and seemed to have been drawn into this demonstration against her will. She was the last of my three visitors to leave the room, and in the moment that we were alone together, before she followed her husband and child downstairs, she said, seeming to be moved out of her reserve by the unaccustomed little excitement, and casting upon me a keen look from her great eyes—

"Are you not afraid of sleeping so far from every one? Or do you prefer it?"

I am not at all nervous; but I was enough impressed by her almost eager manner to answer rather shyly—

"No, I don't prefer it. But there is nothing to be afraid of, is there?"

She glanced towards the door, and, saying hurriedly, "Oh, no, of course not! I hope you will be comfortable, Miss Christie," she left the room.

Afraid! No, of course I was not afraid; I never had minded sleeping away from everybody else; and, if burglars were to break into the Alders, they certainly would not expect to find anything worth stealing in the turret. I wished Mrs. Rayner had not put the idea into my head, though. I was not so strong-minded as to be proof against fear even at second-hand, and ever since the sensation caused by that great jewel-robbery in Derbyshire I had been very careful to hide away my watch, my one bracelet, and my two brooches under my pillow at night. But I was too happy in my new abode to trouble myself long with idle fears. I found that, by opening out my screen in a particular position, I could completely hide the bed and wash-hand-stand, and make myself a real sitting-room; then I sat down by the fire in one of the arm-chairs and gave myself up to the enjoyment of this new piece of good fortune; and I was still gazing into the fire, with my feet cosily warming—the nights were already cold enough for that to be a luxury—on a hassock close to the fender, when I heard Sarah coming up the stairs. I knew her footstep, and I would rather not have heard what I considered her ill-omened tread on this first evening in my new room. For I knew that Sarah disliked me, and even the fact that she had brought me up some coals to replenish my fire, which was getting low, did not reconcile me to her presence; I could not help thinking of the cold, grudging manner in which before tea she had announced to me my change of residence. I tried to be friendly, however, and, when I had thanked her for her trouble, I said—

"I wonder this nice room has been neglected so long. Has no one ever used it, Sarah?"

"Mr. Rayner used to use it for a study," said she shortly. "I don't know why he gave it up; I suppose it was too high up. That was six months ago, before you came."

"It is a long way from anybody else's room, Sarah, isn't it?"

"Mine is the nearest, and I have ears like needles; so you needn't be frightened," said she, in a tone which really sounded more menacing than consoling.

"It will be rather lonely on a stormy night; the wind will howl so up here," I said, my spirits beginning to sink under her sharp speeches.

"Oh, you won't want for company, I dare say!" she said, with a harsh grating laugh.

"Why, all the company I am likely to get up here is burglars," I answered lugubriously, with my chin between my hands.

The start she gave startled me in my turn.

"Burglars! What burglars? What are you talking about?"

I looked up amazed at the effect of my words on Sarah, whom, of all people in the world, I should have considered strong-minded. It was promotion for me to be soothing Sarah.

"Why, I have more courage than you!" I said, laughing lightly. "I'm not afraid of them. If they came, they would soon go down again when they found there was nothing to take. Would you be afraid to sleep up here alone, Sarah?"

But she hardly took the trouble to answer me except by a nod; her black eyes were fixed upon me as I spoke, as if she would, and almost as if she could, penetrate to my inmost soul. Then, as if satisfied with the result of her scrutiny, she relapsed into her usual hard, cold manner, and, answering my good-night shortly, left me alone.

Then I made up my mind definitely on a point that had often occupied me vaguely, and decided that Mrs. Rayner and Sarah were, in different ways, without exception, the two most unpleasant and disagreeable women I had ever met. And after that I went to bed and dreamt, not of a burglar, but of quite a different person.

The next day was Sunday, and there were two strangers in church who attracted the attention of all the congregation. They were two fair-complexioned, light-haired girls who sat in the Reades' pew, and who had evidently spared no expense on rather tasteless and unbecoming toilettes. I caught myself feeling not sorry that they were ill-dressed, and glad that one was plain and that the one who was pretty was dreadfully freckled; and I wondered how it was that I had grown so ill-natured. Mr. Laurence Reade sat between them, and he shared his hymn-book with the pretty one; and I did so wish it had been with the plain one! And when we came out of church, and he and his sisters and the two girls trooped out together, the breaking up of the group left him to pair off again with the pretty one.

I remember noticing, as Haidee and I walked home together, that the midges teased me more than they had ever done that summer, that the sun was more scorching, and that it was just as dusty as if we had not had any rain at all. It was a horrid day.

Mr. Rayner asked us, at dinner, if we had noticed the two girls with the pretty hair in Mr. Reade's pew, and said that he had heard that the one with the blue eyes was the future Mrs. Laurence Reade, and that it would be an excellent match for both of them.

"I noticed that he paid her a great deal of attention at church, and afterwards they paired off together quite naturally," said he.

And that afternoon the heat and the midges and the dust were worse than ever.

Mr. Rayner complained on the day after this that I was looking paler than before, and threatened to have me sent back to my old room if I did not look brighter in two days from that date. Luckily for me, within those two days my spirits improved a little. The next day Haidee and I passed by Geldham Park in our walk, and saw over the fence Mr. Reade, his sisters, and the two strangers playing lawn-tennis. None of them noticed us that time; but, as we were returning, I observed that Mr. Reade jumped up from the grass where he was lounging in the midst of the adoring girls, as I thought contemptuously, and shook out of his hat the leaves and grasses with which his companions had filled it; as for them, they were too much occupied with him to see anything outside the park.

Haidee and I had to go to the village shop with a list of articles which I felt sure we should not get there. But it was one of Mr. Rayner's principles to encourage local trade, so we had to go once a week and tease the crusty and ungrateful old man who was the sole representative of it by demands for such outlandish things as wax-candles, bloater-paste, and *filoselle*. I had been tapping vainly for some minutes on the little counter, on which lay four tallow "dips," a box of rusty crochet-hooks, and a most uninviting piece of bacon, when Mr. Reade dashed into the shop and greeted me with much surprise. When he had asked after Mr. and Mrs. Rayner, and heard that they were quite well, there was a pause, and he seemed to look to me to continue the conversation; but I could think of nothing to say. So he roamed about, digging his cane into the cheese and knocking down a jar of snuff, which he carefully scraped together with his foot and shovelled back, dust and all, into the jar, while I still tapped and still nobody came.

"He must be at dinner," said I resignedly. "In that case we shall have to wait."

For I knew Mr. Bowles. So Mr. Reade seated himself on the counter and harpooned the bacon with one of the rusty crochet-hooks.

"Convenient place these village-shops are," said he, not thinking of what he was saying, I was sure.

"Yes, if you don't care what you get, nor how stale it is," said I, sharply.

He laughed; but I did not intend to be funny at all.

"I came in only for some"—here he looked round the shop, and his eyes rested on a pile of dusty toys—"for some marbles. I thought they would do for the school-treat, you know."

I thought it was a pity he did not return to his lawn-tennis and his *fiancée*, if that was the errand he came on, and I was determined not to be drawn into another *tête-à-tête* with him, so I turned to leave the shop. But he stopped me.

"Old Bowles can't be much longer over his bacon, I'm sure," said he, rather pleadingly. "I—I wanted to ask you if you were any better. I thought last Sunday you were looking awfully ill."

"Last Sunday?"—and I thought of those girls. "I was never better in my life, thank you. And I am quite well. Mr. and Mrs. Rayner have put me into the turret to keep me out of the damp. It was very, very kind of him to think about it. It is the best room in all the house."

"Best room in the house? Then Mr. Rayner doesn't sleep in the house at all," said he, in a low voice, but with much decision.

I got up from the one chair and turned to my pupil, who was deep in an old story-book that she had found.

"Come, Haidee!"

"No, no; that is revenge—it is unworthy of you," said he in a lower voice still. "Don't let us quarrel again. Mr. Rayner is an angel. No, no, not that!"—for I was turning away again. "He has his faults; but he is as near perfection as a man can be. Then you are very happy at the Alders now?"

"Yes, thank you."

"And you have no great troubles?"

"Yes. I have—Sarah."

"Sarah? That is one of the servants, isn't it? A gaunt, shrewd-looking person? I've often met her on the road to and from Beaconsburgh."

"Yes. She goes out when she likes, I think. She is a very important person in the household, much more so than Mrs. Rayner."

"Oh! And she is a trouble to you?"

"Yes; I'm afraid of her. She doesn't like me. And whenever I used to give her letters to post I never got any answers to them."

"Does Mr. Rayner like her?"

"Like her? I don't think any one could like Sarah, except, of course, her 'young man.' That doesn't count. But Mr. Rayner thinks a great deal of her."

"So a young man's liking doesn't count?"

"Of course Tom Parkes is prejudiced in her favor," said I, preferring that the talk should remain personal.

"Surely it is a compliment to a woman that a young man should be prejudiced in her favor?" said he, preferring that the talk should become abstract.

"He must have finished by this time!" I cried; and a vigorous thump on the counter did at last bring in Mr. Bowles, who declared it was the first sound he had heard.

I was sorry to find that he had several of the things I wanted, as everything he sold was of the worst possible quality; and, while he was doing them up, Mr. Reade found an opportunity to whisper—

"You got my flowers?"

"Yes, thank you; it was very kind of you to send them."

"Bring them," corrected he. "What did you do with them?"

I remembered the fair-haired girl and my resolve to be discreet.

"I put them in water, and when they were dead I threw them away."

"Threw them away?"

"Yes, of course; one doesn't keep dead flowers," said I calmly; but it hurt me to say it, for the words seemed to hurt him. It is very hard to be discreet.

He said no more, but took his parcel and left the shop, saluting me very coldly. I had taken up my parcel, and was going out too, when Haidee's soft voice broke in.

"You've got Mr. Reade's marbles, and he has gone off with mamma's wool and the curtain-hooks, Miss Christie!"

I had not noticed this.

"How stupid of him!" I exclaimed.

He had marched off so fast that I had to run down the lane after him before he heard me call "Mr. Reade!" We laughed a little at the embarrassment he would have felt if he had produced a ball of wool and curtain-hooks as the result of his morning's shopping, and I if I had gravely presented Mrs. Rayner with a bag of marbles. And then, remorseful and blushing, I said hurriedly—

"I did keep one of the roses, Mr. Reade—the one with the note on it;" and then I ran back to Haidee, without looking up. Whether he was engaged or not, I could not be ungracious about those lovely flowers.

Then Haidee and I went home to dinner. I had met Mr. Reade quite by accident, and I had done nothing wrong, nothing but what civility demanded, in exchanging a few words with him; but I was glad Haidee was not one of those foolish prattling little girls who insist upon chattering at meal-times about all the small events of the morning's walk.

CHAPTER IX

Mr. Reade's cruel and prejudiced accusations against Mr. Rayner had not in the least shaken my faith in the kindness and goodness of the master of the Alders; but I felt anxious to prove to myself that the charges he brought against him were groundless. Mr. Reade's suggestion that he let his family sleep in the damp house while he passed his nights elsewhere, for instance, was absurd in the extreme. Where else could he sleep without any one's knowing anything about it? I often heard his voice and step about the house until quite late; he was always one of the first in the dining-room to our eight-o'clock breakfast, and even on the wettest mornings he never looked as if he had been out in the rain.

It often seems to me that, when I have been puzzling myself fruitlessly for a long time over any matter, I find out quite simply by accident what I want to know. Thus, only the day after my talk with Mr. Reade in the shop, I was nursing Haidee, who did not feel inclined to play after lesson-time, when she said—

"Do you ever have horrid dreams, Miss Christie, that frighten you, and then come true?"

"No, darling; dreams are only fancies, you know, and never come true, except just by accident."

I said this because everybody considers it the right answer to give to a child; but I do believe just a little in dreams myself.

She went on gravely—

"But mine do. I'll tell you about one I had two nights ago, if you'll bend your head and let me whisper. I mustn't tell mamma, because she always stops me and says I mustn't speak of what I see; but I can say it to you; you won't tell, will you?"

"No, darling, I won't tell," said I, thinking it kindest to let the child speak out about her fancies, instead of brooding over them, as the shy little thing was too prone to do.

She put her little hand up to my cheek, and, drawing down my face to hers, breathed into my ear, in the very faintest, softest whisper I have ever heard—

"You know that day when we took you up to your new room in the turret?"

"Yes, dear," said I.

"Hush! Whisper," cooed she. "Well, that night Jane put me to bed, just as she always does, in my little room, and then I went to sleep just like I always do. And then I dreamt that I heard mamma screaming and crying, and papa speaking—oh, so differently from the way he generally does; it made me frightened in my dream! I thought it was all real, and I tried to get out of bed; but I was too much asleep; and then I didn't dream any more, only when I woke up I remembered it. I didn't tell anybody; and the next night I wondered if I should have the dream again, and I didn't want Jane to go away; and, when I said it was because I'd had a dream, she said dreams were stuff and nonsense, and she wanted to go and dream at having supper. And then she went away, and I went to sleep. And then I woke up because mamma was crying, and I thought at first it was my dream again; but I knocked my head against the rail of my bed, and then I knew I must be awake. And I got out of bed, and I went quite softly to the door and looked through the keyhole, for there was a light in her room. When she has a light, I can see in quite plainly through the keyhole, and I can see the bed and her lying in it. But she wasn't alone like she generally is—I could see papa's hand holding the candle, and he was talking to her in such a low voice; but she was crying and talking quite wildly and strangely, so that she frightened me. When she talks like that, I feel afraid—it doesn't seem as if she were mamma. And then I saw papa put something on her face, and mamma said, 'Don't—don't! Not that!' and then she only moaned, and then she was quite still, and I heard him go out of the room. And presently I called 'Mamma, mamma!' but she didn't answer; and I was so frightened, I thought she was dead. But then I heard her sigh like she always does in her sleep, and I got into bed again."

"Were you afraid to go in, darling?"

"I couldn't go in, because the door was locked. It always is, you know. I never go into mamma's room; I did only once, and she said—she said"—and the child's soft whisper grew softer still, and she held her tiny lips closer to my ear—"she said I was never to say anything about it—and I promised; so I mustn't, even to you, Miss Christie dear. You don't mind, do you, because I promised?"

"No, darling, I don't. Of course you must not tell if you promised," said I.

But I would have given the world to know what the child had seen in that mysterious room.

Haidee's strange story had roused again in me all the old feeling of a shadow of some kind hanging over the house on the marsh which had long since worn away in the quiet routine of my daily life there. The locking of the mother's door against her own child, her wild talk and crying, the "something on the face" that her husband had had to administer to calm her, and the discovery that he himself did not sleep in the same room, all united to call up in my mind the remembrance of that long talk I had had with Mr. Rayner in the schoolroom soon after my arrival, the story he had told me of her boy's death, and the change it had made in her, and his allusion to "those outbreaks which sometimes cause me the gravest—the very gravest anxiety."

I had understood then that he feared for his wife's reason, but, never having witnessed any great change in her cold listless manner myself, and having seen on the whole very little of her except at meals, all fear and almost all remembrance of her possible insanity had faded from my mind, in which she remained a background figure. But now Haidee's story caused me to wonder whether there was not an undercurrent in the affairs of the household of which I knew little or nothing. What if Mr. Rayner, bright, cheerful, and good-tempered as he always seemed, were really suffering under the burden of a wife whose sullen silence might at any moment break into wild insanity—if he had to wrestle in secret, as, from the child's story, seemed to have been the case quite recently on two successive nights, with moods of wild wailing and weeping which he at first tried to deal with by gentle remonstrance (Haidee said that on the second night, when she was fully awake, his voice was very low and soft), and at last had to subdue by sedatives!

And then a suggestion occurred to me which would at least explain Sarah's important position in the household. Was she perhaps in truth a responsible guardian of Mrs. Rayner, such as, if the latter's reason were really feeble, it would be necessary for her to have in her husband's absences? I already knew that the relations between mistress and servant were not very amicable. Though she treated her with all outward signs of respect, it was not difficult to see that Sarah despised her mistress, while I had sometimes surprised in the wide gray eyes of the other a side-glance of dislike and fear which made me wonder how she could tolerate in her household a woman from whom she had so strong an aversion. That Mr. Rayner was anxious to keep the scandal of having a mad wife a secret from the world was clear from the fact that not even Mr. Laurence Reade, who seemed to take a particular interest in the affairs of the household at the Alders, had ever shown the least suspicion that this was the case. So the secluded life

Mrs. Rayner led came to be ascribed to the caprice—if the village gossips did not use a harsher word—of her husband, while that unfortunate man was really not her tyrant, but her victim.

The only other possible explanation of what Haidee had seen was that Mr. Rayner, kind and sweet-tempered to every one as he always was, and outwardly gentle and thoughtful to a touching degree towards his cold wife, was really the most designing of hypocrites, and was putting upon his wife, under the semblance of devoted affection, a partial restraint which was as purposeless as it was easy for her to break through. This idea was absurd.

The other supposition, dreadful as it was, was far more probable. I was too much accustomed by this time to Mrs. Rayner's listless moods and the faint far-off looks of fear, or anger, or suspicion that I sometimes saw in her eyes, to be alarmed even by the possibility of a change for the worse in her— the thought that she was perhaps scarcely responsible for her words and actions reconciled me somewhat to her cold manner towards myself and to her jealousy of the hold I was surely getting upon Haidee's affection. But my strongest feeling was not for the half-witted wife nor for the unfortunate husband, but for the child herself, the unsuspected witness of her mother's outbreaks of incoherent words and cries. It was strange that these attacks should occur only at night, I thought at first; but then I remembered that day when I had read *Adam Bede* aloud to her in the drawing-room, the tearful excitement into which, apparently without any cause, she had fallen, which her husband's entrance had as suddenly subdued—at least for the time; for how could I tell what had followed when he had led her away into that bedroom of hers which was beginning to have for me the fascination of a haunted chamber?

The immediate result of the child's confidences to me was a great increase of my love for and interest in herself. We became almost inseparable in and out of school-hours; I encouraged her to talk; and she soon fell into the habit of telling me, whether I was listening or not, those long rambling stories which have no beginning, no sequence, and no end, which are the solace of children who have no companions of their own age. When my attention was wandering from these incoherent tales, I sometimes had it abruptly brought back by some flight of her childish fancy, which set me wondering if it had been suggested by some half-forgotten experience. Thus one day, when I was working, and she was sitting on a footstool by my side, with two or three twigs bearing oak-apples which represented, as far as I could judge from her severity to some and her tenderness to the others, the personages of her story, my attention was arrested by the words—

"And so the Prince said to Princess Christie"—the heroine of the story, so named in honor of me—" 'I've brought you some jewels much finer than yours.' But Princess Christie cried and said, 'I don't want them. Where did you get them? I know where you got them. You are a naughty bad Prince, and I won't wear any jewels any more.' "

And I thought of what Mr. Rayner had told me of his wife's hearing, on her return home from a ball, of her baby-boy's death and of her saying she would never wear jewels again. But Haidee had been but a baby-girl at the time; her words must be a mere coincidence. But some of the coincidences of her narrative were less difficult of explanation, for she went on—

"And so Prince Caramel said, 'Very well; I'll send you some more roses if you won't throw them away, and some marbles. But you mustn't cry, you know. I won't have a Princess that cries. I sha'n't look at you in church if you cry. If you don't cry, I'll let you have some jam too as well as butter, and you shall have a ride on the butcher's horse up and down the back-yard. And then I'll put you in a fairy-boat, and we'll fly away—fly away right over the trees and over the marsh, and past Mr. Boggett's and up into the clouds, and live in a swallow's nest, and never do any lessons."

And so on, going off in a wild and unexpected way into all sorts of extravagances, while I thought, with burning cheeks, that my demure little maiden had heard and seen more than I had suspected, and marvelled at the tangle of fancy and reality that grew up from it in her innocent mind. And sometimes she would say, "Let us sing, Miss Christie;" and I would sing some ballad, while she would coo an irregular but not inharmonious accompaniment. And we were occupied in this fashion, sitting by the open window one afternoon, when Mr. Rayner appeared in the garden.

"Go on, go on; I have been listening to the concert for ever so long. It is as pretty as birds."

But of course we could not go on in face of such a critical auditor; so Mr. Rayner, after complaining that he had taken a ticket for the series, and was not going to be defrauded like that, told me more seriously that I had a very pretty voice, and asked why I did not take pity on their dulness and come into the drawing-room after tea sometimes and sing to them.

"And you have never tried secular music with the violin, Miss Christie. I believe you're afraid. Sacred music is slow, and you can't read fast; is that it?"

He was trying to pique me; but I only laughed and pointed out to him that he had had a visitor on the evening when he was to have tried my skill, but that I was quite ready to stumble through any music he liked whenever he pleased, if it were not too difficult.

"I know it is too bad of us to want to trespass upon your time after tea, which we promised you should have to yourself. But it would indeed be a charitable action if you would come and let us bore you by our fiddling and our dull chat sometimes, instead of slipping up to your turret-chamber, to be no more seen for the remainder of the evening. What do you do there, if I may ask? Do you take observations of the moon and stars? I should think you must be too close to them up there to get a comprehensive view. Or do you peep into the birds' nests upon the highest branches and converse with the owners?"

"I do nothing half so fantastic, Mr. Rayner. I do my tasks and read something improving, and then I sit in one of my arm-chairs and just think and enjoy myself."

"Well, we are not going to let you enjoy yourself up there while we are moped to death downstairs; so to-night you may just come and share our dulness in the drawing-room."

So after tea Mr. Rayner got out his violin, and I sat down to the piano; and we played first some German popular songs and then a long succession of the airs, now lively, now pathetic, now dramatic and passionate, out of the old operas that have delighted Europe for years, such as *The Huguenots*, *La Traviata*, *Rigoletto*, and Balfe's graceful *Rose of Castile* and *The Bohemian Girl*. Mr. Rayner played with the fire of an enthusiast, and again I caught the spirit of his playing, and accompanied him, he said, while his face shone with the ecstasy of the musician, as no one had ever accompanied him before.

Doctor Maitland, an old gentleman who, Mr. Rayner privately told me, was now resting from his labors with the proud consciousness that he had seldom failed in "killing his man," came in while we were playing.

He was our nearest neighbor, and he often came in the evening to play chess with Mr. Rayner, who always beat him. He listened to the music with great astonishment and some pleasure for a long time, until he learnt that I was reading at sight, and that I had accompanied Mr. Rayner only once before. Then he almost gasped.

"Good gracious! I should never have believed it. You seem to have the same soul!" he cried, awe-struck.

And after that his astonishment evidently outweighed the pleasure he took in our performance. Mr. Rayner gave me a strange smile as the Doctor uttered his quaint speech, and I laughed back, much amused at the effect of our efforts on a musically ignorant listener. When we had finished, and Mr. Rayner was putting his violin into its case, he suddenly discovered that a corner of the latter was damp.

"This will never do," he exclaimed, with as much affectionate concern as if a friend's well-being had been threatened. "I might as well keep it in the garden as in this den," he went on, quite irritably for him—music always wrought him to a high pitch of excitement. "Here, Sarah," he added, turning towards the table where she had just placed the candles. "Take this to my room—mind, very carefully."

So his room could not be damp, I thought, or he would not allow his precious violin to be taken there. I had said good-night, and was in the hall, just in time to see Sarah, carrying the violin, disappear down the passage, on the right-hand side of the staircase, which led to the study. Now the wing where Mrs. Rayner's room was was on the left-hand side of the staircase. Did Mr. Rayner sleep in the study? I could not let my curiosity lead me to follow her, much as I should have liked to solve this little mystery. I knew all the rooms on the upper story, and, except the nursery where Mona and Jane slept, the cook's room, Sarah's, and the one I had left, they all bore distinctly the impress of having been long unused. So I was obliged reluctantly to go upstairs. When I got to the foot of my turret staircase, however, which was only a few steps from the head of the back-staircase that the servants used, I heard Sarah's quick tread in the passage below, and, putting down my candle on the ground, I went softly to the top of the stairs—there was a door here also, but it was generally open and fastened back—and looked down. I saw Sarah, much to my amusement, give a vicious shake to the violin-case, as if it were a thing she hated; and then I saw her take a key from her pocket and unlock a door near the foot of the stairs. That, then, was Mr. Rayner's room. But, as the door went back on its hinges and Sarah took out the key, went through, and locked it behind her, I saw that it led, not into a room at all, but into the garden.

So far, then, Mr. Reade's guess was right. But there still remained the question—Where did Mr. Rayner sleep?

CHAPTER X

It was the elfish baby-girl Mona who first put me on the track of the solution of the mystery about Mr. Rayner's room. This ill-cared-for little creature, instead of resenting the neglect she suffered, prized the liberties she enjoyed of roaming about withersoever she pleased, and sitting in the flower-beds, and in the mud at the edge of the pond, and making herself altogether the very dirtiest little girl I had ever seen, and objected vehemently to the least attempt at judicious restraint. The little notice she got was neither consistent nor kind. Sarah or Jane would snatch her up, regardless of her shrieks, to shut her up in an empty bedroom, if she showed her grimy little face and tattered pinafore anywhere near the house in the afternoon, when callers might come. But, if they did not see her, they forgot her, and left her to talk and croon to herself, and to collect piles of snails, and to such other simple occupations in her favorite haunts until tea-time, when she generally grew hungry of her own accord, and, returning to the house, made an entrance where she could.

The day after the violin-playing was very wet, and, looking out of the window during lessons with Haidee, I caught sight of her small sister trotting along composedly without a hat in the fast-falling rain. I jumped up and called to her; but she took no notice; so I ran to fetch my umbrella and set off in pursuit. After a little search, I saw her steadily toddling up a side-path among the trees which led to the stables; and I followed softly without calling her again, as, if irritated by pursuit, she might, I knew, plunge among the trees and surrender only when we were both wet through.

The stables were built much higher up than the house, close to the road, but surrounded by trees. I had never been near them before; but now I followed Mona close underneath the walls, where she began dancing about by herself, making hideous grimaces at two windows on the upper story, and throwing up at them little stones and bits of stick that she picked up, all wet and muddy, from the moist earth. I seized and caught her up in my arms so suddenly that for the first few moments she was too much surprised to howl; but I had scarcely turned to take her back to the house when she recovered her powers completely, and made the plantation ring with a most elfish yell. I spoke to her and tried to reason with her, and told her it was all for her good, when one of the upper windows I have mentioned was thrown open, and Mr. Rayner appeared at it.

"Hallo, what is the matter? Kidnapping, Miss Christie?"

"Oh, Mr. Rayner, she will sit in the mud and open her mouth to catch the rain without a hat, and it can't be good for her!" I said piteously.

"Never mind. It doesn't seem to hurt her. I believe she is half a frog," said her father, with less tenderness than he might have shown, I thought.

For the child was not old enough to know that it was wrong to dislike her father, while he was quite old enough to know that it was wrong not to be fonder of his child.

"But you will get your own feet wet, my dear child," said he, in quite a different tone. "Come up here and sit by the fire, while I fetch your goloshes. You have never seen my studio. I pass half my time painting and smoking here when it is wet and I can't get out." He had a palette on his thumb and a pipe in his mouth while he spoke. "You don't mind the smell of turpentine or tobacco, do you?"

"Oh, no, Mr. Rayner! But I won't come in, thank you. I am at lessons with Haidee," said I.

"Happy Haidee! I wish I were young enough to take lessons; and yet, if I were, I shouldn't be old enough to make the best use of my time," said he, in a low voice, with mock-modesty that made me laugh.

He was leaning a long way out of window in the rain, and I had work to do indoors; so, without saying anything more, I returned to the house with my prize.

It was to his studio then that Sarah had taken his violin. I had never heard of this studio before; but I knew that Mr. Rayner was very careful about the condition of the stables, and I could imagine that this two-windowed upper room, with its fire, must be a very nice place to paint in — dry, warm, and light. Could this be where Mr. Rayner slept? No; for in that case he would hardly have asked me to come up and look at his painting. And I should not like to think that he had made for himself a snug warm little home here while his family slept in the damp vapors of the marsh at the bottom of the hill. But that would not be like Mr. Rayner, I thought, remembering the pains he had taken to provide a nice dry room just for me, the governess. Yet I should have liked, in the face of Mr. Reade's tiresome suspicions, to be sure.

That night I was so anxious to find out whether Mr. Rayner did really sleep out of the house, as he had been accused of doing, that I had the meanness to leave my own bedroom door wide open, as well as that at the bottom of the turret staircase, and listen for footsteps on the ground-floor, and the sound of a key in the garden door through which Sarah had taken the violin. But I heard nothing, though I was awake until long after the rest of the household must have gone to bed. And I felt almost as much relieved as if it had been my own father proved innocent of a mean action imputed to him.

On the following night there was a high wind, which shook and swayed the trees and whistled round my turret, and made the door which stood always fastened back at the top of the kitchen-stairs rattle and creak on its hinges. At last I could bear this last sound no longer. I had been sitting up late over a book, and I knew that the household must be asleep, so I slipped downstairs as softly as I could. I had got to the top of the back-staircase, and had my hand on the door, when I saw a faint glimmer of light coming along the passage below. I heard no sound. I drew back quickly, so quickly that my candle went out; and then I waited, with my heart beating fast, not so much to see who it was, as because I did not dare to move. The faint light came along swiftly, and, when close to the foot of the stairs below me, I could see that it was a shaded lantern, and could just distinguish the form of a man carrying it. Was he coming upstairs? For the next few moments I scarcely dared to breathe, and I could almost have given a cry of joy when, by some movement of the head, I recognized Mr. Rayner. He did not see me; he put the key in the lock, turned it, took the key out, went through and locked it after him so quickly and so entirely without noise that a moment afterwards I could almost have thought that I had imagined the dim scene. It had been so utterly without sound that, if my eyes had been closed, I should have known nothing about it. I made the door secure with trembling fingers, and went back to my room again, not only profoundly sorry that Mr. Reade's surmise was correct—for I could no longer doubt that Mr. Rayner did sleep over the stables—but impressed with an eerie dread of the man who could move about in the night as noiselessly and swiftly as a spirit.

When I awoke however in the fresh morning, with the wind gone down, and the sun shining in through my east window, all unpleasant impressions of the night before had faded away; and, when Mr. Rayner brought into the drawing-room after dinner a portfolio full of his sketches and panels, and was delighted with my appreciation of them—I knew something about pictures, for my father had been a painter—I felt that it was not for me to judge his actions, and that there must be some good motive that I did not know for his sleeping far out of the damp, as for everything else that he did.

He proposed to paint me, and I gave him a sitting that very afternoon in the dining-room, which had a north light, though there was not much of it; and he said that he must finish it next day in his studio, and, when I objected to neglect my lessons again, he said the whole family should emigrate thither for the morning, and then perhaps I should be satisfied.

So the next day, at eleven o'clock, he came into the schoolroom with Mrs. Rayner, who wore her usual air of being drawn into this against what will she had, and we all four crossed the garden to the stables, and went up through the harness-room to the big room over the coach-house, which looked even more comfortable than I had expected.

For the floor was polished, and there were two beautiful rugs, a handsome tiger-skin, and a still handsomer lion-skin with the head attached, which Haidee crept up to, drew upon her lap, and nursed all the time we were there. At one end of the room was a partition, and behind this partition I guessed that Mr. Rayner slept. There was a bright fire burning in the tiled fireplace, and there were soft easy-chairs, rather worn by constant use, but very comfortable, and there were pictures on the walls, and there was a dark carved-oak cabinet full of curious and beautiful things, and a writing-table; and lastly there were the easel and a great confusion of portfolios and half-finished sketches and studies. Altogether the room contrasted very favorably with the mouldy-looking drawing-room. Perhaps Mrs. Rayner thought so as she sat down, with one eager intent look round the room, as if she had never seen it before; and then, without any remark, she took out her knitting and worked silently, while I posed again as I had done on the previous day, with my head on one side, and my hands, as Mr. Rayner had placed them, clasped under my chin, while he painted and talked.

"You like those sketches I took in Spain, Miss Christie?"

"Yes—only there are too many nasty black priests prowling about in them."

"Oh, you little bigot! Those black figures are just what the hot, rather glaring Spanish scenes want, to relieve the monotony of bright colors and sunshine. You must tolerate them from a picturesque point of view."

"Very well, but from no other. They remind me of the Inquisition. They all look like Jesuits."

"And where is the harm of looking like a Jesuit? I have a partiality for Jesuits myself."

"Oh, not really?"

"Really. Why not?"

"They are such sneaking, cowardly creatures, always working by indirect, underhand means, and leaving their poor tools to bear the storms they themselves have excited."

"But the poor tools are fit for nothing else. It is the daring, clever brain of the Jesuit that weaves the plot; it is on him that the chief responsibility lies; and that his part of the work has its dangers is proved by the persecutions and martyrdom that many of his order have suffered. You cannot conquer everything in this world by the fists alone; every clever man who has ever made his way—'got on,' as the phrase is—is a potential Jesuit."

"Well, then, I like the poor fellows who don't get on, and who have only their fists, better," said I decisively.

Mr. Rayner looked at me with a half smile.

"Most women begin like that," said he dryly.

Of course I felt rather indignant, as every girl does, at being classed with "most women;" so I said no more, but only pursed up my lips; and I saw in the white face of Mrs. Rayner, who had been listening intently to this dialogue, a faint look of amazement at my presumption.

After two hours' work, Mr. Rayner called us to look at his sketch, which represented a very lovely girl with dark gray eyes a little larger than mine, a red-lipped mouth a little smaller, teeth a little whiter, and a complexion a little creamier in the white parts and a little rosier in the red; and the brown hair coiled on the top was just a little glossier and smoother than mine ever was. It was just a little like me all the same; and I was rather hurt when Mrs. Rayner summoned spirit enough to say that he had flattered me, although I knew it quite well. But Mr. Rayner said gravely that it was impossible for a portrait to flatter a handsome woman, and Mrs. Rayner raised her thin shoulders in a slight shrug and turned to leave the room. Haidee rose to follow her, but paused on the threshold to give a last fond gaze at the lion and to look round for me.

"You are an excellent model, you sit so still. It is a pleasure to paint you for that and—for other reasons," said he slowly and deliberately, as, without looking up, he went on putting finishing touches to the head. "What shall I give you as a reward for remaining so long without blinking or yawning as all professional models do?"

"Nothing, Mr. Rayner; I like having it done. It flatters one's vanity to be painted; and flattery is always reward enough for a woman, they say," said I, laughing and following Haidee to the door.

"I shall find something more substantial than that," said Mr. Rayner, in a low voice, as if half to himself, looking up with a very kind smile as I left the room.

That afternoon Haidee had just run out of the schoolroom at the conclusion of her lessons, when Mr. Rayner came in. He held in his hand an old and shabby little case.

"The poor painter has not forgotten his promise, if he dares to call it a promise," said he, with mock humility. "Now see what you have earned by sitting still."

He drew me to the window and opened the case, keeping his eyes fixed upon my face as he did so. The case was lined with old and worn red velvet, and had evidently not been made for the ornament it contained. This was a large pendant in the form of a heart, which was a blaze of what seemed to me the most magnificent diamonds I had ever seen. The sight of them inspired me not with pleasure, but terror. I drew a long breath of surprise and admiration.

"It is the most beautiful thing I have ever seen," said I at last, not quite able to take in yet the fact that it was meant for me, and hoping against hope that it was not.

"You like diamonds?" said he, in a low voice.

"They are lovely—the most beautiful of all jewels, I think," said I, with a break in my voice.

"Would you like to have your hair and neck and arms covered with diamonds, like a duchess at Court?" asked he, still very quietly, but so that I did not know whether he was speaking seriously or in jest.

I looked up and laughed with rather an effort.

"I? Oh, no! I shouldn't care for diamonds for myself; I should look absurd in them. Diamonds are for great ladies, not for governesses."

"Governesses become great ladies sometimes, don't they?" said he, returning to his usual light tone.

"I think most of them don't," said I, in the same manner.

"Well, without being a great lady, a governess may wear an ornament she has fairly earned, may she not?"

"Yes, if it has been fairly earned," said I, trying to keep up a light tone of talk, though my heart was beating fast.

"And so you can accept this pretty little thing as the reward of your services to a grateful painter and a *souvenir* of our pleasant morning all together in the studio."

"Oh, no—oh, no—I can't indeed!" said I earnestly, pushing from me gently the case he was trying to put into my hand. "Don't be offended—don't be angry with me, Mr. Rayner; but the very thought of possessing anything so valuable would be a burden to me night and day."

Mr. Rayner burst into a long laugh.

"Oh, you simple little creature! I did not think a London lady would be so unsophisticated as to mistake very ordinary paste for diamonds," said he, with much enjoyment. "This pendant, the enormous value of which frightens you so much, is worth about fifteen shillings. It wasn't even worth having a case made for it; see, I have had to put it into an old case which once contained a brooch. No, no, my dear child, you need not be alarmed at the mere money-value of the thing, which is very little. It has a value in my eyes, but for a different reason. Look here."

He turned it over, and I saw on the back a monogram, and the date 1792.

"What are the letters of the monogram?"

I read—"R. G. D."

" 'G. D. R.,' " corrected he—"Gervas D. Rayner—my own initials and those of my father and grandfather before me. That this belonged to my grandmother makes its only value. But I have plenty of relics of her; my wife has jewels enough at the bank which she never wears; so you are robbing nobody and pleasing one old friend—I may call myself an old friend already, may I not?—very much by accepting this. In full family conclave at tea, you shall hear me announce the presentation, and then you will be satisfied, won't you, you modest little girl?"

"But I can never wear such a thing as this, if it is only what you call paste," I objected.

"Wear it under your dress, and then the blaze of it will dazzle nobody," said Mr. Rayner, bending over me and laughing kindly at my reluctance.

So I took it with most ungracious feelings, which I tried to hide, and thanked him as well as I could. True to his promise, Mr. Rayner said to his wife at tea-time—

"I have with the greatest difficulty prevailed upon this proud Miss Christie of ours to accept as a reward of her services as model a twopenny-halfpenny trinket, which she almost told me was not fit to wear."

"Oh, Mr. Rayner!"

He was putting such a different color upon my reluctance, as if I had not thought it good enough. And there is a great deal of difference between fifteen shillings and twopence-halfpenny. I saw Sarah, who was in the room, look at me very sharply, as if she thought governesses had no business to wear trinkets at all; and Mrs. Rayner did not look pleased.

Altogether the beautiful ornament that I had admired so much, but certainly not coveted, had brought me more annoyance than pleasure. It procured me one more little trial that very evening. When I got upstairs, I sat down in the arm-chair which had its back to the door, took the case out of my pocket, and looked at the ornament. It certainly was very splendid, and I thought, as I looked at it and made it flash in the setting sun, that, if this were paste and worth only fifteen shillings, it was great waste of money to buy real diamonds, which cost so much more and looked no better. And, as I was holding it up to the light and feeling at last a thrill of pleasure in its possession, I heard a voice behind me say—

"So that's the twopenny-halfpenny trinket, is it?"

Of course it was Sarah. She had come up to bring me some water, and I had plenty in the jug. Her ironical tone and the hard little sneering laugh with which she finished her speech were too much for my temper. I shut up the case, and said coldly—

"Of course Mr. Rayner would not give any one a thing which really cost only twopence-halfpenny, Sarah."

"No, miss, not for such services as yours."

And she said it in such a nasty tone that, when she had left the room, I threw the case down upon the table and burst into tears.

CHAPTER XI

When I had dried my tears and sat down in my favorite arm-chair to consider my grievances against Sarah, I wondered what had made her take such a strong dislike to me as she seemed to feel. It was true that her manners were not very pleasant or amiable to anybody; but there was a malignity in the way she looked at me, and a spiteful coldness in her tone if she only asked me if I would have any more coals, as if she thought it was a great deal more than I deserved to have a fire at all. But she had never been so rude and harsh before as she was on this night, and I began to think that the reason for all her unkindness was her annoyance at the great consideration shown to me, for I was, after all, only a new-comer, while she, who had been in the family for years, was left in her room on the upper story and was not asked to sit for her portrait. It seemed a very silly feeling in a woman so old and sensible as Sarah was supposed to be, and who was certainly very well off for a servant, to show such a mean jealousy of a governess, who is always supposed to be a lady, even in those cases when everybody knows that she is not one. That is only fair, as her work is generally so much harder and so much more unpleasant than that of a servant. Then I thought of the experiences of the other governesses I had known, and I came to the conclusion that Sarah must have lived in families where the governess was snubbed and neglected as some of my friends had been by their pupils' parents, and so she thought it a shame that I should be so much better treated than most of my sisterhood.

"She is only a crumpled rose-leaf, after all," I thought to myself. "I am getting spoilt, and it is as well that there is some one to let me know that I am no more deserving than other people—only more fortunate. I suppose I ought to be thankful for Sarah!"

Then I thought of what Mr. Rayner had said about wearing the dazzling heart under my dress; and it was really so beautiful, and I was so grateful to him for his kindness—for it was not his fault that the gift had already brought down so much discomfort upon me—that I should have liked to do so; but two reasons prevented me. The one was that, if I had fastened it round my neck by a bit of ribbon and it had accidentally been seen by some one—Mrs. Rayner for instance, not to mention Sarah—I should have felt rather guilty and uncomfortable, as if I had done something to be ashamed of, that wanted excuses and explanations; and that feeling is, I think, a pretty sure sign that one is doing what is not quite right. The other reason was that I already wore a *souvenir* round my neck under my dress, fastened to a watch-guard; it was a little case that I had made out of the back of an old purse, and it contained the bit of paper with Mr. Reade's apology which I had pulled off the rose that evening when I had found the basket of flowers in my "nest."

Now, if I went on stringing around my neck all the letters and gifts I received, I should some day have as many trophies about my person as a wild Indian—only I should not take the pride in displaying them that he did. So I decided to lock up my pretty sparkling heart in my desk, and to be content with the less showy pendant I already wore. Sarah had seen it, of course—at least she had seen the cover, one evening when I had a cold, and she had brought me a cup of arrowroot, by Mr. Rayner's orders, while I was undressing. I had seen, by the eager way in which she fixed her great black eyes upon it, that she was dying to know what it contained, and I was mischievously glad that she could not.

Mr. Rayner had given me the pendant on Saturday. The next day, when service was over, and we were standing about in the churchyard as usual, before Mr. and Mrs. Rayner's departure gave Haidee and me the signal to go home, Mr. Laurence Reade left his party and stood looking at the gravestones, until the gradual moving on of the stream of people who were slowly coming out of the porch brought us past him. Then, as Mr. and Mrs. Rayner stopped to speak to some one, Mr. Reade said—

"Haidee, I'll give you a penny if you can read that epitaph"—pointing to one in worn old-English characters. "Miss Christie, I believe it is as much as you can do; it is more than I can."

And we stepped on to the grass, and Haidee knelt down and slowly spelt it out aloud. Mr. Reade kept his eyes fixed on the inscription as he bent over one side of the tombstone, while I looked at it from the other; but what he said was—

"It seems such a long time since Tuesday."

Tuesday was the day on which he had bought the marbles. I could not laugh over a tombstone before all those people; so I said gravely—

"It is just five days."

"Yes, but they have been such long days," said he, in a low voice.

"Not really," I answered. "The days are getting shorter and shorter now."

"Don't you know how long a day seems when you want to see a—a person, and you can't? But perhaps you see the persons you like best to see every day?"

"I like to see my mother best, and she is a long way off," said I gravely.

"Ah, yes, of course! But I wasn't thinking of one's family."

"Perhaps you were thinking of the pretty girls who were in your pew last Sunday?"

"The Finches—Ethel and Katie? Oh, no, I wasn't! I see quite enough of them. They're coming again, too, to the school-treat. Don't see why they can't be contented with their own tea-fights. No; I was thinking of somebody quite different. Can't you guess who?"

He was looking at me now, and not at the inscription at all. And in the pause which followed his words I distinctly heard Mr. Rayner's bright voice saying archly—

"Laurence seems to have a great admiration for our pretty little Miss Christie; doesn't he, Mrs. Reade?"

I did not hear her answer; but it was given in a displeased tone; and a minute afterwards she called her son sharply and said that they were waiting for him. But they all stayed in the churchyard for some minutes after that, and then I noticed that Mr. Rayner was still talking to Mrs. Reade, and that she seemed very much pleased and interested by what he was saying. I just heard her mention "the Bramleys" and "our branch" in her answers; so I guessed that they were what Mr. Rayner called "up the genealogical tree" together.

This was to be a busy week in the parish. The school-treat, which had been put off this year, first on account of sickness in the village and then because of the wet weather, was now fixed to take place on Saturday; and the following day was to be the harvest festival. This was not a very great occasion with us, being signalized only by a special sermon, the harvest thanksgiving hymns—which would be rather inappropriate this year, as the farmers were grumbling more than usual at the damage done by the late heavy rains—and bunches of corn, which those same "thankful people" rather grudged us, in the church-windows and round the pulpit. The Misses Reade had undertaken most of the decoration of the church, as the Vicar's wife had enough to do in preparing for the school-feast and accompanying sale.

The next day Haidee and I took a longer walk than usual; and, when we returned, Jane met me with a mysterious air in the hall.

"Oh, Miss Christie, young Mr. Reade called while you was out, and asked to see you! He said he had a message for you. And, when I said you was out and offered to give it you, he said he had better write it, as it was important. So he wrote a note for you; and please it wasn't my fault, but Sarah got hold of it, and she took it to Mr. Rayner. I told her it was directed to you; but she wouldn't take no notice."

I went upstairs very much annoyed by this fresh indignity offered me by that hateful Sarah, and hurt and sorry beside, for I was longing to know what the note said. As soon as I got into the dining-room, however, Mr. Rayner came up to me smiling, and put it into my hands.

"Here is a *billet-doux* which has been left for you, Miss Christie. Now whom do you expect one from?"

"From nobody, Mr. Rayner," said I, blushing very much.

This was not a story, because I knew the letter could not be at all the sort of communication he implied, but would contain, probably, some formal message from Mrs. Maitland.

I opened it at once to show that I did not think it of any consequence. It only said—

> "Dear Miss Christie,—My sisters find there is so much to be done for the church that they are afraid they won't be able to do it all. Would you be so very kind as to undertake part? If you would not mind, I will ride over with the work to-morrow after luncheon, about a quarter-past two. Yours sincerely, Laurence Reade."

I think I was a little disappointed in the note; but it was all the better, as I could repeat in quite a careless way what it said; and then, just as I was wondering whether I should tear it up to show that I did not care, I saw that there was something written on the inside leaf, and I put it back into the envelope as if I did not notice what I was doing, and slipped it into my pocket.

Dinner was long that day; when it was over, I went into the schoolroom and drew out my letter again. The words on the inside leaf were—

"Why were you so unkind on Sunday?"

I had no way of sending back an answer; I could only wait till next day at a quarter-past two. But I think I could have sung through the lessons like the heroine of an opera that afternoon.

I had not thought it necessary to mention to Mr. Rayner the time at which Mr. Reade had said he should bring the work; at a quarter-past two we were always in the drawing-room all together. But the next day, the day of all others when it was important that I should stay and hear the explanations about the work I had to do, Mrs. Rayner asked me, directly after dinner, if I would mind writing some letters for her, to go by that afternoon's post. I should have sat down to write them in the drawing-room, but Mrs. Rayner said—

"You would like to be undisturbed, I know. Shall I send your coffee to your room or to the schoolroom?"

I said, "To my room, if you please," and went upstairs trying to swallow the lump in my throat.

It was silly of me; but I liked that half-hour in the drawing-room after dinner, and reading the papers over my coffee, and Mr. Rayner's amusing comments on the news—it was such a pleasant rest.

I had got through one stupid letter—they were not at all important—when there was a knock at the door, and Jane came in, giggling and excited.

"Oh, miss, I've brought you a parcel, and I have made Sarah so wild!"—and she laughed delightedly. "I answered the bell, and there was Mr. Reade on his horse with this; and he said, 'Take it to the schoolroom, please; it's for Miss Christie;' and then he got off, and I showed him into the drawing-room. And I saw you wasn't in there, nor yet in the schoolroom. So when I got into the hall, thinks I, 'I'll be beforehand with old Sally this time!' when out she comes and says, 'Give that to me. I'll give it to Miss Christie.' 'Never mind,' says I, half-way up the stairs—'don't you trouble.' And she made a grab at me, but I was too quick for her, and up I run; and here it is, miss."

And she slapped the parcel down upon the table triumphantly.

"Thank you, Jane," I said quietly. "It is only some work for the church from Miss Reade."

Jane's face fell a little; and then, as if struck by a fresh thought, she giggled again. I cut the string and opened the parcel to prove the truth of my words, and showed her the red flannel and the wheat-ears, which were to be sown on in letters to form a text. But in the middle was another note, and a box wrapped up in paper, both directed to "Miss Christie;" and at sight of these little Jane's delight grew irrepressible again.

"I knew it!" she began, but stopped herself and said, "I beg your pardon, miss," and left the room very demurely.

But I heard another burst of merriment as she ran downstairs. Then I opened the note; it only said—

"Dear Miss Christie,—I take the liberty of sending you a few late roses from a tree in a sheltered corner where the rain cannot spoil them. I hope they won't smell of cigars; I could not find a better box. I will call to fetch the text, if you will let me know when I can see you. Yours sincerely, Laurence Reade."

The roses were in a cigar-box, and as long as they lasted they never smelt of anything but tobacco; but I began to think that perfume nicer than their own.

I was so happy that evening that I was glad when Mr. Rayner asked me to accompany his violin, and I was glad that he chose operatic selections again, for in the passionate and sweet music of *Don Giovanni* and *Il Trovatore* I could give vent to my feelings. I felt that I had never appreciated the beautiful melodies so well, nor helped so efficiently to do justice to them as I did in accompanying Mr. Rayner that night. He was so pleased with my help that he begged me to go on, with "Just one more" and "Just one more," until long after Mrs. Rayner had gone to her room. I was nothing loath; I could have played till midnight. I did not say much in comment between the pieces, when Mr. Rayner asked, "How do you like that?" But I suppose it was easy to see by my face that I was enjoying the music intensely, for he just nodded and smiled and seemed quite satisfied.

The clock had struck the half-hour after ten, which was quite late for the household at the Alders, when he finished playing "*Voi che sapete.*"

"And how do you like that?" asked Mr. Rayner as usual, only that this time he put down his violin, and, drawing a chair close to my music-stool, ran his fingers over the keys of the piano, repeating the melody.

"Do you know the words? '*Voi che sapete che cos' è amore,*' " he sang softly. "Do you know what that means?"

"Oh, yes!" said I, rather proud of showing off my small knowledge of Italian. " 'You who know what love is.' "

I drew my music-stool a little back, and listened while he sang it softly through. I had never known a love-song touch me like that before. I could almost have cried out in answer, as I sat with my head turned away, listening, almost holding my breath lest I should lose a sound. When he had finished, he turned round; I did not move or speak, and he jumped up, walked to the shutters, unbarred them, and threw open the window.

"I am suffocating. Oh for a Venetian balcony!" said he. "Come here, little woman."

I rose and obeyed. He threw a woollen antimacassar round my head and shoulders, and drew me to the window.

"Look up there, child, at the moon through the tree-tops. Wouldn't you like to be in Venice, listening by moonlight to those sweet songs in the very native land of the love they sing about?"

"I don't want to be anywhere but here, Mr. Rayner," said I, smiling up at the moon very happily.

"Why?"

But I could not tell Mr. Rayner why.

"I would give the whole world to be there at this moment with the woman I love. I could make her understand there!"

I was struck by the passionate tenderness in his voice, and suddenly made up my mind to be very bold.

"Then why don't you take her there, Mr. Rayner?" I said earnestly.

As I spoke, smiling at him and speaking as gently as I could, though I felt terribly frightened at my own boldness, his eyes seemed to grow darker, and his whole face lighted up in an extraordinary way. I saw my words had made an impression, so I went on eagerly, pressing nervously the hand with which he was holding mine, for I was still afraid lest my audacity should offend him.

"Mr. Rayner, forgive me for speaking about this; but you spoke first, didn't you? I have so often wondered why you didn't take her away. It seems so hard that you, who want sympathy so much—you know you have often told me so—should have to live, as you say, a shut-up life, on account of the apathy of the woman to whom you are bound."

He seemed to drink in my words as if they contained an elixir; I could feel by his hand that he was actually trembling; and I grew more assured myself.

"Now, if you were to take her away, although you might have a difficulty at first in persuading her to go, and force her, with the kind force you know how to use, to go among fresh faces and see fresh people, I believe she would come back to life again, and see how much better you are than other husbands, and love you just as much as ever. Oh, she couldn't help it; you are so kind and so good!"

Then my heart sank, for I saw I had gone too far. As I spoke, from passionately eager, he looked surprised, puzzled, and then his face clouded over with a cold frown that chilled me with fear and shame. I drew my hand out of his quickly, and stepped back into the room. He followed and took my hand again, and, when I looked up, murmuring clumsy and incoherent apologies, his face was as composed and kind as usual; but I thought he looked rather sad.

"Never mind, little one; you have not offended me by speaking your mind out; don't be afraid. But you don't know, you cannot guess—how should a child like you guess?—how many or how deep a man's cares may be while he is obliged to bear a brave front to the world. I think you would be sorry for me if you knew them."

"I am sorry even without knowing them," I said softly.

He bent down over me and looked into my eyes for a few moments. Then he raised his head, and laughed lightly.

"You are a fraud. Great gray eyes ought to be passionate, and yours are as cold as a lake on a still day. I believe you are an Undine! You have no soul."

"Oh, Mr. Rayner!" I said mournfully, and I turned slowly to the piano to put away the music.

"Never mind; I will do that," said he, in his usual tone. "I have kept you up long enough. Good-night, Undine."

I was almost afraid he would again want to kiss me, and, after offending him once, I should not have dared to refuse. So I shook hands as hastily as I could, took my candle, and ran upstairs. I was very angry with myself for having been cold and unsympathetic—I had not meant to be so at all.

But the fact was I had been thinking the whole evening of Mr. Laurence Reade.

CHAPTER XII

I slackened my pace when I got to the top of the first flight of stairs, and walked softly through the corridor where the nursery was, for fear of waking Mona; and, as I went slowly along the passage leading to the turret stairs, I began to think of what Mr. Rayner had called me, and wondered what he meant by saying I had no soul.

"It wasn't because I am not sorry for him, for he must have seen that I am," thought I. "I suppose I don't show my sympathy in the right way; but I could not very well say more about it without being disrespectful. And I must not forget that Mr. Rayner is not only much older than I, but also my employer."

And so I crept up the turret stairs with my candle, and opened the door of my room.

It was quite a calm night, and I walked in very slowly, yet, as I entered, my candle went out suddenly, as if blown by a gust of wind; and I fancied I heard a slight sound as of a human breath blowing it. I stepped forward quickly, a little startled, and tried to peer into the darkness. But it was impossible to see, for my fire had gone out, the blinds were down and the curtains drawn, and not a ray of moonlight could get in. I stood for a few moments, still frightened, in the middle of the room, and then cautiously made my way in the direction of the mantelpiece, where I kept my match-box. I made a slight noise as I passed my fingers over the different articles there, and, just at the moment that I knocked over a china ornament which fell into the fireplace, above the noise it made as it broke to pieces in the grate I heard a sound behind the screen which stood between the bed and the door, and, turning quickly, I was in time to see a figure come swiftly round it and disappear through the still open door. I could distinguish nothing; nevertheless, suppressing my inclination to scream, I rushed to the door and caught in the air at the figure I could no longer see; but I felt nothing.

Then I crept back into my room, shaking from head to foot, and hardly daring to move in this direction or that, for fear of encountering another dim figure. I closed the door behind me, sick with fear lest I should be shutting myself in with more unwelcome visitors; and, starting at the slight creaking that a board made here and there under my own feet, I again searched the mantelpiece for the match-box. My hands trembled so that it was a long time before I could be sure that it was not there; and then I turned and felt my way to the table; and, after moving most of the things on it, I at last satisfied myself that it was not there either. Then I groped my way to one of the windows—I had not thought of that before—drew the curtains and pulled up the blind. The moon gave only a fitful light, being obscured every other minute by thin driving clouds, and it only served to make shadows in the room which were more fearful to me, in my nervous state, than darkness itself. I had one more search for the matches, but could not find them even now.

It was out of the question to undress by such weird moonlight, fancying dim shapes in every corner and noises behind me whichever way I turned; so I determined to conquer my fears and go downstairs with my candle and get a light below. There were sure to be some matches in the kitchen, and I reflected that enough moonlight would come in over or through the shutters to let me see my way without making a noise.

So I groped my way down the back-staircase, which I had never used before, got safely to the bottom, turned to my left, and felt for a door. The first opened into a big black cupboard where I felt brooms, which I shut again quickly; the second was locked, but the key was in the door, and I softly turned it. This was indeed the kitchen; but the moment I found this out, and gave a sigh of relief, I heard on the floor a sound which I knew too well to be the rush of myriads of blackbeetles; and, as I would rather have faced a dozen dim human figures than have felt under my foot the "scrunch" of one blackbeetle, I had to shut that door too as quickly as I had shut the other.

The only thing left for me was to feel my way back to the staircase, go down the passage at the other side of it, which led past Mr. Rayner's study, and so into the hall, where I knew the exact position of the match-box which stood on the hall table.

My only fear now was that I might meet Mr. Rayner, in the event of his not having left the house yet to go to his room. If I met him, I should have to account for my presence wandering about the house at this time of night, and I felt that I was still too much discomposed by the fright I had received for his sharp eyes not to notice my pallor and my quaking hands; and then I should have to tell him what I had seen, and there would be a search and an explanation, and I should get some one into trouble. For my fears had not gone beyond thinking that it was Sarah or one of the other servants who—

perhaps wishing to give me a fright, perhaps only all but caught in the untimely enjoyment of one of my easy-chairs—anxious to escape detection, had blown out my candle, hoping to slip out in the dark unheard.

However, I got back safely to the bottom of the staircase without seeing or hearing anything, and I was creeping along the passage when I caught the first faint sound of voices. I stopped, then went on again softly, while the sounds became plainer, and I found that they proceeded from Mr. Rayner's study, the door of which I had to pass. I discovered by the thin thread of light it let out upon the passage that this door was ajar, at the same moment that I recognized Sarah's voice. She was speaking in a low sullen tone, and, as I drew nearer, I was arrested half against my will by words which seemed to apply to myself—"Against the stupid baby-face of a chit hardly out of the nursery herself. Governess indeed!"

"Is that all you have to say?" said Mr. Rayner very low, but in his coldest, most cutting tone.

"That's—that's all I have to say," said Sarah, with a choking sound in her voice.

The woman was evidently unhappy; I almost pitied her.

"Then the matter is easily settled. You can go."

"I can go! I go! Do you know what you're saying? Do you think you could replace me as easily as you can such as her?" said she, forgetting all respect due to her master, as her voice, still low, trembled with rage.

"That is my affair. You wished me to choose between the services of an underpaid governess and those of an overpaid servant. I have chosen."

"Overpaid! My services overpaid! My services can't be overpaid!" she hissed out.

"As long as you joined discretion to your other undoubted good qualities, I paid you according to that estimate. Now that you let yourself be swayed beyond all bounds of prudence by trifling feelings of jealousy and spite, like a foolish girl, your value runs down to that level. You are no longer a girl, Sarah, and your position is changed in many ways since then, in most for the better. If you cannot accept the changes quietly, you had better go."

"And you would let me go—for a new-comer?" said the woman passionately.

"I cannot think of sending away any member of my household for the caprice of any other member of it, however valuable a servant she may have been—"

"May have been—may have been! My work is not over yet, and, if I don't work for you, I'll work against you," she broke out in a fury. "I'll—"

"Not so fast, not so fast," said he slowly. "You will find that up-hill work when you have to deal with me, Sarah Gooch."

He spoke in the hard tone I had heard him use once or twice before—a tone which always made me shudder. Then his voice changed suddenly to a genial, almost caressing tone.

"Now do you think you will be able to get on without me as well as I can without you?"

There was a pause. Then I heard Sarah burst into sobs and low passionate cries for pity, for forgiveness.

"Why are you so hard? How can you have the heart to talk like that about my services, as if I was too old for anything but money-bargains? That chit, that Christie girl, that you put before me, will never serve you like I've done."

"The services of a governess are not the same as those of a servant. That is enough about Miss Christie, Sarah."

"Enough and welcome about the little flirt—a creature that keeps diamonds from one man in her desk, and wears round her neck a letter from another which she kisses on the sly! Oh, I've seen her, the little—"

"Nonsense!" said Mr. Rayner sharply. "And what if she does? It is no business of mine."

I heard him rise hastily from his chair and walk across the room; and I fled past like a hare. Trembling and panting, I found my way to the hall table, took out of the box there half a dozen matches, and crept guiltily, miserably upstairs. I had listened, as if chained to the spot, to their talk, and it was only now that I had fled for fear of discovery that I reflected on what a dishonorable thing I had done.

If he had come to the door, thrown it open, and seen me cowering with parted lips against the wall within a few feet of it, how Sarah would have triumphed in the justice of her hatred of a girl who could be guilty of such meanness! And how Mr. Rayner's own opinion of me would have sunk! He would have seen how wrong he was in considering the eavesdropping governess the superior of the devoted servant.

I cried with shame and remorse as I stumbled up the turret stairs, shut myself in my room, and lighted my candle. I did not feel a bit frightened now; I forgot even to turn the key in the lock; this last adventure had swept away all remembrance of the previous one. When at last I began to think collectedly of what I had heard, I felt no longer any doubt, from what Sarah had said about the nature and extent of her services, that she was in reality the responsible guardian of Mrs. Rayner, and that, when she spoke of working against her master if he sent her away, she meant to publish far and wide what he had so long and so carefully kept secret—the fact that he had a wife tottering on the verge of insanity. I did not wonder now so much as I had before at the depth of her jealousy of me. I saw how strong the woman's passions were and how deep was her devotion to her master, and I began to understand that it was hard for her to see so many little acts of consideration showered on a new-comer which she, although her service had been so much longer and more painful, could not from her position expect. And I got up from the chair I had sat down on, trying to forgive her, yet hoping she would go away all the same.

As I rose, I caught sight of my desk, which I suddenly saw had been moved. I might have done that myself in my search for the matches; but it flashed through my mind that Sarah had told Mr. Rayner that I kept diamonds in my desk. But it was locked, and the keys were always in my pocket. However, I opened it and looked into the top compartment, where I kept Mr. Rayner's present. There it was in its case, looking just as usual. Then I opened the lower compartment, with the intention of reading through just once more, before I went to bed, those two notes that I had had from Mr. Reade, one on that day and one on the day before, about the church-work. And the last one, the one that had come with the cigar-box on that day, was not there! A suspicion flashed through my mind which made my breath come fast—Sarah had taken it!

It was Sarah then whom I had surprised in my room that evening! She had managed by some means to open my desk, seen the pendant, and, having made a grievance against me of the fact that I received letters from a gentleman, had taken the letter out and probably shown it to Mr. Rayner on some pretence of having "picked it up," to prove to him by the direction in a handwriting which he knew that I was carrying on a clandestine correspondence with Mr. Laurence Reade. And I remembered that she had already taken the first note to Mr. Rayner. Well, if she had read both the notes—for they were lying together in my desk—she must have seen that they were of a very innocent kind; but how was Mr. Rayner, who had not read them, to know this? I was annoyed and disgusted beyond measure; I could have forgiven her anything, even her meanness in playing spy while I looked at the note which I wore round my neck, but stealing my precious letter. I shed some more tears at the loss of it, wondering whether she would ever take the trouble to restore it, polluted as it would be by having been read by her unkind eyes.

Then I went to bed, very tired and very unhappy; and at last I fell asleep, with my hands clasping the note that Sarah could not get at, which I wore in the case round my neck.

Perhaps the excitement and agitation of the evening had caused my sleep to be lighter than usual. At any rate, I was awakened by a very slight noise indeed, so slight that I thought it must have been the work of my nervous fancy; and my sleepy eyes were closing again, when I suddenly became conscious that there was a light in the room not that of the rising sun.

Fully awake now, and cold all over with this new fright, I saw by the flickering on the ceiling that the light must come from a candle behind the screen; I saw that it was being carried forward into the room, and then I closed my eyes and pretended to be asleep. My fingers were still clinging to the little case; but they were wet and clammy with horror. Was it Sarah? What was she going to do now? To put back my letter? I did not dare to look.

I lay there listening so intently that I could hear, or fancy I heard, each soft step taken by the intruder. Then they stopped; and from the effect of the flickering light through my closed eyelids I guessed that the candle was being raised to throw its light on my face. Still I had self-command enough to lie quite still and to imitate the long-drawn breathing of a sleeping person. But then my heart seemed to stand still, for I felt the light coming nearer, and I heard the faint sound of a moving figure growing plainer, until the light was flashed within a foot of my face. I could not have moved then. I was half paralyzed. Then I noticed a faint sickly smell that I did not know, and a hand was laid very softly upon the bed-clothes.

Still I did not move. I had formed a sort of plan in those deadly two minutes, which seemed like two hours, when the light was coming nearer and nearer to my face. The hand crept softly up, and slipped under the bed-clothes close to my chin, till it touched my fingers clutching the little leathern case. It tried to disengage them; but my clasp of my treasure was like grim death. Then the hand was softly withdrawn. I heard the drawing of a cork, I smelt the faint smell more strongly, and a handkerchief wet with some sickening, suffocating stuff was thrown lightly over my face.

Then I started up with a shriek as loud and piercing as my lungs could give, tore the handkerchief from my face, and confronted Sarah, who drew back, her dark face livid with anger, but without uttering a sound. In her hand she held a little bottle. I tried with a spring to dash it from her grasp; but she was too quick for me, and, with a step back against the screen, she held it out of my reach. Then the screen fell down with a loud crash. My attention was distracted from the woman to it for one moment, and in that moment she made another spring at my neck. But then there was a sound outside which had as many terrors for her as her own hard voice had for me. It was Mr. Rayner, calling sharply and sternly—

"Sarah, come out here!"

She started; then her face grew sullen and defiant, and she stood like a rock before me. Again Mr. Rayner called.

"Sarah, do you hear me? Come here!"

And, as if a spell had been cast upon her which it was vain for her to fight against, she went slowly out of the room, and I was left alone.

I sprang from the bed, locked the door, and fell down against it in the dark and cold in a passion of hysterical sobs that I could not restrain. Then they died away, and I felt my limbs grow numb and stiff; but I had not power to move, and I thought I must be dying.

Then I heard a fall at the bottom of the stairs and a woman's cry, and immediately after a voice outside roused me.

CHAPTER XIII

"Miss Christie!"

It was Mr. Rayner calling softly through the door. I did not answer or move.

"Miss Christie, my dear child, are you there? Are you conscious? Are you ill?"

And I heard the handle of the door turn; but it was locked. I raised my head from the ground, and said, in a weak quavering voice—

"I am not ill, thank you, and I am quite conscious."

"But your voice is weak. Are you hurt? Did that woman hurt you?" he asked anxiously.

"No, no; I am only frightened; I am not hurt. I will tell you all about it to-morrow, Mr. Rayner. I can't talk now."

"But I cannot go away and sleep, my child, till I am quite satisfied that you are all right. Put on your dressing gown, and come out and let me see you and be sure."

But I felt that I could not leave my room again that night.

"I am really quite well, only I cannot come out to-night, Mr. Rayner. I am too much shaken with the fright; I am indeed."

"I will fetch you some brandy-and-water, and put it here for you, outside the door, then."

"No, please don't; I should not dare to take it in. I feel that, if I opened the door, she might get in. If I saw her again to-night, it would kill me!" I sobbed. "Oh, please keep her away!"

I was getting hysterical again.

"She shall not come near you, child; I swear it! You are quite safe. I will lock the door at the bottom of these stairs, and come and let you out myself in the morning," he said, in a low voice.

The thought of being locked in did not reassure me much; but I thanked him and wished him good-night, with a last piteous appeal to him to keep

Sarah away. Then I rose from the floor, stumbled to the table, struck a match and lighted my candle, and put it by my bedside. For the first time I was afraid of the dark. And I lay awake listening, and starting at the tiny cracks the wood made, until at last, worn out, I fell asleep.

The next morning I heard Mr. Rayner unlock the door at the foot of the staircase when I had just opened mine, ready to go down. He waited for me, looking up anxiously, and seemed shocked at my appearance. I had noticed myself, as I was dressing, how white and haggard I looked, and how dull and heavy my eyes were, with black rings round them.

"You ought not to have got up at all. You should have stayed in bed and had your breakfast brought up to you."

I shuddered; I had had enough of bedside visits for a long time, and the thought of being a semi-invalid waited on by Sarah was too much for my self-command.

"Take my arm, child; you can scarcely walk. Come to breakfast; a cup of hot coffee will do you good. And, after that, you shall come into the study, and we will talk. Don't say anything about it at breakfast; it might frighten my wife."

I took his arm, for I really was not quite steady on my feet; and he led me into the dining-room, and put me into an arm-chair instead of the one I usually occupied at prayers. Then Haidee, who had seen at once that there was a change in me, and given me a double kiss as consolation, rang the bell to summon the servants to prayers. I held the arms of my chair, and kept my eyes on the ground and my lips tightly closed that I might give no sign when I saw Sarah's face again; but, when they came in, I knew without looking up that she was not there. And Jane waited at table. Had Sarah gone already? My heart leapt at the thought. At breakfast Mr. Rayner said—

"I am going to propose a holiday for to-day. Both mistress and pupil are looking very seedy, and I think a day's rest from lessons will do both good. My motives are not wholly unselfish, I am sorry to say, for I have the penny-bank accounts to do, and I want you to help me with them, Miss Christie, if you will be so kind as to spare me a couple of hours. I won't keep you longer."

I assented rather nervously. I should have a scene to go through with Mr. Rayner, and an announcement to make which would entail a lot of argument and some persuasion and resistance, which I scarcely felt equal to, shaken as I was.

"At what time will you want me, Mr. Rayner?"

"How soon after breakfast can you come?"

"May I have an hour first to finish some work I have to do? It doesn't matter, if you would rather—"

"In an hour's time I shall expect you in the study, then."

After breakfast, I went upstairs, where I found Jane doing my room. I caught her looking at me shyly, as if I had gone up in interest in her eyes. She must have heard something of the night's adventure—I wanted to know what. She prepared to leave the room when I entered.

"Never mind, Jane; don't go. You have nearly finished, I see. So you are doing the rooms this morning?"

"Yes, miss; I've got to get into the way of it, miss."

She gave a gasp, as if to continue, but stopped.

"Well?" said I, smiling, to encourage her to talk.

"You know Sarah's going away, miss."

"Is she?" said I, unable to keep my face from brightening at the welcome words.

"Yes, miss. Oh, there has been a rumpus, and no mistake! You just should have heard her go on! But she's going, and I'm not sorry, for one."

"What is she going away for?" said I.

"Don't you know, miss?"

She spoke shyly, but was evidently prepared to disbelieve me if I said "No."

"I can guess; but what reason did she give you?"

"Oh, it's all along of you, miss! She burst in to cook and me this morning, and said as she wasn't going to stay in a house where there was such goings on. That was what she said, miss." And she paused, her shyness again getting the better of her anxiety to pour out all she had heard.

"Go on, go on. You know I asked you to tell me," said I gently.

"Well, miss, she said all kind o' things about you; but we didn't take much notice o' them, cook and me; we're used to old Sally. But then she said—she said—"

"Yes—well?"

"She said as how she went up to your room, hearing a noise, and then— as how—"

"Go on."

"Then as how—Mr. Rayner came up and—and wasn't best pleased to find her there—"

"Yes—well?"

But Jane would not go on, but got very red, and fidgeted about with the cloth she was holding. And suddenly, as I watched the girl in wonder, the whole awful truth flashed upon me of the complexion that Sarah had given to the story. I did not speak for a minute—I only felt a strange little fluttering pain that seemed to be round my heart—and then I said very quietly—

"I suppose she didn't tell you that she tried to steal something I wear round my neck; that, when she found she couldn't, she threw a handkerchief steeped in some drug over my face to make me unconscious, that she might get at it more easily; that it was my screams that brought Mr. Rayner upstairs, and that he stood outside and called her till she came to him. Here, I'll show you the very handkerchief."

I had tucked it down in the corner of one of the drawers. It still smelt faintly of the stuff it had been soaked in. Little Jane's face brightened with wonder and downright honest pleasure.

"I'm that glad, miss, I could dance," said she. "She said Mr. Rayner let her fall downstairs in the dark, and went on up without taking no notice—and she really is a good deal bruised, and serve her right. But there never is no believing Sarah. And for her to talk about goings on! Oh, my, we did laugh, cook and me!" And Jane chattered on about Sarah and her many unpleasant attributes till she had finished her work, and left the room with a bright grin of friendship.

So Sarah, after doing me another wrong worse than all the rest in circulating lies to injure my reputation, was going. But she would probably not go at once, and I felt that I could not sleep another night in the same house with her. So I turned out all my things and packed my boxes, as I had determined to do while I lay awake during the past night. I looked into my desk, and found that my note had been replaced! I would announce to Mr. Rayner my determination to go when I went to the study, and ask permission to leave that very afternoon. I was sorry to leave the Alders, Mr. Rayner, and sweet little Haidee; and there was another reason which made the thought of leaving Geldham harder still to bear. But the terrors of the night I had passed through had had an effect upon me strong enough to outweigh every other consideration; even now, by daylight, I could scarcely look round my own familiar little room without a feeling of loathing of the scene of my horrible adventure.

There was another reason for my hasty flight. Sarah was a very valuable servant, as she had insisted, and as Mr. Rayner himself had admitted. Now I was the only obstacle to her remaining, and it was really better that the one of us who could best be replaced should go; and my well-founded fears that she might, after all, be retained in any case helped to strengthen my resolution to go. I had had no salary yet, as I had not been two months at the Alders, but my uncle had given me a sovereign to be put by, in case of emergency, and now the emergency was come. So I packed my boxes, and then went downstairs rather nervously to the study, having in my pocket the drugged handkerchief as a proof that my adventure was no fancy, as I guessed that Mr. Rayner would try to make me believe.

Mr. Rayner said "Come in" when I knocked, got up, placed me in an arm-chair by the fire, and asked me to wait while he spoke to Sam. He left the room, and I cautiously made friends with his big dog, who shared the hearthrug with me. He was very gracious, and I had progressed so far as to slide down from my seat to caress him better, when I looked up and saw Sarah.

I sprang to my feet, with a scream that I could not repress, and darted to the bell.

"Don't!" said she sharply. "At least, wait one moment—give me a hearing. I'll stay here—so. Mr. Rayner'll be here in a minute; he won't leave you for long," said she, in a disagreeable voice. "I can't hurt you. I didn't mean to hurt you last night; and I didn't want to steal your letter either. What should I want to steal a bit of paper for? You see I know what it is. I only wanted to read it. I'm of a curious disposition, and I don't stick at much to find out what I want to know—if it's only trifles. The stuff on that handkerchief wouldn't have hurt you, only made you sleep a little sounder, so as I could take the letter. I'd have put it back. I'm sorry I frightened you. I've come to ask you to forgive me."

She said it in a dry hard tone, not as if she really repented her cruel action a bit.

"No, no; I can't forgive you—at least not yet," I said incoherently. "It wasn't only wanting to steal my letter and to stupefy me, but the way you looked at me, the cruel way—as if—as if you would have liked to kill me," I said, growing more excited as I remembered the terrible glare of her eyes when she sprang at me the second time. "I can't forget it—oh, I can't forget it! And you did something worse than that; you told the cook and Jane that Mr. Rayner was coming up to my room! Oh, that was wicked of you, for you knew it wasn't true!"

"That's that little tattling Jane, I know!" said Sarah vixenishly. "I never said such a thing at all; but she likes to make a story up of everything she hears. You know what a chatterbox she is, miss."

I did know it; but I did not think Jane was likely to have altered Sarah's story much. I was silent for a minute. Sarah began again in a different tone.

"You're very hard upon a poor servant, Miss Christie, and it isn't generous of you. I don't deny that I was jealous of you, and that I wanted to prove to Mr. Rayner that you had letters on the sly from a young gentleman. There now—I've made a clean breast of it! But don't it seem hard that I, who've served him and his well for nigh seven years, should have to go just at the word of a young lady who hasn't been here two months?"

"It isn't at my word, Sarah; I have had nothing to do with it."

"Nothing to do with it? Can you deny that you dislike me?"

"I should never have disliked you if you had not over and over again shown that you hated me, and that it was distasteful to you even to have to serve me. And, as to your going away, I heard about it only this morning through asking Jane why she was doing my room."

I blushed as I said this; but I could not confess to Sarah that the first mention I had heard of her departure was when I was listening outside the door of this very room on the night before.

"Then you don't want me to go away?"

"It doesn't matter to me whether you go or stay, as I have packed my boxes, and am going back to London myself this very afternoon."

Sarah stared. Then she gave a disagreeable laugh.

"You won't go," said she.

"You can go upstairs and look at my boxes," I said indignantly.

"Have you spoken to Mr. Rayner about it yet, may I ask, miss?" said she dryly.

"Not yet; but I am going to tell him this morning."

"Then would you mind, before you go, miss"—she laid a peculiar emphasis on these words—"asking Mr. Rayner to let me stay? It won't matter to you, you see; but it's more to me than I can tell."

And, for the first time during the interview, there was real emotion in her voice.

"But what I might say wouldn't make any difference, Sarah," I remonstrated gently. "You overrate my importance in this household in the strangest way. My words haven't half the weight with Mr. Rayner that yours have." Sarah looked at me eagerly as I said this, but she did not seem satisfied. "That is quite right and natural, as you have been here so long and are so much older too."

She did not like my saying that, I saw, by the tightening of her thin lips; but I certainly had not meant to offend her. However, after a minute's pause, she said again—

"Then, as you won't be afraid of your words having any effect, miss, perhaps you will the less mind asking Mr. Rayner to let me stay."

I shrugged my shoulders at her strange persistency; my words would certainly make no difference, and, as I was going away, she would probably stay; so I said—

"Very well; I will ask him."

"You promise, miss?" said she, with a strange light in her eyes. "Gentlefolks like you don't break their word, I know," she went on quickly. "So, if you'll only say 'I promise,' I shall know I can trust you, and that you bear no malice."

She must indeed be anxious to obtain what she asked when she could stoop so far as to class me with "gentlefolk."

"I promise," said I.

She might have shown a little gratitude for what she had been so eager to get, I thought; but, as soon as the words had left my lips, she drew herself up from her imploring attitude triumphantly, and, with a simple, cold "Thank you, miss," left the room.

Then I felt as if the study had suddenly grown lighter. Before long Mr. Rayner returned. I said nothing about Sarah's visit, and nothing about my own departure, until after I had done the very little there was to do in settling the accounts of the penny-bank. This work had been only an excuse for giving me a holiday, because I looked ill, I felt sure; and, when it was finished, Mr. Rayner sent me back to the arm-chair again and poured me out a glass of wine. I began to feel nervous about my announcement.

"Have you quite got over your cruel fright now, little woman?" said he kindly.

"As much as one can get over a thing like that," I said, in a low voice, my fingers shaking.

"One can't forget it at once, of course; but I hope that a little care and a little kindness will soon drive that unpleasant adventure right out of your head."

"If you mean your care and your kindness," said I, looking up gratefully, "why, you can't give me more than you have given me already, Mr. Rayner. But there are some experiences which one can never forget except away from the scenes where they happened. And, oh, Mr. Rayner," I went on quickly, "you mustn't think me ungrateful or capricious; but I have packed my boxes, and I want to ask you to release me from my engagement and let me go back to London by this afternoon's train! For, if I had to sleep in that room another night, I should go mad!"

He came and sat by my side.

"My dear child," he said gravely, "you can't do that—for our sakes."

"But I must—I must indeed!" I cried piteously. "You don't know, you can't tell what I suffered when I felt her hand creeping up to my throat, and thought I was going to be killed—I did indeed! And then I thought the stuff on the handkerchief was poison. She says it is only something to make you sleep. Is it true, Mr. Rayner? Here is the handkerchief." And I pulled it from my pocket and gave it to him.

"Quite true," said he; but I saw him frown. "It is chloroform, which she got out of my medicine-chest; I missed the bottle this morning. No, that wouldn't have hurt you, child; I don't suppose for a moment she meant to hurt you. But it was a cruel trick, all the same. Do you know"—and he looked at me searchingly—"what she did it for?"

"Oh, yes, she told me! She wanted to get at a letter—from a—from a friend, which I wore round my neck." I felt myself blushing violently, knowing from what I had overheard Sarah say to him on the previous night that he knew all about that foolish pendant. "She wanted to read it, and she couldn't get it without stupefying me, because I was holding it. But I have forgiven her, and promised I would ask you to let her stay. I told her it wouldn't matter what I said; but she made me promise."

"And what made you think what you said wouldn't matter?" asked he gently.

"There is no reason why it should," said I. "But I couldn't have promised to ask you to let her stay if I had not been going away myself. Mr. Rayner, you must let me go."

"I will let you go if you wish it, though the Alders would seem more like a tomb than ever without you now, child, that we have got used to seeing your pretty little face and hearing your sweet little voice about the place," said he sadly, almost tenderly; and the tears came to my eyes. "But you cannot go to-day. Think what people would say of us if it got rumored about that our child's governess was so cruelly treated under our roof that she went away without a day's warning; for every one counts upon you at the school-treat, and I believe our young friend Laurence—don't blush, child—would go off his head, and accuse us of murdering you outright, if he were to hear you were gone. And you would find it difficult, believe me, child, to get another situation, if you left your first so quickly, no matter for what reason. No; you shall have a different room, or Jane shall sleep in yours for a week or so, until your very natural nervousness has gone off; and then, if, at the end of the three months, you still wish to go, why, we won't keep you, child, though I think some of us will never get over it if you leave us too suddenly."

He spoke so sweetly, so kindly, and yet with such authority of superior wisdom, that I had to give way. Then, bound by my promise, I had even to ask again that Sarah should stay, and he agreed that she should at once; and then I, not at all elated at the success of my intercession, begged him to let Jane do as much as possible for me just at first.

But later in the day it was not pleasant to see Sarah's acid smile as she said, when she heard I was going to stay—

"I told you so, miss."

And when I said to her, "I kept my promise, and asked Mr. Rayner for you to stay, Sarah," she answered, "Then I am to stay, of course, miss?" in the same tone. And I was reluctantly obliged to admit that she was.

And, as I looked at her face, which could never seem to me again to look anything but evil, a sudden horror seized me at the thought that I had pledged myself to stay for five whole weeks more in the same house with this woman.

CHAPTER XIV

I took advantage of the rest of my day's holiday to work very hard at the text I was doing for the church. I thought that Mr. Reade might call for it that day, but he did not. And the next day, which was Thursday, I finished it, and rolled it up in paper ready for sending away; but still he did not come to fetch it. Haidee and I did not go far that morning—a long walk tired her now; but in the afternoon, when lessons were over, I sauntered out into the garden, with a book in my hand, and went to my "nest," which I had neglected to visit on the day before—a most unusual occurrence; but Mr. Rayner had forbidden me to go outside the house on that day, as I was rather feverish from the effects of the preceding night's excitement.

I found Mona sitting among the reeds close to the pond, not far from my "nest," crooning to herself and playing with some sticks and bits of paper. At sight of me she slid along the bank and let herself down into the mud below, as if to hide from me. When the child suddenly disappeared from my sight like that, I felt frightened lest she should fall into the water, or sink into the soft slime at the edge which she had chosen to retire into, and not be able to climb the slippery bank again. So I walked daintily through the reedy swamp which was her favorite haunt, and looked over the bank. She was busily burying in the mud, with the help of two little sticks, the bits of paper she had been playing with; and, when I bent down to speak to her, she threw herself upon her back, with her head almost in the water, and began to scream and kick. This uncalled-for demonstration made me think that she knew she was in mischief; and, leaving her for a moment to enjoy herself in her own way, I stooped and picked up one or two of the pieces of paper which formed her toys. There was writing on them in a hand I knew, and I had not made out a dozen words before I was sure that Mona had somehow got hold of a note from Mr. Laurence Reade to me.

Down I jumped in a moment, caring no more now for the mud, into which I sank to my ankles, than Mona herself. I dug up the bits she had buried, and took from her very gently those she was still clutching, though my fingers tingled to slap her. I hope it was not revenge that made me carry her indoors to be washed. Then I searched the ground where I had found her, and discovered more little bits, and under the seat of my "nest" a torn envelope directed to "Miss Christie." I ran in, and up to my room, with my mangled treasure, carefully cleaned the fragments, and, after much labor, at last fitted them into a pretty coherent whole. The note ran, as well as I could make out—

> "Dear Miss Christie,—I am so anxious about you that I must write. Is it true that"—here there was a piece missing—"an accident, that you are ill, hurt? If you are safe and well, will you pass the park in your walk to-morrow, that I may see you and know that you"—another piece missing. "I shall put this on the seat near the pond, where I know you go every evening.
>
> "Yours very sincerely, Laurence Reade."

It was dated "Wednesday," and this was Thursday afternoon; so that it was this morning's walk that he had meant. Oh, if I had only come out here last night and found the letter! I would go past the park to-morrow; but perhaps it would be too late, and he would not expect me then—he would think I was too ill to come out.

So the next morning, in our walk, I took care to pass Geldham Hall, both going and returning; but the first time I saw no one in the park, and the second time, to my surprise, I saw Mr. Rayner and Mrs. Reade sauntering along together under the trees in a very friendly manner. I had noticed that it had gradually become quite natural for the haughty Mrs. Reade to turn to Mr. Rayner as soon as we all came out of church on Sunday, and for them to have a long chat together, while her daughters looked at the people from the Alders as superciliously as before; but I did not know that he visited at Geldham Hall, still less that he and Mrs. Reade were on terms of such intimacy that she leaned on his arm as they walked along, and laughed as he talked in a much more natural and unaffected manner than her dignity generally allowed.

The next evening I had to go to tea at Mrs. Manners', to take part in a final discussion of the arrangements for the school-treat on the following day. Mrs. Manners, who was a very simple kindly lady, greeted me with rather a perturbed manner, and introduced me half apologetically to the Misses Reade, the elder of whom was stiffer and the younger more awkward than ever as they just touched my hand and dropped it as if it had been something with claws. They were icily obliged to me for the text, and said they would not have troubled me on any account, but their brother had insisted on taking it. Then they talked about village matters to Mrs. Manners, ignoring me altogether, until two little middle-aged ladies came in, who had dressed in an antiquated fashion a number of dolls for the sale, and who, on hearing who I was, seemed rather afraid of me. The Misses Reade were very kind to them in a patronizing way; and a shy girl came in, who was better dressed, more accomplished, and who had no worse manners than the Misses Reade, but they evidently looked down upon her from a very great height. I afterwards found that she was the daughter of an attorney, and could not expect to be so fortunate as to meet the ladies from the Hall, except at the Vicar's, which was neutral ground.

I did not think it was at all a pleasant party. They all chattered about parish matters, district-visiting, and the Sunday-school, and the life the curate's wife led her husband—of which I knew nothing at all; and I went to a table at the window, where there were two large albums of photographs, and looked at them by myself. But when Mr. Manners came in there was a little stir among them, and they all smiled at him and left off their chatter, and seemed to look to him to suggest a new topic; and he said the weather looked promising for next day, and they all flew upon this new topic and worried it to death. Then, when he had said a few words to each of them, he came up to me and asked me kindly why I was sitting all alone in a corner, and sat down by me, and told me who the people in the albums were, and showed me some pictures of Swiss scenery, and talked about the places they represented. I almost wished he would not, for the other ladies did not seem pleased.

Then we had tea, and Mr. Manners made me sit by him. He went out as soon as it was over, and we all went back into the drawing-room and wrote numbers on tickets; I forget what they were for, but I remember that there was great confusion because several of the ladies made mistakes, so that, while some numbers were missed out altogether, there were a great many tickets bearing the same number. Mrs. Manners asked me if I should like to come upstairs and see the things for sale, all the rest of the ladies having seen them many times already. So we went up together, and, while we were looking at them, she said nervously—

"You have never been in a situation before, have you?"

"No, never before."

"A governess's position has many trials and difficulties."

"I haven't met with many yet. I have been fortunate," said I, smiling.

Mrs. Manners looked at me as if she wanted to ask more than she dared; but she only said—

"Of course some families are pleasanter to live with than others. But in all there arise occasions when we must pray for guidance"—and I thought of my resolution to go—"and when we must walk circumspectly"—and I thought of the best way of treating Sarah. I only answered—

"Yes, Mrs. Manners"—very gently.

She seemed pleased by my submission, and said suddenly, as if to herself, after looking at me for a few moments—

"An honest open face!"—which made me blush—then, in a quicker, more practical tone—"You have no father, and have always lived quietly with your mother? Of course you write to her often?"

"Oh, yes."

"So that you can have the benefit of her counsel in any difficulty?"

I hesitated. Nobody ever seemed to think of going to mamma for counsel; we always kept things from her that were likely to disturb her, because she had delicate nerves, and used to go into hysterics if anything went wrong. So I said—

"In any difficulty I should have to think and act for myself, Mrs. Manners, because writing to mamma about it would only make her cry. But I have met with no great difficulties in my life so far."

She looked at me again, as if a little puzzled, and then said—

"I hope you will not think I am catechising you rudely; but Mr. Manners and I take a great interest in you, knowing how young and inexperienced you are to have to go out into the world alone. And he thinks I have neglected you a little. But, you see, Mrs. Rayner is so very—reserved, and lives such a secluded life, that it is not easy to form an intimacy. But I want you to feel sure, my dear Miss Christie, that, if you should want a friend's advice at any time, you need not fear to confide in me; and Mr. Manners, being a man and your parish clergyman, could help you in cases where my woman's judgment might be at fault."

I thanked her with tears in my eyes; for, although there was a shade of reserve in her manner, and although I did not think it likely that I should ever experience at the Alders any trial that she could help me in—for I could not confide a family secret, like Mrs. Rayner's suspected insanity, to anybody—yet her manner was so sincere and so earnest that I was touched by it and grateful for it.

Then we went downstairs and finished up the evening with music. The two little middle-aged ladies sang, in thin cracked voices, some duets in Italian—passionate love-songs, the words of which they did not seem to understand. The elder Miss Reade played a movement of Mozart's "Fantasia in C minor"—but I did not recognize it until near the end—and the younger a "Galop de Salon," with the loud pedal down all the time. Miss Lane, the attorney's daughter, sang "Little Maid of Arcadee," which Mrs.

Manners said she should have liked if the words had not been so silly. Then I was asked to play, and I chose Schumann's "Arabesque," and they seemed astonished and a little scandalized because I played it by heart. I heard Miss Reade whisper—

"I don't like her style. That great difference between *forte* and *piano* seems to me an affectation."

While I was playing, Mr. Laurence Reade came in to take his sisters home. When I had finished, everybody looked at us as he shook hands with me in a rather distant manner; but he managed to press my hand before he let it go; so I did not mind. And everybody listened, as he said—

"We heard up at the Hall dreadful reports that you were ill, Miss Christie, and wouldn't be able to come to the school-treat."

"Oh, no, I wasn't ill! One of the servants gave me a fright in the night," said I. "I woke up and found her in my room amusing herself by ransacking my things. Then I screamed with all my might, and Mr. Rayner came up and called her out and scolded her."

This explanation was listened to with profound attention by everybody in the room; and I was glad I had an opportunity of giving it, as I felt sure that some rumors must have got about; and it was better they should hear my version of the story. Then Mrs. Manners said she hoped Mr. Reade would not desert them at the last; and he promised to come and help, but said she must not expect him to sell pen-wipers.

"You are going to have a much grander affair than usual, I hear," he ended—"more like a regular bazaar."

"It sounds ungracious to say so," she returned, rather anxiously, "but I am rather sorry that we have not kept to the old simple custom. Still, when Lady Mills offered a marquee, and to come herself and help to sell, and to bring her friends, we were obliged to make a difference. And then the band from Beaconsburgh—" She stopped, for it was old Mr. Reade who had offered to provide that.

"Ah, that's my father's fault!" the young man put in, laughing. "He's a wicked old fellow, wanting to corrupt the rustic simplicity of the parish in his old age."

His elder sister said "Laurence!" reprovingly. Mrs. Manners went on.

"And, if Lady Mills comes on the drag, she'll bring a lot of idle young men"—Miss Lane and the younger Miss Reade looked up—"and there will be nothing to amuse them, for we have only one set of lawn-tennis—I think we must charge a penny a game for that"—in a practical tone—"and they will expect champagne and—"

"Oh, Lady Mills will bring that!" said Mr. Reade confidently, as if he had been on that drag with those idle young men himself.

"But Lady Mills and her set are not the style of people that Geldham is accustomed to," said Mrs. Manners, in a superior tone.

"Oh, no!" assented Mr. Reade gravely.

"And they will make fun of everything; and the treat is after all for the village-people; and I don't want those fast gentlemen from London to get talking to the village-girls."

"I don't think they will want to do so, Mrs. Manners, I don't indeed," said Mr. Reade.

"They are all good girls, those who will help at the treat—the first class at the Sunday-school."

"Oh, those! Then I am sure you need not be afraid."

"And they will want to amuse themselves, and take up the time of the sellers, your sisters and Miss Christie and—"

"I'll keep them off, Mrs. Manners. The sellers shall not be teased by any impertinent and trifling young men. I'll devote myself to looking after them."

Simple Mrs. Manners, who had been in deep earnest all the time, began to have a suspicion that there was a lurking mirthfulness under Mr. Reade's gravity; so she said severely—

"You will have to work, not to play, if you come, Mr. Reade, and set a good example to the others."

"I will; but I sincerely hope they will not all follow it," said he, in a laughing tone; then he turned and looked at me and made me blush.

And in the slight bustle of departure he whispered to me—

"Wait, and I'll come back and take you home."

But, when I had put on my hat and mantle, and Mrs. Manners had led me down into the drawing-room again, to say a few last words to me, and I was wondering how I could wait until Mr. Reade kept his promise and returned, I heard a ring and Mr. Rayner's voice in the hall. I started and blushed, and Mrs. Manners stopped in her talk and looked at me very searchingly.

"Mr. Rayner must have come to fetch you home," she said coldly.

I would not have missed the walk home with Mr. Reade for the world.

"I am afraid so," I stammered.

She looked colder still at my confusion; but there was only one way out of it, so I burst out—

"Oh, Mrs. Manners, Mr. Reade said he would come to fetch me! What shall I do?"

"You would rather go with him?"

"Oh, yes, yes!"

Her manner changed all at once. She put her arm around me and drew me to the French window.

"There, my dear—run out there and wait at the gate on the left. That's the way they always come from the Hall. It is a little deception, I am afraid; but there—go, child, go! He is a good lad."

So I ran swiftly across the lawn in the dusk, afraid of Mr. Rayner's seeing me, and up the path between the laurel hedges which led to the side gate. The path curved just at the end, and I heard the gate swing to; but I could not stop myself. And, as Mr. Reade dashed round the corner, running too, I fell against him, and then panted out, "I beg your pardon," very much confused. He had caught me by the arms, and he did not let me go, but held them very gently, while he said—

"Miss Christie! Pray don't apologize. Where were you running?"

"I—I was going home," I stammered in a low voice.

"But that is not the way." A pause—then very softly—"Were you coming to meet me?"

"N-o," said I, half crying, and disengaging myself.

It was so humiliating to have been caught running to meet Mr. Reade.

"No? I had hoped you were. For I've been running like a race-horse to meet you."

I said nothing.

"Why did you want to run home so fast alone, when I had promised to come and fetch you?"

"I—I didn't want to trouble you."

"That was very kind of you. But, if I happen not to mind the trouble, may I see you home now I am here? Or would you prefer to go alone?"

"I would rather go alone, thank you," said I, though it was heart-breaking to have to say it. But I thought it was time to show some spirit, for I saw that Mr. Reade did not believe me.

He stepped aside to let me pass, and raised his hat very stiffly; then his manner changed all at once.

"Why, you are crying! My darling, I didn't mean to make you cry!"

I could not stop him—I did try—but he was so much bigger than I that he had his arms around me before I could get away.

"Oh, Mr. Reade, let me go!" I said, frightened.

But, as I held up my face to say it, he kissed me, and, after that, of course it did not matter, for I knew that he loved me and that I was safe with him.

I remember every word that he said to me as we walked towards the Alders that night; but, if I were to write it down, it would read just like the same thing over and over again, and not at all as it sounded to me.

We did not go straight back, but a longer way round, for fear the grass should make my feet wet; and we passed the front gate and went on to the side gate that led past the stables. And there Laurence left me, for I did not want that spiteful Sarah to see him with me. I went through into the shrubbery, so happy that I could scarcely keep from singing softly to myself. But, as I came close to the stables, I left off, for fear Mr. Rayner, who might be in his room, as it was now quite dark, should hear me, and want to know how I got back and why I was so late; and just then I could not have told him. I wanted to slip upstairs to my room without seeing any one, and go straightway to sleep with the remembrance of Laurence and his last kiss all fresh and undisturbed in my mind. Then I thought I should dream of him.

But I was disappointed. For close under the stable-wall I saw two men's figures, neither of them Mr. Rayner's, and one of them held a dark lantern. I was frightened, for they made no noise, and I thought they walked like thieves; so I crept in among the trees and watched them. One of them softly tried the door of the harness-room, through which one had to pass to get to the upper story where Mr. Rayner slept. Then they came away and walked first down the path a little way towards the house, and then up it towards where I crouched among the trees. They sauntered cautiously, but slowly, as if waiting for some one. I did not feel much afraid of their seeing me, for I knew I was well concealed; but I was eager to get out and alarm the house, and I dared not move while they were in sight. But, when they came close, I recognized in one Tom Parkes, Sarah's lover, and in the other, much to my surprise, the gentleman who had visited Mr. Rayner after tea one evening, whose conversation with Sarah in the plantation had so surprised me by its familiar tone.

The moon, which had now risen high, fell full upon his face as he passed, and I had a better opportunity than before of observing him. He was rather short, of slim neat build, fair, clean-shaven, with gray eyes and an imperturbable expression of face. He had an overcoat and a big comforter over his arm, and was, as he had been before, very carefully dressed. When they were just opposite to me, they turned back, and, just as they got to the harness-room door again, Sarah came quickly from the house with a key, let them in, and followed herself. And in another minute Mr. Rayner passed me from the road and let himself in after them. I waited a few moments in wonder at this strange scene; it seemed to me that I was always seeing curious things at the Alders. But I had something pleasanter to think about than mysterious night-visitors, and I ran quickly and lightly down the path to the house, where Jane, very sleepy, and surprised at my being so late, let me in.

But that last adventure spoilt my dreams. I did indeed dream of Laurence; but I dreamt that I was carried away from him by burglars.

CHAPTER XV

Laurence had promised to come for me early the next morning, saying that I should be wanted to help to arrange the stalls.

"I'll bring two of the Manners boys, and say we've come for the benches Mr. Rayner offered to lend for the children's tea," said he.

"Then I'll say Mrs. Manners begs you to come at once, and I'll start off with the boys; and, when we get outside the gate, I'll send them on with the benches and wait about for you."

I wondered why he could not wait for me in the house as a matter of course; but he knew best, and I said nothing.

The next morning I put on a white frock that I had been busily making during all my spare time for the last fortnight, and a broad sash of the palest lemon and pink that I had been saving up for some great occasion. Then I slipped into the garden before breakfast—for there was no knowing how soon after he might come—to gather a flower to wear at my throat. I purposely chose rather a faded little rose, in the hope that Laurence might notice it and get me one himself to wear instead. I was going to put it in water until it was time to start, when Mr. Rayner met me at the window.

"Hallo, Miss Christie, stealing my roses! Well, since you had resolved to burden your conscience with a crime, you might have made it worth your while. But I am not going to permit you to spoil the effect of your pretty frock and destroy the reputation of my garden by wearing such a misshapen thing as that! Never! Come out again with me, and we'll find something better."

This was not what I wanted at all; but I was obliged to follow him, and to seem pleased when he gathered and gave me the loveliest little late tea-rose possible, and then found a beautiful bit of long soft moss to put round it. Laurence would never dare to suggest that this was not pretty enough to wear.

After breakfast, I went into the schoolroom with Haidee; but I was not in my usual soberly instructive mood; and, when I heard the front-door bell ring, I took the *Child's Guide to Knowledge* from Haidee's hand and gravely held it before me for some minutes until she said timidly—

"It begins at 'What is tapioca?' Miss Christie."

Then I felt ashamed of myself, and, making an effort, heard all the rest of her lessons as intelligently as was necessary, and set her a copy in my best hand. Then, just as I was thinking that my reward must be very near now, my heart sank as I heard Laurence's step returning through the hall, and those of the boys with him, while yet I had not been summoned. I wondered whether Laurence had forgotten all about me, and could have burst into tears at the thought that he would soon be helping to arrange the stalls with pretty Miss Kate Finch. But presently, when disappointment had given place to despair, I came to what I suppose was a better mood, and reflected that it was all a just punishment for the careless and neglectful manner in which I was certainly performing my duties this morning. And I went in to dinner with all my bright spirits of the morning very properly chastened out of me.

It was wicked and ungrateful of me; but, when Mr. Rayner said brightly, "Mrs. Manners wanted you to go and help her to prepare for the afternoon's festivities, Miss Christie; but we were not going to let you fag yourself out laying tables for a lot of dirty children, so I said you should come later," I felt for the moment as if I quite disliked him, though it was really only another proof of his kindness and care of me.

After dinner, he himself accompanied Haidee and me to the High Field, where the bazaar and tea took place; Mrs. Rayner was not coming until later. The school-children had been there some time when we reached the field; and some of the rank and fashion of the neighborhood, the quiet people who came as a duty, were making purchases in the marquees. I saw Laurence standing outside the larger but less showy one of the two; he looked very grave and gloomy, and did not come forward towards us immediately, as I had expected. Was he offended because I had not come earlier? Surely he must have known how much I wanted to do so! His elder sister, much to my surprise, came out to meet me.

"We have been waiting for you such a long time, Miss Christie," she said; "we have kept a place for you."

And, although she did not speak much more pleasantly than usual, I thought it good-natured of her, and wondered whether Laurence had spoken to her about me and she was trying to be kind to please him. I followed her into the marquee, which was arranged with one long stall down each side. At one, cheap toys, sweets, and very innocent refreshments were to be sold; the Sunday-school girls stood behind it, presided over by the housekeeper from the Hall. Down the other side was a stall loaded with the usual display of mats, dolls, crochet-shawls, and tatting antimacassars, with here and there a gypsy-table or cushion mounted with wool-work, and a host of useful trifles, which were expected to fetch far more than their intrinsic value.

But the custom of former years, when the sale had been chiefly for the village-people, was not forgotten; and one end was piled up with underclothing and children's frocks and a quantity of cheap crockery and ironmongery, the contributions of Beaconsburgh tradesmen. At this, decidedly the least interesting corner of the whole bazaar, Miss Reade asked me if I would mind standing.

"We chose this part for you, because you said you would like to have plenty to do; and we know you are patient. And I assure you the old women from the village will give you lots of occupation; they always want to turn over everything in the place and buy what they require for nothing."

I think I would rather have sold some pretty things too; but of course somebody must sell the ugly ones, and I really wanted to be useful; so I looked carefully over the things under my charge and examined the price-tickets, which I thought was a business-like way of going to work, when Laurence at last strolled in and came up to me. He shook hands with a loving pressure, but he only said—

"How do you do, Miss Christie? They expected you earlier."

And I felt so much chilled by the commonplace words and the "Miss Christie" that I could scarcely answer. I had not expected him to say "Violet" before everybody, as he had done when we walked home on the previous night; but he need not have used my prim surname at all. But, as he stooped to push under the stall a box that was sticking out, he said, in a very low voice—

"I must speak to you presently. You must make some excuse to get away, and I'll watch you and meet you. I have some bad news—at least, I don't know whether you will think it bad news."

His whisper got so gruff during those last words that I longed to kneel down on the ground by him and put my arms round his neck and tell him not to mind, whatever it was; but I could only say softly, as I bent over a bundle of night-caps—

"Of course I shall think it bad if you do."

And he just glanced up with a look that made me hold my breath and almost forget where I was, and his lips touched my frock as he rose, and I knew that the bad news was still not so bad as it might be.

Just then there was a stir and excitement outside, caused by the arrival of Lady Mills and some of her party. They came into our marquee, and I thought I had never seen any one so beautiful or so winning as Lady Mills herself, with her pretty cream-colored gown covered with lace and bunches of pale roses in her hat and on her dress. The ladies with her were beautifully dressed too, and I saw at once that they were indeed, as Mrs. Manners had said, not the style of people Geldham was accustomed to. They made us all, sellers and buyers, look very dowdy and old-fashioned, and they talked and laughed a little louder than we dared do, and moved about as if they were used to being looked at and did not mind it. There were only two gentlemen with the six or eight ladies, and I heard Lady Mills say to Mrs. Manners that the rest of the men were coming on the drag, and that she had given them strict orders that after a certain time they were to buy up all that was left on the stalls. Mrs. Manners seemed rather distressed at that, and said she did not want the gentlemen to purchase things which would be of no use to them; they had some smoking-caps and embroidered cigar-cases. But Lady Mills laughed, and said Mrs. Manners was too merciful; and then she left our marquee and went to superintend the finishing touches put to the arrangement of her own.

Presently we heard that the drag had arrived, and there was a little flutter among the ladies at our stall. As for me, I knew that these gentlemen, who seemed to be thought of so much consequence, would not want any of the things I had to sell; so I went on quite quietly serving the village-women, with whom I was doing very good business. However, when the gentlemen did lounge in, one of them, who was tall and had a long fair mustache, looked for a long time at the things at my end of the stall and asked the price of a tea-kettle. I thought he was amusing himself; but he bought it and carried it off; and presently two more gentlemen came into the marquee and straight up to my corner, and bought, the one a gridiron and the other a soap-dish.

Then the first one came back and asked the price of so many things that he took too much of my attention from my village customers; and at last I told him he would find some ties and cigar-cases and gentlemen's things farther up the stall. But he put up his eyeglass and looked at me gravely, and said he could not afford to spend his money on trumpery—he wanted something useful; and could I oblige him with a toasting-fork? Then he was so long making up his mind between a penny one and a sixpenny one that I told him he had better buy them both, and, when he had settled which he liked best, he could give the other away. But he said, "That is an extravagant way of going to work," and took the penny one.

When he had gone away, Laurence came up again, and I told him, laughing, about the funny purchases they had made. But he was not at all amused; he said it was tomfoolery.

They came again, though, and some more of them too; and at last the first one of all returned a third time and said he had been entrusted with a sovereign to lay out to the best advantage for a young couple who were setting up housekeeping. I had done such good business with the village-women and these unexpected customers that I had not a sovereign's-worth of ironmongery and crockery left; so he bought up all I had, including two pair of pattens and a number of mouse-traps, and made up the money in holland pinafores.

Presently he came in again with Lady Mills, who asked Mrs. Manners if she could spare her another helper; and, looking down the stall, and seeing me with only a few aprons and children's clothes left to sell, she asked if the little lady in white at the end could come; and Mrs. Manners, looking at me rather gravely and anxiously, as if she was sending me into a lion's den, asked me to go. But the other ladies at our stall did not like it at all.

The other marquee looked like fairy-land. The two stalls had so many beautiful bright things on them, besides a quantity of flowers, and the ladies behind them, in their light dresses, looked so pretty. The village-people did not buy much here, but came in shyly in twos and threes, and talked in whispers. But there were all Lady Mills's party, and a lot of Beaconsburgh people, and members of most of the rich families in the neighborhood. And there was a great deal of laughing and talking going on; and this marquee was altogether a much more amusing place than the other.

Lady Mills, who I thought had sweeter manners than any lady I had ever seen, thrust a big basket of flowers into my hands and told me to walk up and down and ask people to buy them. "Ask the gentlemen," she whispered, with a pretty smile. But I did not like to do that; so I stood with my basket in a corner until the tall fair man who had bought so many things of me came up and gave me half-a-crown for one little bud; and I thought how silly it had been of him to make such a fuss over the toasting-forks when he was ready to give so much for a flower. And then Laurence found me out, and he walked up and down with me, holding my big basket; and I sold my flowers quickly, and was very happy indeed, for Laurence talked and whispered to me, and looked at me all the time as we moved among the crowd, and never once left my side while we were in that tent. He told me everybody said I was the prettiest girl there, which of course was nonsense; but it was very nice to hear him say so. When I had sold all the flowers, he whispered—

"Now let us slip out, and we can talk."

So we tucked my basket under one of the stalls, and went out of the tent and away into a lane near the field; and Laurence's face grew very anxious and unhappy as I asked him what was the matter.

"I shall have to go away, Violet," said he, looking at me very intently.

"Go away! Why—why?" said I, the tears rushing to my eyes. I had not expected anything so dreadful as that.

"My mother has decided—has been persuaded—that she must go away to the Riviera to escape the wet season we are threatened with, and I shall have to go with her."

"But you will come back? You will soon come back, won't you?"

"I don't know. I don't know what may happen while I am away. I don't know what the plots and plans may be of the person who has caused me to be sent away."

"What do you mean? What person, Laurence? Your mother—your sister?"

Laurence looked at me without answering, in the same searching intent way as before, for a minute or two; then he said—

"Listen, Violet. You are such an innocent little thing that I don't know how to tell you what I must."

I could not help looking rather frightened at this opening; and he stopped a little while to comfort me before he went on—

"Last night, when I had left you and got home, I found Mr. Rayner just leaving the Hall."

Mr. Rayner! Then he must have gone on there from the Vicarage, and he must have come straight from the Hall when he passed me to go to his room, as I crouched in the shrubbery. Laurence continued—

"I went straight into the study to speak to my father. You know there is more sympathy between him and me than there is between any of the rest of us, so I went straight ahead and told him all about you, and what a sweet little thing you were; and I asked him to find me some occupation in an office, or on a farm or something, at once, for I must have a home to take you to before the year was out. And the dear old dad said you had a good sweet face, and he should like to have such a daughter; but what would the *mater* say? You know my mother rules him with a pretty tight hand; and he may say 'Yes' to anything when her back is turned, but he daren't say 'No' to her to her face. And my mother has strong prejudices, and wants me to marry some one with money, 'to improve our position in the county.' And I told him I was twenty-four, and old enough to know my own mind, and I didn't care what she wanted. But he begged me not to offend her, and then said, 'She has just been in to tell me something that may have a bearing on the matter. It seems she has set her heart on going to the Riviera, and insists on your going with her. Now supposing I stock a farm for you while you are away, you can step into it directly you come back—I suppose she won't want to be gone more than a couple of months—and you can try your hand at farming for a year or two, and keep it warm for Jack, who wants to take to it, he says. When you are living away from us, you will be more your own master, and your mother will have to submit to your marrying whom you like. So don't say a word to her or to your sisters—you know they always side with her—till you come back.' I didn't much like this; but I could not say 'No' to my father—he has been so good to me—and I couldn't refuse to go with my mother; nevertheless I was half mad all the same, for I know who has persuaded her to this."

"Do you? Who?"

"Mr. Rayner. Haven't you noticed how he has been steadily getting round my mother for the last few weeks, till he rules her as surely as she rules my father? I've watched him, and tried to put her on her guard; but I am no match for him. I wondered what he was doing it for; now I see."

"But I don't, Laurence. Why are you so prejudiced against Mr. Rayner—when he has been so kind to me too? What should he persuade her to go away for?"

Laurence looked at me earnestly.

"To get me away."

"To get you away? Why should he do that?"

Laurence began to speak, but got very red, and stopped.

"He doesn't like me, Violet, and he doesn't want me to have you."

"Oh, indeed you are mistaken, Laurence! He has often praised you."

"Yes; that is his cunning. But I tell you he would stick at nothing to prevent my marrying you; and as long you are under his roof I shall never know a moment's peace," said he excitedly. "He is a bad man—"

"Oh, Laurence, you shouldn't say that! I know him better than you do, and I know that he is goodness and kindness itself."

"Violet, you are no wiser than a child. How can you see the way he treats his wife, and yet call him good?"

"His wife! Ah, I know all about that, but—I must not tell you. Indeed he is not cruel to her, as you think, Laurence. I know all about it; I do indeed."

"Well, then, since I must say it, what do you think of the way he treats you? Doesn't he show he cares for you more than for her? Can't you see that he is making love to you?"

"Laurence!" cried I, aghast. "How dare you say such a thing? What have I done that you should think so ill of me as to think I would let a man who is married make love to me? How could you tell me you loved me, thinking that? I will never speak to you again."

I turned sharply from him, and was back in the field among the people before he could stop me. Tea was being given to the children, and I went to help; but the enjoyment of the day was gone. In a dazed state I was still handing about cake, too miserable and excited to know quite what I was doing, when Lady Mills and Mr. and Mrs. Rayner came up to me. This lady, who had charmed me so much, had in return taken a fancy to me, and had begged Mr. and Mrs. Rayner to let me go home with her to stay until Monday; and they had consented. At another time this invitation would have made me half mad with delight, but now it seemed only to overwhelm me with terror at the thought of going among so many strangers. However, they sent me home to prepare what things I wanted, and told me to make haste.

As I was packing a muslin frock I had never yet worn, and wishing I had something handsomer for the occasion, I suddenly thought of the paste pendant Mr. Rayner had given me. That would look quite dazzling peeping out of the muslin and lace round my throat. So I packed that and a piece of black velvet to wear it on; and I was scarcely ready before Jane came up to say that Lady Mills's carriage was at the gate waiting for me.

But just outside the hall door I met Laurence, with a rose in his hand.

"Violet, Violet, don't go without a word to me! Here—throw away that rose and wear mine."

"I will wear yours," said I; "but I can't throw away this one till it is dead. That would be ungrateful."

"Did Mr. Rayner give it you?"

"Yes."

He snatched out of my hand the rose I had just taken from him, and flung it away.

"I beg your pardon, Miss Christie, for my presumption in thinking you would accept mine after his. Good-evening."

He strode off towards the plantation path, and he would not turn round when I called "Laurence, Laurence!" I could not stay to run after him, even if I had been able to overtake him; so, with tears in my eyes, I plunged into the flower-bed where his rose had fallen and picked it up, and put Mr. Rayner's gently on the ground instead. It was an ungrateful thing to do; but I must do what Laurence wished, even if he did not know it.

And so with a very heavy heart I ran up the path to the carriage, and started on a visit which was to be strangely eventful to me.

CHAPTER XVI

There were four ladies already in the carriage which was waiting for me at the gate—Lady Mills herself, with another more matronly-looking lady by her side, whose name, I already knew, was Mrs. Cunningham; and on the opposite seat were a younger lady with a rather sharp expression, named Mrs. Clowes, who was considered very clever, and an unmarried one some years older than I. I made the third on that seat; but there was plenty of room for us all. We drove back first to the High Field, that Lady Mills might tell the rest of the party to make haste, or they would be late for dinner. There were some ladies on the drag waiting for the gentlemen, who were now amusing themselves by selling off by auction some of the things remaining on the stalls, while the grooms were busy packing into the inside of the drag the curious collection of purchases made by the whole party. There was a dog-cart waiting, with a gentleman in it smoking; and standing by the horse's head, also with a cigar in his mouth, was the tall fair gentleman whose face I now seemed to know the best of all. As soon as we drove up, he came to the side of the carriage.

"You are horribly crowded in there; let me take Miss—Miss Christie in the dog-cart."

"And what will you do with Charlie, Tom?"

"I'll put Charlie behind."

"Charlie is getting used to being put behind," said the eldest lady of all, looking at Mrs. Clowes, and laughing.

"Proper place for a husband, Mrs. Cunningham," said the fair gentleman.

I afterwards found that the gentleman they called "Charlie" was Captain Clowes.

"Well, will you come, Miss Christie?"

"No, Tom; Miss Christie is better where she is."

"She couldn't be better off than with me," said he, in a gravely innocent tone.

Everybody laughed.

"Take my part, Mrs. Clowes. Don't all jump upon me at once when I want to make an impression. Could Miss Christie be safer than with me?"

Everybody glanced rather mischievously at Mrs. Clowes; and I saw a faint color rise in her cheeks.

"Not with Charlie behind," said she; and everybody laughed more than ever.

I was glad Lady Mills would not let me go, though, for I did not care much about the gentleman they called "Tom," and Laurence did not like him either. It was about seven miles from Geldham to Denham Court. The drive seemed to me beautiful, though the country was flat; the rains had kept everything very green, and the sinking sun warmed the landscape with a golden tint. I looked about me and listened to the ladies' talk, but did not say much. Some one said I was silent, and some one else said "Tom" would make me talk; but indeed their conversation was so different from any I had ever heard that I could not have joined in it very well, even if I had known them better. Some of them said things which would have sounded quite wicked if they had said them seriously; but they were all in fun, and they seemed to laugh at everything. They laughed a great deal at Sir Jonas, who was Lady Mills's husband, and she herself imitated the way he would rub his hands and stare up at the ceiling, and say in little jerks he "hoped they had—enjoyed themselves—fine day. Stupid things, bazaars—but bring young people together."

"And keep the old ones away," said Mrs. Clowes, in her sharp tones. And everybody laughed very much.

Denham Court was a pretty place built on the side of a slight hill, with the river Doveney running not far from the foot of it. I was shown up into a room that looked out upon greenhouses and cucumber-frames, and from which I had a view of the river, just at a point where it widened out into a broad expanse like a lake. Just then I had not much time to grieve about my quarrel with Laurence and his cruel conduct about the rose; but I did shed a few tears, and wondered whether he would write and ask me to make it up, and thought that I should not be able to enjoy myself at all in this pretty place without him. Then I shook out my muslin frock and put it on, and, when I fastened the black velvet round my throat, with the beautiful flashing pendant on it, and pinned on one side of the lace edging, a little lower down, the red rose Laurence had flung away and I had meekly picked up again, I looked so much nicer than I had thought it possible for me to look that I could not help feeling that life was not quite a blank, and wishing that Laurence could see me.

I had left my room, and was going along the corridor, when I met a man the sight of whom made me start and turn quite cold. For he looked so much like the mysterious visitor at the Alders whom Mr. Rayner had described as "a gentleman," and whom I had seen two nights before going into the stable with Tom Parkes and Sarah, that I thought it must be he. But this man stood aside for me with the stolidly respectful manner, not of a gentleman, but of a servant; and I hurried past him, feeling quite shocked by the strength of the resemblance; for of course a friend of Mr. Rayner's, however familiarly he might choose to speak to Tom Parkes and Sarah, would not be a man-servant at Denham Court.

In the hall I met a maid who showed me into the drawing-room, which was empty; so I walked to one of the windows which led into a conservatory, and peeped in. The flowers were so beautiful, the scents so intoxicating, that I crept in step by step with my hands clasped, as if drawn by enchantment; and I had my face close to a large plant covered with white blossoms like lilies, when I saw peeping through the big fan-shaped leaves of a plant behind it the fair mustache and eye-glass of the gentleman they called "Tom." He was looking intently, not at me, but at the ornament sparkling at my throat. He looked up when I did, and came round to me.

"Nicely-kept place, isn't it? Sir Jonas is proud of his flowers."

"I never saw any like them. Look at these. Are they lilies?"

"I believe this is called 'Eucharistis Amazonia;' if not, it is something like that. Shall I cut you some?"

"Oh, don't, don't! It would be such a pity!"

"I suppose you wouldn't condescend to wear them?"

"I shouldn't dare to do so. What would Sir Jonas say if you spoilt his beautiful plants?"

"Sir Jonas wouldn't say anything; he never does. Even the gardener, a much more important person, wouldn't say anything to me. I'm a spoilt child here, Miss Christie; so you had better make friends with me, and I'll get you everything you want."

"Make friends! Why, I am not your enemy, am I?" said I, laughing.

"Not at present; but you must be careful. Now I will tell you who is my enemy"—and he stooped and looked at the flower at my throat—"the man who gave you that rose."

I started, and his mouth twitched a little, as if he wanted to smile.

"How do you know it was a man?" I asked, blushing.

"Never mind how I know. I am a magician, and I am not going to give you lessons in the black art for nothing. But look here! I'll tell you how I know, if you will give it to me in exchange for any flower you like to choose in this place."

I shook my head.

"I don't want to exchange it; and I don't care to have lessons in your black art, thank you."

"Now that is your nasty pride, Miss Christie. But I suppose one must not expect humility from a lady who wears such diamonds;" and he glanced again at my pendant, as he had done several times while we talked.

"They are not real diamonds," said I, laughing, and rather pleased for the moment at his mistake. "They are only paste."

He raised his eyebrows.

"Then allow me to congratulate you, Miss Christie, on possessing the very best imitation of the real thing that I have ever seen. I know something of diamonds, and I never was deceived before."

I was looking at him curiously, for he seemed to speak as if he did not quite believe me.

"Look! I will go to the door," said I, for the light was fading, "and then, as you are such a good judge, you will be able to tell."

I walked to the door, and he bent his face down close to mine and examined my pendant carefully. Presently he gave a slight start.

"Am I taking too great a liberty in asking if there are initials on the other side of that?"

"Yes, there are," said I, surprised.

"And will you tell me what they are?"

I hesitated. If this gentleman persisted in thinking the ornament was made of diamonds, he would think it a very strange thing if he found out that it was Mr. Rayner who had given such a costly present to his child's governess; so I said quietly—

"I would rather not tell you."

"I beg your pardon. Will you forgive my curiosity? I have seen only one ornament set exactly like that before; but it was in real diamonds"—and again he looked at me. "I was wondering if it had been exactly imitated in paste by the jeweller who set it, and if the sham twin-brother had, by some curious coincidence, come into your possession."

"How lovely the real one must be!"

"No lovelier than yours, I assure you."

"Then doesn't it seem a pity to spend so much money on real ones?" said I. "What do you think the real one was worth?"

"About fifteen hundred pounds, I believe."

"And you thought I had on an ornament worth fifteen hundred pounds!" said I, laughing heartily. "Oh, if the person who gave it me could know, how he would laugh!"

He caught at my words.

"He would laugh, would he?"

I was annoyed with myself, for I had not meant to let out even the sex of the giver of my pendant. He continued—

"He would be pleased, I should think, to have his paste taken for diamonds."

I did not answer, but only laughed again.

"Have any of the ladies seen it yet, Miss Christie?"

"No; and, for fear they should make the same mistake that you have made, I shall not let them," said I.

And I had raised my hands to take it off when Mrs. Cunningham and another lady came into the conservatory. The elder lady's eyes fell upon the unlucky trinket at once.

"What are you taking that off for, my dear? It is just what you want round the throat."

"Because I have been teased about wearing diamonds, and they are only sham ones; and I don't want to be teased any more," said I rather tremulously.

"Never mind Tom, my dear. Don't take off your pretty pendant for him. They are certainly very like, though," said she, looking first at them and then into my face. "Here, put them on again and snap your fingers at Tom."

I raised the velvet obediently, and the gentleman called Tom came softly behind me and took the ends from my trembling fingers, and fastened them himself round my throat again. He first pretended that he had not got them straight, though, and held the velvet a little way from me to try to look at the back of the pendant. But I was prepared for that; and I put my hand round it, as if fearing it might fall, and would not let him see the initials.

After this first experience of the sensation caused by my one ornament, I watched rather curiously its effect upon the rest of the party, as some of them strolled into the conservatory, and when I met the others in the drawing-room and in the general gathering at dinner. Every one looked at me, the one stranger, a good deal, of course; but I noticed that, while my pendant attracted the attention of the ladies, the gentlemen looked more at me myself, and were not scandalized by my unlucky ornament. Sir Jonas, who was a kind, gray-haired gentleman, and looked nearly old enough to be Lady Mills's father, took me in to dinner; and, although he did not talk much, he encouraged me to chatter to him, and to tell him all about the school-treat, and tried to make me drink a great deal more wine than I wanted.

After dinner, when I was in the drawing-room with the ladies, some of them drew me on to a sofa and pulled me about and petted me just as if I had been a child, and asked me a number of questions about my life at the Alders and "that handsome Mr. Rayner."

"And is it true that he is such a dreadfully wicked man, Miss Christie?" said one.

"Yes, it is; she is blushing," said another.

But I was not blushing at all; there was nothing to blush about. I said, laughing—

"No, he is not wicked. The village-people think he is, because he plays the violin and goes to races. He is very kind."

"Oh, we don't doubt that, my dear!" said Mrs. Clowes, in a demure tone.

"You think I like him only just because he is kind to me," said I boldly. "But I shouldn't like him if he were wicked, however kind he might be."

"And Mrs. Rayner—is she kind and good too?"

"Oh, yes, she is just as kind!" said I.

This was not quite true; but I knew already enough of these people to be sure they would laugh if I said "No;" and it was not poor Mrs. Rayner's fault that she was not as nice as her husband. Presently Mrs. Cunningham took me to the other end of the room to look at a portrait of Lady Mills.

"It is no business of mine who gave you that pendant, my dear; but have you any more ornaments of the kind, and, if so, where do you keep them?" she said gravely.

"Oh, I have no more!" I answered, a little surprised at her manner. "And I keep this in an old case in the corner of my desk."

"Ah, I thought so, from the careless way in which you were going to slip it into your pocket when we caught you in the conservatory. Why, my dear child, I have a set that I value very much—no finer than yours, though—diamonds and cat's-eyes—and I sleep with them under my pillow, and even my maid doesn't know where they are."

I showed my astonishment.

"Believe me, when you travel about on a series of visits, as I am doing now, and are obliged to entrust your dressing-case to a careless maid, it is no unnecessary precaution."

"But I shouldn't take so much trouble with my paste pendant," said I.

She shook her head at me, with a laugh, and said dryly—

"I should with such paste as yours."

And then the gentlemen came in. One of them had brought from town that day a parcel of new waltzes, but the ladies all declined to play them until they had tried them over privately; and the gentlemen seemed so much disappointed that, having turned over the pages and seen that they were perfectly easy, I timidly offered my services. They were really pretty, and, after the difficult music I had had to read with Mr. Rayner, they were like child's-play to me. When I had got to the end of the first, I received an ovation. The owner of the music was in ecstasies, and those who had begun to dance stopped and joined the rest in a chorus of admiration that made me quite ashamed of myself.

"Didn't you know that I am a governess?" said I to one gentleman, laughing and blushing.

"Yes; but we thought you were only for show," said Mrs. Clowes.

And I played the rest of the waltzes, and thought how much nicer it was to play for these people than for those I had met at Mrs. Manners's tea-party. Then the gentleman they called Tom, whose name I had now found out to be Mr. Carruthers, led me away from the piano, saying I was not to be made a victim all the evening for other people's amusement; and, telling a gentleman who was talking to me that he and I were going to have a serious conversation and were not to be disturbed, he took me to a deep window where there were seats, and gave me one, while he threw himself into another beside me.

"How beautifully you play!" said he, leaning over my chair and looking at me. "I never knew such a pretty girl as you take the trouble to learn anything properly before."

I had been so much spoilt that day by flattery that I only answered calmly—

"Why shouldn't pretty people learn things as well as ugly people, Mr. Carruthers?"

"Don't call me 'Mr. Carruthers'; nobody calls me 'Mr. Carruthers'—at least, nobody nice. If you don't yet feel equal to saying 'Tom,' let the matter remain in abeyance for the present. Now, to continue from the point where I lost my temper, ugly people have to be accomplished and good and all sorts of things, to get a little of the attention that a pretty person can get without any trouble at all."

"Ah, but it is different if you have to earn your own living! If you are a governess, for instance, people don't care about what you look like, but about what you know."

He stroked his mustache meditatively, looked at me, and said—

"Of course; I forgot that. I suppose you have to know a lot to teach. I am sure you know more than any woman in this room."

"Oh, no, indeed I don't! They are all a great, great deal cleverer than I am. I couldn't talk as they do."

"Heaven forbid!" muttered he, as if to himself. "They know how to chaff—that's all. Did you ever meet any of them before?"

"Never before to-day."

"I wonder if you know any of the people I know? Do you know the Temples of Crawley Hall?"

"No."

"Have you ever been farther west than this—Staffordshire—Derbyshire?"

"No, never."

He was looking on the ground; he raised and fixed his eyes suddenly on my face as he said—

"Do you know the Dalstons?"

"N-o," said I, rather hesitatingly.

"Not Lord Dalston, with his different crazes? You speak as if you were not sure."

"I am sure I don't know him," said I. "But I was trying to remember what I have heard about him, for I seem to know the name quite well."

In the most gravely persistent manner Mr. Carruthers went on probing my memory about Lord Dalston; but I could not even remember where I had heard the name mentioned before. He had to give it up at last; I believe however that he thought it was obstinacy that prevented my telling him.

When, at last, long past the hour when the household at the Alders retired to rest, we dispersed to our rooms, I made a mistake in my corridor, and found myself in one which led to the servants' wing; and I heard a man's voice that I knew saying persuasively—

"Don't be in such a hurry! She won't be up for half an hour yet, nor my man either. I never get a word with you now."

Suddenly it flashed upon me whose the voice was. It was the voice I had heard talking to Sarah in the plantation, the voice of Mr. Rayner's mysterious friend. And the person he was talking to, and with whom he proceeded to exchange a kiss, was Lady Mills's maid! It was a strange thing, but one about which I could no longer have a doubt. The respectful man-servant I had met before dinner in the corridor and the visitor who was shown into the study at the Alders as a gentleman, and who was yet on familiar terms with Tom Parkes and Sarah, were one and the same person!

I was very sleepy and very much preoccupied with this curious discovery when I got to my room; but, before I went to bed, I put, as I thought, my beautiful but unfortunate pendant safely inside my desk, resolved not to wear it again.

CHAPTER XVII

I got up next morning directly I was called, and was downstairs long before anybody else—but I was glad of that, for I wanted to explore the garden. It was a beautiful, warm, bright morning, and I rejoiced, for it would bring the people to Geldham Church for the harvest-thanksgiving. I went over the lawn, and down the alleys, and round and round the flower-beds, and peeped into the greenhouses, and tried to see through the steaming glass of the hot-houses, which were locked, when, suddenly, turning round one of them, I came face to face with Tom Parkes in his Sunday clothes, with a key in one hand and a basket of eggs in the other. He was evidently disconcerted, and tried by turning to the door of the hot-house to avoid me. But I accosted him at once.

"Tom—Tom Parkes, don't you know me—Miss Christie?" I said.

"Lor', yes, miss, to be sure, so it is! Who'd 'a' thought o' seeing you here?" said he, touching his hat with rather awkward surprise.

"Why, you must have known me, Tom! You looked as if you had seen a ghost!"

"Well, the truth is, miss, asking your pardon," said Tom sheepishly, "that I didn't want you to see me. You see, I've been took on here as extry under-gardener and help, and the head-gardener he don't like Londoners, and I don't want him to know as I'm a London chap. So, if you would be ser good, miss, as not to mention as you've seen me before, I should take it kind."

"Very well, Tom, I won't betray you," I replied, laughing.

And he said, "Thank you, miss," and touched his hat again, and went off with his eggs. I was very much amused by this encounter and the important secret I had to keep. As if my mentioning that I had seen Tom at the Alders would necessarily entail the awful discovery that he was a Londoner!

By this time I thought I had better go in and see if any of the other people had come down to breakfast; and I was sauntering along, when, as I got near the house, I heard two men's voices.

"Bella is getting jealous, Tom."

A grunt in the other voice.

"I say, ain't it rough on the little one?"

Then I heard Lady Mills's voice, and when I got to the door there were eight or ten people already assembled. But the two nearest the door, whom I had overheard, were a gentleman named Cole and Mr. Carruthers. It was Mr. Carruthers who had grunted. Who was "Bella"? And who was "the little one"? And what did "rough on" mean?

The bells of Denham Church, which was close by, had begun to ring before breakfast was over, and Lady Mills wanted to know who was going.

"I am going, for one," said Mrs. Clowes, and she looked across at Mr. Carruthers, who was helping himself to a great deal of marmalade.

"Do try to make up a respectable number," said Lady Mills. "You can do just what you like, you know, as soon as it is over; and people in the country think so much of it. We scandalize the neighborhood quite enough, as it is, by not going to bed at ten o'clock, and other wicked practices. And last week we were only three at church out of a party of seventeen."

"Are you going, Miss Christie? Yes, of course you are. I'll go, if you will find all the places for me," said Mr. Carruthers.

And when we got to church—we mustered eight altogether—he sat by me, and picked out from among the books the biggest church-service he could find, which he put in front of me when the collect was given out, whispering—

"Find it for me, please."

At first I would not take any notice, for it was just like playing in church; but he began making such a disturbance, rustling the leaves of his book, looking over those of his neighbors, and dropping with a crash all those within reach on the ledge before him, that I was obliged to find it for him, and all the other places too during the service, just as if he had been a little boy. But I was very angry all the time, and when we came out I would not speak to him. He came however and walked by my side while I talked to somebody else, and at last he said meekly—

"Have I offended you?"

"Yes," I said; "I think you are very irreverent."

"I didn't mean to be irreverent," he said, in a still meeker tone. "But it is so dull to sit in church and not be able to follow the service, and it looks so bad to be fumbling in one's book all the time and find the place only when the parson is a long way ahead. And you can always find it in a minute."

"You should go to church oftener, and then you could find the places as well as I," rejoined I severely.

"Yes, but I always have such a lot to do on Sunday mornings in town," said he mournfully—"pipes to smoke, and—and other things. But I'll try to go oftener; I dare say it will do me good."

"I don't believe going to church does people like you any good at all," remarked I gravely.

And Mr. Carruthers burst out laughing, and said it was very wrong of me to discourage him just when he wanted to try to be good.

At luncheon I sat between him and clever Mrs. Clowes, who described the sermon in a way that made everybody laugh, and said a lot of amusing and sometimes unkind things, as she always did. Presently, in a rather low voice, she addressed Mr. Carruthers across me.

"Shall I pass you the sherry; or is it true that you have taken to milk and water?" she asked meaningly.

"Quite true," said he. "And you can't think how nice it is—not half so insipid as you would expect, and a pleasant change after too many stimulants. Let me give you some grapes, Miss Christie."

And Mrs. Clowes turned away her head, as if there had been something that hurt her in his answer.

Most of the people spent Sunday afternoon just as if it had not been Sunday at all, except that nobody rode or drove. But some went on the river, and some played lawn-tennis, and some lounged about and read novels; and others, of whom I was one, sat under the trees on the lawn and drank iced champagne, which is quite the nicest thing I ever tasted. I heard the mysterious man-servant give an order to Tom Parkes, calling him, "Here, you, gardener, what's your name?" as if he had never seen him before, and walked up and down Mr. Rayner's garden, and gone into Mr. Rayner's stable with him only two nights before. What a silly fellow Tom was with his little mystery! I pointed out the other man to Mr. Carruthers, and asked if he knew whose servant he was.

"He is mine, and the best I ever had. I've had him six months now, and of late I've given up thinking altogether; he does it for me so much better."

I began to wonder whether this mysterious man-servant was some poor relation of Mr. Rayner's, who had taken to this way of earning his living, but was ashamed of it, and who came privately to see his richer connections, to spare them the talk of the neighbors about what people like the Reades, for instance, would certainly consider a great disgrace. So I said nothing more about him to Mr. Carruthers, who was sitting near me, smoking, and teasing me to read a Sunday newspaper, which I did not think right. So at last he began reading it aloud to me, and then I got up and ran away with Mr. Cole to the fruit-garden, where he gathered plums for me; and we looked at the chickens, and watched the fish in the pond, and threw crumbs to them, which they would not take any notice of, until dinner-time.

Mr. Cole had cut me some beautiful flowers to wear in the front of my frock, for I had resolved not to wear my pendant again; but my muslin gown did not look nearly so well without it, and I thought I would just take it out and see the effect of it at my throat close to the flowers, and then put it away again. But, when I unlocked my desk and opened the shabby case in which Mr. Rayner had given it to me, the pendant was gone. Nothing else had been disturbed; the sovereign my uncle had given me lay untouched in its little leather bag close by; the notes I had had from Laurence, tied up with pink ribbon, were just as I had left them. I searched my desk, my pockets, every corner of the room, though I knew it would be of no use. For I remembered quite well, sleepy as I had been the night before, that I had shut it up in the case carefully, turning it about for a few moments in my hand to watch it flashing in the candle-light.

It had been stolen—by whom I could not guess. I sat down after my fruitless search, trembling and too much frightened to cry. For there is something alarming in a mysterious loss like that, an uncomfortable sense of being at the mercy of some unknown power, apart from the certainty that one of the people about you is a thief. At first I thought I would go to Lady Mills and tell her privately all about it; but my courage failed me; for if my loss got known there would be an unpleasant scene for all the servants and a sense of discomfort in the entire household; besides, several of the servants in the house were those of the guests, and not under Lady Mills's authority. It was just as likely that my pendant had been taken by one of them; and everybody would be indignant at the idea of his or her servant being suspected of the theft. So I resolved to say nothing about it, but to bear my loss, which I felt more than I should have thought possible, in silence. After all, if I could never wear it without exciting more attention than I cared for, and surprising people by my possession of an ornament which they persisted in thinking extremely valuable, it was better that it should have disappeared. I began to think it had already had an unwholesome effect upon me, by my secret wish to wear it again.

So I went downstairs to dinner with a piece of plain black velvet round my throat, told Mrs. Cunningham, who asked why I did not wear my pendant, that I had come to the conclusion that it was too handsome an ornament for a girl in my position, and heard Mr. Carruthers say that the same remark would apply to my eyes.

It was a fine night, not cold, though there was a light breeze; and after dinner some of us went into the garden, and I among them, for I was afraid they would make me play the waltzes again, although it was Sunday. One of the gentlemen did say—

"Let us ask Miss Christie to play for us."

But the lady he spoke to replied, in a rather offended tone—

"We need not always trouble Miss Christie; and I am sure she would rather not be disturbed. I just tried the waltzes over this morning, and they are quite easy."

"Just tried 'em over!" muttered Mr. Cole, who was standing by me in the conservatory. "She was hard at it hammering at the piano all church-time."

It was late in the evening when Mr. Carruthers, who had been in the billiard-room with some of the others, came out and sauntered, with a cigar in his mouth, up to the grape-house, where I was standing with Sir Jonas, who had taken a fancy to me and insisted on cutting me some grapes straight from the vine.

"Lady Mills wishes me to say that Miss Christie will get her death of cold if she comes out of the hot-house into the cold air with nothing round her shoulders," said Mr. Carruthers, when we were at the door.

"Bless me—so she will! Fetch her a shawl, Tom."

"I have anticipated the lady's wants; I always do," said Mr. Carruthers; and he wrapped round my head and shoulders a beautiful Indian shawl belonging to Lady Mills.

"Take her in quickly, Tom. I should never forgive myself if she caught cold," said kind old Sir Jonas anxiously, standing at the door of the grape-house with his knife still in his hand.

"Nor should I," muttered Mr. Carruthers. "Now run, Miss Christie."

I was not a bit cold, and I told him so; but he said, "Never mind—won't do to run risks," and put his arm in mine, and made me run as fast as I could until we were round the corner of a wall, out of Sir Jonas's sight.

"And now," said he, "we'll run another way."

And he took me down a long path between apple and pear trees until we got to a side-gate that I had not seen before.

"I am going to take you for a walk," said he.

"But it is so late, and I am dressed so queerly."

"Never mind. You are not sleepy, are you?"—and he looked down into my face. "No, your eyes are quite bright and—wide awake. And nobody goes to bed here till they are sleepy, which is a very good plan. As for your dress, I think it very becoming—very becoming—quite Oriental. And, as it is too late for anybody else to be about, and too dark for them to see you if they were, I am the only person you need consult."

So we went through the gate and by a narrow foot-path over the grass down to the river. We stopped when we got there, by the boat-house, and Mr. Carruthers said it would be a lovely night for a sail.

"Just down there to the broad," said me, "and along that path of moonlight, up to those trees and back again. Wouldn't it be jolly?"

"Yes, if it were not Sunday," I said timidly.

No other objection occurred to me. He looked down at me, as if hesitating about something, and then said—

"You are right. You see I respect your scruples, if I do not share them;" and he took out his watch. "It is just a quarter to twelve. By the time I have got the boat ready it will be Monday morning, and then there will be nothing against it."

He had one foot in the boat before I could do more than say—

"But, Mr. Carruthers, it is so late. What would Lady Mills say?"

"I'll make it all right with Lady Mills; and you are such a good little girl that nobody will think anything of what you do."

I did not understand this speech so well then as I did later; but it gave me a sense of uneasiness, which however was but momentary, for he talked and made me laugh until he had the boat ready, and we heard the big church-clock strike out twelve.

"Now, unless that clock is fast, our consciences are free. Give me your hand. Step carefully. There you are."

I was in the boat, smiling with pleasure, yet ready to cry out at every movement, for I had never been on the water before.

"There isn't much wind; but I think there is enough to bring us back, so I'll just scull down stream to the broad. Take the lines—so—and pull whichever one I tell you."

I disengaged my hands from the shawl I was shrouded in, and, overwhelmed by a sense of my new responsibility, did as I was told without a word. And, as there was not much steering required, I fell to thinking of Laurence. I had had to talk a great deal during the last two days; but whenever I was not talking my thoughts flew back at once to him, as they did now.

"You are not thinking of me," said Mr. Carruthers quietly.

I started, blushed, and pulled the wrong line at once.

"Never mind," said he meekly—"only it's ungrateful. He isn't half so much absorbed in you as I am."

"Absorbed in me! I was thinking of—of Mrs. Manners."

"Happy Mrs. Manners, to be able to call up such a smile of beatitude on the face of a beautiful girl!"

"Who did you think it was, Mr. Carruthers?"

"If I tell you, you will upset me, or command me to land you at once."

"No, I won't. And you wouldn't pay any attention if I did."

"Let me come and sit by you, and I'll tell you. We can drift."

So he came and sat by my side, and directed our course by splashing in one of the sculls, first on one side and then on the other, as we went on talking.

"Why is it," he asked suddenly, "that a woman never cares for the man who loves her best?"

The question, which was quite new to me, startled me.

"Doesn't she—ever?" I asked anxiously.

"I—I am afraid not," said he, in a very low voice, bending his face to mine with a sad look in his eyes that troubled me.

"But how is she to tell?" I asked tremulously.

"I think she can tell best by the look in his eyes when they are bent on her," he whispered, with a long steady gaze which disconcerted me.

I turned away my head.

"If," he went on, still in the same soft voice quite close to my ear, "she raises her lips to his and then tries to read in his eyes the emotion he feels for her—"

"But I did," said I quickly, turning to him with my heart beating fast at the remembrance of Laurence's first kiss.

Mr. Carruthers drew back, stroked his mustache, and looked at me in quite a different manner.

"You have not lived all your life in the country, Miss Christie, I think," said he dryly.

And I saw in a moment, by the change in his look and voice, what I had done. He had been making love to me, while I was thinking of nothing but Laurence. I put out my hand to his very gently, and said—

"Don't be offended with me, Mr. Carruthers. I dare say all you say is true; but I am so fond of him that I cannot help thinking he does love me best."

I said this just to comfort him, for I could not really have doubted Laurence for the world. He took my hand and kissed it, but not, I thought, as if he cared about it very much, and then he said we had better think about getting back; so he turned the boat round and put up the sail, and, the wind having freshened a little, we got back in a very short time, not talking much; but we were quite good friends again, for my mingled delight and fear amused Mr. Carruthers.

When we landed at the boat-house, the church clock was just chiming the half-hour past one. The lateness of the hour shocked me.

"Never mind," said he. "They are sure not to have all gone to bed yet. I'll take you in by a side-door I know, and you shall slip into the library and open a big book before you. And I'll bring in Cole and one or two others, and say we didn't know what had become of you; and you can pretend to have fallen asleep over a book."

"But why should I do all that?" said I. "I haven't done anything to be ashamed of. You said Lady Mills would not mind."

"No, of course not, my dear child; I'll tell Lady Mills all about it. Don't trouble your head about that. She won't say a word to you, and you need not say a word to her. But none of the other ladies could have done a thing so unusual as you have in your innocence—and—and Sir Jonas would scold you for your rashness, and say you might have taken cold."

"But it wouldn't look innocent to pretend I had never been out at all, Mr. Carruthers. And I wasn't alone; I was with you—so I was all right. I dare say Lady Mills has not gone to bed yet. I'll go and see."

And I ran away before he could prevent me, and found Lady Mills and Mrs. Clowes in the drawing-room, the former looking anxious and grave, the latter hard and angry.

"My dear child, where have you been? We thought you were lost!" Her voice trembled.

"Oh, Lady Mills, I am so sorry! I went on the water with Mr. Carruthers. He said you would not mind; but I ought to have known better when it was so late."

"The later the better, my dear, I should say," said Mrs. Clowes, in her most cutting tone.

But Lady Mills's face was lightening as she looked at me.

"Don't you know, my dear, that Mr. Carruthers is one of the most dangerous men—"

Then she stopped, for Mr. Carruthers had come into the room; and, turning from me to him, she said, in such a stern voice that it made me tremble—

"Tom, aren't you just a little ashamed of yourself?"

And he answered very gravely—

"Perhaps; but that doesn't matter. This inquisition is out of place, Stephana, for it is easy to see that to that child night and day are all the same; and, if I had been my respected father in iniquity himself, she would have been none the worse for my society. It was very sensible of you to come to Lady Mills, child," said he to me kindly.

And he shook hands with me, and Lady Mills kissed me, and Mrs. Clowes gave me a cold little bow; and they sent me off to bed without knowing even then the enormity of the breach of propriety I had committed.

Sir Jonas, who was going up to town the next morning, was to drive me to the Alders, and then go on to Beaconsburgh station. Every one—nearly every one, for Mrs. Clowes never came near me at all—bade me a very kind good-by; and, just as I was sitting in the phaeton, waiting for Sir Jonas to take his place beside me, Gordon, Mr. Carruthers's mysterious servant, came up to me in his stolidly respectful manner, and said—

"I think this is something of yours, ma'am. You must have dropped it, for I found it on the stairs, and I am afraid it has been slightly injured." And he put my pendant into my hands.

I was so much astonished that he was gone before I could even thank him; and then, turning it over in my hands, I found that the little shield on which the initials were engraved had been wrenched off.

Was Gordon himself the thief, and had he repented? Or had the person who took it been ashamed to restore it in person? Or had I really dropped it, and only dreamt that I put it away?

CHAPTER XVIII

When Sir Jonas left me at the gate of the Alders that morning, a sense of desolation crept over me as I walked down the drive, followed by the gaunt Sarah carrying my little trunk—like a jailer rejoicing over a recaptured prisoner, I thought ungratefully to myself as I came in sight of the dark red ivy-covered walls of this house on the marsh, which, though I had lived in it two months, still had mysteries for me.

All the questions which had puzzled me about this household came into my mind again with new force after my short absence, which seemed, with its fresh experiences, to have lasted so long, together with others which had arisen while I listened to the talk of my new friends. Was Mrs. Rayner really mad? If so, how was it that no suspicion of the fact had reached that gossip-loving company I had just left, who had tales to tell of almost every family in the neighborhood? Why had the ladies called kind Mr. Rayner, who always went to church and led the simplest of lives, "dreadfully wicked"? They did not think it wrong to play the violin or to go to races. And why, if they thought him "dreadfully wicked," did they all say they would give the world to know him? What was the relation between Mr. Rayner and Gordon, Mr. Carruthers's servant? Then was Sarah really Mrs. Rayner's guardian; and was she not herself a little mad too? What had become of the wild jealousy of Jane which she had expressed to the stranger in the plantation? And why did she hate me so? Had she stifled her hatred once and for all, or would she—Oh, what would she not do, if her wicked, senseless dislike of me should get the better of her again?

It was better to talk to her than to think of her, and I turned and asked after Mr. and Mrs. Rayner and Haidee. My pupil was not well, and had not got up that day; but Sarah would ask if I could go and see her.

"She caught cold, miss, wandering round the pond late Saturday night, because she said she could talk to you there. Such nonsense! But you know she is full of her fancies."

I was touched by this proof of little Haidee's affection for me, and I wanted to go to her at once; but Sarah said Mrs. Rayner was with her and did not wish to be disturbed. So I went upstairs, having asked, in as careless a manner as I could, if there were any letters for me, and having been told that there were not. Laurence might have sent me just a little note; I had been so longing for one. He had not been nearly so nice since I told him I loved him, I thought to myself mournfully; and I sat with my head on my arms and cried. But I had not much time to indulge my grief, for it was nearly dinner-time, and I did not want Mr. and Mrs. Rayner to see my eyes red and swollen, and to think that my holiday had made me discontented. But I think that Mr. Rayner saw that something was wrong, for he looked at me very closely, and said that I did not look any the better for the change, and that it was plain dissipation did not agree with me. And, as I was still rather pensive and my voice a little tremulous, he asked me only a few questions about my visit and then left me to myself, for which I was very grateful.

In the afternoon I was allowed to go into Haidee's room. It was a cold day, and the room itself and the long corridor which led to it struck me as feeling damp and chilly. It was the first time I had been in the left wing. Haidee's chamber was a little dressing-room without a fireplace, and I wondered why they did not move the child, who was really ill, into another room. She jumped up in bed and clasped her hot little hands round my neck as soon as I came in, and then drew my head down on to the pillow beside her and told me to tell her everything I had done from the first moment I went away. So I made a little story of it all, leaving out the parts it would have been improper for her to hear, such as the behavior of Mr. Carruthers in church, and laying particular stress upon such points of interest as my feeding the chickens and cutting the grapes and the flowers. Mr. Rayner peeped in once, and, after listening to part of my narrative, said—

"I shall want to hear about all that too by and by, Miss Christie; but I shall want another edition, one not revised for the use of infants."

I felt a little disconcerted, for he said this rather mischievously; and I began to wonder whether he would approve of the governess having enjoyed herself quite so much, for I had forgotten to be dignified and prim altogether while I was at Denham Court.

Haidee begged me so hard to have tea with her that I was obliged to consent, the more willingly that Mrs. Rayner, who had never once come in to see her child while I was in the room, had seemed, by the way she greeted me on my return, to have exchanged her attitude of apathy towards me for one of dislike. While we were alone together over our tea, Haidee said very softly—

"Miss Christie, will you please go to the door and see if anybody's listening?"

I went to the door to content her, opened it, and saw that there was no one.

"And now will you listen at the other door—mamma's door?"

This was locked; but I put my head against it, listened, and assured her there was no one there. Then she beckoned me back to her and put up her head to whisper.

"Last night that hateful Sarah made mamma cry. I heard her through the door. Mamma's frightened of Sarah—and so am I. Hush! Somebody is always listening."

But no listener could have heard her soft whisper; even I, with my ear close to her lips, could scarcely catch the faint sounds. I comforted her, told her Sarah would not hurt her or "mamma" either—though I felt by no means so sure of her good-will as I pretended to be—and stayed with her until she went to sleep.

Then I wrapped myself up in a shawl and went into the plantation to look at my "nest." And there, leaning with his back against the tree which formed my seat, was Laurence. I gave a cry of delight and ran forward; but he only raised his hat and said—

"Good-evening, Miss Christie."

I stopped short, overwhelmed with dismay. Then I said, in quite a low husky voice, for I could scarcely get the words out—

"Laurence, why do you speak like that? Aren't you glad to see me?"

"Why should I be glad to see you, Miss Christie? I can't hope to show to advantage in your eyes after the more amusing society you have just left."

"What do you mean? What society do I like better than yours?"

"Oh, you are very kind; and I dare say I do very well as a makeshift when there is no more exciting amusement to be had!"

"Oh, Laurence, how can you say such cruel things? Are you angry because I went to Denham Court, and because I enjoyed myself? I couldn't help it, everybody was so kind. But I thought of you all the time, and I wished with all my heart that you had been there."

"Did you think of me while you were letting Mr. Carruthers whisper to you in the conservatory? Ah, I don't wonder you start! And did you think of me when you were sitting in the window-seat with Mr. Carruthers leaning over your chair, and when you were using the same book in church with Mr. Carruthers, and letting Mr. Carruthers gather fruit and flowers for you, and feeding the fish with him in, oh, such an idyllic manner, and playing his accompaniments, and talking about poetry, and—"

"Stop, Laurence—it isn't true, it isn't true! It was Mr. Cole who gathered flowers and fruit for me, and who looked at the fish with me—not Mr. Carruthers at all. And it was Mr. Standing whose accompaniments I played and who talked about poetry with me, not—"

"Mr. Standing? He's another beauty! You choose your friends well, Miss Christie. I feel I am not worthy to be admitted among the number. I am too dull."

"You are too rude," said I, my spirit rising. "I don't know what you mean by calling them 'beauties;' but none of the gentlemen you sneer at would have thought of insulting me and trying to make me unhappy, just because I sometimes talked to other people."

"No, you tried to be impartial, I see," he sneered again. "But I don't think you succeeded. You were not on the river between twelve and two o'clock in the morning with all the men-visitors at Denham Court, were you?"

"No," said I; then, stung to the quick by his sneers—"I wasn't at Denham Court long enough."

"Oh!" said Laurence, more angrily than ever. He was so angry that he began to speak again two or three times, but only stammered and broke off. At last he said, "You—you were not there long; but you—you made good use of your time; for by this morning the fame of your exploits had spread all over the neighborhood."

"My exploits!"

"Yes. This morning, before you arrived, Mr. Rayner had heard of them."

"Mr. Rayner! Oh, that is not surprising!"

Laurence turned upon me sharply.

"Mr. Rayner has a friend staying there," said I, with sudden caution. I must not let out things concerning the people I was living with which they did not wish to have known.

"Oh, more mysteries! So Mr. Rayner set a spy upon you; I can quite believe it of him."

"I did not mean that. Of course he would not think of such a thing. And there is no need of a spy to watch my actions, for I don't do anything to be ashamed of. And Mr. Rayner knows that, for he has said nothing to me about my conduct, which you seem to think so disgraceful."

"Mr. Rayner! No, of course he would not mind. It is nothing to him whether you endanger your reputation by going out alone late at night with one of the most notorious fast men about town."

"But how could I tell he was notorious, Laurence?" said I—I couldn't be spirited any longer; I wanted to cry. "Lady Mills said afterwards that he was dangerous; but how could I tell before? Nobody ran away from him, and all the ladies seemed fond of him, and rather jealous because he talked to me. And he didn't say wicked things—not half so wicked as the things they said. Oh, Laurence, don't be harsh to me! How could I tell?"

He was touched at last; the hand with which he had been angrily pulling at his mustache dropped, and he was turning slowly towards me, when the church clock and the far-off Beaconsburgh town-hall clock began to strike seven together.

"Oh!" said I, half turning instinctively towards the house.

"What is it?" asked Laurence, suddenly stiffening again.

"Mr. Rayner. I promised to be in the drawing-room to accompany his violin at a quarter to seven."

"Pray don't let me detain you," said he between his teeth. "I am sorry I came at all to disturb you in your meditations upon your late enjoyment. But, as I shall leave Geldham for the Riviera in two days, and shall not have another opportunity of seeing you before I go, I took the liberty of coming round this way to-night to congratulate you on having become an accomplished coquette. Good-night and good-by, Miss Christie. I wish you another pleasant evening with Mr. Rayner."

He shook hands with me, trembling all over with passion, and dashed away through the plantation before I could find voice to call him back. I was too utterly miserable to cry; I sank upon my seat, with a confused sense that all joy and brightness and hope had gone out of my life, since Laurence had left me angry and unforgiving; but I could not think. I sat there staring at the pond until Mr. Rayner himself came out in search of me; and, seeing how unhappy I looked, he very kindly told me that I was tired and should not play that night; but I said I would rather; so we went in, and I sat down to the piano, and he took out his violin.

But the spirit was not in me on this night, and I played the notes loudly or softly as was marked, without a spark of the fire which is the soul of music. At last Mrs. Rayner went out of the room. It was to go and see Haidee; but in my despondent state it flashed through my mind that it was because my heartless playing was spoiling the music, and a tear rolled at last down my cheek on to one of my hands. Mr. Rayner stopped, put down his violin, and said, oh, so kindly—

"What is it, my poor child? I did not mean to make a martyr of you. But I saw you were in a sad mood, and I thought the music might divert your thoughts."

"Oh, it is nothing, Mr. Rayner! Let me go on, please."

"No, child, I am not so selfish as that. It would hurt me more than you. Come and sit by the fire, and I'll bring you Nap to play with."

Nap was his big retriever. Mr. Rayner drew my arm in his, seated me by the fire, and left the room; and I dried my eyes, feeling heartily ashamed of myself. What would he think of a governess who went away on a short visit, did things that shocked people, and came back and cried, and could not play, and made herself a burden to everybody? He came back with Nap at his heels, and a glass and decanter in his hand; then, sitting down by me, he poured me out some wine and told me to drink it.

I began apologetically—

"Oh, Mr. Rayner, I am so—"

"Yes, I know. You are so very sorry that you can't help thinking Denham Court a livelier place than the Alders, and so very sorry that you were obliged to leave a lot of nice, bright, amusing people there to come back to a couple of very worthy, but prosy people who—"

"Oh, no, no, no, Mr. Rayner, not that at all!" said I, alarmed.

"Wasn't that what you were going to say? No, my child, you were going to say something far more civil, but not half so true. We may be worthy, but we are prosy; and why should we not own it? And why should you not own that you enjoyed yourself more at Denham Court than you can possibly do here? Why, that is the very thing you went there for!"

"I ought never to have gone at all."

"Now that is a mistake, my dear child. If you were to remain always boxed up in this dreary old vault, you would soon take to spectacles and a crutch. Take all the amusement that comes in your way, little woman, and, after the first natural reaction, you will work all the better for it. And now tell me all about Denham Court; I've been saving myself up for your description as a little treat, though I've heard something of your doings, Miss Prim, from another quarter."

And this was what Laurence, in his passion, called "spying upon me," when Mr. Rayner owned that he heard what went on at Denham Court!

"I heard, for one thing, that you wore the pendant I gave you."

He seemed pleased at this, I thought.

"Yes, it looked so beautiful with my muslin frock. And, oh, do you know, some of the people thought it was made of real diamonds!"

"Did they really?"

"Yes; I knew you would laugh when I told you that. But now you see it wasn't so silly of me not to know the difference when you first showed them to me, when those people who have worn diamonds and beautiful jewels all their lives were taken in by them. One of the gentlemen, Mr. Carruthers, said he once saw a pendant just like it in real ones, and it was worth fifteen hundred pounds. Do you think it is true?"

"I dare say it is. Stones of that size would be very valuable. To whom did it belong?"

"He didn't say. And it had initials behind it too just like mine."

"How very curious! The same initials?"

"Oh, I don't know! I shouldn't think they were the same."

"I thought he said they were the same."

"Oh, no! He wanted to see the back of the pendant; but I wouldn't let him."

"Why not?"

"Well, you see, Mr. Rayner, I—I thought, if he still went on thinking they were real, as I believe he did, and he were to find out by the initials who gave it me, why—why, he would think you must be mad, Mr. Rayner, to give diamonds to a governess!" said I, laughing. "Fifteen hundred pounds! Why, it would be about thirty-eight years' salary!"

Mr. Rayner laughed too.

"That was very sharp of you," he said. "If he had been as sharp as you, he would have got at it, and found out the initials, if he really wanted to know them."

"But I didn't wear my pendant again."

"Why not?"

"Because people noticed it too much, and—and, Mr. Rayner, it is really too handsome for me."

"Nonsense! Nothing is too handsome for you, child; haven't your new admirers told you that?"

I laughed and blushed.

"But, Mr. Rayner," I went on gravely and rather timidly, "then such a strange thing happened that I must tell you about it. I put my pendant into my desk—at least, I am almost sure I did—on Saturday night, and next day it was gone."

"Well, we must find you another."

"Oh, no! But this is the strangest part. Just before I left this morning, Mr. Carruthers's servant put it into my hand, saying he had picked it up on the stairs. And the little shield with the initials was broken off and lost. Isn't it strange?"

"Well, not considering that they were paste. If they had been diamonds, I should say it was very strange that he gave it back again. You careless little puss, you don't deserve to have any finery at all! What will you do when you have real jewels, if you are not more careful with mock ones?"

"Oh, Mr. Rayner, I hope I never shall!"

"Do you mean that?"

I hesitated.

"I mean they seem to be such a heavy responsibility to the ladies who have them."

"I suppose there were some ladies there with jewelry that made your eyes water."

"They didn't wear much; but I believe some of them had a great deal. One lady—she was the wife of a very rich merchant who wasn't there—had dazzling diamonds, they said."

"And what was the name of the fortunate lady?"

"Mrs. Cunningham."

"What did Mrs. Cunningham think of your pendant?"

"She would not believe it was not real, and she scolded me for my carelessness; but I really did—"

"I suppose she is very careful of hers?" Mr. Rayner interrupted.

"Oh, yes—you don't know how careful! She has one set, diamonds and cat's-eyes—"

By a sudden movement he trod on Nap's tail, and the dog howled. I broke off to comfort him.

"Go on, go on," said Mr. Rayner, touching my arm impatiently.

"What was I saying? Oh, I know—about Mrs. Cunningham's jewels. She has one set of what they call cat's-eyes and large diamonds, which she keeps—"

"That she keeps where?" said Mr. Rayner, yawning, as if tired.

"Oh, that she keeps always concealed about her person!" said I.

"Do you mean it?" he asked, much interested.

"Yes, really. She told me so. And nobody in the house, not even her maid, knows where they are. She sleeps with them under her pillow."

Mr. Rayner rose.

"Well, I don't think even the responsibility of diamonds under your pillow would keep you awake to-night, for you must be tired out."

He was fidgeting about the room, as if he were anxious to get to bed too. But he did not look sleepy; his eyes were quite bright and restless. He gave me my candle.

"Pleasant dreams of Denham Court, madam, though you don't deserve them! What business have you to repeat secrets that have been told you in confidence?"

"Oh, Mr. Rayner, as if it mattered—to you!" said I, laughing as I left the room.

"Yes, it is lucky you told it to me," he answered, laughing back.

CHAPTER XIX

Mr. Rayner was right. I was very tired; and the next morning I overslept myself, and did not come downstairs until breakfast was more than half over. It had been unusually punctual, and, to my surprise, the brougham came round to the door as I went into the dining-room, and I found Mrs. Rayner in outdoor dress at the table.

"Well, Miss Christie, we have all got tired of you; so we are going to leave you all alone at the Alders," said Mr. Rayner, when he saw my astonished face.

And, when he had amused himself a little longer by all sorts of absurd stories about their departure, I found that he was going up to town for a few days, and that Mrs. Rayner was going with him as far as Beaconsburgh station. He was going on business, he said; but he should combine pleasure with it—go the round of the theatres, and perhaps not be back until Saturday. This was Tuesday.

"Would you like to go to Beaconsburgh with us? You have no lessons to do, as Haidee is still in bed. And I dare say you have some little purchases to make; and you can change the books at the circulating-library, and Mrs. Rayner will have a companion to drive back with."

Mrs. Rayner did not receive the proposal with enthusiasm; but he told me to run upstairs, put on my things, and be down before he could count thirty; and I was in the dining-room again, panting and struggling with my gloves, in scarcely more than the prescribed time. There was plenty of room for me on the little seat in front of them in the brougham; but I had great difficulty in dissuading him from sitting outside by the coachman in order to give us more room.

When we got to the station, we found that we were there a great deal too soon. Mr. Rayner walked up and down, talking to the station-master and the people he knew, telling every one where he was going, and asking those among them who had been to London lately what were the best plays to go and see, and if they knew of a really good hotel, not too expensive, within easy distance of the theatres. He said to me once, when I was standing by him—

"If anything should happen while I am away—if Haidee should get worse, or Mrs. Rayner frighten you, or anything—telegraph to me at once at the Charing Cross Hotel. I don't know whether I shall stay there; but if you send it there it will reach me. You will find some forms in my study, and you will just write it without saying a word to anybody, and take it straight to Sam, and tell him to go to Beaconsburgh with it at once. Mind—to Sam; don't trust any of the women-servants."

I wondered he did not entrust this duty to the all-important Sarah; but I accepted the charge without comment.

"What shall I bring you this time?" said he, just before the train came up. "Roses are out of season. Some more paste to match your pendant?"

"Oh, no, no!" answered I. "You know I can't wear it, Mr. Rayner; and it only makes me vain and makes me wish for more."

"Ah, I though so!" said he, half to himself, maliciously. "Well, wishes always come true if one wishes them hard enough. I shall bring you some garnets. That is a most inexpensive red stone, and very pretty."

"Oh, I think I would rather not! I really don't want any jewelry, Mr. Rayner," declared I.

But the train had come up. He said good-by affectionately to his wife and kindly to me; and we saw him off, and then made our purchases and drove back to Geldham. It was rather an uncomfortable drive, for the only remark Mrs. Rayner made was, when I said it was cold—

"Then you had better order them to light the fire in your room early, Miss Christie. Mr. Rayner will upset the whole household if you take cold while he is away."

Then she shut her eyes and went, or pretended to go, to sleep, and I looked at her and thought what an unpleasant person she was, until the hollows in her face and the suffering expression about her mouth touched me. Why did she shut herself up and persist in being miserable, instead of returning her husband's love and changing the melancholy Alders into the cheerful, bright place it might be?

I spent a dull day; for, when I went to see Haidee, Mrs. Rayner instantly left the room, and I could not help seeing that it was to avoid me; so I was obliged to resist the sick child's entreaties for me to stay, and to go back and wander by myself about the house and garden, too miserable in my thoughts about Laurence and his cruel desertion of me to be able to read or work.

At tea-time Mrs. Rayner did not appear. Sarah said that Haidee was worse, and that her mother would not leave her. The evening was very cold, and, as Mrs. Rayner had rather ostentatiously told Jane to light Miss Christie's fire directly after dinner, I went up to my own room as soon as I had finished tea, and sat on the hearthrug, and nursed my sorrow where I could at least be warm.

It was about seven o'clock when Jane came up to say that Haidee was worse, and was crying out for me.

"I think she is going to die, miss—I do indeed," said kind little Jane, sobbing. "They won't let me in there; but I've been listening, for Mr. Rayner's away and Sarah's out, and I don't care not that for Mrs. Rayner!"—and she snapped her fingers contemptuously. "I heard Miss Haidee a-calling for you, miss; and I don't believe she knows what she's saying, poor little dear, and they ought to send for a doctor; but I don't suppose they will. Sarah don't care, and Mrs. Rayner don't dare—that's about it, miss."

And Jane gave me a nod and an expressive look as I went out of the room with her. I knew that the servants, one and all, looked upon their mistress as a poor-spirited thing, while they had some admiration and a great deal of respect for their master. The few orders she gave they fulfilled in a spirit of condescension or neglected altogether, while a word from him acted like a spell upon any one of them.

Thus, he having ordered that Mrs. Rayner, being an invalid, was not to be disturbed by sweepings and dustings and noises in the passage leading to her room, no member of the household ever dared to enter the left wing but Sarah, who had entire charge of the long corridor, bedroom, dressing-room, and store-room which it contained, although it was shut out from the rest of the house merely by a heavy baize-covered swing-door with only a bolt, which was seldom, I believe, drawn in the daytime. So that Jane felt like a heroine after having ventured on the other side of that door; and, when we came to it, she stood looking first at it and then at me, as if to touch it again were more than she dared.

"Oh, miss," said she, as I stepped forward to go through, "suppose Mr. Rayner was in there?"

"But Mr. Rayner is in London," returned I, laughing.

"Ah, yes, miss! But he do come back that sudden sometimes he might be a ghost. Of course it's all right for you, miss; but, if he was to know I'd been in there, oh, miss, I should die o' fright! When he's angry, he just speaks fit to cut yer head off."

I laughed at Jane's fears, and pushed open the door, not without difficulty, for it was very heavy, and, Jane's courage having evaporated, she dared not help me. My teeth chattered as I went through this passage, it was so cold; and what was my surprise to find, when I got to the end, that the window had been left open on this chilly and wet October evening! I took the liberty of shutting it, and, returning to the dressing-room door, I tapped softly at it. I could hear Haidee's voice, but I could not hear what she said, and Mrs. Rayner sobbing and calling her by name. I went in softly, and with a shriek the mother started up from her knees; she had been on the floor beside the bed. Haidee knew me, though her cheeks were flushed and her eyes bright with fever, and she wandered in her talk.

I sat on the bed and tried to make her lie down and keep the clothes over her, for the room was as cold as the corridor. Mrs. Rayner was clinging to the rail at the bottom of the little bed and watching me with eyes as glittering as the child's. I felt just a little tremor of fear. Had I trusted myself alone with a sick child and a madwoman on the verge of an outbreak of fury? Her bosom heaved and her hands clutched the rail tightly as she said—

"What right have you to come here? Are you not snug and warm upstairs in your turret? Why must you come and exult over me? You were welcome to my husband. Then you took my child. Can you not spare her to me now she is dying?"

I had heard that one must always talk to mad people as if one thought them sane; so I said—

"Not dying, Mrs. Rayner; don't say that. I came down just to see if I could be of any use. Why don't you take her into your own room? It is so cold in here. And wouldn't it be better to send in for Doctor Maitland? Oh, I forgot! He is away. But you might send Sam to Beaconsburgh for Doctor Lowe."

Her manner changed. As she looked at me, all the anger, all the little gust of defiance faded out of her great eyes, and she fell to sobbing and whispering—

"I dare not—I dare not!"

"May I take her into your room, Mrs. Rayner?"

"No, no."

"Then, if you will allow me, I will take her up into mine. You won't mind her being so far from you, if you know it is better for her, will you?" said I persuasively. "It is so beautifully warm up there that it won't matter if she throws the clothes off her, as she can't help doing, poor little thing; and I'll wrap her up well, so that she shall not take cold on the way."

Mrs. Rayner stared at me helplessly.

"Will you dare?" she asked fearfully.

"Certainly, with your permission."

"You know very well that my permission is nothing," sobbed she.

"And I don't wonder, you poor spiritless thing!" I thought to myself. But I was very sorry for her; and I asked if she would like to have my room for the night, to be near her child.

But she was frightened at the idea; so I wrapped the child up well in a blanket, thinking I would put her in my own bed until her little one could be taken upstairs. I was rather frightened myself at the thought of giving such an order to the awful Sarah, and, just as I was debating with myself whether she would be likely to obey it, she entered the room. I attacked her at once.

"Sarah, I want you to bring Miss Haidee's bed up into my room, if you please. This is too cold for her. Jane can help you, if it is too heavy."

She seemed not to be quite sure whether to be insolent or submissive. She decided for the former.

"And by what authority, miss, do you give orders for moving about the furniture?"

"Your mistress wishes it to be done."

"My mistress! And pray who is that, miss?"

"You know—Mrs. Rayner."

"And is that all the authority you have, miss?"

"No," said I boldly; "more than that—Mr. Rayner's!"

The women both started, and Sarah took up the bed and without a word went out of the room. I turned to Mrs. Rayner.

"Don't be alarmed about Haidee," I said gently. "I'll take great care of her. And, if you will just give your consent, I will send for a doctor on my own responsibility."

The poor thing stooped and kissed one of the hands I held round her child.

"Heaven bless you, Miss Christie!" she murmured; and, turning away, she sank down upon the empty space where the bed had been, and burst into a flood of tears.

She would not listen to the few incoherent words I said to comfort her; and I was obliged to leave the room with tears in my eyes, and carry my little patient upstairs. I could not go very fast, for the burden was rather heavy for a small woman like me; and by the time I got upstairs the bed was ready and Sarah had disappeared.

And now how to get a doctor? For I was seriously alarmed about the child. To expect any more help from Sarah was out of the question. I went down to the nursery, called Jane, who was just going to bed, and asked her where Sam slept.

"In the village," said she.

Nobody slept at the stables now that Mr. Rayner was away, except the old gardener, who would certainly never reach Beaconsburgh before daybreak if I sent him out at nine o'clock at night. Jane was too young to be sent all that way alone at night, the cook too old. There was only one thing to be done; I must go myself.

"Go and ask cook, if she is not asleep, to lend me her big round water-proof cloak, Jane," said I, "and bring me one of Miss Haidee's Shetland veils."

She ran away, astonished, to fetch them; and then, seeing that I was in earnest, she helped quickly and well to make me as like a middle-aged countrywoman as possible by buttoning my cloak, fastening a garden-hat round my head like a poke-bonnet, and attaching my veil to it. Then she tied up my umbrella like a market-woman's, and let me out, giggling a little at my appearance, but promising faithfully not to leave Haidee till my return, and to "stand up to Sally" if she interfered.

I felt rather frightened at the boldness of my undertaking as I heard the hall door close upon me, and realized that I had nothing in the world but my umbrella and my wits to protect me all the long three miles and a half of road to Beaconsburgh. The moon was at the second quarter, but did not give much light, for it was a cloudy night, raining now and then. I was not sorry for this, as I was the less likely to be recognized, and it was not the sort of weather to encourage late loiterers. I passed two or three villagers, only one of whom walked unsteadily; but none of them took any notice of me; and I had got past the last of the Geldham cottages, and on to a piece of straight road up a hill, where there were no houses in sight, when I heard the sounds of a vehicle coming along at a good pace behind me. It slackened to come up the hill, and I, to keep up my character, bent over my umbrella, and walked more slowly. But this subterfuge had an undesired effect.

"Hallo, my good woman! Would you like a lift up the hill?" cried the driver; and my heart leapt up, for it was Laurence's voice.

In a moment I felt like a different woman; my blood seemed dancing for joy, my pulses beat more quickly, and the spirit of mischief came into me so that I wanted to laugh aloud.

"Ay, ay!" I grunted out slowly; and, waiting until the cart came up to me, I climbed with his help and with seeming difficulty, carefully keeping my cloak over my hands, on to the seat by his side.

"All right?" said he; and again I grunted "Ay, ay!" and on we went.

Oh, how happy I felt to be again by his side! But it was rather hard not to be able to take the hand that was nearest to me, and nestle up to his shoulder, and tell him how miserable I had been since last night, when he had rushed away with the dreadful threat of not seeing me again. Well, now he should see me again; he could not help himself. I felt rather nervous as to what he would say when I did discover myself. Was he still angry? Would he insist upon my getting down and going the rest of the way on foot? Or would he say more unkind things to me? Or would he be pleased to see me, and forgive me?

He was not in a very conversational mood. Was he thinking of me, I wondered, or was it only that in my disguise I did not promise to prove an entertaining companion? He asked me if I was going to Beaconsburgh, and I said "Ay, ay!" again. I knew very well that a real countrywoman would not say "Ay, ay!" and I was surprised that it did not strike Laurence himself as a strange sort of answer.

I began to get impatient for him to know me. I looked at him furtively; he was evidently not at all curious or interested about his companion. But he looked very grave and thoughtful; and presently, to my exceeding comfort, he pulled down over his wrists two little uncomfortable woollen cuffs that I had made, and that he had bought of me at the sale. I remembered them quite well; we had had a struggle to get them over his wrists, as I had made them a convenient size, too large for a woman and too small for a man. It seemed to me that he handled them lovingly. Upon this encouragement I spoke.

"Aren't you going to talk?" said I, in my natural voice.

We had passed the hill, and were going along at a good pace; but he gave the reins such a jerk that the horse stopped.

"You won't be cross with me again, will you?" said I, anxious to pledge him to good temper while he was in the first flush of his joy at meeting me; for it was joy.

He slipped the reins into his right hand and put his other arm around me and kissed me, Shetland veil and all. And so we made it up without a word of explanation.

I told him my errand, and he told me his. His father had gone up to town that day to arrange for the disposal of some shares in order to purchase a farm for Laurence a few miles off, which was to be stocked, according to his promise, while his son was away. He was to return by a train which reached Beaconsburgh about ten o'clock, and Laurence was on the way to meet him.

"We will call at Doctor Lowe's first, and then you shall go on with me to the station and see my father," said he.

I protested a little that I ought to go back with the Doctor; but of course he carried his point.

"What do you want a farm for, Laurence?" I asked, as we waited outside the station.

I remained in the cart holding the reins, for fear my quaint appearance should excite curiosity regarding young Mr. Reade's companion if I got out and went into the station with him. But he stood by my side holding my hand under my cloak while we talked in a low voice.

"What do I want a farm for? Why, to have a home for you and something to live on, of course! I know something about farming, and it doesn't matter if I do lose a little just at first."

"But why did you want to go on preparing a home for an 'accomplished coquette,' whom you said last night you were never going to see again?"

"One isn't answerable for all one says to a tormenting little witch like you," said Laurence, laughing. "You didn't suppose I was really never going to see you again, now did you?"

"I shouldn't have cared," said I.

"Ah, I was right about the coquetry! You wouldn't have told such a story as that before you went to Denham Court. I was coming to see you to-morrow evening. I've had to be away all to-day over at Lawley, and I have to be there again to-morrow with my father; but in the evening I shall call at the Alders and ask boldly for Miss Christie. So mind you are not out."

"I shall not promise."

"And we will have a good long talk together, since, thank Heaven, Mr. Rayner is away; and I will give you an address where a letter will reach me."

We were so intent upon our conversation that I did not notice that there was a man standing very near to us during the last part of it. As Laurence finished speaking, he turned his head, and suddenly became aware that the train had come in while we were talking.

"By Jove! Wait for me, darling," he cried hastily, and then dashed off so quickly that he ran against the man, who was dressed like a navvy, and knocked his hat off.

When he returned with his father, who greeted me very kindly, he looked pale and anxious.

"Do you know who that man was I ran against?" he whispered.

"That navvy?"

"It was no navvy. It was Mr. Rayner."

"Laurence!" said I incredulously.

"I tell you it was—I swear it! What was he doing, skulking about in that get-up? He came down by this train. He must have overheard what we were saying. Now mark what I say, Violet—I shall not see you again."

"But, Laurence, how could he prevent it? You will come to the house and ask for me—"

"Listen, Violet," he interrupted. "If you do not see me to-morrow night before seven o'clock, be at your 'nest' without fail at half-past."

"Very well, I will, Laurence—I will. I promise."

But nothing would reassure him.

"I tell you it will be of no use, my darling—of no use. We must say good-by to-night, for I shall not see you again."

CHAPTER XX

During the whole of the drive back to Geldham it was old Mr. Reade who talked to me, and not Laurence, who drove along, silent and grave, pulling my cloak affectionately up to my throat every now and then, and watching me as I talked to his father, but scarcely speaking himself at all. When we got to the gate of the Alders, he jumped out, carefully lifted me down, and, telling his father to drive on home, as he should walk the rest of the way, he came inside the gate with me.

"Violet," he said very gravely, "I am afraid I have been foolish in agreeing to my father's wishes, and I am more anxious about you than I can tell. The Alders is no fit place for you. I can see quite well now what I could not when I was blinded by my passion last night, that you are so good and innocent that evil seems to have no power over you; but yet— And—and it is just that which makes you so sweet; and I don't want to spoil it, open your eyes, and all that." He was playing nervously with my hand, holding it against his breast, and looking into my eyes so miserably, poor fellow! "Look here, Violet!" said he suddenly, as if struck by a happy thought. "If any man, while I am away, tells you you are nice, and tries to make you think he is very fond of you—no matter who it is—Mr. Rayner or—or my father, or any man—don't take any notice, and don't believe them."

But poor Laurence was more innocent than I if he thought I did not know what he meant. He was jealous of Mr. Rayner, and I could not persuade him how absurd it was.

I said, "Very well, Laurence;" but he was not satisfied. He went on trying to justify himself—not to me—he wanted no justification in my eyes—but to himself.

"What could I do, when my old dad offered to do so much for me, but let him have his way? But it was wrong, I know. Our engagement ought to have been open from the first; and his weakness in not daring to face my mother was no worse than mine in giving way to him. And now I am tortured lest my weakness should be visited on you, child; for I cannot even write to you openly, and, if I enclose letters to you to my dear old blundering dad, you will certainly never get them."

"Why not send them to Mrs. Manners, Laurence? Then they would be quite safe. And you don't mind her knowing, do you? I think she guesses something already," said I, smiling, remembering how she sent me to the gate to meet him on the previous Friday evening, the very night when he first told me he loved me.

He caught at the suggestion eagerly.

"That is a capital idea, my darling! I'll go to her before breakfast to-morrow morning and ask her to look after you as much as she can while I am away. I don't think she is very fond of my sisters—I wish they were nicer for your sake, my darling, especially Maud. I wish some one would marry her; but no one is such a fool."

"Oh, Laurence, she is your sister!"

"I can't help that; I wish I could. Alice, the little one, isn't half so bad; it is only being with Maud that spoils her. If ever you get Alice alone, you will find she is quite nice."

I had already had proof of that, and I told him so.

"But one can't confide in her, because she would tell everything to Maud, and Maud to my mother. You have no idea what the tyranny of those two women is like; my father dreads and I avoid them. My mother thinks she holds my destiny in her hand; but she is mistaken; and within the next six weeks she must find it out; for, if she wishes to stay abroad longer, she will have to stay alone. By the third week in November I shall be back in England, and before the month is out you must be my wife, my darling."

"Oh, Laurence, so soon!"

"So soon? Why, it is a century off! I shall be gray-headed if we wait another week. I am not sure where we shall stay; but to-morrow night I will bring you an address that you can always write to. It is that of a friend of mine—I forget the number of the street, but you shall have it; and I shall be sure to get your letters. Now, if anything happens to alarm you, or you are ill, or anything, you are to write at once, and I will return to Geldham without delay. And, my darling—"

We were interrupted by the sound of a carriage coming up the drive; it was Doctor Lowe's brougham returning from the house. I went to the carriage-window, and he told me that Haidee was suffering at present only from a bad feverish cold, but that we must be careful with her, for it might turn to something worse, and he should call again to see her in the morning. He said that the child's chest was weak, that the damp place was the worst thing for her, and that he should like to see her parents to advise them to take her away to some drier climate, as soon as she was well enough to be moved.

"Mind, she mustn't be moved yet," said he. "She is very well where she is—nice warm room, high out of the damp. But the lower part of the house strikes like a vault."

"What would he say if he could go into the left wing?" I thought to myself.

"There was only a silly little servant up there with the child. She says that is your room."

"Yes, Doctor Lowe."

"And is it true that Mrs. Rayner sleeps on the ground-floor?"

"Yes, quite true."

"Well, then, you may think yourself lucky, young lady. For, if I lived in that house, I should let the people I wanted to get rid of sleep at the bottom, and keep the top for myself."

"Mrs. Rayner will have the ground-floor of the left wing to herself."

"Ah, well, there is no accounting for tastes; and, if Mrs. Rayner has a fancy for building her own sepulchre, why, there is nobody very eager to prevent her, I dare say!" said he dryly.

The Doctor was an old bachelor, famed for his rudeness as much as for his skill. Mr. Rayner did not like him, I knew; and on that account I had had at first some doubts about sending for him; but, as he was well known to be by far the best doctor in Beaconsburgh, I had resolved to risk it. Now I began to repent having done so.

"Is that young Reade? Is that you, Laurence?" said the Doctor, peering out of the carriage-window into the deep shadow of the trees behind me.

Laurence came forward.

"Yes, Doctor Lowe."

"Oh, ah! Come to inquire about the sick child, I suppose?"

"No, Doctor Lowe. I drove back from Beaconsburgh with my father and this lady, after calling upon you, and I am saying good-by to her, as I am going abroad and shall not see her again until a few days before she becomes my wife," said he, in a low voice, but very proudly, with his hand on my shoulder.

"Wife, eh?"—incredulously.

"But it is a secret."

"Oh, ah, of course!"—knowingly. "So this is the Miss Christie I've heard so much about!" And he deliberately put on his spectacles and stared at me in the faint moonlight. "Well, she wouldn't have turned the heads of the men when I was young."

We both laughed at the old man's rudeness.

"I have no doubt heads were harder to turn then, Doctor Lowe," said Laurence dryly.

"Well, take care some one else doesn't turn hers while you are away!" said the Doctor, glaring at him ferociously; and he told the coachman to drive on, and drew up the window sharply.

This last hit struck poor Laurence as an evil omen; and, when I told him that I must go in now, and that I should see him again on the morrow, he flung his arms around me in such distress that I did not know what to say to comfort him.

"See what clever Doctor Lowe thinks of your Mr. Rayner, Violet," said he, looking anxiously into my eyes. "Now listen, my darling. Don't trust him, don't trust anybody while I am away, and don't believe what anybody may tell you about me. What would you do if they showed you the certificate of my marriage to another woman, Violet?"

"Oh, Laurence, you are not going away to be married, are you?"

"No, child, no; and, if any one tells you so, you will know it is a lie. And, if you get no letters, and they tell you I am dead—"

"Oh, Laurence, don't!"

"Why, that will be a lie too! I shall be alive and single all the next six weeks, and at the end of that time I shall come back and marry you; and, if you want me, I shall come back before, my own darling! Good-by, good-by!"

He kissed me again and again, then tore himself from my arms, and dashed away without daring even to look at me again; and, tearful and trembling, I turned to go back to the house. But Laurence's terrible excitement had communicated itself to me, and I staggered down the drive, hardly able to see where I was going; and, when I had got to the bottom, with only the lawn at the side and the gravel-space in front between me and the house, I stopped for a moment, and clung to a birch-tree for support while I dried my eyes before presenting myself at the front door. I had told Jane to come down and open it for me when she heard my ring; and I hoped with all my heart that it would be she, and that that horrid Sarah would not have taken it into her head to sit up, for I did not want her to see my tear-stained face.

But, just as I was going to leave the shelter of the trees and cross the gravel-space to the portico, I stopped, for I saw in the gloom a figure making its way across the lawn towards the back of the house. It was coming from the path among the trees which led to the stables. I strained my eyes, but there was a cloud passing before the moon, and I could only see that it was a man, and that he was carrying what looked like a small trunk; and it seemed heavy.

Who could it be at this time of night? For it was between eleven and twelve o'clock. Was it Tom Parkes paying a late visit to Sarah, knowing the master was away? Or was it the mysterious servant Gordon, thinking Mr. Rayner was at home? Or was it a burglar? But then a burglar, I argued to myself, would hardly be likely to carry things to the house he was going to rob, but rather to take things away; and the trunk he was carrying seemed to be heavy already. He had disappeared behind the back of the house by this time, and, as I was curious to know what would happen next, I waited, trembling, creeping in among the trees, and in a few minutes had the satisfaction of seeing him reappear, followed by Sarah. And, the cloud having passed over the face of the moon, I saw that it was indeed Tom Parkes; and then I would have given the world to know what he had brought her.

The impression which Sarah's talk with the stranger in the plantation had given me of Tom's desperate wickedness had faded a good deal from my mind by this time; but this strange sight revived it. What if Tom—placid, stolid-looking, honest-faced Tom, as I had once thought him—were in reality a thief? And what if Sarah, in her master's absence, had been persuaded by him to take care of stolen property? There had been something stealthy in his manner of sneaking across the lawn in the shadow with his burden which had suggested this thought; but, on the other hand, was it not much more probable that he had been turned off at Denham Court, and had brought some of his own personal property, intending to take up his abode at the Alders for a few days, in the master's absence? The all-powerful Sarah might even dare that, relying upon her power of making herself unpleasant for the rest of the household to keep her secret.

They disappeared up the stable path, and I took the opportunity to dart across the gravel-space to the front door and ring as gently as I could. Jane came down in a few minutes, very sleepy, and let me in.

"Sarah's been asking where you were, miss, and, as I let the Doctor in, I told her you came back with him. I guessed as you'd come back safe, miss, when the Doctor said as how a young gentleman was with you," said Jane, with elaborate archness.

I told her to go to bed as fast as she could; and, when I had followed her upstairs and seen her into the nursery, I went softly to the head of the kitchen stairs, and, as I heard no sound and saw no light, I slipped down with my candle. The side-door by which Sarah and Mr. Rayner used to go to and from the stables was ajar, and just inside was a small old brown portmanteau. I did not dare to go all the way down to inspect it closely, as I own I should have liked to do; but in the view I got of it, as I held my candle over my head and peered at it curiously, it struck me that I had seen it before somewhere. Then I turned and fled guiltily upstairs to my room. Haidee was sleeping, and looked less feverish than when I went away. Jane had built up the fire carefully, so that it might keep in all night, and placed the drink the Doctor had ordered on a little table beside the child. Her bed had been placed at the right-hand side of the fireplace, facing the door, and my screen had been put round the back to shut out all draught from the windows. I was very tired, and the moment I laid my head on my pillow I fell soundly asleep, and did not wake until the morning.

Haidee was already awake, and undoubtedly better.

"How did you sleep, darling?" said I, sitting on the bed and kissing her.

"Oh, beautifully, Miss Christie! I hardly ever woke up once, and when I did I watched the beautiful fire; I could just see it when I lay with my head so. It is so nice and warm up here. I wish mamma was up here; I should like to be up here always. I think I should have nice dreams up here, not like the ones I have downstairs."

And she closed her eyes, as if to shut out the thought of something.

"You shall stay up here till you are quite well again, darling," said I, inwardly resolving to beg that she might sleep in my room permanently.

"Miss Christie, you know you dream sometimes with your eyes wide open, just as if you were awake? I dreamt a dream like that last night."

"That was because you were ill, darling. When people are ill, they dream like that."

"Do they—quite plain, like as if it was all quite real?"

"Yes; sometimes they think they see people and talk to people."

"That was like my dream. I dreamt it was while I was looking at the fire that the door there opened quite gently and softly, just as if it moved quite of itself, and then I saw papa's face, and he had in his hand something red and sparkling; and, just when the door came quite wide open, I thought I sat up in bed, and he looked at me. And then the door seemed to shut quite softly again, and I didn't hear anything—and that was all."

"That wasn't really a dream, darling. It was just a fancy because you were ill."

"Not a dream! Papa didn't really come, did he?"

"Oh, no, darling! Papa is away in London. See, the door is locked."

And I got up off the bed and went to the door, and showed her that it was so. Haidee leant back thoughtfully.

"Dreams are very strange things, I think. And to dream of nice things is just as good as if they really happened. And to dream of horrid things— cries and moans and things—is dreadful!"—and she shuddered.

"You sha'n't dream of anything dreadful while you are up here with me, darling," said I, soothing the little delicate fanciful creature, and wondering whether some of the cries she spoke of had not been real, and not only dreams.

For I was beginning since last night, when I had witnessed her real feeling about her child, to be very sorry for Mrs. Rayner, and to wonder whether I could not draw nearer to her in some way through Haidee, and, through understanding her better, learn to sympathize with her still more. Her misery had seemed so real, and, on the other hand, I had never seen her so utterly broken down and helpless. When once the mask of cold self-control which she usually wore had disappeared, she seemed such a weak thing that it appeared scarcely possible that she could have such a force of obstinacy in her as Mr. Rayner had described her to possess. Mad or sane, I should never be afraid of her again. I only felt utterly sorry for her, and anxious to let her know how much I longed in some way to cheer her dull life. Why was she so reticent to her husband? What if I, being a woman, and having now established, through my care of her child, some claim on her gratitude, could win my way to her heart altogether, persuade her to leave Geldham for a time, and meet Mr. Rayner on his return with the triumphant news that at last his wife was ready to break through her apathy and come back into the world of men again? The thought made my heart beat faster, and I longed to begin my delicate work at once.

But I was disappointed. I had all my meals by myself that day, except tea, which I had upstairs with Haidee, for Sarah said Mrs. Rayner was too unwell to leave her room. When we had finished tea, I still sat upstairs by my pupil's bedside, and my high spirits at the thought of Laurence's expected visit infected her, and she laughed and chattered to me in a fashion very unusual with her. At last I heard the front-door bell ring, and my heart seemed to stand still with joyful anticipation. But no one came upstairs to fetch me, and, after a few minutes' breathless waiting, I ran downstairs, unable to bear the suspense any longer. I met Sarah in the hall.

"Who was that, Sarah?" asked I, too much excited to think of a decent subterfuge.

"Only one of Gregson's boys asking for Mr. Rayner, miss."

Strange that Gregson's boy should come to the front door, I thought. I could not go upstairs again. It was half-past six; and at half-past seven I was to be at my "nest," if Laurence had not come before. I thought that hour would never end. It seemed to me to be getting very dark too. When the hands of the schoolroom clock pointed to twenty minutes past, I put on my shawl, and had opened the window to go out, when Sarah came in.

"If you please, miss, would you mind helping me with the store-list? Mrs. Rayner is too ill to do it, and it has to be posted to-morrow morning."

"Oh, Sarah, won't it do in—in half an hour?" said I breathlessly.

"Mrs. Rayner will want me then, miss. It won't take you more than five minutes."

I followed her out of the room, suppressing my impatience as well as I could. But the task really did not seem to take long. In what appeared to be about a quarter of an hour I was free, and I dashed into the garden, through the plantation, towards my "nest."

I had not looked at the clock again, but surely it was very dark for half-past seven! Yet Laurence was not there! And, as I stood wondering whether something was wrong, I heard the church-clock strike eight. What awful mistake had I made? Was he gone? Should I really not see him again? A bit of paper half hidden in the grass, not on my seat, but under it, caught my eye. It was a leaf torn from a pocket-book. On it was scrawled in pencil, in Laurence's handwriting—

> "Good-by, my darling! Remember what I prophesied last night, and, if no other warning will serve you, take this one. I called at the Alders at seven, and was told by Sarah that you were tired out with watching by Haidee, and were asleep. I come here to-night, and you are not here. I know it is a trick, and I know who is at the bottom of it. When I left you last night, there were two men in a cart outside the stable-gate of the Alders. If anything happens, write. Write to me at

the following address." Then followed the address, and the scrawl ended with—"I have spoken to Mrs. Manners. Good-by, my darling! Take care of yourself for the next six weeks, and you shall never need to take care of yourself again.

"Your devotedly loving Laurence."

I kissed the note, thrust it into the front of my frock, and fled into the house and into the schoolroom. Sarah was just turning away from the mantelpiece; and by the clock it was just four minutes past eight.

How the time had flown between my leaving the schoolroom with Sarah and my going into the garden!

CHAPTER XXI

I sat down by the table as soon as Sarah had left the schoolroom, and rested my head in my hands. I did not want to cry, though a few tears trickled down between my fingers at the thought that I should not see Laurence again before he went away; but I wanted to put the events of the evening together and find out what they meant. There was only one conclusion to come to: Sarah had deliberately prevented my meeting him. The ring I had heard had been Laurence's; and, after sending him away by means of a falsehood, she had had another ready for me when I asked who it was. "Gregson's boy"! I had thought it strange at the time that the carpenter's son should come to the front door, and now I felt sure that he had not been there at all.

I looked again at Laurence's note. He had called at the house at seven, he said. Now I distinctly remembered that, after I had heard the bell and met Sarah, I came into the schoolroom and found that by the clock it was half-past six. I had sat there until twenty minutes past seven, and during that time there had been no other ring at the hall door. And I had noticed how very dark it was getting; then, just as I was opening the window to go out, Sarah had come in and asked me to help her with the store-list, and I had been free in a very short time; yet on my arrival at my "nest," the church clock had struck eight.

Sarah must have put the schoolroom clock back.

I had found her just now turning from the mantelpiece, and I could not doubt that, her object being gained, she had been putting the clock right again. This malicious persecution frightened me. Was I safe in the same house with a woman who would take so much trouble merely to prevent my having a last interview with my lover?

There had been a matter-of-fact deliberateness in the way she had answered me about the bell and asked me to do the list which had the effect of alarming me still more than the savage manner in which she used to look at and speak to me when she was jealous of some new proof of the consideration with which I was treated at the Alders. This was Wednesday, and Mr. Rayner would probably not be back before Saturday. What new proof of animosity would she manage to give me in those three days? That she would not let this opportunity of showing her rooted dislike to me go by I felt sure. I remembered how earnestly she had begged to stay, and wondered whether the wish for a chance of playing me some unkind trick had had anything to do with it; for Sarah was not likely to have forgiven me for having been the cause of her threatened dismissal. It was of no use to speculate upon what she might do; if she grew too intolerable, I could telegraph to Mr. Rayner, and he would find some means of bringing her to reason.

I turned again to Laurence's note to divert my thoughts from her, and wondered why, in those few hurried lines to me, he had thought it worth while to mention that he saw two men in a cart outside the stable-gate when he left me on the previous night. What meaning could the incident have to him? It had one to me, certainly; but then it was because I had seen Tom Parkes bring in the little portmanteau, and then return across the lawn with Sarah. The mention of this cart revived my curiosity regarding the past night's adventure. I could make nothing of it myself; but I thought I would write to Laurence and tell him what I had seen; and, if he knew anything more, my information might lead him to an explanation of the whole occurrence. I was still staring at the note when Sarah came in again, this time to bring me my candle, an office she seldom undertook. I saw a look of disappointment and alarm come over her face as her quick eyes fell on my note, and when I got upstairs I took the precaution to learn the address I was to write to by heart before enclosing this farewell note with Laurence's first, which I still wore round my neck.

The next morning I received a letter from Mr. Rayner. He had been to the Gaiety Theatre on the very night of his arrival in town, and sent me a crumpled programme of the performance, with some comments which did not interest me very much, as I had not seen any of the actors and actresses he mentioned, having been only once to the theatre in my life. I laughed to myself at Laurence's fancy that he had seen Mr. Rayner in the dress of a navvy at the station that night. The letter, which had been written at four o'clock on Wednesday, said further that he was going that evening to the Criterion Theatre, where he hoped to be better entertained. He said he had written to Mrs. Rayner, and sent his love to Haidee by her, but that he enclosed a second portion to me to give her, as she was not well. Then he gave me a message to deliver which I would much rather not have been entrusted with, and at breakfast I said to Sarah—

"Mr. Rayner has sent a message to you in a letter I have just received from him. He says, 'Tell Sarah not to forget the work she has to do in my absence.'"

As I looked up after reading this out to her, I saw that her face had turned quite livid; the old hatred of me gleamed in her eyes, and I wished Mr. Rayner had written to her himself, instead of making me deliver a message which appeared so distasteful to her.

She said, "Very well, miss;" and I wondered what work it was.

I spent most of the day by Haidee's bedside. I did not see Mrs. Rayner, for she appeared neither at breakfast nor at dinner, and to my inquiries Sarah gave the same answer as before—that she was not well enough to leave her room. She could not even see any one either, Sarah said, when I asked if I might read to her; and I was obliged to see my hopes of gaining her sympathy fade away, and to recognize the fact that either she would not or Sarah would not allow me a chance of breaking down the barrier of reserve between us. I could let her see that I had not forgotten her, though; and, seized by a happy thought, I went in search of an old knife and a basket, and went into the garden to gather her some flowers.

It was about four o'clock in the afternoon; the leaves and grass were still wet, for it had been raining hard all the morning, and the mist was rising already from the marsh. There were scarcely any flowers left now, but by wandering into remote nooks of the garden, and by stepping in among the plants and spying out every blossom hidden under the leaves, I managed at last to collect enough for a very fair October bouquet. I took them into the house, and it suddenly occurred to me that they would make a better display in a large wire-covered vase that stood on a whatnot in the drawing-room. So I ran in there, with my frock still tucked up, the gardening-knife in one dirty hand and my basket of flowers on my arm. I had my hand still on the handle of the door, when I saw there was a gentleman in there, standing at the window, looking out into the garden. I slipped back hastily, hoping to escape before he could catch sight of me; but he turned, crossed the room quickly, and stopped me.

"Miss Christie!"

It was Mr. Carruthers.

"They told me you were out."

Sarah's work, thought I.

"No; I was only in the garden."

There was no help for my appearance now, so I quietly took the pin out of my frock and let it down while he went on talking.

"I am very, very glad to see you. You are looking very well. I am afraid," said he, still holding my hand, "you have not been missing any of us much."

"Well, you see I had known the people there only two days," said I seriously.

" 'The people there'! As if I cared how little you missed 'the people there'! When I say you have not been missing any of us, I mean you have not been missing me."

"But I haven't known you longer than the others," said I, smiling.

"But you have known me so much better than the others," said he deprecatingly.

"I am not quite sure of that."

"Didn't you talk to me more than to the others?"

"Yes."

"And walk with me oftener than with the others?"

"Yes."

"And didn't you like me better than the others?"

"I think I did—yes, I did."

"All that is very tepid. I can't think why you don't like me, when I like you so much."

"Oh, you did not understand me, Mr. Carruthers! I do like you very much; but—"

"There—you have spoilt it all with that unkind 'but'! Don't you think me handsome? I am considered one of the handsomest men about town, I assure you."

"Not really?"

This slipped out quickly, for I thought he was in fun. I afterwards found out, to my surprise, that it was true; but I did not learn it then, for he looked very much amused, and said—

"That is blow number two; but I am not going to be crushed. Don't you think me good?"

"Oh, no!"

"Why not, Miss Christie?" said he, pretending to be in despair.

My chief reason was that, if he had been very "good," he would not have made Lady Mills angry with me by taking me on the river late at night; for he had shown later that he knew it was not considered right. But it would have seemed ungenerous to recall that when it had all passed over; so I only said—

"I know from the way they talked to you and of you that they did not think you very good, and that you did not wish to be thought so."

"But I am going to reform after what you said on Sunday."

"Oh, no, you are not!" said I, shaking my head. "You say so only because it amuses you to see how much you can make me believe of the things you tell me."

"Do you judge all the people you know as severely as you do me, Miss Christie?"

"Yes, quite," said I gravely.

"Oh—er—the gentleman who gave you the red rose, for instance?"

He said this in a mock-bashful tone, looking at the carpet, as if ashamed to meet my eyes. I could not help getting red, and I think he knew it without looking up.

"Or—or perhaps he—never does anything wrong?"

"Oh, yes, he does, Mr. Carruthers!" said I, with a bright idea in my head—he had been laughing at me long enough, I thought. "He did very wrong in thinking he need be jealous of any of the gentlemen I met at Denham Court."

Mr. Carruthers raised his head and looked straight at me. I am not sure that he was not a little annoyed as well as amused, though he laughed very good-temperedly.

"I will never make love to you any more, you ungrateful girl!" said he.

"Make love! Do you call that making love?" said I, laughing.

"It is not the best I can do by any means; but I shall be very glad to show you—"

"You need not take that trouble, thank you; I will take your word for it," said I, laughing again.

I had learnt to answer him back in his own way; and I think he was a little surprised at the progress I was making.

"You are too quick of fence for me," said he, shaking his head. "Well, don't you want to know what has been going on at Denham Court?" he asked rather suddenly, in a different tone.

"Oh, yes! But there has not been time for much to happen. I left there on Monday, and this is only Thursday."

"There has been time for a very serious misfortune to happen, for all that," said he gravely. "Last night Denham Court was broken into, and

Lady Mills and Mrs. Cunningham and Mrs. Carew and some of the other ladies had all their most valuable jewelry stolen; and a quantity of gold plate was taken too."

We had been standing by the window all this time, I playing with the flowers in my basket. I went on mechanically twisting a chrysanthemum in my fingers after he had finished telling me this startling story, but I did not know what I was doing.

"Last night, did you say?" said I at last, in a frightened whisper.

"Yes, last night. Sit down," said he kindly, putting me into a chair. "This seems to have quite overwhelmed you. Why, child, your very lips are white! Let me ring for some—"

"No, no!" I interrupted, starting up. "I am quite well; I am not going to faint. Don't—don't ring. Tell me all about it quickly, please. When did you find it out? Have they caught the thieves? Do they know—"

"Stop—I can't tell you all at once. The thieves have not been caught yet, and we don't know who they are. The robbery was discovered this morning."

"This morning! Who discovered it? How?"

"Now don't get excited, and I will tell you all about it. This morning a ladder was found lying underneath Lady Mills's dressing-room window, which had been opened by smashing one of the panes from the outside. It was Lady Mills's maid who first gave the alarm by a cry at sight of the open window when she went into the dressing room this morning, after calling her mistress. Lady Mills ran in; they looked out together, and saw the ladder lying underneath. The dressing-room has two doors; the one which does not lead into the bedroom had been unlocked and left open by the thief, to pass into the house by. But, at first sight, nothing seemed to have been disturbed. The dressing-case was locked and in its place; a strong tin case in which Lady Mills kept the greater part of her jewels was still in the locked-up wardrobe. But, on moving it, they found that the lock had been burst open, and it was entirely empty. Jewels, cases and all, had disappeared. By this time the head-gardener had come into the house saying that he hoped all was right, but that he had gone to the tool-house in the morning with one of the under-gardeners, a man named Parkes—"

"Tom Parkes?"

"Yes. He keeps the key of the tool-house. And they had found the door forced in, and a file and one of the ladders gone. Of course the alarm spread quickly all over the house; and then the other losses were discovered one by one. There is the mysterious part of it. Everything had been done so methodically and so neatly, even to locked doors being found still locked, that it was not until after careful examination that the stolen things were missed. Lady Mills and Mrs. Carew found their dressing-cases locked; but, when they opened them, each found that the most valuable of the contents were gone. The butler and Sir Jonas himself examined the plate-chest together. That was locked too, and, on first opening it, they congratulated themselves on its having escaped. But, on removing that part of it which is in constant use, they found that the gold plate, which is used only now and then, and some solid silver cups and candlesticks had been taken. But the loss which has caused the greatest sensation is Mrs. Cunningham's. She came into the breakfast-room quite white and scarcely able to speak, with some pebbles and a piece of cotton-wool in her hands. She declares that she carried about on her person, sewn up in wash-leather and cotton-wool, a very valuable set of diamonds and cat's-eyes; that it was not until long after she discovered her other losses that she cut open the leather, just to make sure that her greatest treasure was safe; that she found the jewels gone and the pebbles she produced in their place. The poor woman was so hysterical that it was a long time before she could tell us all about it. She declares that she slept with them under her pillow, and that no one in the world knew where she kept them, for that she never mentioned the fact to any one—"

"Oh, but that is not quite true, Mr. Carruthers! For she told me."

"So she said," said he, looking at me steadily. "But you could never have repeated such a thing to any one who could make a wrong use of the knowledge."

"Oh, no! The only person I spoke of it to was Mr. Rayner."

"Mr. Rayner!" said he quickly. "You could not have chosen a worse person to entrust the secret to, I am afraid."

"What do you mean?"

"Why, he is the most talkative man I know. I have met him at Newmarket several times—a bright amusing fellow enough, but the last man to whom I should tell anything I did not wish to have repeated for the amusement of the next person he met."

"Oh, but he would not repeat a thing like that!" said I earnestly. "He scolded me for telling him, and said such confidences should never be repeated, no matter to whom."

"That's all right," said he, much relieved. "Then I shall tell Mrs. Cunningham you didn't mention it to any one. The poor woman is half out of her mind; it was she who sent me over here to-day, to find out whether you had spoken about it in the presence of any one who could use the knowledge. For my part, I thought it very likely she had only imagined she had spoken to you about it; but I wanted an excuse for coming; so I gained my object, and put her under an obligation at the same time."

I did not pay any attention to the implied flattery in these words; I was too much interested in the robbery.

"And is no one suspected?" I asked, with trembling lips.

"At present we know nothing, and we suspect a different person every minute. The robbery had been so well arranged, and was carried out with such discrimination—for nothing but the best of everything was taken—that at first the servants were suspected of complicity. But my man Gordon, who has no end of sense, suggested that it was only fair to them all to have their boxes examined at once. This was done, but no trace of anything was found. Of course that does not prove that they may not have given information to the thieves, whoever they were. There has been a gang of navvies at work on the railway close by for the past fortnight, and a hat belonging to one of them was found in the garden, and has been identified already; but it seems that the friends of the man it belongs to can prove that he passed the night drunk in the village. So at present we know absolutely nothing. Gordon told me privately that he doesn't believe either the servants or the navvies have had anything to do with it, and he pointed out the resemblance between this and a robbery which took place some time ago at the house of another of my friends, Lord Dalston, whom I had been staying with not long before. He believes that it is the work of a regular jewel-robber, and that very likely he got a discharged servant to supply him with information. I pointed out to him that no servant who had long left could have given him such precise details as he seems to have had concerning the jewels of the ladies who were only visiting there, for instance. But I could not convince him. As for Mrs. Cunningham's, that really seems marvellous, because she is a cautious sort of woman. I suppose her maid somehow found out the secret, and then told it to—Heaven knows whom."

"I suppose so," said I mechanically.

I was trying to put together what I had just heard and what I had already known. Mr. Carruthers rose.

"I need not trouble Mrs. Rayner at all now that I have seen you," said he.

"Mrs. Rayner!" I repeated, in the same mechanical stupid way.

"Yes. When the servant told me you were out, she said I could see Mrs. Rayner. I did not want to disturb her, knowing that she has the reputation of being an invalid. But she insisted."

"Wait one moment," said I, as he took my hand. "Are you quite sure, Mr. Carruthers, that the robbery took place last night?"

Before I uttered the last words, his eyes suddenly left my face, and were fixed on some object behind me.

I turned, and saw in the doorway Mrs. Rayner, paler and more impassive than ever, and Sarah. All the doors at the Alders opened noiselessly, and they had overheard me. And, as I looked at Sarah's face, my heart beat faster with fear and with suspicion become certainty, for I knew that I was on the right track.

CHAPTER XXII

In his astonishment at Mrs. Rayner's ghostlike entrance and appearance, Mr. Carruthers had not paid much attention to the end of my question, and I determined to try to get another opportunity of putting it to him. He expressed his sorrow to Mrs. Rayner at having caused her the trouble of receiving him when she was evidently suffering, and said that he had ventured to call to tell Miss Christie about a great robbery which had taken place in the house she had so recently visited, Denham Court. Nothing but physical suffering could have explained the impassive stolidity with which she listened, her great gray eyes staring straight in front of her, to the account of the robbery. She made no comment until it was over; then she turned to him and asked, with a faint expression of relief—

"Then nobody was hurt?"

"Oh, no, there was no collision at all! They vanished like spirits, leaving no trace."

"I am very sorry they were not caught. My husband has been in town since Tuesday morning, and I am nervous while he is away," said she, like one repeating a lesson.

All this time Sarah stood by her, smelling-bottle in hand, as if prepared for her mistress to faint. Yet to my eyes Mrs. Rayner did not look worse than usual.

When he rose to go, I accompanied Mr. Carruthers to the door, where a dog-cart was waiting for him; but Sarah, whose duty by her mistress's side was suddenly over, followed close behind, and I had no chance of suggesting to him my own suspicions about the burglary. When he had gone, I reflected that it was better for me not to have said anything to a comparative stranger to implicate one of the servants in the house where I was living until I had consulted Mr. Rayner.

To give vent to my excitement over the important secret I fancied myself on the track of, I wrote to Laurence. With Sarah about, a letter was a thing requiring caution, as the event proved. I was so sensible of this that I contented myself with giving an account of Mr. Carruthers's visit and of the robbery at Denham Court, only saying, in conclusion, that it might have some connection with what he had seen, and that I had something to add to that. I said that I would write more fully as soon as I had an opportunity of going to Beaconsburgh to post my letter myself; and then I said a great deal more concerning different things which were perhaps really less important, but which were much pleasanter to write about.

The postman called for the letter-bag at six every evening; so I waited at the schoolroom window until I saw him come up to the house and heard Sarah give him the bag; then I ran out into the hall, as if I had only just finished my letter, and put it into the bag which he held. Sarah could not even see the direction as I put it in, and I congratulated myself upon my artful strategy; but I might have known that she was not to be baffled so. I had stood at the door and watched him turn into the drive, and returned to the schoolroom in a flutter of excitement at my own audacity, when from the window I saw Sarah flit after him. I dashed out on to the lawn, and got into the drive just in time to see the postman fasten up the bag and go on again, while Sarah, saying something about "a misdirection," put a letter into her pocket; and I knew that it was mine. With my heart beating fast, I walked up boldly to her.

"What did you take my letter out of the bag for, Sarah?" said I, half choking with anger.

"It's not your letter, miss. What should I want with any letter of yours?" said she, looking down at me insolently. "It's a letter to my sister that I've forgotten to put the number of the street on."

I knew quite well that this was a falsehood, but I could not prove it; for I had indeed been too far off to recognize my letter when she put it into her pocket, and my moral certainty counted for nothing. She knew this, and stalked off defiantly to the house with my letter, while I crept back to the schoolroom, and sobbed bitterly at the tyranny I was suffering from this hateful woman.

Well, it would soon be over now—that was a comfort. I would tell Mr. Rayner all I had seen on Tuesday night, and about the cart Laurence had met outside—perhaps I would not mention it was Laurence who saw it—and about Parkes's wishing to avoid me at Denham Court. I should not dare to suggest to Mr. Rayner any doubt about Gordon, who seemed to be in some way a personal friend of his. But now, with all my thoughts turned to jewels and jewel-robberies, I could not help thinking again about that strange disappearance of my own pendant while I was staying at Denham Court, and its restoration by this man. Then his treating Tom Parkes as a stranger at Denham Court, when I had seen them together one night at the Alders, seemed to me now a rather suspicious circumstance. I congratulated myself on having been so cautious in my letter to Laurence that Sarah would not learn much by reading it, and wondered when I could make an excuse to go to Beaconsburgh, to post one to him with my own hands. It seemed very hard to be cut off in this way from the relief of opening my heart to him; but it would be all right on the morrow, when Mr. Rayner came back— she would not dare to annoy me then.

But the next morning, to my great disappointment, I got another letter, saying he should not be back until Monday afternoon. I had written to him on Wednesday, and he had got my note. He said, as I mentioned that the weather was bad and the fogs had begun to be thick, it would be better for Mrs. Rayner to leave the ground-floor and sleep upstairs.

"I expect you will have difficulty in persuading her to leave her own room," the letter went on; "but I am so anxious about her, for it seems to me she has looked paler than ever lately, and I feel so sure she would be better on a higher floor that I beg you, dear Miss Christie, to use all your powers of persuasion to induce her to move. Tell her that it is only for a time, that she shall go back to her old room as soon as the weather is warmer again; tell her I wish it, tell her anything you think likely to affect her. I have great trust in your diplomatic powers, little madam, and I anticipate the happiest results from them in this instance. I have given Sarah orders by letter to prepare the big front spare-room."

I was delighted with this letter; it made me for the moment angry with Mrs. Rayner for her persistent ignoring of his kind feeling towards her. But, when I remembered her agony over her child on the night of Haidee's illness, and the settled melancholy I now knew how to detect under her cold demeanor, pity got the better of me again, and I was glad to have an opportunity at last of doing her some good. She was always supposed to be attached to her room on the ground-floor, and Mr. Rayner wrote as if it would be difficult to persuade her to move. But I had two powerful weapons in her husband's loving letter and her affection for Haidee, and I resolved to use them well.

As I was dining alone, I was just wondering how I could get at her, when the opportunity presented itself, as if at my wish.

"Mrs. Rayner feels well enough to have tea in here with you, miss, this afternoon," said Sarah.

That then would be my chance. But I reflected that I could not be very persuasive at tea-time, subject to the chance of our common tyrant, Sarah, pouncing down upon us. I went out after dinner and sat, in spite of the damp, on the seat at my "nest" for a little while, trying to invent subtle plans for inveigling Mrs. Rayner into the drawing-room or the schoolroom for an uninterrupted *tête-à-tête*. As I sat there, I heard some one coming along the path from the house. The trees between were not yet bare enough for me to see through; but, when the steps had gone by, I crept through the branches, peeped out, and saw Sarah getting over the stile into the path which led to the high-road. I ran indoors, asked Jane where Sarah was, and learnt that she had gone to Beaconsburgh to get some groceries; I had noticed a black bag in her hand.

I seemed to breathe more freely at once. Now was my time for seeing Mrs. Rayner. I was a little shy about going into the left wing without an invitation; she might be asleep, or she might not wish to be disturbed. I thought I would reconnoitre first. So I went into the garden with my knife and basket, as if to cut flowers, gathered a few China asters, and ventured round, past the drawing-room window, through the wet rank grass and the swampy earth, to the left wing. I had put on my goloshes, but they were not of much use, for I sank into pools that came over my shoes.

Still I went on, through an unwholesome mass of fallen and decaying leaves, to the dark yews and laurels that grew round Mrs. Rayner's window. I had never ventured here since the evening of my arrival, when I had strayed this way in my explorations, and been startled by my first dim view of Mrs. Rayner's pale face at the window of what must be her room. Again I pushed aside the branches of the now almost leafless barberry-tree and looked for the second time at the gloomy window, overhung by an ivy-bush which now seemed to fall lower than ever. There was no face looking out this time; a broken gutter-pipe had caused the rain-water to form a sort of slough under the window, so that I could not go close to it; but I went as near as I could, singing, and cutting off little branches of yew, as if not knowing where I had strayed. My ruse succeeded. Just as one of the branches I had pulled down towards me swung back into its place, Mrs. Rayner's white face, looking astonished and alarmed, appeared at the window. I smiled good-morning to her, and made a show of offering her my flowers. I wanted her to open the window. This she seemed reluctant to do. But I stood my ground until at last she put a hesitating hand upon the fastening. When the window was just a few inches up, I said, opening upon a point where I knew we had sympathy—

"Sarah has gone to Beaconsburgh. I saw her off. I hope she will be a very long time."

I was right. She opened the window, which was a little above the level of my head, more confidently; and I saw that it was barred inside.

"Haidee is so much better to-day, Mrs. Rayner, I think she might come downstairs for a little while to-morrow into the dining-room, if we make a good fire there. She was asking to-day why you did not come up and see her, and I told her you were not well enough. She is very anxious about you."

"Give her my love," said Mrs. Rayner, with a faint smile. "I could not do her so much good as you have done." There was a plaintive expression of helplessness in these words which touched me. "Thank you, Miss Christie."

"I am so glad she is better," remarked I, venturing impulsively into the slough that I might stretch my hand up to the window-ledge. "I think it did do her good to go upstairs. The lower part of this house is damp, you know; Doctor Lowe said so."

She seemed to shrink back into herself a little at these words; however, she said—

"You have been very good to the child. It was best for her to go."

"Yes, I think it was. Don't you find that the mist from the marsh makes your room very cold this weather, Mrs. Rayner?"

She looked at me in a frightened irresolute way, and then she formed with her lips rather than spoke the words—

"Yes—rather cold—now."

"Wouldn't you be more comfortable in one of the rooms upstairs while the fogs last?" I insinuated shyly.

But I saw that her breath was beginning to come fast, and the faint pink to tinge her cheek as it did when she was excited.

"Did any one tell you to say that to me?" she asked, in a whisper.

"I told Mr. Rayner, when I wrote, that we had a slight fog here on Tuesday night, and this morning I had a letter saying that he thought it was bad for you to sleep on the ground-floor when the mists had begun to rise high, and that he had told Sarah to prepare the large front spare-room for you."

Instead of looking grateful for this proof of her husband's thoughtfulness, she became agitated, and at last her agitation grew almost uncontrollable; she trembled and clung to the bars inside the window, and I saw that her forehead was wet with the effect of some strong emotion—it looked like fear.

"At last—at last! I have been here too long," she gasped.

I thought that the effect on her nervous temperament of making her leave the room against her will would outweigh any physical good the change might do her. The wild look was coming into her eyes which I had seen there twice before, and I was afraid of her being seized with a paroxysm while I stood there on the other side of the barred window, powerless to help her; so I said gently—

"Of course Mr. Rayner would not wish you to go if you did not wish it."

But she shook her head, and, putting her face between the bars to be closer to me, she said, in a low broken voice—

"Do you know what his wishes mean when Sarah carries them out?"

I stood looking up at her, appalled. Her terror was so real that it infected me, and for the moment I almost shared the poor lady's mad belief that there was a conspiracy against her. But her next words restored me to my senses.

"Are you against me too?" she asked piteously. "I always thought you were; but then you were kind to my child—and I don't know, I don't know whom to trust!"

"You may trust me, dear Mrs. Rayner, indeed," said I earnestly. "I would not have suggested your leaving your room if I had thought it would cause you so much pain. Indeed, I did not know you were so much attached to it."

She shuddered. There was a pause, during which she stared at me steadily and searchingly. But I had no cause to fear her poor mad eyes, so I returned her gaze, and she grew gradually calmer.

"Miss Christie," said she at last, in a whisper, "you have influence in this house. That night when Haidee was ill you made Sarah obey you. If I may trust you, give me this proof—get me one day's respite. Let me stay in my own room till—to-morrow."

Her voice sank till I could scarcely catch the last words.

"I will try," said I softly. "And, oh, Mrs. Rayner, shall I tell Sam to take the dead leaves away in a wheelbarrow? I am sure it can't be wholesome to have them so close to your window."

"No, no, leave them—never mind," said she hurriedly. "You must be in the water. You will catch cold. Go—Heaven bless you!"

She shut down the window in a frightened way, and disappeared into the room. I could not see in, for the window-sill was some eight or ten inches above my head. I turned and splashed my way back, with my teeth chattering, to the house, and changed my wet shoes and stockings, half crying for pity for the poor, helpless, forlorn lady for whom I could do so little.

At tea-time she came into the dining room, and, as Sarah was there, I practised the innocent deception of pretending not to have seen her before that day. I thought it better that the lynx-eyed guardian should not discover that I had found a way of communicating privately with her unlucky charge. So I said again at tea-time that I had had a letter from Mr. Rayner, and that he thought that on Saturday she had better move into the spare-room.

"Saturday!" interrupted Sarah sharply.

"Yes," said I, rather frightened at telling such a story. "Do you think you would like to go to-morrow, or would you rather go to-night, Mrs. Rayner?" I asked gently.

"To-morrow," said she, with a steady look which I took as an acknowledgment; and I turned to Sarah.

"I will answer for it to Mr. Rayner, if there has been any mistake," I said, as modestly as I could, for it was an awkward thing to have to give orders before the mistress of the house, however tottering her reason might be.

"Very well, miss," said Sarah, to my surprise.

For the second time my use of Mr. Rayner's name had acted like a charm; and I wondered how this woman, who had dared so much to cut me off from communication with Laurence, could calmly submit to receive orders from me.

After tea, Mrs. Rayner in her turn surprised me by a warning which seemed to show keen observation. She came and stood by me at the fireplace while Sarah was clearing the table, and once, while the latter was for a moment out of the room, breathed softly into my ear, without turning her head—

"Take care—she hates you, and she is dangerous."

I glanced up quickly; but Sarah was already back in the room, and Mrs. Rayner's face was as impassive as ever.

I was so much used to living in fear of Sarah that the warning did not make any particular impression upon me, and I went to bed neither more nor less afraid of her machinations than usual.

I woke up in the night without being conscious of any cause for doing so. I had started at once into full wakefulness, and I saw that Haidee was sleeping quietly, and that the fire was still alight, but had burnt low; and I thought I would replenish it.

Then, as I raised myself on my elbow, I thought I heard a sound, too faint to be called a noise, outside the door. So I kept quite still and listened intently. I heard nothing for some time, then again a muffled noise as of something being shuffled softly from one stair to another, then again no sound. The turret staircase was uncarpeted; it had once been polished, but the beeswax had worn off long since and had not been renewed. I got out of bed softly, lighted my candle by putting a match to the dying fire to avoid the noise of striking it, crept to the door, and literally put my ear to the keyhole. And, after a few moments, I heard the same soft shuffling again. It might be Nap, Mr. Rayner's retriever, trying to find a stair softer than the rest to lie upon; yet they were surely too narrow for him to make the attempt.

Whoever or whatever it was seemed to be making its way down by very slow degrees, until it seemed that it must be about six or seven stairs from the top. I screwed up my courage and resolved to give the intruder, human or otherwise, a fright. All the locks were kept in good condition at the Alders, and there was not such a thing as a creaking door in the place. I turned the key without the least noise, then the handle, and flung open the door, stamping my foot and brandishing the candle. I heard Haidee scream; I had forgotten her.

My plan succeeded only too well. A figure which had been crouching on the stairs sprang up. It was Sarah.

Before I had time to do more than recognize the savage frightened face, her foot slipped, and, with a piercing cry, she fell backward down the stairs. The staircase had one turn. I, trembling at the door, saw her long thin hands clutching and struggling to save herself at the corner; but she failed, and I heard a heavy thud, and then a groan. She had fallen headlong to the bottom.

For one second I leaned against the wall unable to move; then, trembling so that I could scarcely find the top stair, I stepped forward to go down. But on the second stair my foot suddenly slipped, and, if I had not been going very slowly because of my agitation, I must have fallen. On the next stair I slipped again; on the next to that, putting out my foot very cautiously, I found a string fastened across.

With a sudden suspicion, I sat down without advancing farther, and slid my hand along the stair. It was slippery; so were the others. The turret staircase was dark even by day; if I had been running downstairs at my usual pace, nothing could have saved me. It was a trap set by Sarah, if not for getting rid of me altogether, at least for seriously injuring me. She was greasing the stairs one by one when I had heard her; in her alarm at my sudden appearance she had sprung up, her foot had slipped on the greasy plate below which she had been using, and she had fallen herself a victim to the trap she had laid for me. And, as the horrible truth broke upon me, I heard another groan and a murmur I could not distinguish.

Sick at heart, and for the moment almost as helpless as she, I crawled down the stairs, wondering and fearing what spectacle would meet my eyes at the bottom.

CHAPTER XXIII

All the stairs below where Sarah had slipped were safe and in their usual state. At the bottom, an almost senseless heap, lay Sarah, with one arm twisted under her and her head in a pool of blood. She was moaning, with closed eyes, and did not know me even when her eyes opened and she stared round her.

The noise of her fall had by this time brought out Jane from the distant nursery; and she ran for the cook, who was an older and more experienced woman, and who indeed proved useful in this emergency. It was past midnight; but, late as it was, I was obliged to send Jane into the village for Sam, to tell him to take one of the horses and ride as fast as he could to Beaconsburgh for the Doctor. Meanwhile the cook declared her belief that one of Sarah's arms was broken, for she fainted when it was touched; and then, having discovered that the blood was flowing from a great gash at the back of her head, she bound it up as well as she could to stop the bleeding. Then I ran downstairs for some brandy, which we put to her lips from time to time, but in vain tried to make her swallow. And then we sat in the cold, in the dim light of a candle, both of us crouched on the floor, the cook supporting the wounded woman against her knee, I a little way behind, lest she should recover full consciousness and know me.

It was a ghastly thing to be sitting there with that horrid stain on the floor within a few feet, listening to the feeble moans of the wretched woman whom we hardly expected to live until help came, holding our breath when for a few moments the moaning ceased, I thinking of the awful retribution her malice had brought down upon her, not daring to speak to tell her I forgave her, lest my voice should have some terrible effect upon her wandering mind. And so we sat shivering not with cold alone, until the front-door bell sounded through the silent house, and Jane, who had not dared to come upstairs again since she went to send off Sam, opened the door, and we heard the Doctor's heavy tread on the stairs.

It was Doctor Lowe. He called first for more light. Jane brought a lamp, and he signed to her to go away. After asking me whether I was hysterical, and hearing me answer "No," he told me to hold the lamp while he made his examination. He said afterwards that I had strong nerves; but nothing but fear of him kept me steady at my post, as, with averted head, I heard the sharp little cries the wounded woman gave two or three times. The cook had been right; the arm that lay under Sarah was broken; the Doctor could not tell yet whether her spine was not injured too. He cut off her long black hair and strapped up her head, which had received a gash which might affect the brain, he said; and he set and bandaged the broken arm. Then we brought a mattress, and very carefully lifted her on to it, carried her to her room, and put her on the bed.

"Who is going to sit up with her?" asked he.

"I will," said I, but added doubtfully, "if—"

"If what?" said the Doctor, turning upon me sharply.

I drew him a little apart and said—

"Doctor Lowe, do you think the sight of any one she disliked very much would be bad for her?"

He looked at me very keenly as he answered—

"No. She won't be able to recognize anybody; but I warn you she will be restless. How did the accident happen?"

"She fell downstairs."

"The staircase leads to your room, doesn't it? How came she to be there at this time of night? Why don't you tell me the truth, and save me the trouble of making stupid guesses?"

I told him the truth, and his only comment was—

"And don't you think the moral of that is that you should leave this place as soon as possible?"

"I sha'n't stay here long," said I, smiling, and thinking of Laurence.

"Oh, you think that young f-fellow at the Hall is going to marry you?"

"Yes."

"Well, I tell you frankly, I wouldn't take a wife from this house."

"But then you wouldn't take a wife from anywhere, Doctor Lowe. If you did, you would think more of the girl than of the place she came from, just as Laurence does."

"You have a sharp little tongue. I pity Laurence when he comes home late."

He asked after Haidee; but I could not let him see her, as the staircase was not yet ready; so, after giving me instructions about the treatment of Sarah, he left the house.

There was a fire already in her room, for she was by no means the ill-used creature she liked to think herself. I seated myself in a chair beside it, prepared to watch until early morning, when the cook had promised to take my place. Before long the patient began to grow restless, as the Doctor had predicted; she turned her head from side to side, tried to raise her broken arm, which had been set and bandaged tightly down, muttering and moaning incoherently. Presently she was quite quiet, and I hoped she had gone to sleep. I think I must have dozed myself for a few minutes, when I was startled into full wakefulness by a low hoarse cry of "Jim!"

She had managed to move her head so that her great black eyes, glittering now with fever, were fixed full upon me; and my heart beat fast, for I thought she must know me. But she repeated, still staring at me—

"Jim!" Then she added in a whisper, "They are after you, Jim! It's about the check. You must be off to-night. Go to the old place. I'll put 'em off, and I'll let you know."

Then more mutterings and exclamations, and before long she began again to speak coherently—

"It's too risky, Jim. I'll do it, if you want me to; but it's putting yourself in danger as well as me. All right, I'll pass it."

Then she broke out passionately—

"It's an ill thing you're going to do, James Woodfall. What do you want of a lady for a wife? Her money's none so much, and, as for her pretty face, it's the face of a fool. I'm twice the woman to look at that she is, and I'm only twenty-five; and I've stuck to you through thick and thin. Why don't you marry me, Jim?"

And it flashed across me, as she went on addressing to me reproaches, coaxings, encouragement, and defiance, that she was living over again some long-past passages in her life—passages, I could not but gather, of a very questionable character. For it was plain that this Jim, or James Woodfall, who occupied all her thoughts had been a very bad man indeed, and that Sarah had assisted him in every way in his wicked deeds.

"Don't go for that, James," she said once imploringly. "It'll be a lifer if they catch you; and they've had their eye on you lately. There's many a safer way of getting money than that."

Another pause, and then came a speech which chilled me with horror.

"Dead men tell no tales, Jim," said she, in another fearful whisper. "It's easy done, and it's safer. What's an old man's life that you're so shy of touching him? You've done many a riskier thing. Why do you always turn coward at that?"

I could scarcely sit and watch this woman-fiend after that. I seemed to see murder in her fierce fiery eyes; and I shuddered even as I moistened her dry lips and touched her burning forehead. She rambled on in the same style, mentioning other names I had never heard, and not a word of me or Mr. and Mrs. Rayner, or even of Tom Parkes, until she broke out angrily—

"Jim's mad about that little Christie girl, Tom, and he says he'll marry her in spite of everything, and I've got to bring it about," she hissed between her teeth.

What awful confusion in her mind was there to connect me with her criminal lover of years before? There suddenly woke up in my mind the remembrance of the evening when, hidden in my "nest," I had overheard a conversation between her and Mr. Rayner's mysterious visitor, who had afterwards turned out to be Mr. Carruthers's man-servant, and I remembered that she had then expressed jealousy of some man called "Jim." Was it the same man? How was it that he never appeared? I had thought at the time that she must mean Tom Parkes, and that the woman she was jealous of was Jane; but, on the whole, she got on well with Jane; and the only person in the house against whom her animosity took any serious form was myself. And now she fancied this "Jim" wanted to marry me—and I had never even seen him!

She was rambling again into the present, though, for the next speech that caught my attention was—

"It's a good weight, Tom—Jim might have lent you a hand. The water's deep in the cellar; but it won't hurt the jewels, and the plate'll clean. Come on."

Was it the Denham Court robbery that was on her mind now? I held my breath while she went on—

"Tom, that sneaking Christie girl's got wind of it somehow. Jim's that gone on her he won't listen to me; and, if I don't prevent it, she'll be his ruin."

Again that strange confusion of my name with that of the unknown Jim! My brain seemed to be getting as much confused as her own. I held tightly to the arms of my chair as I listened to her ravings, as if in a futile attempt to steady body and mind. I was mad to discover who this James Woodfall was, and I left my chair, and drew, as if fascinated, nearer to the bed as she said—

"Take care, Jim. You risk too much. There must be some thief-taker in the world clever enough to recognize the forger James Woodfall in the jewel-robber—"

At that moment, while I listened with pulses beating high and eager eyes for the name, the door opened, and the sick woman, distracted by the noise, cried, "What's that?"

It was the cook come to take my place. But the reaction from the high-pressure tension of my nerves during the last few hours was too much for me. I fell fainting to the floor.

The next morning I awoke late, with a headache and an unpleasant feeling of having gone through some horrible adventure. I told Haidee, who had been very much alarmed, poor little thing, by my antics at the door when I frightened Sarah, and by the noise of her fall, a much modified story of the whole occurrence, and then ventured down the stairs very cautiously; but Jane, instructed by the cook, had already removed the grease and made them safe again.

But I never again went down those stairs at night-time without a shudder.

I telegraphed to Mr. Rayner to inform him of the accident, without, of course, mentioning the cause, as soon as the Doctor's early visit was over— he said she was suffering from brain-fever, and ought to have a regular nurse. I received a telegram from Mr. Rayner before dinner-time—

"Am much distressed about accident. Give her every care. Have sent off an experienced nurse already."

And by the afternoon train she arrived—a silent, middle-aged woman, the very sight of whom inspired respect, which in my case amounted to awe.

The fright in the night had made Haidee rather feverish again, so that I thought it better to delay her coming downstairs yet another day. But she got up and sat by the fire in my room, and I sat with her during a great part of the day. Just before dinner we heard a light unaccustomed step on the stairs and a knock at the door, and Mrs. Rayner came in. Seeing her in the full light of my four windows, I was shocked by the change in her since I had first come to the Alders, little more than two months before. Her cheeks were so wan and hollow, her eyes so sunken in their sockets, and her lips so drawn and livid that I seemed to be looking at the face of a dead woman. She made little reference to the previous night's adventure, only saying—

"I hear Sarah is ill. I had to go in search of my breakfast myself this morning. I hope she is better."

But the look on her worn face of relief from a hated burden belied her words. She had not dared even to visit her child while that harpy was about. I was sorry Sarah's illness had been caused by me; but I could not feel much sympathy with her; her wandering speeches of the night before had shown her real cruel, vindictive self too plainly.

When we were called to dinner, which Mrs. Rayner said she would have with me to-day, I went down first, in order to leave her with her child for a few minutes. At the foot of the turret stairs, where a mat had been put to hide the traces of the horrible stain, I found the elfish Mona, as dirty as usual, playing with a large bunch of keys—Sarah's housekeeping keys. I thought they would be safer in my care than in Mona's; so I took them from her, not without a struggle and many tearless screams and howls on her part. I did not come much into contact with this young person now, as, when neither Mr. nor Mrs. Rayner appeared at meals, she had hers in the nursery with Jane, which she much preferred, as it did not entail so much washing and combing.

I thought to myself how much annoyed Sarah would be if she knew her keys were in my possession; but I was glad I had found them when, later in the day, after tea, Jane came to me and said Mrs. Saunders, the nurse, could not drink the draught ale from the cask, and wanted some bottled stout.

"And cook says, 'What shall we do?' miss. She's making such a fuss about it."

"Where is the bottled stout kept, Jane?" said I, thinking of my keys.

"It's either in the cellar, miss—but Mr. Rayner keeps the key of that—or else in Sarah's store cupboard."

"That is in the left wing, isn't it?"

"Yes, miss."

"Very well, Jane. I have found Sarah's keys; so I will look in there and see if I can find any," said I.

I did not much like taking this task upon myself; but it would not do to offend the nurse; and I thought it better to venture into Sarah's domain myself than to trust the duty to Jane.

"Oh, and, if you please, Miss Christie, could you get us out some candles and some moist sugar? They are in there I know, for Sarah went to Beaconsburgh for them yesterday."

I said I would; and, lighting a candle, I rather nervously pulled open the heavy door of the left wing and entered that mysterious part of the house sacred to Mrs. Rayner. Oh, how cold it was as the door closed behind me! I was growing nervous after the adventures I had had lately, and I did not like to hear the muffled thud of that door as it swung to after me. The store-room was the first door on the right, I knew; and I tremblingly tried the keys until I came to the one which opened it. I shivered. It was colder than ever in there, a great big bare room, with shelves and cupboards, and old hampers and boxes, and odds and ends of lumber. I could not help thinking how angry Sarah would be if she knew I was in the room, where no member of the household but herself ever ventured, and which had therefore grown into an importance it did not deserve, for it was a very ordinary apartment, and the cupboard I first opened, in search of candles and moist sugar, was a very ordinary cupboard, with the usual store of jams and pickle-jars and household stores of all kinds, except, of course, I thought angrily, as I shivered again with the cold, the candles and moist sugar of which I was in search. I opened another cupboard, I searched on the open shelves, but could not find either of the things I wanted.

At last I caught sight of a black bag lying on the floor; it looked like the very black bag Sarah had had in her hand when I saw her start for Beaconsburgh on the previous day; perhaps she had not taken her purchases out yet. I took it up; but suddenly my attention was diverted by the fact that in one of the boards of the floor on the spot where it had lain there was a tiny ring. If I had not had my attention very much on the alert in this unaccustomed place, it would have escaped my notice. As it was, I put my finger through it, and found that it raised a trap-door.

I raised it only a few inches, and shut it again directly—not that I had no curiosity about it, but that I had also some fear. An unsuspected trap-door in a house so full of surprises as the Alders had an interest of a rather appalling kind. At last I gathered up my courage, and little by little raised the door and put it right back, not without a horrid wonder whether there was any spring in it which would shut me down if I ventured on the ladder I saw below me.

The rush of cold air when the trap-door was wide open seemed to take my breath away. I held my candle over the opening, and saw that some three feet below the ladder was green and slimy, and that a foot below that there was water. Was it a well? Suddenly there flashed through my mind Sarah's words in her delirium of the night before—"The water's deep in the cellar." I looked about me for something to try the depth of the water with, for go down I must. I found a rod that looked like those used for the bottom of window-blinds, and cautiously, candle in hand, ventured on the ladder. It was quite firm.

As soon as I was on the bottom dry step, the fourth from the top, I saw that I was in a large cellar, on one side of which were empty wine-bins which looked rotten and green. Above the level of the water the walls were green too. There was a tiny grating high up, from which down to the water there was a long green streak, as if water continually ran down there. I heard the drip, drip at intervals while I stayed. The cellar ran to the left—under Mrs. Rayner's room, I suddenly thought with horror. Did she know that she might as well be living over a well? I tried the depth of the water; it was between three and four feet. Then I looked through the rungs of the ladder I was standing on, and thought I saw something behind it. Putting out my rod, I felt something soft which shook at the touch. I peered round the ladder and saw, on a big deal table the top of which had been raised to about eight or ten inches above the water's level, the little brown portmanteau I had seen Tom Parkes carry across the lawn, the same that I had afterwards discovered inside the back-door. And I remembered now where I had seen it before—stowed away at the bottom of a cupboard in the room I had occupied at Denham Court. I knew it by an old Italian luggage-label, "Torino," which I had noticed then.

It was within arm's reach through the rungs of the ladder. With trembling fingers I opened it—for it was not even fastened—and, to my horror, drew out from a confusion of glittering things with which it was half filled a serpent bracelet I had seen Lady Mills wear. I put it back, closed the portmanteau with difficulty, and clung to the ladder, overwhelmed by my discovery.

Again my brain seemed to whirl round, as it had done on the previous night when Sarah had been on the point of revealing James Woodfall's other name. My candle slipped from my fingers, fell with a hiss and a splash into the water below, and I was in darkness.

CHAPTER XXIV

I gave one cry as my candle fell, and then, instinctively shutting my eyes, as if to hide from myself the dreadful fact that I was in darkness, I felt my way up the ladder out of that dreadful cellar into the store-room above. It was seven o'clock, and only just enough light came through the one little grated window high up in the wall for me to see that there was a window there. But, once on the store-room floor, I crawled cautiously round the square hole I had come up through until I came to the door, which I shut down with a strong sense of relief. Then I groped about, stumbling over hampers and boxes now and then, and scarcely able to repress a cry at each fresh obstruction, until I came at last to the door. I had left it unlocked; and the moment after I touched the handle I was on the other side. Luckily I had slipped the keys into my pocket at first sight of the black bag; and, after long but impatient fumbling, I managed in the dark to fit in the right one and to turn the lock securely. Then I groped my way along the passage; and I never in all my life felt such a thrill of heart-felt thankfulness as I did when the great baize-covered door swung to behind me, and I found myself once more in the lighted hall.

I flung myself into a chair, overwrought and exhausted by what I had suffered in the left wing, and it was not for some minutes that I noticed an envelope directed simply, in Mrs. Manners's handwriting, to "Miss Christie, The Alders," which lay on the table beside me. I tore it open, and, scarcely glancing at her kind little note saying she had received the enclosed when she called at the Beaconsburgh post-office that afternoon, pressed Laurence's letter to my lips again and again before I opened it. It said—

"Nice, Friday.

"My own sweet Violet,—I had hoped to find a letter from you waiting for me on my arrival here; but I know very well it is not your fault that I am disappointed, even if I do not hear from you for a whole week—for I will never doubt my darling again. I have had the battle with my mother prematurely, and gained the victory. I intended, as you know, to break my resolution to her gently; but she herself hurried the *dénouement*. We broke the journey at Paris, stopping there last night. As soon as we got there, I opened my writing-case and wrote a tiny note to my darling, just to tell you how I walked up and down the deck of the steamer and sat in a railway-carriage, thinking of you and the last look I had into your beautiful loving gray eyes in the drive on Tuesday night—such a long time ago it seems! I left the room for a minute to order something to eat, with my letter closed up and directed to you on the table, ready to be enclosed to Mrs. Manners. When I came back, I found my mother there; she had torn open my letter and was reading it. Then we had a scene. I asked for my letter, and she tore it up and flung it into the fireplace, with some words about you that sent my forbearance to the winds, and I told her she was speaking about my future wife.

" 'Your future wife,' answered she, drawing herself up to her full height and rolling out her voice in a way that always reduces my father to nothingness, 'is Miss Langham of Greytowers.'

" 'You have been misinformed, mother. In such a matter it is always best to get your information at first hand. Your future daughter-in-law is Miss Violet Christie, the most beautiful girl in Norfolk or out of it. And as for Miss Langham, if you are so bent upon having her for a daughter-in-law, and she doesn't mind waiting, you can save her up for Jack.'

"I expected a lot more nonsense; but she was so much taken by surprise that that speech broke the back of the difficulty; and now, though she receives all my attentions frigidly and we are getting along very uncomfortably, she knows her control over her eldest son is at an end. I only wish, my darling, that my promise to my father had not prevented my telling her this while we were still in England, for I begin to fancy this journey 'for her health' was nothing but a trick—a plot, for there were two in it—for getting me away from you. However, I suppose I must live through the two months now somehow, as I promised her. She will keep me to that.

"But I am in a fever of anxiety about you. I will not distress you by a lot of vague suspicions that are rising in my mind to torture me; but I beg of you, my beautiful gentle love, to let me know every little event that happens at the Alders. I pray Heaven you may have very little to tell. And now I entreat you to comply with this my earnest, solemn request. Don't trust your letters to any one to post—don't even post them yourself—but give them to my youngest sister, to send on to me. She teaches in the Sunday-school. Get Mrs. Manners to send you up to the Hall on some pretext on Sunday; get Maud alone, and you will find she will do what you ask. Tell her to remember her last promise to me in the conservatory, and I'll remember mine.

"Keep this letter where no one can get at it—not in a desk—if you don't tear it up. I feel already such a hunger for a sight of your sweet face—I can't think of the touch of your little clinging hands about my throat without the tears rising to my eyes. I think I must jump into the sea if I cannot find some means of getting back to you sooner. Good-by; Heaven bless you! Write to me; don't forget. Keep safe and well, till you are once again in the arms of

"Yours devotedly for ever and ever,

"Laurence."

It was new life to me, it was heart-felt unutterable joy, to read this and put my cheek against the signature, to tuck it inside my gown and feel that I was in possession of the most precious treasure the whole world could produce, the first real long letter from the man I loved.

I went into the dining-room, took it out again, and began kissing each line in turn, I was so silly with happiness. I had got to the middle of the second page in this fashion, when the iron bar which fastened the shutters suddenly fell down and swung backwards and forwards almost without noise. I thrust my letter hastily back into my gown and stared at the shutters, too much startled to think what could be the reason of this, when one of them slid softly back, and a man was in the room before I could get to the door. With a cry of relief, I sprang towards him.

"Oh, Mr. Rayner, how you frightened me! I thought you were a burglar."

"My poor dear little girl, I often come in this way to save kicking my heels at the door; but I wouldn't have done it, frightening you out of your wits, if I had known you were in here. I thought everybody would be occupied with the two invalids. And how are you, little woman?"

I was so delighted to see him back once more, to feel that at last there was some one to look up to and trust in the house again, that I laughed and cried together as he shook my hands and patted my shoulder, and told me that it would never do to leave me at the Alders in his absence again; he should have to take me with him. I laughed.

"Why, I am too useful here, Mr. Rayner! I don't know what they would have done without me, with first Haidee ill, and then Sarah. You see, as Mrs. Rayner is never well enough to give any directions, I was obliged to take a good deal upon myself; and I hope you won't be angry when you hear all I've done."

"No, my child, I am sure I shall not," said he, helping himself to some cold beef on the sideboard—there was no regular supper at the Alders, but there were always meat and biscuits on the sideboard after tea for those who cared for them. "How is Mrs. Rayner?"

I told him that she was no better and no worse, and that she had moved to-day into the front spare-room.

"To-day?"

"Yes. She was so reluctant to leave her own room that I took the liberty of telling Sarah I would answer to you for delaying the change this one day. Was it too forward of me?" I asked timidly.

"No," said he very kindly, drawing me into a chair beside him at the table; "I give you full permission to use my authority in any way you think proper."

"Thank you, Mr. Rayner. And, oh, I don't know what you will say, but I made Sarah take Haidee's cot up to my room! The dressing-room in the left wing is so very cold. And then I sent for Doctor Lowe. Was that right? I had heard he was the best doctor in Beaconsburgh."

I asked this rather nervously, for I knew Mr. Rayner disliked Doctor Lowe. But he was in too good a humor to find fault with anything.

"All that you have done is perfectly right, and always will be, in my eyes; so you need never fear what I may say to you, child. Have you any more news? I want to hear all about Sarah's accident, and whether you were very much alarmed when you heard about the robbery at Denham Court."

"I have a lot to tell you," I said hesitatingly; "but I won't tell you any of it to-night, Mr. Rayner, because it is all bad, miserable news, and I won't spoil your first evening. It is bad enough to come back to a house as full of invalids as a hospital. But it will all come right again now you are back."

Mr. Rayner laughed, and seemed much pleased. He put his hand on mine, which was lying on the table, and looked into my face very kindly indeed.

"Do you think so, my child? Are you so glad to see me again?"

"Yes, indeed I am. You can't think how dull the place is when you are away. There is nobody to talk or laugh, and one creeps about the house as if one were in a Trappist monastery, and didn't dare to break the sacred silence."

"Thanks, my child; that is the very prettiest welcome home I have had for—years," said he, with much feeling in his voice.

And he kept me a long time chatting to him and listening to his account of what he had seen in London, until at last I grew very sleepy while he finished the story of his adventures; and I said I must really go to bed, or I should never be able to get up in time for breakfast. As it was, the clock struck eleven before I went upstairs.

The next morning at breakfast the talk was chiefly about the robbery at Denham Court. Mr. Rayner had read the accounts of it in the newspapers, besides the bare mention of it I had made in my letter to him; but now he wanted to hear all we had heard, and whether we were very much alarmed by it. Mrs. Rayner said very little, as usual; and I only told him Mr. Carruthers's story, reserving the suspicious things I had seen for when I should be able to talk to him alone. The opportunity soon came.

I went into the schoolroom after breakfast, thinking I would employ the hour and a half there was to spare before church-time in just beginning my letter to Laurence. But I had not got beyond "My own dearest Lau—" when Mr. Rayner came in and smiled in a mischievous manner that brought the color into my cheeks when he saw what I was doing. I put away my letter at once, so I do not know how he guessed to whom I was writing.

"Am I disturbing you?" said he.

"Oh, no! I was only writing a note to pass away the time."

"Well, and now for all the 'bad, miserable news' which was too overwhelming for me to hear about last night."

"Oh, Mr. Rayner, I don't know where to begin, and it seems ungenerous to tell it you now, as the person it concerns most is ill and unable to answer for herself!"

"Well, trust to my generosity, child," said he gravely. "I suppose you mean Sarah. Has she been annoying you again?"

"Oh, yes! But that is not the worst. If it had been only that, I would not have told you anything about it until she was well enough to defend herself. Indeed I am not so inhuman as to have any vindictive feeling against the poor woman now, when her very life is in danger. But I must tell you this, because I know something ought to be done, and you will know what it is."

"Tell me first how she has annoyed you, and—how the accident happened."

"She stopped a letter of mine by running after the postman and getting it out of the bag by some excuse or other."

"When was that?"

"On Wednesday."

"That is the most unwarrantable thing I ever heard of. I knew the woman was prejudiced against you; but one has to forgive old servants a good many things, and I never guessed she would dare so much as that."

"Oh, don't be so angry with her, or I shall never dare to tell you the rest, Mr. Rayner!"

And it required several questions and guesses on his part to draw out from me the account of the accident to Sarah, and the inevitable suspicions as to how it came about. Mr. Rayner turned quite pale when I came to my slipping on the stairs and catching my foot in the string, and he looked up and out of the window from under his frowning brows with an expression of hard fury that made me instinctively move away from him on my chair, it was so terrible, so merciless. And I had still so much that I must tell him! It was with averted head that I whispered all the suspicious things I had seen and heard connecting Sarah and Tom Parkes with the Denham Court burglary—my view of Tom carrying something across the lawn; his returning with Sarah; the fact of two men in a cart having been seen outside—I did not say by whom, but I fancy Mr. Rayner guessed; my seeing the brown portmanteau inside the back-door; and lastly my discovery of the portmanteau in the cellar under the store-room, and my recognition of it and of the bracelet I took out of it at haphazard as having both come from Denham Court.

Mr. Rayner listened with the deepest interest, but with some incredulity.

"My dear child, it is impossible—at least I hope from my soul it may turn out to be so! Poor old Sarah is, I acknowledge, the worst-tempered and most vindictive woman alive. But the accomplice of thieves! I cannot believe it." He got up and walked about the room, questioned me again closely, and then remained for a few minutes in deep thought. "She would never dare! Sarah is afraid of me, and to bring stolen goods into my house would be a greater liberty than even an old servant would take, I think."

"Ah, but you were away, Mr. Rayner! She may have reckoned upon getting the things out of the house before your return," I suggested.

"And Tom Parkes, too, a fellow I have a great liking for, and whom I have trusted with money too over and over again," he went on to himself, scarcely noticing my interruption.

I wondered Mr. Rayner did not ask me for the store-room keys and go himself to prove at least one part of my story; but I did not like to suggest it, half fearing, coward that I was, that he would ask me to go with him to that dreadful cellar.

"Don't say a word about this to any one, child," said he at last. "I must sift the matter to the very bottom. It is possible that they may both have been cheated by some clever knave into assisting him innocently. But didn't you say you saw Tom Parkes carrying what you took for the portmanteau on Tuesday night?"

"Yes, Mr. Rayner."

"But the burglary was on Wednesday! No, no; you may depend there will be some explanation of the matter as soon as Sarah is able to give an account of herself. In the mean time I will make inquiries, and I will set your mind at rest as soon as possible." He remained silent again for a little while, then shook his head, as if to dismiss all disagreeable thoughts, and said, in his usual bright tone, "And now I have a little bit of news for you, which I hope you will think neither bad nor miserable. How would you like to leave the Alders for a short time, and spend a couple of weeks on the borders of the Mediterranean?"

I looked up at him in bewilderment, which amused him.

"You look at me as if you thought me a magician who could transport you against your will to the uttermost parts of the earth by a wave of my wand. This is how it is. I have to see one of Mrs. Rayner's trustees on important business at once. He is staying at Monaco, which is, as you know, not far from Nice, where, I learnt by a letter from Mrs. Reade the other day, she and her son are staying. But I dare say that is stale news to you, and anyhow it is a matter of no consequence."

This was said so mischievously that I could not help growing very red indeed and being thankful when he went on—

"Having to go there myself, I thought the change might do my wife good; and this morning I tried every inducement to persuade her to go, but in vain, as I expected. But for Haidee some change is absolutely necessary, as the Doctor told you. And, as I cannot look after the child entirely by myself, I pondered as to who could do it for me, and I decided upon you."

"Oh, but," I began, the impossibility of my travelling alone over Europe with Mr. Rayner and Haidee being clear even to my not very wise brain.

"Now listen, and hear how cleverly I have managed it. Haidee goes to look after her papa, Miss Christie goes to look after Haidee, Mrs. Christie goes to look after Miss Christie."

"My mother!" I exclaimed.

"Yes. I went to see her yesterday, and proposed the plan to her, not forgetting to put in a word about our friends at Nice. She was delighted, and asked your uncle's consent at once. We have already settled that she is to meet us at Liverpool Street on our arrival in town next Friday morning."

"Next Friday!" said I, utterly bewildered. "And leave Mrs. Rayner all alone here?"

"Unless you can persuade her to go with us. You can wheedle a bird off a bough, and I really believe you have more influence with her than I have."

Indeed it seemed so; for I had often wondered how she could be so obstinate with him, when to me she always seemed as weak as a reed.

"There, child," said Mr. Rayner, taking a letter from his pocket and putting it into my hands. "You don't seem able to take it all in. Read that."

It was a letter in my mother's handwriting. I opened it, still utterly bewildered. It said—

> "My darling Violet,—Your kind friend Mr. Rayner is waiting; so I can pen you only these few lines; and I don't know how to express my feelings at his generous offer. He says I am to write to you and persuade you to go; but I do not think you will need much persuasion. He has directed me to provide an outfit for you at his expense, and bring it with me to Liverpool Street Station, where I am to meet you on Friday, though I don't like starting on a journey on a Friday. Heaven be praised for sending us such kind friends! I have no time for more, as Mr. Rayner is waiting. With best love from your uncle and cousins, in the fond hope of seeing you very soon,
>
> "Your affectionate mother, Amy Christie."

My dear mother! It was just like her to see nothing so very extraordinary in this offer, to take it as a matter of course, and thank Heaven for it in the most simple-minded way, while it troubled me somewhat still. I read the letter twice through, and then tried deprecatingly to thank him for the outfit he had got her to provide.

"Oh, does she mention that? I told her not to do so," said he, laughing.

"You don't know my mother. When she has anything to tell, she can't resist telling it. This letter is just like her. But she has done two things she never in all her life did before—dated her letter and put no postscript."

CHAPTER XXV

As soon as we came out of church that morning, I found an opportunity of speaking to Mrs. Manners, and asked her shyly if she could give me any message to take that afternoon to Miss Maud Reade at the Hall.

"Laurence told me to ask you," I whispered timidly; "it is because he particularly wants my next letter to be enclosed in hers. He didn't say why; but he is very emphatic about it."

"Dear, dear," said kind Mrs. Manners anxiously, "it is a pity young people cannot get on without so many subterfuges! I don't know whether Mr. Manners would approve. But there—I promised Laurence I would help you—and there is no harm in it—and so I will. Come up to the Vicarage after afternoon service, and I'll give you a packet of tracts for her."

I thanked her; but she had already turned to reproach a deaf old woman bent with rheumatism for not coming to church oftener, and to promise to send her some beef-tea jelly next day. I made my way to where Mr. and Mrs. Rayner were standing, the former advising old Mr. Reade to send his plate, which was known to be valuable, to the bank at Beaconsburgh for safety.

"Jewel-robberies are epidemic, you know, and I dare say we haven't seen the last of this series yet," said he. "There was Lord Dalston's, and now Sir Jonas's; but they never stop at two. You remember some years ago, when there were five big robberies within six weeks? I shouldn't wonder if the same sort of thing occurred again."

"They wouldn't try for my little store; it wouldn't be worth their while," said Mr. Reade, with undisturbed good-humor. "If Laurence were at home, perhaps I'd get him to send the lot off; but I can't see after things myself; and, if I put 'em all in a cart and packed 'em off to Beaconsburgh, the chances are they would all get tilted into a ditch. So they must take their chance in the old chest at home. I've given Williamson a blunderbuss—but I think it frightens him more than it would a thief—and I sleep with a revolver at my bedside; and a man can't do more."

"Don't you think the thieves will be caught, Mr. Rayner?" asked Gregson, the village carpenter, timidly. It was rumored that he had fifteen pounds and a pair of silver muffineers hidden away somewhere; and he turned to Mr. Rayner, who always took the lead naturally in any discussion, with much anxiety.

"Not in the least likely," answered Mr. Rayner decisively. "Why should they be? They might be if they had their equals in wits pitted against them; but they haven't. The ordinary detective has the common defect of vulgar minds, want of resource. The thief, if he is clever enough to be a successful jewel-robber, has the abilities of a general. The bolder he is, the more certain he is of success. The detective, in spite of repeated failures, believes himself infallible. If I were a thief, I should commit robberies as nearly as possible under the detective's nose. That astute being would never suspect the man who braved him to his face."

"Ah, it's very fine to talk," said one acute villager, who thought Mr. Rayner was really going too far; "but, when it came to the detective being there, you'd be about as bold as the rest of us, I'm thinking."

Mr. Rayner laughed good-humoredly enough, and said perhaps he was right; and I heard the acute villager bragging of having put down Mr. Rayner, who, he said, was a bit bumptious for just a gentleman-fiddler, and wasn't so much cleverer than the rest of 'em, he guessed, for all his talk.

At dinner Mr. Rayner tried again to induce his wife to go to Monaco, and encouraged me to join my persuasions to his, which I did most heartily. But to all we said she only replied steadily and coldly that she disliked travelling, did not feel well enough to undertake a journey, and preferred remaining at the Alders. She added, in the same parrot-like tone, that she thought the change would do me and Haidee good, and that it was very kind of my mother to go.

After dinner I ran upstairs to my room, and, opening the door softly, found Haidee dozing by the fire. So I sat down to write my scarcely-begun letter to Laurence.

I first told him how happy his letter had made me, and then, obeying his injunction to tell him everything that happened at the Alders, I gave him a full account of the way Sarah had prevented our meeting on Wednesday evening, and of her stealing my letter out of the bag on Thursday, of Mr. Carruthers's visit to tell me of the robbery at Denham Court, of the accident to Sarah on Friday night, of her ravings about a bad man named James Woodfall, of Mr. Rayner's return, and of his intention to take Haidee, my mother, and me to Monaco in a few days.

The hope of seeing Laurence again soon had by this time swallowed up every other thought concerning the journey; and I was eager for Friday to come, that we might start.

Then I told him that I had some very grave suspicions about the robbery, that I had told them to Mr. Rayner, who did not think so seriously of them as I did, but that he said I ought not to repeat them to anybody until he had thoroughly sifted the matter, and I had promised not to do so.

"So now you are not to be anxious about my safety any more, my dearest Laurence. For Sarah, the only person who wished me harm, is too ill to move, and is in danger, poor woman, of losing, if not her life, at least her reason, the Doctor says. And Mr. Rayner has promised not to go away again for more than a day at a time, either on business or for pleasure. There seems a curious fatality about his absences, for both these dreadful robberies that have frightened everybody so much lately, the one at Lord Dalston's and the one at Denham Court, have happened while he was away, with no man in the house to protect us against burglars or our fears of them. I think your prejudice against Mr. Rayner ought to break down now that through him we are to meet each other so soon; for when we are at Monaco you will come over and see us, won't you? My mother is very anxious to make your acquaintance, though she does not know of our engagement, for I dare not tell her any secrets. I think Mr. Rayner must have guessed it though, for he says little things to tease me and make me blush. And you see he does not try to prejudice me against you, as you thought he would. But he might try, and everybody else in the world might try, for years and years, but they would never succeed in changing the heart of your own ever loving

"Violet."

I had said at dinner that day, in answer to Mr. Rayner's inquiries, that I was not going to afternoon service, but I had not mentioned that I was going to the Vicarage. I felt sure that I should blush if I did, and then Mr. Rayner would guess my visit had something to do with Laurence; and I did not want to be teased any more. So, when five o'clock came, and I knew that service must be over, I put on my outdoor things, kissed Haidee, who was now awake, and slipped softly downstairs and out by the schoolroom window. I was not afraid of leaving that unfastened, now that Mr. Rayner had come back again.

Mrs. Manners met me in the hall of the Vicarage, took me into the drawing-room, and gave me a packet of tracts, two or three of which had names lightly pencilled on them, as specially suitable to certain of the parishioners, as, "The Drunkard's Warning"—Mrs. Nabbitts; "The Cost of a Ribbon"—Lizzie Mojer. These I was to deliver to Miss Maud Reade for distribution in her district this week.

"Tell her to notice that I have marked some specially," said Mrs. Manners, as she gave them to me; and I rather wondered how the persons they were directed to would take the attention.

I thought that, in spite of her hatred of subterfuge, Mrs. Manners seemed to enjoy the little mystery which hung over my engagement. She kissed me very kindly as she sent me off, and told me I was to let her know when Sarah was well enough to be read to, and she would send something to be read which might do her good. I promised that I would; but I hope it was not impious of me to think, as I could not help thinking, that she was too wicked for any of Mrs. Manners's good books to have much effect upon her.

I went through the side-gate of the Vicarage garden, where I had run against Laurence on that happy evening which seemed so long ago, although in truth only eight days had passed since then, and my heart beat fast, and I walked slowly, for it seemed to me that Laurence must be coming round the corner again to meet me; but of course he did not; and I quickened my pace as I crossed the park to the Hall.

The mist was growing very thick, although it was only a little past five; and I knew I must make haste back, or I might risk losing my way, short as the distance was between the Hall and the Alders.

I rang the bell, and asked for Miss Maud Reade; and the servant who opened the door, and who, I felt sure, was the Williamson who was afraid of the blunderbuss, showed me into the drawing-room. There was no one there, for they were all at tea.

This was my first entrance into Laurence's home; and I was so much agitated between pleasure at being in the house he lived in and shame at feeling that by some of the inhabitants at least, if they knew all, I should be looked upon as an unwelcome intruder, that I sank into a chair and buried my face in my hands. It was a very comforting thought, though, that I was sitting on a chair that Laurence must certainly have sat upon; and then I wondered which was his favorite, and tried one that I thought likely, to see if any instinct would tell me if I were right. I had not made up my mind on that point when the door opened and Miss Maud Reade came in.

She was a girl of about sixteen, with a weak but not disagreeable face; and she shook hands with me rather timidly, but not unkindly.

"Mrs. Manners asked me to bring you these tracts for your district, Miss Reade. She has marked some for people she thinks them specially suitable for," said I, giving her the packet.

"Thank you; it is very kind of you to take so much trouble," said she.

"Oh, it is no trouble at all!" I answered.

There was a pause of rather awkward constraint; and then I said in a whisper—

"Laurence—your brother—told me to come and see you, and to ask you to put a—a letter from me to him inside yours. He said I was to tell you to remember your promise, and he would remember his; he underlined that."

Miss Reade's constraint broke up at once, and she grew as much excited and as mysterious as I.

"Did he? Then he hasn't forgotten!" she said, in a hissing whisper. "I suppose you know what it is; it's about getting Mr. Reynolds to come here next winter. Oh, do keep him up to it! I'll do anything in the world for you— that won't get me into trouble with mamma or Alice—if you will!"

"I will. I'll remind him again in my next letter—or when I see him. I'll say, 'Don't forget to invite Mr. Reynolds in the winter.' Will that do?"

"Oh, yes, that will do beautifully! But it is a long time to wait," sighed the girl.

I thought she was much too young to be in love, when she was still in short frocks and wore her hair in a pigtail; but I was obliged to help her, in return for the service I wanted her to do me.

"I have brought my letter," said I mysteriously. "Shall you be writing soon?"

"I have a letter ready now, and I will put yours inside and give it to a gentleman who is here, and who is going back to London directly after tea, and I will ask him to post it at once."

"Oh, thank you!" said I; and tremblingly, with fear lest the dreaded Alice should get hold of it, I put my letter into her hands, and soon afterwards left the house.

The fog was already so much thicker that I wondered whether the gentleman with our letter would be able to find his way back to London that night, and even whether I could find mine back to the Alders. I must be sure to keep to the drive in crossing the park. But, before I got to that,

I lost myself among the garden-paths, and walked into a flower-bed; and I began to think I should have to find my way back to the door and ask ignominiously to be led to the gate, when I heard voices on my left; and I made my way recklessly in their direction across grass, flower-beds, and everything. I could not see the speakers yet, for there was a hedge or something between us; but I could distinguish that they were the voices of a young man and a young woman of the lower class. Thinking one of them at least must be a servant at the Hall, and able to direct me, I was just going to speak through the hedge, when a few words in the man's voice stopped me.

"I have had enough of you Norfolk girls; you are too stand-off for me."

It was the voice of Tom Parkes.

"Yes, to such weather-cocks as you," answered the girl, with rough coquetry. "Why, you were keeping company with that ugly Sarah at Mr. Rayner's; and, now she is ill, you want to take up with me. Oh, a fine sweetheart you'd make!"

But she was not as obdurate as these words promised. It seemed to me, with my suspicions concerning Tom already strong, that in the talk which followed he managed with very little difficulty to find out a good deal about the ways of the household, and also that he spoke as if he had learnt from her a good deal already. Presently I heard the sound of a kiss, and he promised to come and see her again on Wednesday; and then they went away; while I, seized by a sudden inspiration, found my way not to the park, but back to the house, which was less difficult.

I asked for Miss Maud Reade again; and this time she rushed out of the drawing-room and met me in the hall as soon as I was announced, and whispered—

"They are all in there. Come into the library."

"May I have my letter back, just to put in something I have forgotten?" said I.

"Oh, yes; here it is!"—and she drew it from her pocket. "Write it here. I will give you a pen. Why, how white you look! Has anything happened?"

"Oh, no, no, nothing, thank you!"

I wrote on a half-sheet of paper, which I carefully folded inside my letter, these words—

> "A man who was at Denham Court, and about whom I have
> strong suspicions, is hanging about the Hall now. He is
> coming here again on Wednesday night."

I put my letter into a fresh envelope, and put the torn one into my pocket that it might not be seen about; then I begged Miss Reade earnestly to send the letter off at once, as there was something in it of the utmost importance; and she whispered again, "Remember—Mr. Reynolds in the winter!" and, having this time got Williamson to show me as far as the beginning of the drive across the park, I made my way in safety, but slowly and with much difficulty, back to the Alders.

I slipped through the schoolroom window, which I had left unfastened; and, as soon as I was inside, I heard Mr. Rayner's study door open, and his voice and that of Tom Parkes in the passage leading from the hall. Mr. Rayner was speaking in his usual kind and friendly way to him, and I thought to myself that it would be useless for me to tell him what I had just heard, which, after all, was nothing in itself, and only became important in connection with the suspicions I already had of the man—suspicions which Mr. Rayner himself refused to share. And, when Tom Parkes had said, "Well, good-night, sir," and gone in the direction of the servants' hall, and Mr. Rayner had returned to his study, I ran upstairs and prepared for tea, at which meal I felt rather guilty, but said nothing of my expedition or its results.

That evening Mr. Rayner kept me in the drawing-room accompanying his violin, and talking, until after Mrs. Rayner had gone up to the room she now used on the upper floor. He described to me the beauties of the Mediterranean shore, and said that I should be happier there than I had ever been in my life—which I could easily believe when I thought how near I should be to Laurence. He asked me if I was not anxious to see the pretty dresses my mother had been commissioned to get for me, and told me I should look like a little princess if I were good and did just what I was told.

"There is no fear of my not doing that, Mr. Rayner," said I, smiling. "But you must not give me too handsome dresses, or I shall not feel at home in them."

"You will soon get used to them," said he, with a curiously sharp smile. "There is nothing that women get used to sooner than fine clothes and beautiful jewels, and pretty idleness and—kisses."

Certainly I liked Laurence's kisses; but the tone in which Mr. Rayner said this grated upon me, and brought the hot blood to my cheeks uncomfortably. He saw the effect his words had upon me, and he jumped up and came towards where I was standing ready to light my candle.

"You look hurt, my child, but you have no reason for it. Don't you know that all those things are the lawful right of pretty women?"

"Then it is a right a good many of them are kept out of all their lives, Mr. Rayner," said I, smiling.

"Only the silly ones," he returned, in a tone I did not understand. "Well, I will explain all that to you on our journey to Monaco."

He looked very much excited, as he often did after an evening spent with his violin; and his blue eyes, in which one seemed to see the very soul of music, flashed and sparkled as he held my hand.

"Don't be surprised at what I have said to you this evening. You have brought me luck, and you shall share it. This journey shall take you to the arms of a lover who will give you all the things I spoke of and more—a thousand times more!"

That was true indeed, I thought to myself (but did he mean what I meant?) as I tore myself, laughing and blushing, away and ran upstairs. There was more delight in the mere fact that Laurence preferred me to any other woman in the world than in all the beautiful gowns and jewels that ever princess wore. And I went to sleep that night with my hands under my pillow clasping his letter.

Haidee left my room next day for the first time, and spent the afternoon by the dining-room fire. Soon after dinner Mr. Rayner came in with his riding-boots on, and asked with a smile if I had not a letter to send to the post. He was going to ride to Beaconsburgh, and, if I gave it to him, it would go a post earlier than if I put it into the bag for the postman to fetch.

"No, I have no letter, thank you, Mr. Rayner," said I, with a blush.

"Not a line for—Nice, to tell—some one you are coming?" said he archly.

"No," answered I, shaking my head.

"You posted that one yesterday yourself, didn't you, Miss Christie?" whispered little Haidee, putting her arms round my neck.

Mr. Rayner heard the whisper.

"Yesterday?" asked he quickly.

"I—I gave a—a note to Miss Reade to put with hers," said I.

A curious change passed over Mr. Rayner. The smile remained on his face, which had however in one second turned ashy white. He said, "All right, my dear," in his usual voice, except that I fancied there was a sort of hard ring in it, and left the room.

"Was it naughty of me to say?" said Haidee, feeling that something was wrong.

"Oh, no, my darling!" I answered.

I too was afraid I had displeased Mr. Rayner by going to the Hall, without saying anything about it to any one, in what must seem a sly, underhand manner; and I wished Laurence had not enjoined me to send my letter in that way.

That evening, at tea-time, Mr. Rayner announced that he had found a letter waiting for him at the Beaconsburgh post-office which obliged him to go to Monaco a day sooner.

So Haidee and I must be prepared to start on Thursday morning.

CHAPTER XXVI

On Tuesday afternoon, while I was helping Haidee to dress her doll in the dining-room, there was a ring at the front-door bell, and shortly afterwards Jane came in, looking rather frightened, saying a gentleman was in the hall asking for Sarah.

"And I've told him she is ill, Miss Christie; but he won't believe me; and he won't go away, and Mr. Rayner is out; and please will you speak to him?"

I got up, and, following her into the hall, found, not a gentleman, but a respectably-dressed man, who very civilly apologized for disturbing me.

"I beg your pardon, ma'am; but are you Miss Rayner?"

"Oh, no!"

"Mrs. Rayner?"

"No. Mrs. Rayner is an invalid, and I am afraid you cannot see her. I am the governess. If you have any message for Mr. Rayner, I will give it to him; or, if you like, you can write him a note, and it shall be given him when he returns."

"Thank you, miss."

Still he hesitated.

"Would you like to wait for Mr. Rayner? He will be back in about an hour."

"Thank you. Could I speak to you in private for a few minutes, miss?"

"Oh, yes, certainly! Will you come in here?" — and I opened the door of the schoolroom.

He followed me in and shut it carefully.

"I am the brother of Sarah Gooch, miss, who is a servant here."

I nodded assent.

"I've been abroad and worked myself into a good position, and now I want my sister to leave service. And I don't want the other servants to know

I'm her brother. It may be pride; but perhaps you'll excuse it, miss. Would you mind sending for her without saying it's her brother wants her?"

How could I break the fact of her illness to the poor man?

"Oh, please be prepared for bad news! I'm so sorry!" said I gently. "She is ill—very ill."

To my surprise, he looked more incredulous than unhappy. He said very suddenly—

"She was quite well last Friday afternoon."

"Yes—an accident happened to her on Friday night. She fell down a flight of stairs and injured herself severely. If you will only wait until Mr. Rayner comes, he will speak to you. Sarah is a very old servant in this family, and much respected, and she has every possible care, I assure you."

But he still seemed more curious than anxious about her, I thought.

"She has been in the family a long time then? Excuse me, miss, but I've been away so long that she is almost like a stranger to me, and I had great difficulty in finding her out. But I'm very glad to hear she is thought so well of."

"Oh, yes! Mr. Rayner has the greatest confidence in her."

I did not want to say anything disagreeable about the woman now that she was ill, especially to her brother, whose affection did not seem very warm as it was.

"Ah, that's the great thing! We've always been a family to hold our heads high, and I couldn't hear anything to please me more about her. But I expect it's little use my coming home and wanting her to keep house for me. She was a good-looking girl, and I've no doubt she's looking forward to marrying on her savings, and then we shall be just as far apart as ever. Do you know, miss—if it's not troubling you too much, and you won't take it a liberty—if she's got a sweetheart?"

I hesitated. The man's cold curiosity seemed so unlike the warm interest of a brother that I began to wonder whether I was right in giving him the information he wanted. My doubts were so vague and his questions so very harmless, however, that, when he said—

"I beg your pardon, miss—of course it is not for a lady like you to interest yourself in the likes of us—"

I broke out—

"Oh, pray don't think that! Sarah has an admirer, I know—"

I stopped. I could not say anything reassuring about Tom Parkes.

"Ah! An honest hard-working fellow, I hope, who'll make her a good husband."

He was more interested now, and was looking at me very searchingly.

"I can't speak to a man's prejudice behind his back," said I slowly; "but—"

He was very much interested at last, and was waiting impatiently for my next words, when Mr. Rayner quietly entered the room. There had been no ring at the front door. He looked inquiringly at the man, whom I was just going to introduce as Sarah's brother, when the latter anticipated me by saying quietly—

"From Scotland Yard, sir."

"Scotland Yard?" echoed Mr. Rayner inquiringly. But the name did not seem new to him, as it did to me.

"Yes, sir; I've been sent after a woman named Sarah Gooch, from information received that she was in your service. Mr. Gervas Rayner I believe, sir?"

Why did he not own he was her brother? I thought to myself.

"Yes, that is my name. But what on earth do you want with my servant, Sarah Gooch?"

The man glanced at me. Mr. Rayner said—

"Go on. Never mind this lady; she is as much interested in the woman as I am. What do you want with my old servant Sarah?"

"Suspected of complicity in the Denham Court robbery, sir—some of the property traced to her."

I started violently. This man, then, was not Sarah's brother at all, but a detective who had been trying to extract information from me by a trick! Mr. Rayner stared full in his face for a few moments, as if unable to find words; then he exclaimed, in a low voice—

"Impossible!"

"Sorry to shake your trust in an old servant, sir; but proof is proof."

"But what proof have you?" asked Mr. Rayner earnestly.

"Last Friday afternoon, between half-past four and twenty minutes to five, your servant Sarah Gooch was seen to give the contents of a black bag to a man in Beaconsburgh. The fact excited no suspicion. The man took the next train to London, travelling second-class. But south of Colchester he was seized with a fit; he was taken out at the next station, the bag he had with him examined for his address, jewels found in it, and the police at Scotland Yard communicated with. The man escaped; but, on inquiries being made, witnesses were found to prove conclusively that the biscuit-tin which contained the jewel had been handed to him in a street in Beaconsburgh, on Friday afternoon, between half-past four and twenty minutes to five, by a woman who was identified as Sarah Gooch."

I remembered seeing Sarah pass through the plantation on Friday afternoon, on her way to Beaconsburgh, with the black bag. But I was too horror-stricken to speak, even if I had not been, now that the blow had fallen, as anxious to screen her as Mr. Rayner himself was to prove her innocence.

"But I cannot believe it!" said Mr. Rayner. "She is a rough, harsh woman; but I have always found her honest as the day."

"She may have been instigated," suggested the detective. "It's wonderful what things women will do for their lovers, and she had a lover—not of the best possible character."

Mr. Rayner gave a quick glance at me, and I felt guilty, for it was indeed I who had given this piece of information.

"Do you know his name?" asked Mr. Rayner.

"I am not in a position to state it yet; but we have our suspicions," said the man cautiously.

Mr. Rayner gave no sign of incredulity; but I knew his face well enough now to be able to tell that he did not believe him.

"The main point now is, having traced the jewels to the woman Sarah Gooch, to find out how they came into her possession. I must ask you to let me see the woman and question her. Taken by surprise, she may confess everything."

"You shall see her," said Mr. Rayner gravely, "and then judge for yourself whether she is in a state to answer questions. I will ask the nurse if you can see her now. Miss Christie, would you mind going up with me and watching in her place while Mrs. Saunders comes out to speak to me?"

We went up together, scarcely speaking a word; and I sent out the nurse to him and stood watching in her place. Sarah, looking more hideous than ever with the white bandage round her head and against her leather-colored face and black hair, was turning her head from side to side, and moaning and muttering feebly. The only words one could catch seemed to refer to the pain she was in. Then the door opened, the nurse re-entered, and the detective, with Mr. Rayner behind him, peeped in. A glance at the hollow face and dry lips of the sick woman might have satisfied him that her illness was no sham; but he watched her and listened to her mutterings for some minutes before he retired. I left the room as quickly as I could—the sight of the ghastly figure of the guilty woman sickened me.

"You see," Mr. Rayner was saying as I got outside, "she is quite unable at present to speak for herself. I hope, and indeed believe, that, when she can do so, she will be able to clear herself of anything worse than perhaps the innocent passing of the stolen goods from one rogue to another, without herself having the least idea of the crime she was being made to participate in. I will do all in my power to assist the course of justice. The doctor will be here in the morning, and he will tell you when she is likely to be able to give an account of herself. In the mean time you shall spend the night here. Miss Christie, will you kindly tell Mrs. Jennings to prepare the room next to mine and Mrs. Rayner's?"

The name "Mrs. Jennings" for the moment puzzled me; then I remembered it was that of the cook, and I wondered why he had not said Jane. His room and Mrs. Rayner's! Did Mr. Rayner then sleep in the house since his wife's change of apartment?

The cook grumbled a good deal when I gave her the order. What was the house being turned topsy-turvy for? Why had Mr. Rayner just sent Jane off to Wright's Farm to pay the corn-bill, to-day of all days, when there was a visitor and more to do? Telling her she might stop the night too, if the fog came on, as it was doing, when he might have known she wouldn't want telling twice when that hulking young Peter Wright was about the farm! She knew what it was; Jane would not be back till late to-morrow afternoon, if she was then, and—

And so the cook went on, until suddenly Mr. Rayner appeared upon the scene, and she broke off in her complaints, startled.

"I am afraid I have entailed a good deal of trouble upon you, cook, by thoughtlessly giving Jane permission to spend the night at the farm if the fog grew thick; so I have just asked Mrs. Saunders to take her upstairs duties till Jane comes back, in return for which you will be kind enough to watch by Sarah during her unavoidable absences."

This silenced the cook at once. It was a just punishment for her grumbling, for there was no duty she would not rather have undertaken than that of watching by the unconscious Sarah even in her quiet moments. She said to me afterwards that the nurse was very good; directly Sarah began to talk or grow excited, Mrs. Saunders always managed to hear, and came in to relieve her from the unpleasant task of listening to the sick woman's ravings.

I left Mr. Rayner talking to the cook, and went back to Haidee in the dining-room. When tea-time came, Mr. Rayner entered with the detective, whom he now addressed as "Mr. Maynard," and treated as a distinguished guest. Mr. Maynard talked rather interestingly when his host drew him out, and was elaborately courteous to Mrs. Rayner, whose cold manner rather overawed him, and to me. He went to his room early, and, when Mrs. Rayner had gone to hers, I remained in the drawing-room putting the music in order, as Mr. Rayner had told me to do.

"This day's events have upset me more than you can imagine, child," said he, passing his hand through his hair wearily. "That vixen Sarah has always seemed honest—and yet I don't know what to believe."

"And, you know, the portmanteau I found in the cellar," I whispered timidly.

Mr. Rayner started.

"Good Heaven, I had forgotten that! Or rather I had dismissed it from my mind as a fancy brought about by the excitement of Sarah's accident, and hastily connected in your mind with your view of poor old Tom Parkes carrying a box across the lawn. Where are the store-room keys, child?" asked he excitedly. "We must go at once to the cellar, and— Heaven help us if what I took for your fancy should prove to be the truth!"

I tremblingly produced the keys, which I carried about with me; and, much against my will, I accompanied Mr. Rayner into the left wing. He took the keys from me; but he was so very excited that he could not find the right one to fit into the door, and I opened it for him. We crossed the store-room. There lay the black bag on one side of the trap-door, where I had put it down on catching sight of the little ring in the floor. I put my finger through this and raised it again, not without a shudder at the remembrance of my last visit, and Mr. Rayner went down hastily, while I held the candle for him to see by.

"No, my child, I see nothing," said he, as he peered about.

"Look through the ladder; it is behind there," said I.

Mr. Rayner looked through it, then looked round it, stretched his arm out, and again raised his face to mine, this time however with a look of unutterable relief.

"Thank Heaven, it was your fancy, child!" said he. "There is nothing there."

"Not a deal table?" I gasped.

"No—nothing but water."

"Perhaps the water has risen higher and covered it?"

"Come down yourself and see. Or are you afraid to come down again?"

"No, I am not afraid," said I uncertainly.

He came up and took the candle from me, while I descended. The water, I knew by the number of steps which were dry above it, was at the same level as before. I looked through the ladder and round it. Table and portmanteau had utterly disappeared. As I looked up suddenly, Mr. Rayner's face, distorted by the weird light thrown on it by the flickering candle, seemed to me to wear a mocking smile which made the handsome features hideous and alarming.

"Let me come up," said I sharply.

He held out his hand, and, when I, trembling and tottering, reached the top of the ladder, he flung his arm round me to support me. But I was so sick with the horror of finding my story—my true story—disproved, and with the fancy I had had on looking up at Mr. Rayner's face, that I slid from his arm, ran out of the store-room, along the passage and through the swing-door, and leaned against the hall-table to recover myself. Mr. Rayner was at my side in a few minutes, and, almost unconsciously, I let him lead me back into the drawing-room. He brought me some brandy-and-water and made me drink it, and bathed my forehead, and told me gently not to be frightened, for I should soon be out of this dreary place and among beautiful scenes where I should forget the gloom of this sepulchral, dead-alive house, which was turning my poor little brain.

"But indeed I did see the portmanteau the first time!" said I piteously.

"Yes, dear child, I know," said Mr. Rayner.

But I saw he did not believe me; and the tears began to roll down my cheeks.

"You must not cry, you must not cry! You will spoil your pretty face if you cry," said Mr. Rayner almost angrily.

I knew he hated the sight of anything ugly or distressing—it was part of an artist's nature, he said; so I forced back my tears as fast as I could, and tried to smile.

"There is my lovely girl again!" said he, stopping in front of me—he had walked up and down the room while I wept. "We will never mention Sarah's name again when once we are away from her, little one," said he. "But until we go, or until our respected friend Mr. Maynard goes, I am afraid she must still occupy a good deal of our thoughts. She will certainly not be able to submit to any cross-examination on his part to-morrow, or for a long time to come—if she ever is," said he gravely. "And in the mean time he will try to trump up a story and to criminate as many persons as he can, just to show his superiors that he has not wasted his time here. And certainly he will leave our poor Sarah without a rag of character."

"But, do you know, Mr. Rayner, I don't think Sarah has always been as nice a woman as you suppose," said I timidly. "From what I have heard her say, I think, when she was young, she must have had some horrid friends who made her do all sorts of wrong things; and that is why I cannot be as much surprised as you are at her doing wicked things now."

"Did you tell Mr. Maynard that?"

"No, I only answered his questions. He said he was her brother—and of course I did not want to make him doubt his own sister. But, Mr. Rayner, I want to ask you something. Have you ever heard of a James Woodfall?"

He was sitting by me on the sofa, with his head turned away. He did not answer my question at once. Then he said very quietly—

"Did Mr. Maynard ask you that?"

He turned slowly as he said so, until his eyes met mine.

"Oh, no! I heard Sarah say the name when she was delirious—the first night—Friday night," I whispered.

"Oh! Was he a friend of Sarah's?"

"Oh, yes! I think she must have been in love with him when she was young, and he must have been a very bad man who made her do anything he liked; and the most curious part of it is that she—she mixes his name up with the people she knows now," said I, lowering my voice still more.

"How?" asked Mr. Rayner. "Whose name does she mix his up with?"

"Why, with—with mine, Mr. Rayner!" said I, blushing uncomfortably at the very thought. "She kept saying in her ravings that this wicked forger—for she said he was a forger—James Woodfall, was in love with me and wanted to marry me, and that he wanted her to help to marry this common thief to me. Wasn't it dreadful to have to listen to that?" whispered I excitedly.

"Did she say James Woodfall was a common thief?"

"No, I gathered that from what she said. Did you ever hear of him, Mr. Rayner?"

"Yes, I have heard of him, and I believe he is alive now," said he.

"Then I believe that she is in love with him still, and that he is at the bottom of this dreadful robbery!" cried I, much excited. "Oh, Mr. Rayner, couldn't you find out from Sarah where he is now, while the detective is here, and get him caught?" I said breathlessly.

Mr. Rayner shook his head thoughtfully.

"I am afraid not, my dear child. If James Woodfall is the man I mean, he will never be taken alive," said he.

CHAPTER XXVII

Mr. Rayner slept that night in the dressing-room leading out of the large front room which his wife now occupied. I met him coming out of it as I went downstairs to breakfast the next morning. I spent the hours until dinner-time in my own room, packing and preparing for the journey the next day.

It was curious, I thought, that I had not heard again from my mother, who would naturally be overflowing with excitement about such a great event. I had written a long letter to her on Monday, and put it into the post-bag, with no misgivings as to its safety now that my enemy Sarah was ill. It was a very pleasant thing to think that I should soon be with my mother again, and that in a few days I should see Laurence; but there was a less bright view to be taken of the expedition, and from time to time, in the midst of my happy anticipation, it troubled me.

It seemed an unkind thing, in spite of her obstinate refusal to quit the Alders, to leave delicate Mrs. Rayner alone in this dreary place, the gloom and damp of which had evidently had much to do with the morbid state of mind she was in, with no companions, and no other inmates of the house, except a weird child who was not fond of her, two servants, a sick-nurse, and a delirious invalid. I had noticed faint signs of nervous agitation in her manner lately when the coming journey was alluded to, and I had caught her eyes fixed upon mine sometimes as if she had something to say to me which she could not bring herself to the point of uttering; and the strange perversity of the poor lady, who seemed now mad, now sane, puzzled me more and more.

The Doctor, for whose verdict Mr. Maynard was waiting, did not come that day until just before dinner; and then his report was as gloomy as possible. He did not think it probable that Sarah would ever recover her reason, and the only change she was likely to get from her sick-room was to the county lunatic asylum. On hearing this, the detective, who had spent the morning in making inquiries, in searching Sarah's boxes, and even her room, at Mr. Rayner's suggestion, in examining every corner of the housekeeper's room in which she generally sat, and of the store-cupboard under the stairs, which was also under her charge—but I do not think he went into the left wing, where the large store-room was—having failed to make any discovery, wished to return to town that afternoon; but Mr. Rayner pressed him to stay, saying that he would drive him over to Denham village that afternoon, and, in the character of a friend of his, come down from town for a few days, he could examine the scene of the robbery and make inquiries without any one's suspecting who he was, and perhaps pick up some scraps of information which would save him from the reproach of having made a journey in vain.

"Do you know enough about railways to pass for an engineer, or inspector, or anything of that sort?" asked Mr. Rayner. "You know, of course, that suspicion has fallen upon a gang of navvies who are at work upon the line near there; but, although there have been detectives among them since, not one has been sharp enough to discover anything yet."

The man seemed a little shy at first of interfering in a branch of the work of watching which had been put into other hands. But he was rather put upon his mettle by the allusion to the fact that his journey had been so far a failure. And Mr. Rayner whispered to me in the hall, with his eyes twinkling, when the detective was already seated in the dog-cart at the door, that he had put that fellow up to discovering something—it did not matter what, wrong or right. He said they should be back early, as the fog was rising already, and, in order to repay Mr. Maynard for detaining him, there was to be dinner at half-past six, instead of the usual tea at half-past five. And, in the very highest spirits, Mr. Rayner patted my shoulder, told me to save myself up for next day, and that he had a present to give me on the journey, and jumped into the dog-cart.

I went back into the dining-room, where the cook was clearing away the luncheon; Jane, as she had predicted, not having come back yet. Mrs. Rayner was sitting by the fire, with Haidee on her lap.

"Are you unhappy at the thought of losing her so soon?" said I softly, leaving my seat and kneeling by her side, as soon as the cook had left the room.

Mrs. Rayner looked at me earnestly, and then whispered—

"No, I am not unhappy about her, but about you."

"About me, Mrs. Rayner!" I exclaimed, in astonishment.

"Hush!" she whispered softly. She took her arms from her child's neck, and told her to go and play; and Haidee obediently walked to the window, where her doll was lying on the floor.

"It is as much as my wretched life is worth to warn you," whispered she, taking the hand I had laid on her lap, and clasping and unclasping her own about it nervously. "You are kind-hearted, and innocent as a child—I see that now," she continued, her eyes wandering restlessly about the room.

I began to be afraid of a fit of hysterics, or worse; and I begged her not to talk if it fatigued her, and asked her if I should fetch some eau-de-cologne. She shook her head.

"I am not hysterical—don't be afraid of that," said she, turning her great eyes upon me, as if in reproach. "I only want to tell you this—when you arrive in London to-morrow, if your mother is not waiting at the station, insist upon going to her house before you go farther. Do not on any account enter another train without her. Call the guard—make a disturbance at the station—do anything rather."

"But how can I?" said I gently. "I cannot insist against Mr. Rayner. He would not listen. You know that, when he tells one to do a thing, there is such a strong authority about him, one must do it."

"Try, try!" said she earnestly. "I believe you have the power, if you have the courage. You have thwarted his wishes as nobody else has ever dared to do—in sending for Doctor Lowe, in taking Haidee upstairs. Try once more. It is not Sarah's safety that is concerned this time, nor Haidee's, but your own. For Heaven's sake, try!"

She lay back in the chair, her face, neck, and hands all wet with the violence of her feeling and her unaccustomed vehemence. Yet her voice had never once risen above a whisper that could not have been heard at the other end of the room. She raised her head again, and read with unexpected penetration the look on my face.

"I am not mad, Miss Christie," she said quite quietly. "Think me mad if you like—if your mother meets you at Liverpool Street Station. But, if not, remember my warning; it may have cost me my life."

She shook off my hand and lay back again, as if wishing for rest. And I remained on my knees beside her, not knowing what to think, whether she was mad or sane, whether I should follow her advice or dismiss her words as—no, I could not think them idle; that she herself had been in terrible earnest as she uttered them I could not doubt. What then? She wanted to make me distrust her husband. She had not spoken like a jealous woman; she was too cold, too indifferent for jealousy. What strange fancy was this of hers about the journey? If my mother should not be at the station waiting for us, which was very likely, as she was seldom punctual, I should still have Haidee with me. I should naturally suggest waiting for her; but, if she did not come soon, probably Mr. Rayner himself would either send or go to my uncle's house in search of her. What had I to fear with Mr. Rayner, my best and kindest friend, next to Laurence, in the world? Why should a morbid fancy of his poor, sickly, fanciful wife trouble me?

And yet the impression her words had made upon me was so strong that I determined, if my mother should not arrive at the station shortly after us—that she would be there already was too much to expect of her—that I would ask Mr. Rayner to let me take a cab to my uncle's house and fetch her myself.

Mrs. Rayner scarcely spoke for the rest of the afternoon; that unusual burst of vehemence seemed to have exhausted her.

The fog, which had been hanging about us for days, grew so thick as the afternoon wore on that we had to have the lamps lighted much earlier than usual, and it was quite dark when, at about half-past four, there was a ring at the front-door bell. The cook came in to say that a boy from the village wanted to speak to Miss Christie; and I went into the hall and found a little fellow of about ten whom I did not know, who told me that Mrs. Manners, who was at the school-house, had sent to ask me to come to her at once, as she wished to speak to me about the dole. This was a yearly distribution of clothing and money among the very poor people of the parish, which took place in November. It was rather strange that Mrs. Manners should want to speak to me about it, I thought at first, as I was not a district visitor. However, of course I must go; and I went back into the dining-room and told Mrs. Rayner about it.

"Don't go, Miss Christie," said she at once. "It is some trap, some trick; Mrs. Manners never sends messages but by her own boys. Don't go."

"I don't like not to go," said I hesitatingly. "It may be something of importance, and Mrs. Manners has been so kind to me. Please let me go, Mrs. Rayner."

She shrank into herself, and leaned back again as the cook reappeared at the door, saying the boy said Mrs. Manners's message was—would I make haste?

"Of course you can go, Miss Christie," said Mrs. Rayner listlessly.

I ran upstairs and was down again ready for my walk in a few minutes. The boy was evidently prepared to accompany me; and the fog was so thick that I was glad of it, for he was more used to the turns of the road than I; and even he had to go very slowly and to keep close to the hedge. He kept urging me to make haste, however, and I followed him as fast as I could, while he turned every other minute to see that I was still behind him.

The school was about half a mile from the Alders, among the first houses of the village. When I stumbled against a milestone which was, I knew, not far from our destination, the boy said—

"Here, miss, take care! This way."

And, taking a corner of my cloak, he led me round into a path which branched off to the left.

"But you are going wrong," I said. "It is straight on, I know—not up here. This is the way to Dunning's Farm, half a mile off."

"It's all right, miss," said he. "I'm afraid of our being run over along the high-road now we're so near the village. Come on, miss; it's all right."

He was very impatient; and I followed him, not without some misgivings. We had groped our way up this lane for what seemed to me a very long time, when the boy stopped and whistled.

"What are you doing that for?" said I sharply.

But the boy, who, by making but a few steps forward, was lost to my sight in the fog, whistled again. I stood for a moment trembling with terror. Then the boy exclaimed angrily—

"Why, he ain't here!"

"He! Who?" I cried, in alarm; and at that moment I heard a crackling of branches, and saw dimly through the fog, a few yards in front of me, the figure of a man crashing through the hedge, and leaping down from the field into the road.

Smothering a cry, I turned, and ran I knew not whither. It was Tom Parkes or Gordon, who had decoyed me out here to punish me for my discoveries, which Sarah must have told them about.

I heard the boy say, "Thank ye," and then the footsteps of the man coming nearer to me. My only hope was that I might perhaps escape him in the blinding fog by crouching under the hedge till he had passed; but, to my horror, he was coming as slowly and as cautiously as I. I had found my way to the hedge and knelt down close under it, my face almost in among the briers and thorns. He passed me; I could see the vague form as it went by. But in my joy at the sight I drew a sharp breath; he turned back, groped for me, found, and raised me to my feet, all without a word. I closed my eyes and shuddered. For the first moment I felt too exhausted by the excitement of those awful minutes to struggle much. I could only feebly try to push him off, crying brokenly—

"Don't—don't hurt me!"

"Hurt you, my own darling! Look up at me. Heaven help me, I have nearly frightened you to death!"

I looked up with a cry, and flung my arms round his neck. It was Laurence, his face so haggard and so dirty as to be scarcely recognizable; but he told me, as he kissed me again and again, that I must not mind that, for he had travelled night and day without a moment's rest since he got my letter on the morning of the previous day.

"And, thank Heaven, I am in time, in time!" he cried, as he pressed me again in his arms.

"In time for what, Laurence? I should have been near you in two days," said I wonderingly. "We were to start to-morrow morning."

"To-morrow morning! Just a few hours more, and I should have lost you!" cried the poor fellow in such agony of horror and relief at the same time that only to see him in that state brought the tears to my own eyes.

"Lost me, Laurence? Oh, do tell me what you mean!" I cried piteously.

"Oh, Violet, are you still so innocent as to think that that man would have brought you to me?"

"Why not?" asked I, in a whisper.

"Because he loves you himself," said he between his teeth—"if the feeling even you inspire in such a man can be called love. Your innocence would not have protected you much longer. Oh, I was a fool, a blind fool, ever to leave you, for father—mother—anybody in the world! But I did not know quite all until your own sweet naïve letter opened my stupid eyes."

"Oh, Laurence, Laurence, what dreadful things are you saying?" I cried, shaking with fear even in his arms.

"Never mind, my own darling; you are safe now," said he very gently. "I didn't mean to frighten you. I ought to have warned you long ago; but I could not bear to—"

"But, Laurence, my mother is going with us. Didn't I tell you that? I had a letter from her—"

"Which she never wrote. On my way back to London, I telegraphed to your mother to meet me at Charing Cross Station, and there she told me she had never seen Mr. Rayner and never heard a word of the journey to Monaco."

This blow was too much for me; I fainted in his arms. When I recovered, I found that he had carried me some distance; and, as soon as I began to sigh, he put me down and gave me some brandy-and-water out of his flask.

"I'm always wanting that now, I think," said I, trying weakly to smile as I remembered that two or three times lately Mr. Rayner had given it to me when I seemed to be on the point of fainting. "You are the first person who has made me go off quite, though," I said.

And poor Laurence took it as a reproach, and insisted on our stopping again in the fog for me to forgive him. We were making our way slowly, in the increasing darkness, down the lane to the high-road.

"But what am I to do, Laurence?" I asked tremblingly. "Shall I tell Mr. Rayner—oh, I can't think he is so wicked!—shall I tell him you have come back, and don't want me to leave England?"

"Not for the world, my darling," said he, quickly. "Nobody in Geldham—not even at the Hall—knows I have come back. That is why I had to send for you on a pretext, and frighten you out of your life. The boy I sent for you did not know me. I got here in a fly from the station only a few minutes before I met him, and sent him off with the promise of a shilling if he brought you back with him."

"Ah, that is why he was so anxious not to lose sight of me for a moment! But what is all this mystery about, Laurence? Why don't you go to the Hall and see your father?"

"Ah, that is a secret! You won't mind waiting till to-morrow to know that, will you, darling?"

"Oh, yes, I shall! I want to know now," said I coaxingly. "Won't you trust me with your secret?"

He did not want to do so; but I was curious, and hurt at his refusal; and, when he saw the tears come into my eyes, he gave way.

He had been so much struck by the postscript to my letter, telling him of a suspicious-looking man whom I connected with the Denham Court robbery hanging about the Hall, and promising to visit it again on Wednesday, that he had obtained, by telegraphing to the chief of the metropolitan police, a force of constables to lie in wait about the Hall that night. He had appointed a trustworthy person to meet them at Beaconsburgh station and conduct them to a rendezvous he had appointed in the park, where they were probably waiting now. He was going to station them himself, under cover of the fog, in places round the Hall, among the shrubs, where they would be well concealed, and yet be near the approaches of the house, especially on that side where the strong-room was. The fog might work for them or against them; it might throw the thieves—if indeed they came, which was a matter of chance—into the constables' hands, or it might help them to escape. That must be left to fortune.

"And you know you said in your letter that Sarah was always raving about a bad man named James Woodfall, who seemed to have a great influence upon her and to be mixed up in everything evil she talked about. Well, I have brought down among the constables a man who knew James Woodfall, and swears he could identify him. This Woodfall used to be a clever forger, and got caught only once, when he was quite a lad; but he has been lost sight of for years. There is only an off-chance of his having anything at all to do with this; but I mentioned his name to the chief constable, and he thought it worth trying. So now, my darling, you know everything, and you must keep my secrets, every one, like grim death. As for your journey, don't be alarmed. I shall be in the same train with you; and your mother will really meet you at Liverpool Street Station, for I have told her to do so."

Laurence insisted on seeing me home. We had crept along the high-road until we were close to the cottage nearest to the Alders, when we heard the sounds of hoofs and wheels, and men's voices halloing through the fog. Laurence opened the gate of the cottage garden and led me inside till they should have passed.

It was the dog-cart, with Mr. Rayner on foot leading the horse, and Maynard still in it.

"Lucky you are going to stay the night!" Mr. Rayner was saying. "I wouldn't undertake to find my way to my own gate to-night."

CHAPTER XXVIII

We followed the dog-cart at a safe distance, which was not very far off in the fog, until it stopped at the stable-gate. Then we slipped past quite unseen on the other side of the road, while Mr. Rayner was busy opening the gate; and at the front gate Laurence left me, and I groped my way down the drive as fast as I could, and got in some minutes before Mr. Rayner and his companion. And, as I could rely upon the silence of Mrs. Rayner and the cook, I said nothing to anybody else about my excursion.

We were about an hour over dinner, and, when Mr. Rayner had been to the cellar—not the dreadful store-room cellar—himself to get out a bottle of port, he asked Mr. Maynard if he was fond of music.

"Well, I'm not much of a dab at it myself, though I used to tootle a little upon the cornet when I was a boy," replied the detective, whose language had grown a little easier and was less carefully chosen as he knew us better. "But I don't mind a tune now and then."

"Ah, you are not an enthusiast, I see!" said Mr. Rayner. "Now I can never be happy long without music. Did you ever try the violin?"

"Well, no; that is rather a scratchy sort of instrument, to my mind. Give me the concertina," replied Mr. Maynard genially.

"Then I won't ask you to listen to my music," said Mr. Rayner. "I'm only a fiddler. However, I think I must console myself for this disgusting weather by a—a tune to-night; but I'll be merciful and shut the doors. My wife and Miss Christie will entertain you, and—let me see, it is half-past seven—at nine o'clock I'll come and inflict myself upon you again, and we can have a game at backgammon. Do you care for backgammon?"

Mr. Maynard having declared that he did, Mr. Rayner asked me if I could go into the drawing-room and hunt out *La Traviata* and Moore's "Irish Melodies." I went obediently, and was on my knees turning over the great piles of music that stood there, when he came in and softly shut the door. Before I knew he was near I felt something passed round my neck and heard the snap of a clasp behind. I put up my hand and sprang to my feet, startled.

Mr. Rayner, bright and smiling, drew my hand through his arm and led me to a looking-glass. Flashing and sparkling round my throat was a necklace of red jewels that dazzled me by their beauty.

"Don't I keep my promises? I said I would bring you some garnets. Do they please you?"

But they did not at all, after what Laurence had said; the magnificent present filled me with terror. I put up both hands, tore them off, and flung them down with trembling fingers, and then stood, panting with fright at my own daring, wondering what he would do to me.

He did nothing. After looking at me for what seemed to me a long time, while I stood trembling, at first proud and then ashamed of myself, without the least sign of displeasure he picked up the necklace, slipped it into his pocket, and said quite gently—

"That is very pretty spirit, but is rather ungrateful, isn't it? Never mind; you shall make amends for it by and by. Now will you go and help Mrs. Rayner to entertain our lynx-eyed friend? You shall come back and fetch me at nine o'clock. Run along now, my dear."

He gave me a gentle little tap of dismissal, and, rather crestfallen, I returned to the dining-room. But neither my entertaining powers nor Mrs. Rayner's were called into play; for Mr. Maynard was already rather drowsy, and, after sleepily muttering "Bravo—very good!" as the last sounds of Schubert's "Adieu" died away on Mr. Rayner's violin, he had to make an effort to listen to a selection from *Rigoletto*, and during some airs from *Martha* which followed I heard the regular breathing of a sleeping person from the arm-chair where he was sitting. But I was paying little attention to him. The door being shut, I had gone closer and closer to it, as if drawn by an irresistible fascination, as Mr. Rayner seemed to play the "Adieu" as he had never played it before. Every note seemed to vibrate in my own heart, and nothing but fear of his displeasure if I disturbed him before nine o'clock kept me from returning to the drawing-room, where I could have heard each plaintive passionate note unmuffled by the two doors between. When the last note of the "Adieu" had died away, and Mr. Maynard's coarse voice had broken the spell by his "Bravo—very good!" I listened for the next melody eagerly, and was struck with a chill sense of disappointment as an air from *Rigoletto* followed.

It was not that I did not care for that opera, though it is scarcely one of my favorites, but a certain hardness of touch, which struck me at once as being unlike the rich full tones Mr. Rayner generally drew from his loved violin, grated upon my ear and puzzled me. Of course Mr. Maynard did not notice any difference, and muttered approval from time to time indiscriminately.

But my glance stole from him to Mrs. Rayner; and I could see that she also was struck by the curious change of style in her husband's playing. It was as brilliant as ever; the execution of one of the difficult passages in the arrangement of *Martha* was clever, more perfect than usual; but the soul was not there, and no brilliancy of shake or cadenza could repay one for the loss. It did not sound like the playing of the same man, and my interest in the music gradually died away; and, after watching Mrs. Rayner curiously for some minutes and noting the intentness with which, sitting upright in her chair, she was listening to the violin and at the same time keeping her eyes fixed upon the slumbering Maynard, I gave myself up to my own agitated thoughts.

What was going on at the Hall now? Had the constables been able in the fog to find their way safely to the park, and would the thieves come, after all? Would they catch Tom Parkes? Would Gordon prove to be mixed up in it? Above all, would they catch the dreaded James Woodfall, whose influence seemed so strong and the memory of his name so fresh, though he had not been seen for years? It was an awful thing to think that I, by my letter to Laurence, had set on men to hunt other men down. I began to hope, even though I felt it was wrong to do so, that Tom Parkes would make his escape; he had never done me any harm, and I had rather liked him for his good-natured face. As for the unknown James Woodfall, the case was different. From Sarah's words and the eagerness with which the police had snatched at the least chance of catching him, it was plain that he must be a very desperate criminal indeed, for whom one could have no sympathy. I hoped with all my heart they would catch him; and I was rather anxious to see what such a very wicked man looked like. Poor Tom Parkes was probably only a tool in the hands of this monster, who had made even the terrible Sarah a submissive instrument of evil.

And then I fell to thinking very sadly of what Laurence had told me that day about the deception practised upon me concerning the journey to Monaco, and I remembered Mrs. Rayner's warning. Could it be true that Mr. Rayner, who had always been so kind, so sweet-tempered, so patient, who had always treated me almost as if I were a child, and who had borne my rudeness in the drawing-room just now with such magnanimous good-humor, could really be such a hypocrite? There must be some explanation of it all which would satisfy even Laurence, I thought to myself—almost, at least; for that letter from my mother, which she had never written—could that be explained away? My tears fell fast as this terrible proof rose up in my mind. How could he explain that away? But one's trust in a friend as kind as Mr. Rayner had proved to me does not die out quickly; and I was drying my eyes and hoping that a few words from him would make it all right, when suddenly the silence round the house was broken by a howl from Nap, Mr. Rayner's retriever, who was chained to his kennel outside.

Mrs. Rayner started. Still Maynard slumbered. I looked at the clock; it was seven minutes to nine. Another and another howl from the dog, followed by loud and furious barking. We two women sat staring at each other, without a word. I would have spoken; but Mrs. Rayner glanced at the sleeping detective and put her finger to her lips. Still the sounds of the violin came to us from the drawing-room without interruption.

When nine o'clock struck, I jumped up, much relieved, opened and shut the door softly, crossed the hall, and turned the handle of the drawing-room door. It was locked. I tapped; but there was no answer. He was playing a brilliant concerto, and I supposed he had not heard me. I knocked again and said softly—

"Mr. Rayner, it is nine o'clock. You told me to come at nine."

Still there was no answer, which I thought strange, for his hearing was generally very sharp indeed. It was of no use for me to stand there knocking if he would not hear me, or did not yet wish to be disturbed; so, after one more unsuccessful attempt to attract his attention, I took a lamp from the hall-table and went into the schoolroom. It was now ten minutes past nine. Nap was barking more furiously than ever. I knew by the mist there was all through the house how dense the fog must be outside; but I was so much struck by the noise the dog was making that I unfastened the shutters and opened the window about an inch to listen.

The fog was blinding. I could not see a yard in front of me. I heard nothing but Nap's barking for a minute; then I saw the dim glow of a lantern and heard a muffled whisper through the fog—

"Who's that?"

"It is I—Violet Christie. Is that you, Laurence?"

"Hush! All right!" he whispered back. "Let me in."

He got in softly through the window, and, rather to my alarm, a middle-aged man in plain clothes, also with a lantern, followed him. Laurence himself looked more alarming than any thief. His face was ghastly white with fatigue, and dirtier than ever through long watching in the fog. He listened for a minute to the violin, then said quickly, but still in a low voice—

"Who is that playing?"

"Mr. Rayner," I answered.

He turned sharply to the other man, who nodded as if to say it was just what he had expected.

"How long has he been playing?" asked Laurence.

"Ever since half-past seven."

He turned to the other man again.

"A trick," said the latter simply.

"Who is with him?" asked Laurence again.

"Nobody," said I, surprised and rather frightened by these questions. "Mrs. Rayner and Mr. Maynard are in the dining-room."

"Maynard?"

"Yes. He is asleep."

The middle-aged man gave a snort of disgust.

"Hasn't Mr. Rayner been in the dining-room at all, dear, this evening?" asked Laurence gently.

"Not since dinner. I left him playing in the drawing-room at five-and-twenty minutes to eight, and he told me to call him at nine. He has been playing ever since."

"But it is past nine!"

"Yes. When I went to the drawing-room door just now, I found it locked, and I knocked; but he did not answer."

"Will you go and knock again, and say you wish to speak to him particularly, dear?" said Laurence gravely.

I hesitated, trembling from head to foot.

"Why?" asked I, in a low voice.

"Because we want to speak to him particularly," said the other man gruffly.

But I looked at his hard face and panted out—

"You are a policeman, I know! What do you want with Mr. Rayner?"

"Never you mind, my dear; we won't hurt you. Just go and say you want to speak to him."

"No, I won't!" I cried—not loudly, for my voice seemed to grow suddenly weak. "Whatever you think he has done, or whatever he has done, I will never help to harm Mr. Rayner!"

The man shrugged his shoulders, walked to the window, and whistled softly. Laurence put me into a chair, whispering "That's a brave girl!"—but with such an anxious, stern face. And the other man came back into the room, followed by a policeman with his staff ready in his hand.

"We must break open the door," said the elder man.

I started from my seat. I wanted to rush to the drawing-room door and warn Mr. Rayner; but Laurence prevented me, whispering gravely—

"My darling, you must leave it to us now."

Every word, every movement had been so quiet that the music still went on while they opened the schoolroom door and crossed the hall. I stood watching them breathlessly.

The three men, Laurence, the most stalwart, foremost, placed themselves against the drawing-room door, and by one mighty push burst it open. I ran forward to the doorway just in time to see Gordon, Mr. Carruthers's servant, fling down the violin and rush to the opposite window, the shutters of which were unfastened. But I heard the crash of glass, and at the same instant two policemen dashed through the shattered French window, seized and handcuffed him. Then he stood between them, white and immovable, without a struggle.

"It's no go. We know you're one of the gang," said the middle-aged man. "Game's up. We've got your leader."

"What leader?" asked Gordon calmly.

"James Woodfall."

"It's a lie!" snapped out the immovable Gordon. "Jim Woodfall wouldn't let himself be nabbed by such as you."

"Why not? We've got you."

The man did not answer.

"All his fault for getting soft on a girl! Wish I had her here!" Gordon muttered presently.

He caught sight of me at the doorway and shot at me a sort of steely look that made me shudder. But I did not connect myself with his words. I was too bewildered to think or to understand clearly what was going on until I saw him, handcuffed as he was, quietly draw a tiny revolver from his pocket and, without raising it, point it at Laurence. With a scream I rushed forward into the room and flung myself in front of Laurence, and I heard a report and felt something touch my arm—I did not know what at first—and Laurence sprang forward with almost a yell. But he was encumbered with my form; and, before he could put me down, Gordon had wrenched himself away from his captors, and, snarling, "I meant to have done for her!" had dashed through the open window out into the fog and darkness.

I knew by this time that I was shot in the arm, for the blood was trickling through my sleeve; but the wound did not pain me much yet—I was too much excited for that, and too much occupied with Laurence's pitiful distress. He did not attempt to join in the hopeless chase of the escaped Gordon, but put me on a sofa, tore off the body of my frock, and bandaged my arm himself.

"Tell me what it all means, Laurence," said I. "I am not badly hurt—I am not indeed—and I want to understand it all. Did you catch the thieves? Who were they? Have they really caught James Woodfall? And I hope—oh, I hope poor Tom Parkes has escaped!" I whispered; for the middle-aged man had not joined in the pursuit, but stood on the watch, half in and half out of the window.

"Tom Parkes has been caught, and James Woodfall has escaped, I am afraid," said Laurence.

"Then he was there! Tell me all about it," I said anxiously.

"Won't to-morrow do?" pleaded poor Laurence earnestly. "I am afraid, if you get so much excited, your arm will get inflamed, and I ought to be setting off for the doctor now."

"No, no; you couldn't get to Beaconsburgh to-night, you know you couldn't. It wouldn't be safe," said I. "Your bandaging will do quite well until the doctor comes as usual to see Sarah to-morrow morning. Now tell me quickly all about the robbery. Did you find the policemen in the park?" Then suddenly I sprang up from the sofa. "Where is Mr. Rayner? Why was Gordon here instead of him? Oh, Laurence, my head seems to be going round! I don't understand it at all. I am getting quite bewildered. Why was it?"

"Let me tell you about the robbery. You will hear and understand it all in time," said he very gravely and gently. "I found the policemen in the park and stationed them in the shrubbery, and I stood myself, with that man over there and one other, as close as possible to the back entrance of the house; and there we waited until nearly half-past seven, when a man came up through the fog and tapped at the door. One of the maids opened it, by appointment as it turned out, for she was expecting him, though I don't believe the poor girl suspected what his real business was; for it was Tom Parkes. And, when they went inside, Tom went last, and left the door ajar. A few minutes later another man came up and slipped in so quietly, so quickly, that we could hardly have sworn in the dense fog to his going in at all. Then presently Tom and the girl came out. He said good-by to her without as much delay as she would have liked, walked a few steps away until she had shut the door, then returned and crept alongside the wall of the house until he was under the strong-room window. There were four of our men stationed very close to that, and their chief, who was with me, crept along easily under cover of the fog, which was as thick as ever, to join them. I followed with the other man. In a few minutes we heard a soft whistle from the strong-room window, as we guessed. Tom answered by another, and we saw a third man come up and join Tom. I was so close that I saw a bundle let cautiously down from the window by a cord. Tom handed it to the third man, whom we allowed to walk off with it—followed however by two policemen—in order to watch the further proceedings of the other two thieves. Another bundle was let down, which Tom carried off himself; and then we watched anxiously for the next movement of the man in the house. The strong-room window is about twenty feet from the ground; but the man jumped down and landed on his feet. In an instant five of us were upon him, but, though I think each of us in turn thought we had caught him, he eluded us all and got clear away, and in the fog escaped us. But that man at the window there, who has been so many years in the force, recognized him and identified him as James Woodfall, and I recognized him too."

"You, Laurence! I didn't know you had ever seen him!" I cried.

At that moment the elderly man left the window.

"It's of no good, sir, I'm afraid. The one rogue's got off as clear as the other. Can you tell me where Maynard is, miss?"

I got up from the sofa and led the way into the dining-room. Mrs. Rayner was still sitting, pale and upright, with staring gray eyes, Maynard still sleeping. The other detective shook him, and glanced at the wine.

"Drugged," said he shortly.

With a few vigorous shakes he succeeded in rousing Maynard, and, when he began to look around him in a dazed way, the other said sharply—

"Pretty fellow you are to be hoodwinked like that, and drink and sleep quietly under the very roof of one of the greatest scoundrels unhung!"

"Who?" said the other, startled. "Mr. Rayner?"

"Mr. Rayner! Yes, 'Mr. Rayner' to simple folk like you; but to me and every thief-taker that knows his business—the missing forger, James Woodfall!"

CHAPTER XXIX

As the detective pronounced the name "James Woodfall," I gave a cry that startled them all. Shaken as my trust in Mr. Rayner had already been, the shock seemed in a moment to change the aspect of the whole world to me. I shrank even from Laurence as he would have put his arms round me, and my wild wandering eyes fell upon Mrs. Rayner, who sat with her hands tightly clasped and head bent, listening to the proclamation of the secret which had weighed her down for years. And, as I looked at her, the scales seemed to fall from my eyes, my dull wits to become keener, and part of the mystery of the house on the marsh to grow clear to me.

I sank down upon the floor beside her, and she put her thin wasted arms round my neck and kissed me without a word. And the three men quietly left the room. We did not say much even then.

"Oh, Mrs. Rayner," I whispered, "it is terrible for you!"

"Not so terrible to me," she whispered back wearily. "I have known it for years—almost ever since I married him. But don't talk about it any more," said she, glancing furtively round the room. "He may be in the house at this moment; and they might search and watch for months, but they would never catch him. But he will make us suffer—me—ah, and you too now! You were so unsuspicious, yet it must have been you who set Laurence Reade upon the track."

"Not of Mr. Rayner. Oh, I never thought of such a thing!" I whispered, shuddering.

And I told her all about my suspicions of Tom Parkes, my visit to the Hall, my letter to Laurence, and all I said in it.

"Mr. Reade has shown energy and courage," said she. "But he will suffer for it too. You don't know that man yet. He will never let Laurence marry you. Even if he were in prison, he would manage to prevent it."

Luckily Laurence himself tapped at the door at that moment, for Mrs. Rayner's gloomy forebodings were fast increasing the fever of my overwrought mind. He came to say that the constables had returned to the house, having failed in the fog to find any traces of Gordon, or of—of any of the others. He was going to return with them to the Hall, where they would sleep, leaving Maynard to pass the night at the Alders, as his missing host had invited him to do, and a couple of constables to keep watch in turn, though there was nothing less likely than that the—the persons they were in search of would return to the Alders that night. Then he said very gently to poor Mrs. Rayner—

"Will you forgive me for what I have done in all innocence? I had some vague suspicions, the reasons for which I will explain to you presently; but indeed I never thought to bring such a blow as this upon you."

"It is no blow to me," said she, raising her sad eyes to his face. "That man—my husband—would have got rid of me long ago, but that he hated violence and dreaded it. Everything short of that he has tried," she whispered; "and it is not my fault that my wretched life has lingered on in spite of him."

Laurence ground his teeth.

"The wretch!" he said, in a low voice. "But he shall pay for it now. I'll ransack the whole world till we have unearthed him."

"You will never do that," said she calmly. "He dares too much for that. He is no coward to lie hid in a corner," she went on, with a sort of perverse pride in the man for whom every spark of love was long since dead. "He will brave you to your faces and escape you all. But you have done your best. You are a brave man, Mr. Reade. You would help me if you could. Good-night."

She shook hands with him, and left the room. He turned to me quickly.

"You must both leave this place," said he. "The long-continued suffering has almost turned that poor lady's brain. But she is safe from that vile wretch now; and you too, oh, my darling, thank Heaven!"

There was a tap at the door, and the voice of the elder detective said—

"Are you ready, sir?"

"All right," said Laurence; and then added, in a voice for me only, "I'm not ready a bit. I should like to stay and comfort you for ever. Take care of your poor little wounded arm. Good-night, good-night, my darling!"

I heard him leave the house with the constables. Then, exhausted by the events of the day and night, I just managed to crawl upstairs to my room, and, throwing myself upon the bed without undressing, I fell into a deep sleep which was more like a swoon. In the early morning I woke, feeling stiff and ill, undressed, and got into bed; and when the sun had risen I got up with hot and aching head, and found that my arm was beginning to be very painful.

Haidee and I had breakfast alone, for the cook told me that Mr. Maynard had already started for London; and I was just going to see how Mrs. Rayner was when Doctor Lowe arrived on his daily visit to Sarah. As soon as he saw me he ordered me off to bed, and then, after making him swear secrecy, which did not make much difference, as the story would certainly be all over the neighborhood and in the London newspapers before long, I let him draw from me an account of the greater part of the events of the previous day. He said very little in comment beyond telling me that I was "a little simpleton to be so easily humbugged," and that he had always mistrusted Mr. Rayner, but that now he admired him; and then, strictly forbidding me to leave my bed until his visit next day, he left me.

Jane came up to me soon after. She had only just come home from Wright's Farm, and was full of curiosity excited to the highest pitch by the vague account that the cook, who was deaf and had not heard much, had given her of the events which had taken place in her absence. I told her that there had been a robbery at the Hall, that the man who had asked to speak to me was a detective, and that he and Mr. Rayner had left the Alders.

My faith in the latter was gone altogether; but my affection for him was gradually coming back again. The fearfully wicked things that he had done I had only heard about; and how could the impression so given outweigh that much stronger one of his constant kindness to me? And to think that it was I who had drawn down justice—for it was justice, I sorrowfully admitted—upon him caused me bitter remorse.

Laurence told me, in one of the little notes he kept leaving for me all day long, that it was expected that Mr. Rayner would brave everything and return to the Alders sooner or later, if only for a flying visit, and that, in consequence, the search of the house which must take place was to be postponed, and the place watched, with as much caution as possible, from the outside. By letting the life at the Alders go on as usual, it was hoped that he might be lured back under the impression that he was not expected to return there. Laurence had telegraphed to my mother to tell her that I was quite safe and the journey put off, in order to allay her fears about me.

Mrs. Rayner brought one of these notes up to me late in the afternoon. In addition to her usual pallor, she had great black rings round her eyes; and, in answer to my inquiries, she confessed that she had not slept all night.

"I have something to tell you," she whispered in my ear. "Mrs. Saunders drinks, and is not a proper guardian for Sarah. She is afraid of Mr. Rayner;

but last night, knowing he was not in the house, she was in nearly as excited a state as her patient, and was very rough with her. Sarah's room is nearly opposite mine, and I opened my door and heard what sounded like a struggle. Maynard, who was in the room next to the dressing-room, either did not hear or did not like to interfere. But now he is gone; and I ought to be used to terrors, but I am afraid;" and she shuddered.

"Surely there is nothing to be afraid of if you lock your door, Mrs. Rayner?"

"I have no key. Will you leave your door open and the door at the foot of the turret staircase? I know you must not leave your bed; but it will be some comfort to know you are within hearing."

I promised; and that night, when Jane came up to my room for the last time, I made her leave the doors open when she went down.

The sense of being on the alert made me wakeful, and two or three times during the night I rose and stood at the top of my staircase, listening. And the third time I did hear something. I heard a faint cry, and presently the soft shutting of a door, then steps in the corridor below, and whispering. I crept half-way down the stairs; the whispering continued. I got to the bottom, and recognized Sarah's voice muttering to herself. I would rather have again faced Gordon with his revolver than this madwoman; but I was so anxious about Mrs. Rayner that, after a few minutes spent in prayer, I ventured out from the doorway, and found Sarah crouched in a corner muttering to herself. The wretched woman started up on seeing me; but, instead of attempting to approach me, she hung back, moving her still bandaged head and her one free hand restlessly, and saying —

"I've done it — I've done it! He'll come back now. I've done what he wanted. He can marry the Christie girl now. It's all right. He'll come back again now."

With a terrible fear at my heart, I dashed along the corridor to Mrs. Rayner's room and went straight in. The atmosphere of the room was sickly and stifling. I went up to the bed. Mrs. Rayner was lying with a cloth over her face! I snatched it off. It was steeped in something which I afterwards learnt was chloroform. Thank Heaven, she was alive! — for she was breathing heavily. I rushed to the two windows and flung them wide open, pulled the bell-rope until the house echoed, and moved her arms up and down. The cook and Jane came in, terribly alarmed, in their night gowns. I left them with Mrs. Rayner while I ran downstairs for some brandy.

There was some on the sideboard in the dining-room, I knew; and I was returning with it, and was just outside the dining-room door, when I caught sight of a man in the gloom at the end of the passage leading from the hall. He had come from Mr. Rayner's study, and disappeared in a moment in the darkness. It was impossible to recognize him; but I could not doubt that it was Mr. Rayner.

Where was he going? Was he going to escape by the back way? Did he know the house was watched? I made a step forward, anxious to warn him; but he had already disappeared, and I dared not follow him.

I crept upstairs, too much agitated to be of any use any longer; but happily Mrs. Rayner was already recovering, and the brandy-and-water restored her entirely to consciousness. I spent the rest of the night in her room, after I had, with the cook's assistance, persuaded the unhappy lunatic who had done the mischief to return to her own room, where we found, as I had expected, Mrs. Saunders in a stupid, heavy sleep, half in her arm-chair and half on the floor. The cook declined to watch in place of her for the remainder of the night, but as a precaution locked the door on the outside and took the key away.

"Now, if Sarah wants to do any more mischief, let her try it on Mrs. Saunders," said she.

I could scarcely approve of this way of settling the difficulty; but happily no harm came of it; and Mrs. Saunders profited by the lesson, and kept pretty sober after that.

This woman, having been sent from town by Mr. Rayner, had taken upon herself in some sort the authority formerly held by Sarah in the household, and she now suggested that Mrs. Rayner had better go back to her old room in the left wing, saying she would take charge of it for her as Sarah had done. The poor lady came up herself to my room, where, having made my arm much worse by my expedition in the night, I was lying in bed the whole of the next day.

"Why do you go back if you don't wish to do so, Mrs. Rayner?" I asked.

"I expect it is by Mr. Rayner's orders," she whispered.

And, my strong suspicion that he was in the house acting like a spell upon me, I said no more.

But I was curious to know what was the mystery that hung about that bedroom in the left wing which no one was allowed to enter but Mrs. Rayner, Mr. Rayner, and Sarah; and I resolved that, as soon as I could, I would try to induce Mrs. Rayner to let me go in there.

As I lay thinking of all the strange and horrible events which had filled my life lately, the thought of Mr. Rayner lying concealed in his own house, perhaps hidden in some cellar the existence of which was unknown to every one else, came uppermost in my mind. It was the most dreadful blow I had ever experienced to have my respect and affection for a kind friend turned suddenly into horror of a great criminal. But I would not believe that he was all bad. How could a man who was so kind and sweet-tempered have no redeeming points at all? And it was I, who had never received anything but kindness at his hands, who—innocently indeed—had drawn down this pursuit upon him. There were only two things that I could do now. I could pray for him, as I did most earnestly, that he might repent of what he had done, and become in very truth all that he had seemed to me; and I could perhaps let him know how the thought that it was I who had brought down justice upon him tormented me.

A possible means of communicating with him occurred to me. In spite of the Doctor's prohibition, I sprang out of bed, got my desk, and wrote a note asking his forgiveness, and giving him a full explanation of the way in which, in all innocence, I had written the letter which had led to this pursuit of him. I told him the house was being watched, and was to be searched before long, and begged that, when he had got away, he would find some means of letting me know he was in safety. "I do pray for you every night and morning. I can't forget all your kindness to me, whatever you have done, and I don't wish to do so," I added, as a last thought in a P.S. And then I put on my dressing-gown, and, when I heard nobody about, slipped down by the back staircase to his study, where I put the note, directed simply to "G. Rayner, Esq.," just inside the drawer of his writing-table, and crept guiltily upstairs again.

Mrs. Manners came to see me that afternoon; Laurence had confided nearly everything to her, and she was much more severe upon Mr. Rayner than I—quite unchristian, I thought, and rather angry with me for not being as bitter as herself against him.

"Don't you know he wanted Sarah to kill his own wife that he might marry you, child, and, when Sarah was taken ill and couldn't do it, he wanted to run away with you?"

"Yes; but, as he was prevented from doing either of those things, it is easier to forgive him. Don't you think I ought to try to forgive him, Mrs. Manners?"

"I don't know, I am sure, child," said she, after a little hesitation. "But I think it ought to require an effort."

Then she told me that, when Laurence had heard that morning through Jane of the night's adventure, he had gone to Dr. Lowe and insisted upon Sarah's removal to the county lunatic asylum that very day; and I never saw the poor creature again.

When Mrs. Manners had left me, and Jane had come up at four o'clock with a cup of tea, I insisted on getting up and being dressed, as I wanted to see Mrs. Rayner, and find out whether she had heard of Sarah's departure. I heard that she had gone to her old room in the left wing, and, having taken the precaution to wrap a shawl round me before entering that long cold passage, I passed through the heavy swing-door, the very sight of which I hated.

I was opposite to the store-room door, when it was softly opened, and, without being able to make any resistance, I was drawn inside by a man's arm. I looked up, expecting to see Mr. Rayner, and was horror-stricken to find myself in the arms of Gordon, the man who had shot me. It was so dark already in the store-room, lighted only by one little high window, that, his back being turned towards it, I could not see his face.

"Don't tremble so," said he—his voice was always hard, but he did not mean to speak unkindly. "I meant to do for you before I left this house; but this has saved you." And he showed me my letter to Mr. Rayner.

"Do you know where he is?" I asked eagerly.

"No, ma'am," said he, in his respectful servant's manner; "but I should say that he is on his way to America by now, where he meant to have taken you."

"Me? America?"

"Yes, ma'am. Miss Haidee was to have been left at Liverpool Street Station, and brought back to the Alders."

"But I wouldn't have gone."

"I beg your pardon, ma'am; but I don't think your will would have stood out against James's—Mr. Rayner's. And, if this letter had not shown you to be loyal to him, I would not have left you here alive. I am surprised myself, knowing how set he was upon having your company, that he did not come back and carry you off with him. But I suppose he thought better of it, begging your pardon, ma'am. I may take this opportunity of apologizing for having once borrowed a trinket of yours while you were staying at Denham Court. But, as it was one which I myself had had the pleasure of assisting Mr. Rayner to procure from Lord Dalston's, I thought it wisest to pull off the little plate at the back, for fear of its being recognized by Mr. Carruthers, in whose service I was when I was first introduced to Lord Dalston's seat in Derbyshire."

"My pendant!" I cried. "It—it was real then?"

"Yes, ma'am. I had to remonstrate then with Mr. Rayner for his rashness in giving it you; but nothing ever went wrong with him—daring as he is— till you came across his path, ma'am. He was too tender-hearted. If I did not feel sure that he is by this time on the high-road to fresh successes in the New World, I would shoot you dead this instant without a moment's compunction."

I shuddered, glancing at his hands, which were slim and small, like those of a man who has never done rough work. I saw that he had got rid of his handcuffs.

"I have nothing to keep me here now, ma'am; so I shall be off to-night: and, if you care to hear how I get on, you will be able to do so by applying to my late master, Mr. Carruthers."

He led me courteously to the door, bowed me out, and shut himself in again, while I went on, trembling and bewildered, towards Mrs. Rayner's room.

I knocked at the door. At first there was no answer. I called her by name, and begged her to let me in. At last I heard her voice close to the other side of the door.

"What do you want, Miss Christie?"

"May I come in, Mrs. Rayner? I have something to tell you."

"I can't let you in. Can you speak through the door?"

"No, no; I must see you. I have something very important to say about Mr. Rayner," I whispered into the key-hole.

"Is he here?" she faltered.

"No; he has gone to America," I whispered.

She gave a long shuddering sigh, and then said—

"I—I will let you in."

She turned the key slowly, while I trembled with impatience outside the door.

When I found myself inside the room which had been a mystery to me for so long, nothing struck me at first but a sense of cold and darkness. There was only one window, which was barred on the inside; the fog still hung about the place, and the little light there had been all day was fading fast, for it was five o'clock. But, as I stepped forward farther into the room,

I drew my breath fast in horror. For I became aware of a smell of damp and decay; I felt that the boards of the floor under the carpet were rotten and yielding to my feet, and I saw that the paper was peeling off the wet and mouldy walls, and that the water was slowly trickling down them.

"Oh, Mrs. Rayner," I cried, aghast, "is this your room—where you sleep?"

"I have slept in it for three years," said she. "If my husband had had his will, it would have been my tomb."

CHAPTER XXX

The heartless cruelty of Mr. Rayner in allowing his poor submissive wife to live in a room such as he would not for the world have kept horse, or dog, or even violin in shocked and repelled me, and wrung from me the cry—

"The villain!"

"Hush!" said she. "He may be listening to us now."

"I don't care!" cried I passionately. "I am glad if he hears—if he hears me say that this morning I hoped he would escape, but that now I hope they will find him, for they cannot possibly punish him as he deserves. Oh, Mrs. Rayner, and I—I sleeping up in the turret to be out of the damp! How you must have hated me!"

"I did once, I own," she whispered, sinking into a chair and taking the hands I stretched out towards her. "But it was foolish of me, for you did not know—how could you know?"

"But why did you stay? Why did you say nothing about it? And why were you not glad to go upstairs, instead of begging as you did to remain here?"

"Because," she whispered, her nervous agitation coming back again, "I knew that while I remained down here they would not kill me outright; they could not let me die down here and introduce doctors and strangers to examine into the cause of my death into this room. I knew that a change of room was my death-warrant; and so it would have been, but for the accident which happened to Sarah on the very night when, but for you, I should have been sleeping upstairs ready to her hand."

I staggered back, suddenly remembering the message Mr. Rayner had in his letter told me to give to Sarah. It was this—"Tell Sarah not to forget the work she has to do in my absence." And I remembered also the grim way in which she had received it. Could he have meant that?

Mrs. Rayner continued—

"He hates violence; all was to have been over by his return, and he free to marry you."

"But he couldn't. I was engaged to Laurence, Mrs. Rayner."

She gave a little bitter smile.

"And do you think that, with Laurence away and Mr. Rayner here, you could have withstood him? In spite of his soft manners, he has a will that acts like a spell. I tell you," said she, twisting my fingers nervously, "though you say he is in America, and Laurence Reade says I shall never be in his power again, his influence is strong upon me even now. There is no peace, no freedom for me as long as he lives."

"Mrs. Rayner," said I suddenly, "may I ask you if what Mr. Rayner told me when I first came is true—that you were rich and he poor, and that he lived on your money?"

"No, it is not true. I had a little money when he first married me, which he ran through at once."

"And is it true you once wrote books, and had a little boy whose death made a great change in you?" said I slowly, watching her face.

"No; I never had any child but Mona and Haidee."

"Then what did he—"

"What did he tell you so for? He delights in making up fantastic tales of that sort, and often in making me bear witness to the truth of his inventions; it is part of his wild humor. When he went away to carry out a robbery, he would let me know what he was going to do—just to torture me."

The dead calmness with which she told me all this was maddening to me.

"Why did you bear it? Why didn't you rebel, or run away, while he was engaged in a robbery, and tell a policeman?"

"If Sarah had killed me, and you had married Mr. Rayner," she answered slowly, staring straight at me, "you would have understood why."

And the power this man exercised over every one who came much in his way became in a moment clear to me, when I saw by what different means he had on the one hand cowed his gentle wife and the fiery Sarah, and on the other gained a strong influence over such different women as

Mrs. Reade and myself. But the revelation was more than I could bear. I said faintly—

"May I go to my room, Mrs. Rayner? I—I am not well."

And she herself led me very slowly—for I was indeed weak and ill, half with the pain of my arm and half with misery and disgust—up to my bed in the turret-room.

Before the end of the day I heard that Mrs. Saunders had disappeared, without any warning or any application for payment of her services, as soon as Sarah had been taken off to the lunatic asylum. She had spared us any pangs of self-reproach on her account, however, by taking with her Mrs. Rayner's watch, and also the cook's, which had been left in the rooms of their respective owners.

"She doesn't expect to see Mr. Rayner again then," I whispered to Mrs. Rayner, who came to my bedside to tell me the news, "or she would never dare to do that."

And, persuaded by me, Mrs. Rayner, now relieved of any dread on Sarah's account, returned to the front spare-room, which, however disagreeable the remembrance of Sarah's mad attempt on her life might be, was at any rate healthier than the dungeon in the left wing. There was really nothing to keep the poor lady at the Alders now, as I told Laurence by letter that evening all that Gordon had said to me in the store-room, and the idea gained ground that Mr. Rayner had gone to America. But she insisted upon remaining until I was well enough to be moved, an event which I had myself retarded by rashly leaving my room three times since I had been told to keep to my bed.

Next day, which was Saturday, Laurence wrote to say that he had himself searched the store-room and Mr. Rayner's study, but had found no trace of Gordon beyond a pair of handcuffs placed neatly in the middle of the store-room on the top of a pyramid of biscuit-tins and pickle-jars, with a sheet of paper saying that the late wearer begged to return them with thanks to the police, who might perhaps succeed in making them stay longer on the wrists of a simpler rogue than their obedient servant, F. Gordon.

Those days that I spent in bed were a miserable time for all of us. The suspense we were all in—never sure whether Mr. Rayner was in America or whether he might not be really close to us all the time. The bits of news brought us from hour to hour by the awe-stricken Jane—first that there was a large reward offered for his capture; then rumors, which always proved to be false, of his having been caught; then complaints of the number of people who came just to look at the outside of the house that the ugly stories were being told about! For the facts fell far short of the accounts which were freely circulated—of there being a cellar full of human bones, supposed to be the remains of Mr. Rayner's victims, under the Alders; that the household consisted entirely of women whom he had married at one time or another; and so forth.

Meanwhile the fog still hung about the place, and Nap, the retriever, howled every night. When Monday came, I, anxious to be declared convalescent as soon as possible, and to be able to avail myself of Mrs. Manners's invitation to stay at the Vicarage, persuaded Doctor Lowe to let me go downstairs. It was about twelve o'clock when I left my room, and I had made my way as far as the corridor below, when I became aware of an unusual commotion on the ground-floor, doors being opened and shut, the sobbing of a woman, excited whisperings between Jane and the cook, and then a heavy tramp, tramp of men's feet through the hall and along the passage to Mr. Rayner's study.

I went to the top of the back staircase, descended a few steps, and looked over. The gardener and Sam were carrying between them a door, on which something was lying covered by a sheet. The cook opened the study-door, and they took it in. A horrible dread filled my mind and kept me powerless for a few moments. Then I ran along the corridor, down the front staircase, and met little Haidee with awe on her childish face.

"Oh, Miss Christie," she whispered, clutching my arm in terror, "they've found papa!"

Jane ran forward and caught me as I tottered in the child's clasp. Before I had recovered sufficiently to go to Mrs. Rayner in the drawing-room, Laurence and Mrs. Manners arrived, having heard the ghastly news already. They took us over to the Vicarage at once, and I never entered the Alders again.

In the evening Laurence told me all about the discovery. The gardener, who had done little work for the last few days beyond keeping the gate locked and driving away with a whip the boys who would swarm over when they got a chance, "just to have a look at the place," had been attracted that morning by the shrill cries of Mona, who, now more neglected than ever, spent all day in the garden in spite of the fog. He ran to the pond, where she was nearly always to be found, and whence her cries came, fearing she had fallen in. But he found her standing in the mud on the edge of it, screaming, "Come out, come out!" and clutching with a stick at an object in the water. It was the body of her father, entangled among the reeds.

The down-trodden grasses and rushes at that corner of the pond nearest to the stile which joined the path through the plantation to the path through the field beyond told the story of how he must have missed his way coming through the plantation in the dense fog of Wednesday night, on his way back from the Hall to the Alders, slipped into the pond, and been drowned out there in the fog and darkness, while his dog Nap, hearing his cry for help, had tried in vain, by howling and barking, to draw attention to his master's need.

It was an awful thing that night to lie awake in my strange room at the Vicarage, and picture to myself the dead Mr. Rayner lying at the Alders, the sole occupant, with the exception of the woman hired to watch by him, of the big dreary house where he, with his love of fun and laughter, had seemed to me to be the one ray of brightness.

I heard next day that two passages, booked in the name of "Mr. and Mrs. Norris," had actually been taken by him on board a ship which left Liverpool for New York on the very Thursday when we were to have started on our journey "to Monaco." The tickets were found upon him and also the necklace, which proved to be a valuable ornament of rubies that had belonged to Mrs. Cunningham, which he had clasped round my neck on the night of his death, but which I had flung upon the floor. These were the only ones, of all the stolen jewels, which were ever recovered, with the exception of the diamond pendant, which I sent back to its owner, Lord Dalston. Upon the house being searched, the candle which had fallen from my hand when I first went into the cellar under the store-room was found under the stagnant water there, and also the brown portmanteau, which was identified as one belonging to Sir Jonas Mills; but the jewels, with the exception of a stray drop from an ear-ring, had disappeared.

I heard about Gordon, as he had told me I should, through Mr. Carruthers, who, long before the impression these events made had died away, received a letter dated from New York, in which Gordon, in a very respectful manner, apologized for the inconvenience his sudden disappearance might have caused his master, who had, he could not doubt, by this time learned the reason of it through the London papers. Mr. Carruthers would find that the bills he had commissioned him to settle in Beaconsburgh on that unfortunate Wednesday afternoon had been paid, and he begged to forward him the receipts; he had also left the silver-mounted flask to be repaired at Bell's, and the hunting-stock at Marsden's. He had given up service for the present and taken to a different profession, as he felt, if he was not taking a liberty in saying so, that it would be impossible for him to find in America a master who gave him in all respects so much satisfaction as Mr. Carruthers had done.

Nothing more has ever been heard of Gordon under that name; but some time afterwards a representative of the United States Congress, who was described as a rich West India merchant, made a great sensation by a very impressive speech upon some financial question; a rough sketch of him in a New York illustrated paper fell into the hands of Mr. Carruthers, who sent it to Laurence, and under the trimly-cut mustache and hair parted very much on one side we fancied we recognized something like the clear-cut features and bland expression of our old friend Gordon.

I was married to Laurence before the trial of poor Tom Parkes and of the subordinate who had been caught removing the plate from the Hall. I had to give evidence, and I was so much distressed at having to do so that Tom, good-natured to the last, called out—

"Don't take on so, miss. Lor' bless you, you can't say any worse than they know! It's only a matter of form."

He took a stolid sort of glory in his iniquities, pleaded "Guilty" to the charges brought against him of taking an active part in all three robberies, and exulted especially in the neatness of the execution of the robbery at Denham Court, where the various articles stolen were being quietly abstracted one by one at different times by Gordon for two or three days before the Tuesday, when they were finally carried off by Mr. Rayner, and taken by him and Tom to the Alders, where Sarah had received them, as I had seen.

As to what had become of the jewels afterwards, Tom professed himself as innocent as a child; but, whether this was true or not, nobody believed him. He was sentenced to fourteen years' penal servitude, and he did not hear the sentence with half so much concern as I.

Poor Mrs. Rayner never entirely shook off the gloomy reserve which had grown round her during those long years of her miserable marriage.

Kind-hearted Sir Jonas Mills was among the very first to come forward to help her; and, by his generous assistance and that of other friends, she went to live abroad, taking Haidee with her, and Jane, who proved a most devoted servant and friend.

Laurence and I, who were married before she left England, undertook the care of poor little savage Mona, who has grown into almost as nice a child as her sister. And now I have one of my own too.